THE SPORRAN CONNECTION

THE SPORRAN CONNECTION

Peter Kerr

ISIS
LARGE PRINT
Oxford

First published in Great Britain 2007
by
Accent Press Ltd.

Published in Large Print 2007 by ISIS Publishing Ltd.,
7 Centremead, Osney Mead, Oxford OX2 0ES
by arrangement with
Accent Press Ltd.

British Library Cataloguing in Publication Data
Kerr, Peter 1940–
    The sporran connection. – Large print ed.
    1. Burns, Bob (Fictitious character) – Fiction
    2. Police – Scotland – Fiction
    3. Forensic scientists – Scotland – Fiction
    4. Murder – Investigation – Scotland – Fiction
    5. Scotland – Fiction
    6. Sicily (Italy) – Fiction
    7. New York (N. Y.) – Fiction
    8. Detective and mystery stories
    9. Large type books
    I. Title
    823.9'2 [F]

    ISBN 978–0–7531–8028–0 (hb)
    ISBN 978–0–7531–8029–7 (pb)

Printed and bound in Great Britain by
T. J. International Ltd., Padstow, Cornwall

To the real Bob Burns,
wherever he is now.

CHAPTER
ONE

Well, OK, it *was* more than ten years old, but so what? It only had twenty-thousand on the clock, genuine, and it looked as if it had just rolled out of the showroom. Immaculate paintwork gleaming white, even the tyres buffed up to a deep black lustre that you could comb your hair in. And let's face it, even if it was just the basic, entry-model Ford Sierra, some low-profile rubber on a set of sporty alloys, along with a snazzy *Cosworth* boot badge and a brace of rally seats (all nicked from one of the wrecks in the police-car graveyard, of course), and this motor would be the business. Young Andy Green was well chuffed.

Yeah, that old bloke had really looked after this wee beauty. Treated it like a baby. Never took it out in the rain. Scarcely *ever* took it out of the garage since his wife died a couple of years back, according to the neighbours. Too bad about his old lady snuffing it, right enough. But still, it's an ill wind . . .

Andy flicked an imaginary grain of dust off the dashboard, adjusted his fake Ray-Bans, lowered the driver's window and stuck his elbow out, adopting the customary cruiser-poser's position. This performance

1

was for the benefit of two demure-looking young ladies in a Renault Clio, which he now proceeded to overtake in a tyre-smoking scream of maximum revs. He glanced in his rear-view mirror, electing to interpret the young ladies' one-fingered salutes as a sign of approbation, and trying hard to convince himself that he was unable to lip-read their concerted yells of, "*WANKER!*"

Stuff them, anyway. After all, he wasn't just another country bobby doing the school crossing patrols at a one-horse place like Haddington any more. He was in the Edinburgh CID now — a bona fide big-city dick. So, who needed ten-a-penny hick slappers like that pair?

His hand was drawn downwards to the shelf under the dash, where a persistent rattle was beginning to get on his nerves. He groped about for a moment until his fingers lighted on the offending object. A music cassette! The old guy must have missed it when he was giving the car the pre-sale once-over. Andy glanced at the title on the inlay card. *SPIKE JONES AND HIS CITY SLICKERS*. Who the blazes were they? Only one way to find out. He slipped the tape into the slot on the fascia and tweaked the volume right up.

A revolver shot rang out, then another . . . and three more!

Startled, young Green ducked, then jumped — first bashing his nose on the steering wheel, then bouncing his head off the roof.

"Bugger me — I nearly filled ma breeks!" he wheezed, his pulse pounding.

2

The taped gunshots reverberated into a loony chorus of *You Always Hurt The One You Love* — virtuoso gargling and what sounded like the tuned inventory of a saloon bar full of percussive nutcases blasting from the car's speakers. Andy Green had never heard anything like it. Then, remembering that the old guy had made a point of mentioning that the car was almost out of juice, he pulled off the road and into the Esso service station on the western edge of town.

He continued to marvel at the musical mayhem escaping though his open driver's window, a bewildered look contorting his face while he began to dispense petrol from one of the self-service pumps. So distracted was he that he hadn't even noticed the glamorous young woman behind the wheel of a red Alfa Romeo Spider drophead, parked over by the carwash. She watched Andy closely for a few moments, then drove unhurriedly over and stopped at the pump opposite him.

Andy Green noticed her then all right. Wow! Talk about your drop-dead, classy babes. This one had it all, and then some!

And she made sure that young Green saw just enough of it to hold his interest in eye-popping mesmerism, her concessions to modesty confined to the limits of decency by the brevity of her skirt and the depth of her neckline. She slunk cat-like from her car.

Andy watched her approach him, his grip on the pump trigger tightening with every thrust of her swaying hips, the nozzle rattling in the Sierra's filler pipe in time with each sensuous click of her stiletto

3

heels. Inside his car, meantime, the City Slickers were inflicting grievous musical harm on a song called *Laura*.

Andy swallowed hard. He was peering at his own features gawping back at him from the mirror lenses of the Alfa Romeo woman's sunglasses. He jerked his head towards the car window. "Ehm, not exactly ma own taste in music," he gulped, his hose hand trembling. "The tape was in the car when I picked it up, like. Yeah, I'm more into, well, Status Quo — *Rockin' All Over The World* — that more kinda sophisticated stuff." He watched his face flush in the woman's reflector shades, while his fingers gave the fuel trigger one involuntary squeeze too many. "Aw, bollocks!" he yodelled as the petrol spilled down the front of his trousers. "Ma mother'll give me pure bloody hell for this!"

The Alfa Spider woman lowered her glasses and flashed Andy a dark-eyed look that had him wobbling at the knees. "Screw up, *piccino mio*," she whispered huskily, "and you're dead meat. *Capeesh?*" With that, she turned and sauntered back to her car, pausing before slithering into the driving seat to look back at her stunned quarry, while drawing a rigid, crimson-nailed forefinger slowly and deliberately across her throat.

Young Green was transfixed. He stood there with the dripping petrol gun in his hand, gaping at the red coupé sweeping out of the forecourt and away into the westbound flow of traffic. Robot-like, he placed the nozzle back in its holder, glancing down at his

4

petrol-soaked trousers as he did so. It was only then that he caught a glimpse of something propped against the bottom of the pump casing. It was a paper carrier bag.

Must belong to the foreign babe in the Alfa Spider, he figured. Hey, right enough, she had been toting it when she zeroed in on him — except, not surprisingly, it hadn't exactly been the paper poke that he'd been concentrating on.

Bending down, he opened the bag and peeped inside. His heart skipped a beat. Was this what it seemed to be? Nah, it couldn't be. Not *real*, anyway. With eager fingers, he rummaged through the bag's contents. Jeez, it *was* what it seemed to be. And real an' all! Holy shit!

Looking furtively around, he opened his car boot and locked the bag safely inside. Take no chances. His eyes darted again towards the few other forecourt customers. Right, nobody had noticed what had happened, he was sure of that. But what the *hell* was he gonna do now? His mind was in a spin. He sprinted to the side of the road and peered on tiptoes westward. Just as he thought — the red coupé was long gone. Not a moment to lose. He dashed over to the filling station shop.

"Pump Number Two, was it, sir?" the girl at the cash desk smiled. "That'll be thirty pounds and thirty-five pence, please."

Andy slammed his Visa card on the counter. "The open-top Alfa Romeo Spider that was out there a minute ago," he panted, "— did the woman pay by credit card? I need her name and card number."

"No, she didn't pay by credit card, sir." The girl smiled another frustratingly-calm, Esso-trained smile. "Collect the coupons, do you, sir?"

Andy shook his head impatiently. "Cash, then — did she pay by cash? Have ye got her car registration number on yer receipt pad, maybe?"

"No, not cash either, sir." The girl courteously offered Andy a small brochure. "Have you got a copy of our new Esso Gift Catalogue, sir? You really should save the coupons, you know." Unhurriedly, she pointed to the first page. "See — nice bath towels and nice drinks tumblers. Nice and big, them. Handy for these nice summer days when —"

"Cut the flannel, hen!" Andy snapped. He flashed her his police ID. "The woman must've paid by cheque, right? Quick, gimme a look at her cheque, then. This is CID business!"

"No, not by cheque either, sir." The girl stuffed Andy's declined gift coupons into her blouse pocket, the professional smile fading from her face. "See, the bird never even came intae the shop, 'cos she never even bought petrol or nothin'."

"Thanks a bloody million," Andy grunted. He rapidly scribbled his signature on the Visa slip. "A great bloody help *you've* been!" Glancing up, he looked the girl squarely in the eye. "Do ye know who the bird was, by any chance? I mean, have ye seen her in here before, like?"

The Esso girl tilted her head towards her slowly raised shoulder. "Search me, Kojak," she said flatly, then handed Andy his receipt. "In this game, ye see one, ye see them all, pal. Have a nice day now."

Headlights blazing, horn blaring, another millimetre or two of rubber scorching off his car's tyres, Andy Green departed the filling station in belated hot pursuit of the mysterious woman in the red Spider. A moment later, a white Ford Sierra almost identical to his hurtled into the forecourt from the opposite direction, its perspiring driver glancing anxiously at his watch. He clumsily rammed a tape into the car's cassette player as he skidded to halt at Pump No 2.

FIVE MINUTES LATER — THE VILLAGE OF DIRLETON, THREE MILES WEST OF NORTH BERWICK...

Detective Inspector Bob Burns was not a happy policeman. Squinting into the morning sunshine, which was already flooding the porch of his pantiled cottage, he focused a half-shut, bleary eye on the lanky silhouette standing with his finger poised a mere inch from the bell push.

"Touch that button again, Green, and I swear I'll break your bloody finger off!" He drew back the sleeve of his dressing gown and checked his watch. "Hell's teeth! What the blazes do you think you're playing at, waking me up at this ungodly hour on a Sunday morning, for Christ's sake? And a bank holiday weekend, at that!"

7

"Ehm, well, it's nearly quarter to ten, Chief," Andy Green flapped. "I mean, I thought ye'd maybe be up, like. Like gettin' ready to go to church . . . or something like that, like . . ." The words faded, and he lowered his eyes apprehensively as his boss grabbed him by the shirt front and yanked him forward till their noses were almost touching.

"Now then, boy," Burns muttered, the morning-after whiff of garlic and red wine hitting Green's olfactory organ with all the subtlety of a right hook and leaving him in no doubt as to the reason for his superior's patent ill humour, "tell me that I didn't hear you saying those words when I opened the door just now. Tell me that I didn't *really* hear you say that you'd come to report that you'd found a paper poke at the North Berwick filling station." The menace in his voice intensified with every syllable. "Just tell me that my ears were playing dirty tricks on me, Green, and I might *just* manage to curb this overwhelming urge I've suddenly got to return you to the lowest possible echelon of the uniformed mob first thing tomorrow bloody morning!"

Andy Green coughed, a surge of foreboding gripping his throat — a suffocating feeling exacerbated by the pungent proximity of his boss's heavy breathing. "I c-can't, skipper," he stammered, blinking, then coughing again.

Bob Burns' hold on Green's shirt tightened. "You c-can't, skipper, what? Come on, boy — I'm waiting!"

"Ah-ehm, I can't tell a lie, sir . . . in the immortal words of Abraham Lincoln, when . . ." He hesitated. Timorously, he produced the paper carrier bag from behind his back and held it aloft. "When his father felled him with a tree trunk for shooting President Kennedy, or whatever."

Without even giving it a second glance, Bob Burns brushed the bag aside. He took a deep, deliberate breath, trying hard to recover his naturally placid and patient demeanour. "Look, lad," he said quietly, summoning up unplumbed reserves of restraint, and releasing his grip on Andy Green's shirt. He laid both hands on the young fellow's shoulders and turned him slowly through one-hundred-and-eighty degrees. "Look out there and tell me what you see."

Andy shaded his eyes with his forearm. "What do I see? Hmm, let me see now." For a silent moment or two, he contemplated whether, in fact, this might be a trick question. Then, having arrived at no firm conclusion, he answered positively, "Nothin!" Cringing, he awaited the inevitable bollocking. But none came.

Instead, Bob Burns gave Green's back a congratulatory pat, then murmured, "Precisely, Andrew. Nothing. Nothing, that is, except the blooming roses and twining clematis clambering in gay profusion over the trelliswork arch at the cottage gate. Nothing, except the idyllic expanse of the village green unfolding beyond. Nothing, except the ruins of the old castle sleeping peacefully behind the shady curtain of ancient yew and sycamore over on the far side of the green there. Nothing . . ." He cupped a hand to his ear and closed his eyes. "Ah-h-h . . . Now, tell me, what do you *hear*?"

Andy duly cupped a hand to his own ear. He cocked his head and listened. "Nothin' again?" he ventured, prudently opting to plump for the same answer that had served him so well in the visual test only just concluded.

"Precisely." Bob Burns' voice exuded an almost eerie calm. "Nothing. Nothing, that is, except the glorious song of that blackbird rising from the depths of Archerfield Wood behind the old inn there. Nothing, except the drowsy chirping of sparrows in the high beech hedge by the lane here. Nothing, except the contented drone of a bumble bee lumbering nectar-laden homeward from that clump of honeysuckle tumbling over the wall of the little stone church there. Nothing . . ."

"Yeah," Andy concurred with a fatalistic lift of his shoulders, "a real nothin' place, this Dirleton, eh, boss?"

"Quite right, lad." Bob's tone was changing again, however. His vocal pitch was rising, nervous tension increasing palpably as he proceeded to articulate loudly, "And that is the *exact* reason why I came back to live here, in the nothingness of my native village, after more years than I care to remember *existing* in a dump of an attic flat in Stockbridge, with the wholesome, screaming bedlam of a thousand Edinburgh schoolkids assaulting my lug holes every morning, and the health-promoting guff and din of a gridlock of poison-spewing, engine-revving cars and buses exploding upwards from the bloody street all bloody day and most of the bloody night!" He was nicely wound up now — shouting, even. "And now you turn up in my little haven of tranquil nothingness at some god-awful

10

hour on a Sunday morning to break the news that you've found a paper poke! *Well*, I can tell you this for nothing, Green —"

The disconsolate DC Green tried to interject. "But, boss," he pleaded, pointing at the upheld carrier bag, "it's got —"

But Bob wasn't interested. "You can take your damned poke and hand it in at North Berwick nick, which is what you should have done in the first place." He paused to draw breath. "Or, better still," he spluttered, puce-faced, "you can take your bloody poke, roll it up with whatever's inside, and stick it sideways right up your fucking ar —"

"Ah, good morning, Andy! Brought the breakfast rolls, have you? Magic! What a pleasant surprise!" It was the ever-effervescent Doctor Julie Bryson, breezing through the front door of the cottage in a swirl of white lace, and plucking the carrier bag from Andy's still-raised hand. "How thoughtful of you." She gave Andy a teasing wink. "Sucking up to your boss, huh? Never mind, your secret's safe with me." She raised a make-believe cup to her lips. "Coffee or tea for you, Andy?" Then, shaking the carrier bag, she giggled, "Oo-ooh, this *is* heavy. Brought the bacon and marmalade and things as well, have you?"

Andy Green smiled sheepishly, but said nothing. He was thinking plenty, though — his thoughts confined almost exclusively to the tantalising flashes of the Doc's tanned bouncy bits, which were revealed every time her negligee moved in the light summer breeze. Ace thrup'nies . . . especially for a forensic scientist, he mused longingly. Mmm, a real wee stotter she was, right enough. Small, but perfectly formed. Jeez, imagine the Chief managing to pull a wee belter like her . . .

"OK, Green, when you've quite finished perving Doctor Bryson," Bob told him curtly, "you can put your eyes back in their sockets, then take your paper bag back and do what I told you to do with it." He cut off Julie's attempted objection with a wave of his hand. "No, DC Green *won't* be joining us for breakfast. He's got other more *pressing* matters to attend to . . . haven't you, lad?"

"If you say so, boss," Andy mumbled. He pulled a little-boy-lost face for the benefit of Doctor Julie, then looked down at his feet. "But I think I'll follow your first suggestion, skipper — if, ehm, that's OK with you, like. I mean, it would be a helluva waste to ram all that stuff up my ar —"

"Aa-aa-ee-ee-ee!" Julie squealed as she sneaked a little peek inside the bag. Shocked, she let it slip from her fingers, allowing the contents to spill out and scatter over the flagstones at her feet. "What on *earth* is that?"

CHAPTER
TWO

MULBERRY STREET, LITTLE ITALY, NEW YORK — A BACK ROOM IN THE "MAMMA SIRACUSA" PIZZA AND SPAGHETTI JOINT — MONDAY, AUGUST 5 — 12.30p.m. . . .

Physically, Massimo "Messina Max" Plantano was definitely a Little League player — in outward appearance, at any rate. But what he lacked in altitude, he more than compensated for in attitude. Massimo Plantano thought big. He always had. B-I-G was how they spelt survival in the back alleys on the west side of the Bowery when he was a kid. The only son of poor Sicilian immigrants and the youngest of a family of thirteen, Massimo soon learned that there was only one way up from the bottom of the heap in the Big Apple. And if that meant pain and suffering, then so be it.

He was only nine years old, legend has it, when he experienced his first broken leg. It belonged to his best buddy, Giorgio Guardione, another kid of Sicilian extraction. Because of his lankiness, Giorgio was known to his Little Italy contemporaries in New York as *il giraffa*, the giraffe. Bodily, Giorgio was the very antithesis of little Massimo, but, unfortunately, did not possess an IQ to match his height. Nor did his unusually (for an Italian) rangy limbs afford him as much agility as the shorter members of the Scorpione

Rosso Gang, of which he — because of his superior stature, no doubt — purported to be leader. However, Giorgio's distinct lack of nimbleness, both corporal and cerebral, was soon to lead to his downfall.

Writhing among the trash cans, where he and the other Red Scorpion members had been engaged in a game of back-street baseball, Giorgio screamed in agony at his best buddy: "Hey, Massimo! What the fuck? Why you hit me on the shin wid the baseball bat, man?"

Massimo looked down at the big fellow (a hitherto unknown experience, which the little guy was soon to develop into a lifelong obsession) and said without emotion, "Because ya didn't jump outa the way fast enough, that's why. So, get used to the feelin', piece-a'-shit loser!"

Giorgio wailed and clutched his shattered tibia.

Massimo pulled a cigar butt from behind his ear, stuck it in the corner of his mouth and drawled, "And somethin' else ya better get used to, Giorgio pal — ye're lookin' up at the new leader a' the Scorpione bunch, get it?"

"But why, Massimo?" Giorgio howled. "Why you doin' this to me, man? I'm your best buddy, for Chrisakes!"

Raising his elbow to rest it on the end of the baseball bat, Massimo twisted his face into a thin, humourless smile. "Yeah, and lucky for you that you *are* my best buddy, giraffe boy." He spat the cigar butt into the gutter beside Giorgio's head. "Yeah, lucky for you, otherwise I'd a' broke the other fuckin' leg as well!"

14

From that day on, everybody knew for sure that pain and suffering meant nothing to Messina Max Plantano — his trick being to make sure that he wasn't ever the one on the receiving end.

But that was forty years ago, and a lot of bad blood had passed under (and over) the Brooklyn Bridge since then. Today, Max was in reflective mood. Today was the twentieth anniversary of the death of his father; or, to be absolutely accurate, the twentieth anniversary of the day when what remained of his father's bloated corpse had been fished from the East River. Date of death, unknown. Cause of death, lead poisoning — if a gutful of shotgun pellets could qualify as such.

Max pushed his lunch plate to one side on the big mahogany desk that was the nerve centre of his "business" empire, then reached over and hit the intercom button . . .

"Kitchen? . . . *Si*, boss here . . . Hey, listen up! Tell that bum Angelo the meatballs is lousy. They stink! What's he usin' for meat? Garbage already? Tell him, no kiddin', my old man — God rest his pieces — had a dog could crap better meatballs than this!" Grimacing, he pushed the plate further away. "And don' gimme no goddam excuses, OK! Just tell Angelo go fix me a salami sandwich . . . Yeah, salami on rye, and hold the goykins. Even a bum cook like Angelo can't screw *that* up!"

There was a knock on the door. A pretty blonde head with big blue eyes and an innocent smile appeared round it. "Sorry to interrupt, Mr Plantano, but Ah couldn' get through on the intercom. Ah guess you was usin' it?"

"You're new, ain'cha?" Max grunted.

"Why, yessir, Mr Plantano. The agency sent me round this mornin' to fill in for a while. Somethin' about the reg'ler girl needin' a urgent operation. Appendectomy, was it?" The girl placed a forefinger on her cheek and looked thoughtfully heavenward. "Well now, Ah had a cousin took appendicitis once and —"

"Yeah," Max cut in, "that was the other chick's problem here also. Appendicitis — somethin' like that." He pulled a who-the-hell-cares? shrug.

Although the room had no window, and the only electric light was a green-shaded banker's lamp on his desk, Max was wearing dark glasses. He felt naked without them. He took them off.

"But come on in, honey. Lemme have a look at the rest a' ya."

The girl stepped bashfully inside and stood by the door, blushing.

"Hey-y-y, not bad at that," Max drooled, giving her the once-over — twice. "In from the sticks, are ya, baby?"

The girl batted her eyelashes. "Tennessee, sir. Smithsville, Tennessee."

"Tennessee, huh? Well now, I like southern belles. Yeah, southern belles make me feel, like ... ring-a-ding-ding!" Without taking his eyes off her, he took a large cigar from a box on the desk, cut the end and lit up. "What's yer name, baby face?" he enquired through a billowing blue haze.

"Why, Lulu-May, Mr Plantano sir."

"And don' tell me — yer surname's Eventually, right?" Max let rip with a guffaw, Lulu-May's obvious embarrassment merely adding to his enjoyment. "Anyway, honey," he eventually wheezed, "what can I do for ya? . . . if that ain't a stoopid question."

"There's a call for you on line one, Mr Plantano sir," said Lulu-May, ignoring the lewd remark. "From Scotland, England, I think." She checked her notepad. "Yeah, that's right. A Miss Laprima Frittella, the lady said. Callin' from Edinburrow."

"OK, put her through," Max grunted. He pensively rolled his cigar between thumb and fingertips, while checking out Lulu-May's rear elevation as she wiggled towards the door. "One thing, sweet lips," he called after her, then glanced at his podgy cigar mitt, "— ya know anything about shorthand work, do ya?"

Lulu-May paused in the open doorway and shook her head.

"Good," Max smirked. "Come back later and I'll give ya a practical demonstration." With a self-satisfied smirk, he lifted the phone and waited to be connected.

"*Pronto* . . . Max?"

"Laprima, baby!" Max was euphoric, his spaghetti bowl of bonhomie filled to overflowing. "*Ciao, bella! Come stai?*"

"*Sto bene, grazie. E tu?*"

"*Bene, bene*, I'm feelin' good. But speak American, baby, huh? Now, what's the low line on the latest drop ya done over there?"

"I made the connection with the new messenger boy yesterday."

"Ya gave him the groceries?"

"Sure, no problem. Yeah, he arrived right on time, playing your favourite song, just like you said."

"Beautiful! So, uh, what time is it wid ya in Scotland?"

"Five-thirty, Monday evening."

"Beautiful! So, uh, the boy delivered the groceries to the correct address already, yeah? I mean, ya checked it out, baby, right?"

Silence.

"Hey, speak to me, Laprima baby! Come on, don' mess around, OK? Hello! Hey, cut it out, honey — ye're givin' me heart attacks here."

"It's, uh . . . just that there's been a slight problem . . . delivery-wise."

Silence.

"Hello . . . you still there, Max?"

Max was breathing fast. "*Yeah*, I'm still here!" he growled. "I just been swallowin' a sonofabitch blood pressure pill! Now, what the hell kinda goddam problem ya got delivery-wise?"

Laprima was breathing fast now too. "The problem, Maxie — to give it to you straight from the shoulder — is that, uhm, the messenger boy didn't actually, well, *make* the delivery."

"Aw, ye're jivin' my pants off, right, baby?" Max had more pathos in his voice than Al Jolson singing Mammy. "Hey, Laprima *bellissima*, tell me ye're only jivin' my pants off here, *puh-leez* . . ."

Laprima steadied herself. "Sorry, Maxie. It's no gag. I checked with the customer by phone at close of business today. And, uh, no dice. No delivery."

Max swallowed another blood pressure pill. He was thinking baseball bats. "OK, baby," he said softly, his voice breaking with bottled-up frenzy, "ya know who to contact. I want that piece-a'-shit messenger boy should get what's comin' to him, and I want you should get my groceries back *prontamente. Capisci?*" Max's voice was trembling now. He lowered it to a malignant whisper. "Ya wouldn't want that sweet little doll face a' yours messed up bad for good, now would ya, honey?"

Laprima Frittella had known Massimo Plantano long enough to realise that he meant business. She knew only too well what happened to anyone in the organisation who didn't match up to the boss's high standards of lowlife thuggery. She was shaking in her slingback stilettos, and she knew that Max knew it. She tried to sound composed. "Maxie sweetheart, you know I'd never do anything to cross —"

"SHUT yer goddam face when ye're answerin' MY questions!" Max erupted. "And don' gimme none a' that never-do-anything-to-cross-me crap! Nah, too many money-grabbin' broads tried to feed me that smooth-talkin' baloney before, and I never swallowed none a' it, right! Ya get where I'm comin' from?"

"Yeah, of course I do, baby. I just —"

"BUTTON yer cake hole, I said! You deaf or somethin'? Now listen, and listen good. I want that thievin' bum messenger boy wasted, and I want them groceries back, OK? And in addition also, I want the

19

deal for that item a' merchandise ye're buyin' for me closed, and closed but FAST. Do I make myself understood, *carissima mia?*"

"Well, sure, you know I'll do my best, Maxie honey, but —"

"ZIP it! You was doin' yer best today, ya dumb bitch, and all ya done was lose the friggin' groceries, for cryin' out!"

"OK, OK, Max, I won't foul up again, I promise you. Just — just gimme a break, huh?"

Max released a sinister little chuckle. "Hey-y-y, ya sound real terrified, baby. *Real* terrified. Yeah-h-h," he breathed, "I like that. Ya know I do, doll face." He laughed aloud, then yelled down the phone, "Now get this screw-up in Scotland fixed, babe, or I gonna personally see to it that ya go on a Loch Ness Monster hunt in a one-woman, concrete submarine!"

"I get the message, Max."

"You better, sweetness. And don't forget to clinch the buyin' deal on that piece a' merchandise. I NEED THAT SPORRAN, AND I NEED IT *PRONTO!*"

CHAPTER
THREE

LOTHIAN AND BORDERS POLICE HQ, FETTES AVENUE, EDINBURGH, SCOTLAND — MONDAY, AUGUST 5 — 7.30p.m. . . .

Bob Burns yawned, closed his eyes and leaned back in his seat. "So much for a so-called bank holiday," he grumped. "The first Monday off in yonks, and it's totally bloody wasted!"

Andy Green sat fidgeting at the other side of the desk. "I mean to say, skipper," he whined, his face a picture of disillusionment, "a hundred thousand quid. There must be a reward for turning in *that* kind of boodle. Even ten per cent. That would be, let me see . . . one per cent would be . . . no, start again . . . a hundred pounds multiplied by . . . no, that's not right either . . . divide a hundred by —"

"Oh, for Pete's sake, save yourself the bother!" Bob barked. "First, we'll have to find out who *owns* the damned money before you start getting your knickers in a twist about a bloody reward!"

"Yeah, but that's what I mean. I mean, I had to borrow four grand to buy that motor, and if I could get my hands on some reward spondoolicks . . . I mean, why aren't we putting out posters and ads and everything, asking the owner to come forward, instead of just sitting here waiting?"

"Don't be such a twonk. Do you want this place overrun by every bare-faced liar in the country? Hell's teeth, put that kind of info about and we'll have the buggers lining up with their hands out from here to Princes Street in no time flat!"

Eyes downcast, Andy began to twiddle his thumbs, his bottom lip protruding sulkily. He thought for a while, then muttered, "I didn't need to hand it *all* in, you know. I could've stuffed a few of the wads in my Davy Crockett at the filling station, like."

Bob opened an accusing eye. "Who's to say you didn't? You're certainly daft enough."

Andy rose to the bait. "Aw, honest, boss, I never nicked a single note. Cub's honour."

Bob Burns closed his eye again. "I hope not, boy. Sooner or later, the owner of that dosh is gonna turn up, and if there's any missing . . ."

The phone rang. Bob sat up, groaned, stretched himself, then answered it.

"Burns here . . . Hi, Julie . . . Aye, still here — awaiting developments, you might say . . . No, bugger all yet . . . The Alfa Romeo car? . . . No, all Green remembers is that it was red and looked new . . . The carrier bag? . . . OK, bring it along and you can tell me about it. Cheers."

He replaced the receiver and shook his head wearily. Looking over at Andy Green, he asked himself, "Why me? Why am I lumbered with a bampot mystery like this? Why not a nice interesting murder case, preferably with *him* as the victim?"

"Heh, Chief!" Andy piped up, his mien suddenly more optimistic. "Finders keepers!"

Bob glowered at him. "You what?"

"The filling station loot!"

"Come again."

Andy Green's eyes were fairly glinting now. "The one hundred grand. I mean, maybe, if the money isn't claimed within a certain time, I'll get to keep the lot!" He rubbed his hands together. "Yeah, I reckon there's some kinda rule like that. You know, just like the time my old lady found that umbrella on the bus. She handed it in at the lost property office, see, and after about, well, a few weeks or months I think it was, she got the umbrella to keep. She's still got it, an' all." He could hardly contain his delight. "A tartan one it is, with a handle like a duck's head, and it opens up automatic-like when you press the wee —"

The door opened. "Oh dear, have I interrupted something?" It was Julie Bryson, looking slightly taken aback. "Sorry, I should've knocked." She looked at her watch. "I didn't think you'd still be in conference, or whatever you call it."

Bob assured her it was OK, then stood up to fetch her a chair. "Young Green here was just talking in his sleep as usual, daydreaming about a one-hundred-K windfall." He shook his head again and had a quiet laugh. "Remind me to keep an eye open for winged porkers landing on my bird table the next time I put some crumbs out."

"Oh, I don't know about that," Julie countered. "There *is* some law about lost things becoming the property of the finder, if still unclaimed after a certain period of time, isn't there?"

Andy Green latched on to this with unbridled enthusiasm. "That's *just* what I was sayin', Doc! And just think, a hundred thousand nicker. Here, with that amount of spon, I could buy maself a *real* Ford Sierra Cozzie, and buy my Mum and Dad's council house for them, and put a deposit on a suave wee *pee deter* for maself here in the smoke. Somewhere handy for the nightlife, like. For takin' birds back to an' that. Aw, yeah," he drooled, "I can see it all now. There'd be —"

"Spare us the sordid details," Bob butted in. "And just remember, you've got enough on your plate holding down your job as a *probationary* detective constable without drifting off to Wonderland on police time." He turned to Julie. "Right then, you said you had something for me — something about the carrier bag."

Julie handed him the empty bag. "Recognise anything?" she asked, touching her nose.

Bob scrutinised the bag thoroughly. "I recognise a brown paper bag." He hunched his shoulders. "But then, that's the sort of observant stuff we Detective Inspectors are paid for."

"No, I mean smell it, silly!"

Bob held the bag to his nose and sniffed. "Ah, I've got it now. It smells like brown paper."

"Inside, for heaven's sake. I meant smell it inside!" Julie snatched the bag from him and held it over his face, as if feeding a horse. "*Now* what do you recognise?"

24

"The smell of used bank notes," came the muffled reply.

"Anything else?"

Bob inhaled again, deeply. "Yeuch!" He pulled the bag away, gagging. "What the hell's that pong? It's sweet, it's sickly . . . enough to make you puke!"

Julie tutted in exasperation and promptly passed the bag to Andy Green. "Come on, Andy, you try!"

It only took one sniff. "I recognise that," he said with a self-congratulatory grin. "It smells of you, Doc. Well, ehm, that expensive perfume you always wear, I mean to say."

"*Femme* by Rochas," Julie confirmed through clenched teeth, wheeling round to glare at Bob. "Remember? You gave it to me for my birthday."

"Yeah, well, of course," Bob blustered. He fingered his shirt collar and darted a don't-you-dare-bloody-snigger glance at Andy Green. "It's just that, uhm, it was the unusual circumstances that threw me for a minute there. I mean, let's face it, I don't usually have a paper bag over my head when you dab it all over, do I?"

Julie dipped her head coquettishly. "I won't tell, if you won't."

Andy Green stuck his tongue firmly in his cheek and commenced a detailed survey of his fingernails.

Bob reckoned it was time to switch smartly from defence to attack. "Is that all your highly-educated forensic crew can come up with," he snapped at Julie, "— the particular exotic fragrance of the paper bag? Brilliant!"

"Well, you didn't exactly give us a helluva lot to go on, did you! A hundred wads of ten used, one-hundred-pound notes. All different breeds — Bank of Scotland, Bank of England, Royal Bank of Scotland, Clydesdale Bank, the full set. And no specific clues to go for, like blood, fingerprints, Semtex, for example!" Julie was well nettled. "Be fair! What in heaven's name do you expect? Miracles?"

Bob raised his hands. "OK, OK, I'm sorry, OK?" He looked up irritably at the wall clock. "To hell with it — we'll go over the whole boring bit just once more, then I'm damn well calling it a day!"

"Aw, thank God," Andy Green groaned. He massaged his midriff. "Ma belly thinks ma throat's been cut."

Julie patted the young Detective Constable's knee. "Never mind, Andy, I'm sure your skipper will treat us to a nice, juicy pizza at Mamma Roma's when we finally get out of here tonight." Then, noting Bob's scowl, she promptly added, "On CID exies, of course!"

Bob chose to ignore that speculative remark. "Right, Green," he said, getting straight down to business, "run it past me one more time. You were at home with your folks in Haddington, looking through the used car pages in the *Evening News* on Saturday night, right?"

That had been it, Andy Green confirmed, and he had noticed this ad for a low-mileage, one-owner Sierra. A North Berwick phone number, it was. The old boy on the other end had said to come down first thing in the morning. There had been a lot of interest, so if he really wanted the car, he'd have to be sharp. After all, it wasn't every day that a Ford Sierra, in mint nick, with only — .

"Aye, aye, aye," Bob cut in, "you can skip all the propaganda about the car. Just get on with it, for God's sake!"

Duly admonished, Andy resumed his narrative . . .

One of his mates had picked him up at eight o'clock on Sunday morning, had driven him the ten miles or so over the Garleton Hills to North Berwick, and had dropped him off at the pre-determined address in Saint Baldred's Road. The old gadgie hadn't even been out of his scratcher yet, so Andy had stood blethering to a couple of neighbours while he waited for the codger to get into his day threads and fish his teeth out of their tumbler and that. Anyhow, it had only taken a quick gander at the Sierra to persuade Andy that this was the motor for him. Pure, dead brilliant it was! All the same, he had taken it for a wee spin, just so's not to appear too keen, like, then did the business there and then. Four-and-a-half big ones. Only one thing, though — the old gadgie hadn't been too chuffed about taking a cheque; not until Andy had slipped him an eyeful of his CID ID, that is. "Magic, that!" Andy enthused. "Open, Sesame Street!"

"Just get to the filling station bit, will you," Bob Burns yawned, before settling back and closing his eyes again. "Just get to the bit about the mysterious bird in the Alfa Romeo Spider . . . this fantastic drop-dead cutie in the wonderful drophead coupé."

"Aw, heh, nice line, Chief!" Andy Green was impressed. "Poetry as well, eh!"

"Hmm, they didn't tag him Robert Burns for nothing," Julie quietly remarked.

"Anyway," Andy went on, "I'd just started listenin' to the tape —"

"Wait a minute," Bob frowned, "you didn't say anything about a tape before."

"Not important, boss. Just a tape the old bloke left in the car."

"Let *me* be the judge of whether it's important or not. What tape was it, anyway?"

Andy reached into his inside jacket pocket. "This one — Spike Jones And His City Slickers. *Spike Jones Murders Again*, it's called."

Bob took the cassette and looked at the cartoon of a zany bunch of musicians on the inlay card. "I remember this stuff from when I was a nipper," he smiled. "It's stark, raving bonkers. Just as a matter of interest, though, which track were you playing when the Spider lady drew alongside?"

Andy craned his neck to look at the cassette box. "When she drew alongside, ye say? Ehm, that one." He pointed to the list of titles. "*You Always Hurt The One You Love*. Weird . . . but good! I mean, musical gargling an' that. Dead brilliant!" He scratched his forehead. "And musical fartin' an' all. Yeah, I wonder how they do *that*."

Bob shook his head in despair. "A trombone, Green," he stated flatly. "They do it with a trombone."

28

Andy Green thought about that for a couple of moments. "Gee!" he eventually gasped, consciously restraining the fingers of his right hand from going on an exploratory trip to his backside. He was deeply confused, and looked it. "But — but where do they stick the mouthpiece, then?"

Bob Burns groaned and buried his face in his hands.

"I think, Andy, it's what's called, in musical circles, an unorthodox embouchure," Julie advised, deadpan.

"Aw, right enough," Andy concurred, none the wiser. "There ye go, then."

Bob's face emerged jaded from behind his hands. "And there's nothing more you can tell us about this bird in the red Alfa," he droned, "other than that she was a right stotter of a Spanish type, with a half-American, half-foreign accent, correct?"

"What about the actual words she said?" Julie prompted. "Was it all in English, for instance, or —?"

"Hey!" Andy snapped his fingers and sat up. "Now you mention it, she did call me something Spanish at that! Uhm, let me see now . . . *Pinocchio?* . . . No, not exactly that . . . Yeah! *Cappuccino*, that was it!"

Julie joined Bob in a questioning frown. Then her face lit up. "Wait a mo, it wasn't *piccino*, by any chance? Or even *piccino mio*, maybe?"

"Yeah, *that* was it! Spot on, Doc! Peach — peach, eh, whatever you just said. Magic!"

"So, what the hell does that mean in Spanish?" Bob asked. "Daft numpty?"

"Italian," Julie said, "not Spanish. A familiar term, *piccino mio*. It's Italian for 'kid', or 'sonny boy'. That sort of thing, you know?"

"Don't screw up, sonny boy, or you're dead meat," Andy muttered reflectively. "Bloody charming, eh?"

"So, an Italian-American bird, then." Bob raised a cynical eyebrow. "That narrows it down to about twenty million or so, I suppose."

"Come on now!" Julie objected. "There can't be that many newish Alfa Romeo Spiders on the road in *this* country. Why don't you check with the main dealers?"

"That's already in hand."

"The ferry ports too? And the Channel Tunnel people?"

"Them as well." Bob leaned forward and planted his elbows firmly on the desk. "But I still think the best bet is just to wait for the Spider woman to show her hand. That hundred grand was meant for *somebody*, and when she discovers that the particular somebody hasn't got it, she'll break cover, never fear." He then turned back to Andy Green. "You reckon she had about a five minute head start on you when she left the North Berwick Esso station, do you?"

"Yeah, and I went like shit to try and catch her, but no chance. Nah, she was well away. That's why, when I got to the crossroads at the far end of Dirleton, I decided to double back and report to you, skipper. She could've been headin' in any direction on any one of half-a-dozen roads by that time. Know what I mean?"

"Hmm," Bob pondered, "and ten minutes later, I called the traffic cops and put out an APB on her. But nothing."

Julie couldn't resist a little dig. "What do you expect at that time on a Sunday morning? Most of your traffic boys would still be busy having a post Saturday-night kip in a nice, quiet layby somewhere."

Bob pretended not to have heard that quip. Accurate as it may have been, he didn't want Andy Green's professional innocence defiled. Thinking hard, he tapped the bridge of his nose with his thumb. "I must confess, though, I'm really surprised the Spider woman, or someone, hasn't been back at the filling station to ask questions about that paper poke."

"And you're quite sure nobody has?" Julie checked.

"Yep, we've had a succession of plain-clothes lads hanging about the place round the clock, posing as pump-maintenance guys, a gardener, night watchman, you name it. The North Berwick uniformed blokes are keeping a weather eye open, too." He stroked his chin and mumbled, "The lack of action's beginning to bother me, mind. Nobody dumps a hundred thousand smackers at a petrol pump and just forgets about it. No, something about this whole thing stinks."

"Of *Femme* by Rochas, dare I say?" Julie hazarded.

"Mmm," Bob mused, "*cherchez la femme* . . ."

The phone rang. Julie answered it: "DI Burns office . . . Uh-huh? . . . I see . . . Right you are, I'll put him on." She handed Bob the phone. "This could be the action you've been looking for, Kemosabe. It's the duty sergeant on the incident desk. The North

Berwick police have just reported finding a young guy tied up in the boot of a white Ford Sierra. He's been shot . . . dead!"

FIFTY MINUTES LATER — THE CAR PARK OF TANTALLON CASTLE, TWO MILES EAST OF NORTH BERWICK . . .

"Pretty spectacular backdrop for a murder," Bob Burns observed as he parked his unmarked Omega behind the clutch of police panda cars guarding the cordoned-off white Sierra.

"That's a jewel of understatement, if ever I heard one," said Julie, taking in the stunning panorama. She stepped from the car and stood for a moment to savour the view over the wide, still waters of the Firth of Forth. The evening sun had painted the guano-blanched crags of the Bass Rock a pale pink and had illuminated in fiery red the sandstone bulk of the castle ruins that dominated the coastline from the clifftops just ahead.

Bob was already striding over to the scene of the crime, with DC Andy Green following faithfully a couple of paces behind. A uniformed officer stepped forward from the little huddle of bobbies standing by the Sierra.

"DI Burns, I presume," he said and offered Bob his hand. "Inspector Dave Murray, E-Division, Haddington."

Bob quickly concluded the formalities, then asked, "OK, what have you got for us, Dave?"

He ushered Bob and his little entourage over to the murder vehicle. "Everything's just as my boys found it.

Nothing's been touched. The photographer's already taken some preliminary shots, but he'll snap whatever else you want, of course."

Bob Burns looked down into the car's open boot, a lump rising in his throat at the sight of the trussed-up body so brutally robbed of life. The victim's lips were frozen in a grimace of terror, glazed eyes staring from his mask-like face.

"Shot through the head where he lay, by the looks of it," Bob said, unable to conceal the disgust he felt. "Poor young bugger. Didn't stand an earthly."

Julie came forward to take a closer look. "Whoever did it gave him a good going-over first, though." She pointed a finger. "Look, the severe bruising and the lacerations to the side of the face here . . . and there, the swollen lip." Gingerly, she peeled back a torn flap of blood-soaked shirt. "And the grazed skin and subcutaneous discolouration on his rib cage there. My God, somebody's really sunk the boot in with a vengeance!"

"Hmm, and I don't like the angle his left leg bends at below the knee," Bob muttered. He leaned over and touched the awkwardly upturned foot. There was a nauseating crunch of bone on splintered bone as the misshapen limb flopped over and came to rest the wrong way round on the floor of the boot. "How the hell . . .?" Bob winced. "The bastards must have set about it with a jemmy or something!"

Julie pulled on a pair of surgical gloves. "May as well have a closer look at one or two bits and pieces while we wait for the rest of the team to get here," she said, slipping professionally into forensic scientist mode. She studied the victim's face, then remarked, "You know, Andy, at first glance, he's not at all unlike you."

The fingers of Andy Green's right hand were already kneading his Adam's apple. "Aye, well," he replied shakily, "but he's a bit paler than me, like."

"Yeah, but a hole in the head'll make that difference every time, son," Bob advised. "The anaemic skin tone kinda goes with the state of health, if you catch my drift."

Julie shot him a reproachful look. "Tasteless remarks aside," she said, "I meant the blue eyes, fairish hair, general boyish demeanour, that sort of thing." She stretched over the corpse and picked up a small leather pocketbook that was lying open in the far corner of the boot. "Now, what have we got here?" Her fingers carefully probed the inner folds of the wallet. "Mmm, no money, anyway. The killer obviously took care of that." She then pulled out a passport and flipped it open.

Bob peered over her shoulder. "So, who was he?"

Julie found the relevant page. "Gaetano di Scordia. Italian. Born Palermo, 1979."

"He doesn't look like an Eyetie to me," Andy Green croaked, dry-mouthed. "I mean, the blue eyes an' that."

"Ah, but he's Sicilian, you see," Julie pointed out.

"Yeah," Bob agreed, "it'll be the old Norman genes."

Andy Green loosened his tie. "Who — who's Norman?" he stammered. "I thought ye just said the stiff's name was Guy somebody." He nodded frantically towards the Sierra's boot. "And, anyhow — look, he's not even wearin' jeans!"

By now, Julie was leaning into the car through the open driver's window. She re-emerged with a small, rectangular object in her hand.

"Well, well, well, guess who just happened to be lurking in the cassette player. Spike Jones And His City Slickers, no less!" She held the tape up to Bob. "*Spike Jones Murders Again* — yet again, would you believe?"

"Stick the cassette back in the machine and switch it on," Bob told her with more than a hint of urgency. "I think you may just have stumbled on the motive there."

Julie did as instructed, and instantly the serene old walls of Tantallon Castle were being battered by crackpot melodic salvoes of *You Always Hurt The One You Love*.

"There you are then, Green," Bob shouted to Andy above the musical mayhem. He pointed down at the dead body. "Now we know who was *really* meant to pick up the hundred grand from the Spider woman, don't we?"

Without diverting his eyes from the grizzly contents of the boot, he attempted to lay a comforting hand on his sidekick's shoulder, but his fingers encountered only fresh sea air.

Andy Green had already swooned into an untidy heap of gangly arms and legs, his complexion matching his surname, if not the luckless Gaetano di Scordia's deathly pallor . . . yet.

CHAPTER
FOUR

THE MEDITERRANEAN ISLAND OF SICILY —
A HILLSIDE OVERLOOKING THE HISTORIC
PORT OF MESSINA — TUESDAY, AUGUST 6 . . .

Young Franco Contadino had decided to knock off
early for lunch. Business in his little workshop down
there on the outskirts of town was even slacker than
usual today. And besides, it was just too darned hot for
work. *Merda!* how he hated being a blacksmith in the
summer; even more so than in winter, if that were
possible. All that messing about with bench grinders,
electric hacksaws, oxyacetylene cutters and welders;
the perpetual smell of metal filings and the smoke of
red-hot steel in your nostrils; the spark burns on your
hands and arms; and, worst of all, the heat — the
incessant, suffocating heat of the forge that had you
sweating like a pig with malaria, even on the coolest of
days.

But it wasn't cool today. *Dio!* it was a scorcher —
one of those oppressively sweltering summer days when
even the butterflies were too done in to take off.

Breathless after the ten minute climb up from the
road where he had parked his van, Franco slumped
down on a crumbling stone wall beneath an ancient
carob tree, unintentionally disturbing a small gecko that
had been snoozing in the rubble, and sending it

scurrying off in search of a more private retreat. Not that that would be too difficult to find . . .

Franco opened his bottle of water and took a long, reviving slug. Ah, that was better! He breathed in deeply. At least there was an occasional puff of air up here; a rare little swirl of refreshingly tepid air rising up from the Straights of Messina, carrying on its breath the salty tang of the sea and the faint scent of tamarisk. Why, you could scarcely even hear the traffic on the crowded coastal *autostrada* from this height. Close your eyes, and it could be twenty years ago . . . except that there was no cockerel crowing on the roof of the little house now, no hens clucking and scratching contentedly in the dust by the door, no white-haired grandmother calling the family in from the field for the midday meal. *Che stupendo!* He could smell that glorious aroma of freshly-baked bread even now.

But those days were gone, never to return. Franco had grown to accept that long ago. Even his own father had had to leave this little farm to find work in the town when scarcely much more than a boy himself. That was just the way of things in Sicily.

The boom of a cannon echoed up from Messina's *campanile* belltower far below. Automatically, Franco checked the time on his wristwatch. Twelve noon. Everyone would be busy preparing for the lunchtime rush at the *Ristorante Bella Siciliana* back in Edgeware Road by this time. He turned his head to look at his grandparents' little farmhouse, in ruins now and neglected, save for the old grape vine and pink bougainvillea that clambered in unrestrained competition over the rickety pergola outside the kitchen window, more or less as they had always done.

Franco smiled to himself. That little heap of stones, or rather his dreams of what he would do with it one day, had been what had sustained him during those first homesick months in London. Ah, London — where the streets are still paved with gold, and where there's still a fortune just waiting for every young Italian waiter who's willing to work his *culo* off and look after the pennies. Oh yes, that was what they had all said all right, but it hadn't taken him long to find out the truth about London . . . and himself.

Sure, he had worked hard and long, seven days a week and every hour that the boss could throw at him, the slave-driving old *bastardo*. And, sure, he had been making decent enough money — well, decent enough compared to the pittance his father had been paying him as an apprentice blacksmith, on those weeks when he could afford to pay him anything at all, that's to say. But London, like any other big city, can be a false friend. It welcomes the poor stranger with open arms, seduces him with promises of riches, then uses its many other temptations to claw back from the unwary everything it has given — and often much, much more.

Looking back on it now, Franco could only admit that he had been a mug; the classic engineer of his own demolition, you might say. At first, he had done little else in London but work and sleep, and maybe, whenever he could snatch a moment, try to bone up on his English. And, sure enough, the money had soon started to accumulate in his Bank of England account. After all, he'd had precious little time to spend any of it, and his only notable expense was the criminally-large slice of his wages that *il padrone* docked off every week for the rent of a cramped room above the restaurant; a dingy, damp dump of an attic that he had been obliged to share with an ever-extending family of mice and a pair of racing cockroaches that always managed to outpace him on a nightly three-metre sprint across the linoleum floor between the bedside cabinet and the wardrobe.

And then along came love, or what he mistook for it. Kate O'Flaherty exploded into his life like a fiery-haired bombshell, when she breezed into the restaurant for a Guy Fawkes Night theme party with a bunch of giggling girlfriends from the Neasden fireworks factory where they all worked. Kate was dressed as a Roman candle. Franco was smitten. Perhaps it was the reflection in her Irish eyes of the fibre-optic "sparks" spraying out from her green tinsel wig that had bewitched him. Or maybe it was just the predictable effect made on his Latin libido by the bounty of Kate's Celtic curvaceousness, poured incredulously as it was into that long, red tube of a dress. Some firework! Franco could hardly wait to light this one's touchpaper.

After a long year of self-imposed carnal continence, the virile young *Siciliano* was more than ready to launch himself into an incontinent bender of epic proportions, and the lusty and willing Miss O'Flaherty was just the love laxative required.

But, sadly, it was to be, "Hello, Kate — *arrivederci*, prudence!" Franco had popped his cork, and the genie of *la dolce vita* cheerfully escaped the bottle. In only a few, wild weeks of serious nightclubbing and general hell-for-leather hedonism, Franco's hard-won savings, a sub of a month's wages and a recklessly-negotiated overdraft of a thousand quid had disappeared — to be followed swiftly by *carissima* Kate.

He was in debt, ditched and disconsolate, and suddenly feeling a long, long way from home. Yet, home was the last place he could go now. For one thing, he didn't have the fare, and, more importantly, how could he tell his doting parents that he had been so *stupido*? What now of all his extravagant boasts of returning one day to Sicily with enough money to turn the old family farm on the hillside into the swankest country restaurant on the island? And what were his great promises of providing for his *Mamma* and *Papà* in their old age going to be worth now?

Thoroughly depressed and increasingly desperate, he had then decided to pawn the only thing of value that he possessed, the gold pocket watch that his grandfather had left him, and to recoup his losses via that optimistically-fast route so well trodden by many an émigré Italian waiter — the path to the bookie's shop.

And that, by the fickle ways of fate, was how Franco Contadino came to be sitting alone on this deserted Sicilian hillside today, not only still skint, but even deeper in hock than ever.

CHAPTER
FIVE

THE DEACON BRODIE TAVERN — THE ROYAL MILE, EDINBURGH, SCOTLAND —WEDNESDAY, AUGUST 7 — 5.45p.m. . . .

Bob Burns had arranged to meet Julie Bryson here for an after-work drink. Not *his* choice of rendezvous, it had to be said. He looked around the bar. Nothing *that* wrong with the place, mind you . . . if you liked all that "genuine Auld Reekie" repro kitsch. He held his pint up to the light. Hmm, and the beer *was* good, you had to admit that.

He took a luxuriant gulp of his favoured Belhaven Best, then burped discreetly into the funnel of his fist. "*Toujours la politesse,*" as the French say. Yeah, and there were plenty of them about these parts of the Edinburgh Old Town at this time of year. Camera-toting French, Germans, Japanese, Americans, and Aussies with elastic-sided boots as well. Take your pick, the area was crawling with touristy rubbernecks of every stamp and tint. God, and it would only get worse, the closer the International bloody Festival loomed.

With that melancholy thought in mind, he tapped into the conversation of a pair of chiffon-neckerchiefed chrysanthemums standing one-hand-on-hip further along the bar. They were sipping rosé spritzers through pastel cocktail straws and dragging histrionically on gold-tipped Black Sobranies, while loudly discussing Chekhov's *Uncle Vanya* in London luvvie-speak.

Jesus, they were here already, Bob said to himself. The organisational vanguard of the Festival Fringe artyfarties, up checking on the doss-down capacity of the back room of the Cowgate Scout Hut, or some other hole-in-the-wall "theatre", while mincing about town as if they owned the Royal Lyceum Theatre itself. He chuckled into his pint glass. "You've got to laugh, right enough!"

Of course, he knew that Julie loved all this "annual cultural invasion" crap. It forced Edinburgh to lighten up, was how she put it — to loosen its staid, old corset strings for a few all-too-short weeks of the year. But then she would, wouldn't she? After all, she was from Glasgow, and (paradoxically, the Edinburgh corset-wearers would say) from a genteel family background that had taught her to appreciate such "better things in life'. Bob heaved a what's-the-bloody-difference sort of shrug. Hell, the nearest *he*'d got to culture, as a kid in an East Lothian farmworker's cottage, was being allowed to stay up late in front of an old black-and-white telly on weekend nights to watch Andy Stewart on *The White Heather Club*.

"And is that supposed to make me some kind of lesser being?" he muttered. "Nah, not bloody likely!"

"It's the first sign, you know . . ."

"Uh?"

"Talking to yourself . . . the first sign of going *aff yer heid*, as we say in Kelvinside."

42

"Aye, well, it's a prerequisite of qualifying for the police pension," Bob replied, covering his embarrassment by giving Julie a peck on the cheek. "Welcome to Stratford-on-Forth, by the way."

Julie, meantime, was hailing the barman. "Hi, Julian!"

"Hi, sweetie. The usual, is it?"

"Yes, a spritzer please, Jools. Rosé if poss."

Bob rolled his eyes ceilingward.

"So prithee, sire," Julie puckishly smiled as she made herself comfortable on a high stool (never an easy straight-skirt exercise for one so petite, but one which, as she was well aware, Bob was always grateful to witness), "whence cometh my eagle-eyed prince of sleuthery this fine day?"

Glowering over the rim of his glass, Bob grunted, "If you're asking where I've been, the answer's North Berwick. Yeah, and a right bugger of a day I've had too, if you must know!"

"Forsooth! Methinks mine eyes smell onions. I shall weep soon," Julie enunciated, her head thrown back in mock commiseration, her forearm pressed theatrically to her brow. "Oh, how full of briers is this work-a-day world."

"OK, OK, you can cut the Thespian act," Bob said sotto voce, while deliberately turning his back on the two chrysanthemums, who were already beginning to show a discomforting interest in Julie's spontaneous performance, "unless, of course, you're trying to be talent-spotted by the two fairy godfathers there." He lowered his voice still further and added out of the corner of his mouth, "And anyway, it was *working*-day world, not *work-a*-day. If you must quote the Bard, just make sure you get it right, eh!" He allowed himself a self-satisfied smirk. "You weren't the only one forced to swallow Shakespeare by the shovelful at school, you know."

"Oo-oo-ooh, bully for you," Julie warbled in over-done deference, "and touché, I'm sure!" She clinked her glass against his and pouted, "Oh, well, I suppose you'd better tell me all about your bugger of a day, then, hadn't you?"

There wasn't a helluva lot to tell, Bob glumly confessed; not in a positive sense, at any rate. He'd gone over the whole business again and again with the newspaper boy who reckoned he'd seen the Gaetano di Scordia bloke being bundled into his car by two "foreign-looking gadgies" outside a North Berwick boarding house on the evening of the murder. But there had been nothing else about them that the kid could remember, except that the car that had closely followed the white Sierra away from the boarding house just might have been one of these new Fiat Puntos. *And* it had foreign plates . . . maybe. The kid hadn't been able to say for certain what colour the car was either; maybe light blue, maybe pale grey, maybe even dirty white. He'd been too far away, and he hadn't paid that much attention to the incident, anyway. He had assumed it was just a normal bunch of piss-artist golfers having a lark about. That sort of thing happened all the time in North Berwick during the holiday season.

"Mmm, foreign heavies, a Fiat car, foreign number plates," Julie recapped. She gave Bob an impish look. "You don't think it would be overstating the bleedin' obvious to say that we're *probably* looking at an Italian hit squad at work here, do you?"

Bob frowned at her — a bit like a grumpy old guard dog with a thorn in his paw, Julie thought, just waiting for a chance to transmit his ill humour to the first available ankle. She decided not to push her luck with further attempts at levity.

"Hey, it could be a lead, though," she said with exaggerated optimism. "You know, find the Fiat and maybe find the —"

"We found the bloody Fiat," Bob butted in, eyes closed, eyebrows arched, "just a mile or so along the coast from Tantallon Castle, hidden in a gully running down to the shore."

"So?"

"It'd been torched, totally frazzled — presumably sometime during Monday night. A family of picnickers came across it this afternoon and reported it at North Berwick police station on their way home. There's a gang of bobbies doing a hands-and-knees search of the spot right now. But ..." He raised a pessimistic shoulder and took another slug of his pint.

"What about the landlady at the boarding house? Hasn't she managed to come up with anything yet?"

"Zilch! Well, nothing that she hadn't already told us in her original statement, that is. The Gaetano di Scordia guy booked in late on Saturday night, rushed out in a big hurry on Sunday morning without even

45

taking breakfast, then came back about an hour later —
looking really hot and bothered, she said. Never left his
room for the rest of the day. She heard him making
some calls from the pay-phone in the hall at various
times during Monday. Sounded pretty frantic, she
reckoned. Couldn't understand a word of it, though.
All in Italian. Next thing, she goes out shopping in the
afternoon, and when she comes back, the guy's bolted
the course . . . and without paying his bill, either."

"And you've still found nobody, other than the paper
boy, who saw what happened when he left?"

"Nobody. We've spoken to all the other boarding
house guests again, but it was such a glorious afternoon
on Monday that they were all at the beach, on the golf
course, or wherever. The local fuzz have done a
door-to-door interview sweep round the whole
neighbourhood, and they've drawn a total blank as
well." Bob lowered his eyes and gazed morosely into his
beer.

"It's a real baffler," Julie concurred.

"It's a real bastard," Bob corrected.

Julie opened her handbag and stirred about inside.
"Never mind," she said, readopting an optimistic tone,
"I've got something here which might just give you a
tiny lead, if . . ." She stopped talking, her attention
caught by something on the TV in the corner of the
bar. "Hey, I know that place. I used to go there with my
parents." She waved at the barman. "Julian! Hey, Jools!
Turn the telly sound up, huh? I want to catch this thing
on the Six O'Clock News, OK?"

46

"In an exclusive interview for the BBC, a spokesperson for the selling agents confirmed today that a formal offer for the purchase of the island of Muckle Floggit, off the west mainland of Scotland, has been accepted by the present owner, "eighties punk rocker, Sid Sloth. The spokesperson would give no details of the purchaser's identity, other than that he's from Italy and is a universally-renowned name in the world of the arts, who intends to spare no expense in the sympathetic development of the island's many natural assets for the primary benefit of its resident population. Although strenuously denied by his personal manager in Milan, rumour is rife among the eighty-five inhabitants of Muckle Floggit that the new owner is, in fact, the world-famous tenor, Luciano Pavarotti. As one delighted islander, ferryman Angus MacGubligan, put it . . ."

"If yon big operatic chiel really has bought the place, it is bound to be the best thing to happen here in the Hebrides since the BBC dubbed *Noddy* into the Gaelic for the TV. Yes, for it will give this wee island chust the kind of refined image it deserves, after all them years of being invaded every August by gangs of skin-headed scruffs hoping to catch a peep of yon Sloth eejit stotting about all over the place up at the big house there. Aye, we'll not be sorry to see the end of yon crew of chunkies at all!"

"A positive Angus MacGubligan there. Pavarotti or not, however, the islanders will be hoping that the new owner, whoever he is, will prove to be significantly more conscientious than his various predecessors with regard to providing them with such much-needed fundamental amenities as running water in their cottages, hygienic sewage facilities, mains electricity and even some form of eco-friendly refuse disposal. Another priority for the new "Baron Floggit", if he is to win the hearts of the local populace, will be making good the catalogue of neglect suffered by the island's infrastructure during the tenures of a long line of absentee landlords. Angus MacGubligan again . . ."

"I chust want to say that us folks of Muckle Floggit here is all looking forward to welcoming the new laird, and to assisting him in spending his — ehm, to *helping* him with his ideas of improving our bonnie wee island."

"So, not for the first time in living memory, the stoical inhabitants of this most scenic of Scotland's Western Isles prepare for a change of what might still be described as a *feudal superior*. But whether the change will be for better or for worse remains very much to be seen. This is Martin Metcalfe for BBC News, Muckle Floggit in the Inner Hebrides."

Bob's mobile phone chirruped. "Hello, yes?" His brow furrowed. "What the hell do *you* want, Green? I thought I told you to . . . Uh-huh . . . Aye . . . Jesus wept! . . . And you haven't sent them to DVLA yet? . . . No? Well, your natural flair for total disorganisation may have paid off for once, *if* we can regard your life being spared as something profitable, that is." He listened to what Andy Green had to say for a couple of seconds, then barked, "No, you can't bloody well go home to your mum's place in Haddington now. There's no telling what the old guy came out with when he was being kneecapped, so just stay put! . . . That's right, you'll have to kip in the office tonight. Goodnight!"

A look of foreboding was clouding Julie's naturally sunny countenance. "What was that all about? Andy Green dropped another clanger, has he?"

"Yes and no." Bob's expression was a mix of exasperation and gloom. "The old bloke Green bought the car from — he's been found by his neighbours, lying unconscious on his kitchen floor. Been there since last night, it seems. Both legs smashed. Lamped by a baseball bat or the likes, with a hefty scud on the back of the head for good measure."

"Dead?"

"Nah, not quite, but not a kick in the arse off it. He's in an ambulance en route to intensive care right now."

Julie looked puzzled. "So how's Andy Green involved?"

"It appears that the assault on the old geezer bears all the trademarks of the modus operandi employed in the murder of the young Italian at North Berwick. And if the bird in the red Alfa Spider *is* mixed up in this mess, it could be that she'd made a mental note of the number of Green's car when she deposited the hundred grand at the filling station on Sunday. So, when the hit squad came up empty-handed at Tantallon Castle on Monday, maybe the word was relayed back to her, she

49

rumbled the mistake and checked out the ownership of Green's Sierra with the Driver and Vehicle Licensing Agency. Something along these lines, anyway."

"Ah, so there hadn't been time for the old guy's car to be registered in Andy's name, is that it?"

"Whether there would've been time or not is immaterial, because Green had forgotten to send off the bloody change of ownership slip in any case. And talk about luck of the devil — the old bloke hadn't even torn off the seller's bit, so Green still has that section of the form too!"

Julie looked anxious. "But I remember Andy saying that he showed the old chap his CID identity to ease any doubts he might have about accepting a cheque. So, if the old boy was *that* way, it's more than likely he made Andy write his name and address on the back of the cheque."

"He did. And that's why I told Green to hit the sack in HQ tonight, just in case the old guy succumbed to a bit of gentle persuasion before his lights went out." Bob tapped his leg. "Your knee bone's connected to your tongue bone." He flipped open his mobile phone, punched in some numbers, then moved in close to use Julie as a human telephone booth.

"Hello. DI Burns here. Detective Sergeant Yule please . . . Jimmy? This latest North Berwick thing . . . Yeah, send a couple of our lads out to Haddington smartish to put a cover on DC Green's parents' house. Advise the local nick what's going on, of course, but tell them to keep a low profile. No panda cars scooting about the place like dodgems, OK?" Bob dipped his chin and shielded his mouth with his hand. "Oh, and Jimmy, better tie the necessary bits of red tape together and fix our boys up with peashooters. Get me? . . . Good lad."

Julie looked worried. "Buying that car could yet prove to be a *lot* more expensive than Andy thought, huh?"

Bob nodded his head, sighed, then asked, "Anyhow, what was so interesting about all that stuff on the box just now? You're surely not suggesting that old *Nessun Dorma* himself could be the Mr Big behind the North Berwick Italian connection, are you?"

"No, no, not at all. No, it just interested me because Mum and Dad used to take me to the island of Muckle Floggit for summer holidays when I was a kid, that's all. Rented a cottage, went sea fishing in a wee boat, cooked the porridge on the peat fire, went hill walking on Ben Doone. Yeah, all that sort of idyllic stuff, you know." Her expression then changed from reflective to frustrated. "There *was* something about that news item, though . . ."

"Sorry, can't help you. What I know about the Hebrides you could write on the back of a postage stamp." Bob nudged Julie's arm. "But come on, you were about to dig some enlightening item or other out of your handbag before those memories of a privileged Glaswegian childhood wafted you off to Bonnie Prince Charlieland."

"Oh — right — yeah. I got all carried away there for a minute. Sorry." Julie delved into the handbag again and pulled out a small, cellophane envelope. She handed it to Bob. "OK, what do you make of that, Kemosabe?"

Bob held the envelope up and looked at the contents. "It's half a raffle ticket, isn't it? Something like that, anyway." He handed it back and shrugged. "What's this all about?"

"One of my forensic mates found the ticket about an hour ago, under the driver's seat of the white Ford Sierra that the young Italian guy was bumped off in. I really don't know whether it's a raffle ticket or not, but first things first." Julie opened the envelope and passed it back to Bob. "Take a good sniff."

Bob obliged, then leaned forward and nuzzled his nose behind Julie's ear. He sat back again and returned her knowing look.

"*Femme*," they confirmed in concert, "by Rochas!"

Julie nodded her head. "Yes, the same scent as Andy's paper bag with the hundred K in it."

"The hand of the Alfa Romeo Spider woman?" Bob asked rhetorically.

"Snap!" said Julie. "And if you'll permit me just one final Shakespearean quotation . . . All the perfumes of Arabia will not sweeten *her* little hand!"

"It's beginning to look that way," Bob conceded. "Yeah, our mysterious bird in the red roadster threatens to relegate poor old Lady Macbeth to the rank of junior Sunday school teacher." Thinking, he stroked his chin, then held his hand out. "Give us another look at that raffle ticket, will you? Now then," he murmured, "what's this printed on it? *A-M-F-F-C*. Some obscure amateur football club, maybe? And then it says, *Ten*

Pounds Paid." He turned the envelope over. "Look, there's some numbers scribbled in pencil on the back of the ticket."

"Yes, I wondered at first if it might be a phone number, but it doesn't seem to add up to a British one. Then I thought, the way things are panning out, you might want to get one of your desk-bound gumshoes to check it out with the Italian telephone company. As I said, it might just give you *some* kind of a lead."

Bob looked intently at the numbers again. "Wait a minute," he said, suddenly inspired, "this isn't a phone number, it's a bloody bank account number! *YES!*" He clenched his fist and punched the air. "Better look out, *Signorina* Macbeth, the Edinburgh polis are right up your Spider's gearbox!" He stood up and gave Julie an uncharacteristically public cuddle. "You're a genius, Doctor Julie darlin'! And listen, if this little lead of yours comes up trumps, I'll treat you to a night out of a lifetime in — in —"

"Muckle Floggit," Julie whispered, her eyes flitting back and forth between the cellophane envelope and the TV set.

Bob was bamboozled.

Julie was elated. "Muckle Floggit — that's it!" she beamed. "Old Angus on the telly there . . ." She slapped her thigh. "I should've twigged!"

"What the blazes are you on about now?"

"The ticket. It's not for a raffle, it's for a boat! The initials — *AMFFC* — I can remember what they stand for now. It's the *ARDENSTOOSHIE and MUCKLE FLOGGIT FERRY COMPANY!*"

CHAPTER
SIX

Pushing up his dark visor, Franco Contadino shut off the taps on the gas bottles and hung the welding torch on its hook. Instinctively, he attempted to wipe the sweat from his forehead with the back of his hand; an exercise about as fruitful as trying to dry a saturated sponge with a wet sack. A small, curly-tailed mongrel dog trotted in through the wide doorway, cocked his leg at the anvil, haughtily back-heeled a few token puffs of dust at the object of his urinary signature, then proceeded nonchalantly on his way.

Franco's very soul was filled with empathy, his heart with envy. How he would have loved to be in a position to do what that little mutt had just done. He stepped outside, where the heat seemed even fiercer than at the height of day. The late afternoon sun was blasting the full force of its rays against the drab, ochre walls of the workshop, as if reminding mere mortals of its infinite power, before descending to a resting place somewhere beyond the fire island of Volcano out there beneath the western horizon. Franco pulled the roller shutter only half way down, in hopes, no matter how futile, that the listless air of the city might yet steal into the workshop and dilute the metallic fug that hung suffocatingly inside.

He crossed the street into the air-conditioned tobacco smoke of the scruffy little bar, only half-heartedly acknowledging the greetings of the jovial, though down-at-heel, gathering of neighbourhood characters. Noisy post-mortems were still being carried out on the dismal performances of every national soccer team (except Italy's) which had taken part in the European Championships a few weeks earlier.

Franco had heard it all before. He lifted his glass of ice-cold beer from the bar and ambled over to stand alone by the open door. Dolefully, he stared over at the faded, flaking paint on the walls of the little flat-roofed building opposite. The decrepit, back-street blacksmith's shop with humble house attached. The centre of Franco's universe. The sum and substance of his life. *Dio*, what a hole to have got into. It had taken his father nearly thirty years of slaving away for somebody else just to save the deposit to put down on that little business, then only ten years to work himself into an early grave trying to keep up the payments. And now it was Franco's turn.

But what else could he do? He'd had to bum the money from his mother to get back from London for his father's funeral, and he knew she really didn't buy all that stuff he'd told her about being mugged outside the restaurant in Edgeware Road and having all his savings snatched from his body belt. A wistful smile traversed his lips. His Mamma would never let on, though. Too proud of her son, and too protective of his feelings. He shook his head and shrugged resignedly. Italian mothers! *Si*, and their Italian sons!

The trouble was, it was only after he had agreed, at his mother's behest, to take over the little business after his father's death that he began to discover just what a financial mess it was in. And his Mamma didn't even know. His father had never told her, and Franco wasn't about to tell her now. All his mother had ever wanted was enough lira in her purse every day to buy the basic necessities of life from the little food store on the corner. Her husband was a businessman, after all. He was his own boss, a man to be looked up to in the community, and she was proud of him. And she was proud of her son, too, working as a waiter — no, the *head* waiter — in a high-class London restaurant, from where even the Queen of England ordered her favourite pizzas. So, what did Maria Contadino need with luxuries? In her husband and son, heaven had blessed her with all the riches she could ever have wished for.

How could Franco tell her the truth? He hadn't the heart to break the news that they were staring bankruptcy in the face, that repairing the occasional old metal gate or welding patches on the rusty exhaust pipes of a few passing bangers wasn't even paying for her daily shopping excursions along to the *minimercato*, far less persuading the bank not to carry out its threat to repossess the house and workshop. The heartbreak of losing her husband may not quite have done for her completely, but the shame of losing face in the eyes of her neighbours almost certainly would.

Franco was near his wits' end. He had even asked the bank manager about the chances of putting up his grandparents' old farm as collateral for an increase in his overdraft limit, but the bastard had only laughed. What was a heap of rubble and a muddle of impoverished little fields stuck away up there in the hills worth to anyone? *Santo cielo*! he'd scoffed, you couldn't even get within a kilometre of the place unless you were on a donkey, or unless you were a goat! *Si*, and only a goat would lend money against that ruined hovel. "*Va all' inferno!*"

And go to hell Franco gladly would . . . if he could afford the ticket out of here. After all, stoking fires for the devil couldn't be any worse than sweating his balls off in that smothering hellhole across the street — *and* there would always be the offchance of a wild orgy or two to look forward to at the end of a shift for *il diavolo*. He stuck his hand in his pocket and fished out a jangle of coins. *Merda!* he didn't even have the money to get a bus downtown, never mind flash enough of the stuff about to be able to pull some sexy *ragazza*.

"*Ay, Dio!* I ask you!" he shouted, an outstretched hand raised imploringly to the skies. "Why are you doing this to me, man? I'm only twenty-three years old, for fuck's sake, and already you're making me live like a monk! Hey, God, listen to me, uh! Is this a way to treat a healthy Sicilian boy?"

"Don't push your luck, *piccino*," a one-legged man guffawed, pausing to slap Franco's back as he crutched his way out of the bar. "You could end up with a refrigerated she-dragon like mine waiting for you at home!"

It was all right for old Hopalong to laugh, Franco silently griped. At least he'd got a life pension for having had his pin ripped off by a crane down at the Messina docks. And what had *he* got for having had his holy-all ripped off by an Irish slag in London? A life sentence of skintness in this stinking *culo* of purgatory, that's what!

He thrust his spread palm heavenward again. "*Uno favore, Dio!*" he yelled. "*Solo uno favore, eh!*" He thumped his brow with the heel of his hand. "Come on, God. It's not too much to ask, man — just one little favour for your boy Franco here, OK!"

Meanwhile, the phone was ringing vainly in his little workshop opposite . . .

MANHATTAN ISLAND, NEW YORK — THE LUXURY PENTHOUSE OF A FIFTH AVENUE APARTMENT BLOCK OVERLOOKING CENTRAL PARK — EARLY AFTERNOON THAT SAME DAY . . .

Massimo Plantano had risen late today; at 1pm instead of his normal noon. But then, he had been up later than usual last night; until 6am instead of his normal 5, tweaking and tugging the reins of his burgeoning business bandwagon from his hot seat in the bullet-proof backroom of the *Mamma Siracusa* trattoria on Mulberry Street. There had been more things than usual to attend to last night, too; vital things, international things, things that had been meticulously planned to keep him half-a-dozen steps ahead of those doodly-squat palookas in the FBI. This was one egg that he'd been sitting on for a long time, a golden egg, which was just about ready to hatch. Yeah, he could feel it in his goddam ass!

"So, keep tryin', ya dumb Eyetalian broad!" he hollered from the bathroom. "Can't ya see I'm tryin' to have a friggin' shave here, for cryin' out?"

His wife dutifully did his bidding, re-dialling the number without even bothering to silently mouth the thoughts of loathing that were running through her mind. He would soon be gone for the day again, the vile little runt. Then she would have the place to herself, as usual. Lonely? Sure, she got lonely . . . sometimes. But what was lonely in a palace like this, compared to the gruesome dungeon of a basement room in that lousy Little Italy slum where she'd had to sit and wait for him — sometimes for days and nights on end — when they were first married thirty years ago? And her only a green kid, just come over from Syracuse in Sicily and missing her Mamma bad. Now, *that* was lonely!

She listened to the number ringing out, her thoughts drifting . . . Married? Messina Max Plantano had never known the meaning of the word, not in *any* way. *Si*, if only his never-ending procession of floozy hangers-on knew the real truth about the mighty-atom Italian stallion. Stallion? Him? In his dreams, maybe!

Max shuffled into the lounge, patting after-shave onto his face. It was a face that bore the expression of a man who had demanded something today, expected it to happen yesterday, and was ready to cancel all your tomorrows for you if he didn't get his way.

"Ain'cha got through to the sonofabitch *yet?*" he barked. "And where's the goddam coffee? Ya know I feel like shit 'til I get my coffee in the morning! What the hell's happenin' here? Ya anglin' for a goddam servant next or somethin'? Here, gimme that, for Chrisakes!" He grabbed the phone and rammed it to his ear.

"Like I told you," his wife said blandly, "it's ringing out, OK?"

"Chicken-shit Eyetalian telephones!"

"Maybe he's gone home already."

"*Home* ya say? He lives in the friggin' place, the goddam peasant! What time a' day is it over there, anyway?"

His wife hunched her shoulders. "Who knows? Maybe eight o'clock or something, I guess. Maybe he's gone out for the night."

Fuming, Max slammed the handset down, picked it up again and punched the buttons, laboriously reading the numbers off the phone pad as he went along. "Lemme see . . . uh-hu . . . then it's . . . five . . . then one . . . and five. Yeah." He glared at his wife. "Maybe ya done it wrong. Maybe ya been diallin' the goddam

Pope or somethin'!" He listened impatiently for the connection. "Half-assed, piece-a'-shit Eyetalian telephones!"

BACK IN MESSINA, SICILY, MEANTIME . . .

Franco Contadino leaned his shoulder against the door frame of the bar, emptied the dregs of his glass down his gullet and lounged cross-legged, deliberating whether or not to blow some more of his few remaining lira on another beer.

"Oy, Franco!" one of the neighbourhood kids shouted from across the street. "Wake up, *amico*!" He pointed to the workshop, then held his thumb to his ear, his little finger to his mouth. "Business so good you don't need to answer your phone these days, eh?"

Franco gave him a bored nod of acknowledgement. Damned phone — should've pulled the shutter right down, then the little bastard wouldn't have heard it. More than likely only somebody chasing up yet another unpaid bill.

He placed his empty glass on a table inside the door and started to saunter over to the workshop.

"Franco!" someone shouted after him from the bar. "Where the hell are you going, man? A good movie is starting on TV in here. Swedish — on the satellite. *Molto culturale, si?*" He winked, gripped his bicep, then made the usual phallic lunge with a clenched fist. "*Ay-y-y, formidabile!*"

Franco automatically turned tail and began to walk briskly back, only to stop half way, thinking better of it. What the hell did *he* need with a hard-core porn movie

61

at a time like this? It'd be like showing a red-hot heifer to a hobbled bull. He turned again and proceeded once more at an unhurried pace towards his workshop. With luck, whoever was trying to get through would have rung off before he got there. Then again, the money-grabbing shit on the other end would only phone back in the morning. *Cristo*, what a life! He ducked under the roller shutter and into his airless cell.

"OK, OK, I'm coming!" he grouched as he lifted the phone. "*Pronto!* Messina Lunatic Asylum here. Ground floor ward for those with suicidal tendencies. To whom do you wish to speak?"

"What the . . . who the fuck?" The owner of the voice with a Bowery accent was clearly harassed. "Sonofabitch, hoss-dick telephone system! Hey, what number is this I'm callin' here, for cryin' out?"

"Messina *quindici, quindici, sette* —"

"Messina, Italy?"

"*Si, signore*." Franco repeated the number, in full this time.

"Yeah, that's it, that's what I been diallin' here already. But hey . . . wait up a goddam minute there! What's wid the asylum crap? Ain't that the friggin' Contadino place?"

Franco's heart sank. He recognised that refined phraseology. Uncle Massimo! At least, that was what Franco had always known him as — although, in truth, he was only some kind of distant cousin of his father's. There were hundreds of them, mostly in the States, but Uncle Massimo's lot were the only branch not to have retained the old Sicilian family name.

It had been Massimo's own father, old Primo Contadino, who had changed it when he first arrived in New York as a young man between the two world wars. He was one of the genuine "with-out-papers" WOPs, and proud of it, so he could have given the immigration people on Ellis Island any name he wanted. He chose the surname that he did, according to family folklore, because he believed that Primo Plantano — or Top Banana, as some steerage-class intellectual had translated it for him on the boat over — had more "class" to it for a new American than his old clan handle, which tagged him in English, he was similarly advised, as Head Ploughboy, or Number One Boor, even. And that was why Primo duly christened his only son Massimo — the "Greatest" — a carefully chosen epithet, which, in Primo's estimation, placed the lucky infant even higher up the much-esteemed banana tree than his old man.

This curious predilection for descriptive sobriquets was one that had been inherited, and developed in his own peculiar fashion, by Massimo himself, as Franco was about to discover.

"*Si*, this is the Contadino place. Franco speaking."

"Now we're talkin'! Hiya, Frankie boy! Hey, how ya doin', kid?"

"*Lo zio* Massimo?" Franco hesitantly enquired. "Uncle Massimo?"

"You bet yer cute little Eyetalian ass it's yer Uncle Max! So how's it goin', boy?"

Franco tried to sound enthusiastic. "*Sto bene, grazie. E tu? Come stai?*"

"*Bene, bene, bene!* Yeah, yeah, I'm just fine and all. But, hey, let's speak American, huh? Talk 'capital A', know what I mean, Frankie boy?"

Franco knew what he meant all right. He'd had his ear bent with all this "capital A" bullshit just six months ago at his father's funeral; a solemn family occasion, for which Uncle Massimo, the self-styled godfather of the clan, had deigned to make one of his rare but much-trumpeted transatlantic pilgrimages back to "the old country".

"Yer old man was a good guy," Massimo had murmured to Franco at the graveside, "but a grade-A mug . . . a world-class schmendrick. Know what I'm sayin' here, kid?"

Franco had tried to ignore him, the exact minute of his father's laying-to-rest hardly seeming an appropriate time to discuss the finer points of his character, good or bad, with a New York hoodlum, family elder or not. But Massimo had persisted . . .

"I'm tellin' ya, Frankie boy, that guy in the box down there coulda made it big. He coulda gone all the way to the top wid me in the States. I told him many times, no shit — get yer ass over here to the Big Apple, cousin *mio*, and I'll show ya the stairway to heaven, but fast!"

Which would have been one sure way, Franco had told himself at the time, of his old man ending up in a box even sooner than he had.

"Yeah," Massimo had gone on, "I loved that guy, Frankie. Loved him like the brother I never had, ya know — even if he was a goddam loser." Then, laying a gold-dripping hand on Franco's arm, he'd said, "And

64

in addition also, that's why I love you, kiddo — like the son I never had. Capeesh?" He'd raised his padded, camel-hair shoulders and dropped the corners of his mouth before elucidating, "My old woman, see — zero conception capabilities. She don't have the guts for makin' no *bambinos*, get me? And that's why, boy, you got it comin' to ya, but good. Yer old Uncle Messina Max Plantano is gonna look after ya. Hey, I owe it to yer mamma!" Max had then smiled in a curiously sentimental way. "Yeah-h-h, little Maria Lampedusa, the sweet thing," he reflected. "Hmm, she shoulda married me, the dumb bitch!"

Massimo's egotistic monologue had then been interrupted by the priest commencing the benediction, the most emotional moment in the whole ceremony, for which Massimo hadn't even seen fit to remove his beige velvet fedora or Gucci shades. And he wasn't silent for one second longer than was politely expedient, either . . .

"So, whadda ya wanna do wid yer life now, Frankie boy?"

Franco had muttered that he didn't really know, but that he reckoned his mother would expect him to stay at home and carry on the family business. This revelation had rendered Massimo almost speechless — but not almost enough . . .

"Ya *what*! Come on, get real, baby! Why the fuck ya wanna bust yer buns knockin' shit outa bits a' scrap iron for piece-a'-shit peanuts? For hey, if knockin' the goddam shit outa whatever is what turns ya on, yer Uncle Max got a position for ya in his organisation right now. It's, like, one of our in-house *specialities*, see? Yeah, and moreover, I can always use a natural, right?" He'd then paused to stretch up and elbow Franco heartily in the kidneys. "Ya get where I'm comin' from . . . son?"

Franco's somewhat curt reply that, thanks all the same, but he'd have to think about the offer had either satisfied Massimo for the present, or had put him off the idea completely. In any event, the topic of Franco going to work for him had never been raised again that day. Massimo had flown back to New York the following morning, with the subject, as far as Franco was concerned, as dead and buried as his father.

Until today's phone call, that is . . .

"Ya didn't answer my question, kiddo. What's wid all the loonatic asylum baloney? Ya diversifyin' yer business activities or somethin'?"

"No, no, Uncle Massimo." Franco released an embarrassed little laugh. "No, no, just a little *stratagemma* to confuse the creditors, that's all."

"I knew it. That sonofabitch trashcan-fixin' business is down the goddam tubes already, right?"

"Well, things could be better, I'll admit that, but —"

"But nothin'! As from right now, your worries is over, OK?"

"*Scusi*, but I don't understand what you're saying to me. I mean —"

"Hey-y-y! Didn' I tell ya when they planted your old man that old Uncle Max was gonna look after ya? Sure I did, and when Messina Max Plantano says he's gonna friggin' do somethin', he friggin' does it, right? Yeah,

66

and don' you ever forget that, Frankie boy. Now, listen up here. I gotta nice piece a' action cookin' and I gonna cut ya in for a slice, all right?"

"*Si, grazie*, but —"

"Tomorrow ya fly to London, England."

Franco flipped. "Not *London*! No, no, I got problems in London — the bank, the bookie, the —"

"Screw piece-a'-shit London problems! Ya got problems in London, yer Uncle Max's boys gonna fix 'em, OK? So settle." Max then went all confidential. "Now, the low line is I need ya in Limeyland. And furthermore already, I gonna give ya a new identity to go wid yer new life, capeesh?"

Franco didn't like the sound of this. "New life? B-but, Uncle Massimo," he stammered, "my Mamma — she's old, she's frail, she's nearly blind, she needs a hysterectomy. I can't just up and leave her. She — she would —"

"SCREW yer mother!" Max screamed. "I'm talkin' FAMILY here! Now zip yer lip and listen up, for Chrisakes!" He lowered his voice to a malevolent croak. "Ya know what a sporran is, kid?"

"A sporran?" Franco gulped. "Uhm, some kind of Scottish thing for stashing your money in?"

"Correctóla! Yeah, and I have just bought me the biggest sonofabitch sporran in the whole mother-humpin' world. And what's more also, yer Uncle Max is puttin' *you* in charge of it, Frankie boy. Oh yeah-h-h, now ya gonna get yer mitts on some *real* dough!"

Franco pricked up his ears. "Dough? You mean dough, as in . . . ?"

"As in money, kiddo!" Max rasped out a throaty laugh. "Yeah, money — as in, you fill my sporran, I'll fill yours."

Franco was growing nervier by the moment. Whatever Massimo was on about in that "capital A" double-talk of his, it was a cert that this sporran business would be more bent than a couple of metres of *luganega* sausages. "Well, I don't know, Uncle Massimo," he flustered. "I, you know — I think maybe —"

"DON'T think! NOBODY in the outfit thinks, except ME! UNDERSTOOD?" Max lowered his voice again. "OK, so how does forty Gs grab ya?"

"Gs, as in . . .?"

"Grand. Like, forty thousand dollars . . ."

Franco's nerviness was fading fast. "*American* dollars?" he falsetto'd.

"Is there some other kind? Hey, and that's just for *antipasto*. Handle my sporran right, baby, and ya gonna be fingerin' plenty more mazooma where that came from."

Forty thousand American dollars! The thought of all those lovely greenbacks made Franco's sphincter twitch. And even more to come! *Gesù!* he would have those blood-sucking bastards at the bank off his back in no time.

Max was becoming impatient. "Are ya still conscious there, kid? Speak to me, huh!"

But Franco was momentarily dumbstruck. He managed a whimper.

Max liked the sound of that. "OK, Frankie boy," he crooned, "just unlax and listen real good. First, ya gonna dye yer hair blonde — tonight. Then ya gonna go to the Etna Travel Bureau in Messina first thing tomorrow, right? Ask for Luigi Truffaldino. He's ma main man there. Luigi gonna give ya a envelope, and in that envelope gonna be everything ya gonna need for the London trip — like money, new passport, airplane ticket, everything." A sudden thought then struck Max. "Hey!" he exclaimed, a trace of panic in his voice, "ya *can* speak Scotch, can't ya?"

Franco emerged from his daze. "English," he replied, "Scotch is English. Well, sort of. *Si*, I heard it in the London restaurant sometimes. Football fans. Strange lingo. Every second word is *fuckin'*." Sensing his uncle's creeping anxiety, he then attempted to convey a measure of reassurance. "*Si, si*, but I can handle it, though."

"Yeah, ya friggin' hear one friggin' Limey, ya hear 'em all, I guess," was Max's muttered response. "Anyway —"

"Uhm, sorry," Franco interjected timidly, "but, uh, did you say something about a new . . . identity?"

"You bet yer sweet Eyetalian butt I did, boy. All sorted, as they say in Limeyland. Hey-y-y, for Messina Max Plantano, no *problema!*"

This was all going too fast for Franco. "But my picture in the new passport . . . with blonde hair?"

"Sure! Like I said already — all sorted. Unlax. No *problema!*"

69

Franco fingered his wavy locks. "But — but my hair. It's still black. I don't understand. I mean, how did you manage to get a picture of me with . . .?"

"Look, Frankie baby, don' talk dumb, huh! They don' call me Messina Max for nothin'. Why, I got connections in the old country that knows before you do what time ya gonna take a dump in the mornin', for cryin' out! Organise some kinda new pic for a friggin' passport? That ain't nothin'! No shit, I could fax a crap from here in New York right now and have it curlin' outa yer asshole ten goddam seconds later, *if* I wuz in such a ways inclined." Max went all confidential again. "This is the *organisation* ye're in now, kid. Ya get where I'm at?"

Franco's nerves were beginning to act up again. "So, uhm, what's my new name?" he enquired, a quiver of apprehension in his delivery.

"I thought ya was never gonna ask," Massimo replied, a lift of excitement in his. "It just happens to be one a' the best friggin' numdie plums I ever gave anybody in the outfit."

"*Si* . . .?"

"Yeah, it's, wait for it . . . Dannato Cornamusa!"

A stunned silence at the Sicilian end.

"Hey, ya still there, kid? Speak to me, for fuck's sake, Frankie boy. Just tell me, ain't that one smart-assed name, or ain't it?"

"Dannato Cornamusa? But that means —"

"*I* know what it friggin' means, boy! It was me dreamed it up already! It means — loosely translated into Limey — Goddam Bagpipes, right? Now ain't that a peach? Ya know — sporran, bagpipes, all that Scotch crap? Yeah, and for sure them chicken-shit Limey faggots in plaid skirts is gonna be too dumb to make the subtle lingo connection, right?"

Franco's head was starting to ache. "*Si, si,* right, Uncle Massimo," he mumbled. Dannato Cornamusa, he repeated to himself. *Cristo,* what a bummer! Still, for forty grand, and more in the pipeline, Massimo could call him Gina Lollobrigida if he wanted to. His spirits cautiously recovering, Franco probed, "So, uhm, what happens when I get to London?"

"Relax! All taken care of, Frankie boy." Max croaked out a self-congratulatory chuckle. "Hey-y-y, but that's *Danny* boy now, right?"

"Mmm, *si* . . ." Franco still had lingering doubts.

But they were the last thing on Max's mind. "OK," he breezed, "ya gonna be picked up at the airport by my Limeyland lootenant — a real foxy broad wid the travellin' name of Laprima Frittella." The smugness came oiling down the line. "Another handle of my own creatin', it goes without sayin'."

Franco had never had a full-blown migraine before, but he knew well enough that there's a first time for everything. "Laprima *Frittella?*" he queried. "But that means —"

"*I* know what it friggin' means!" Max let rip with a delighted guffaw. "Laprima Frittella! Now, tell me, kiddo, ain't that moniker a goddam kick in the mother-humpin' coconuts, or ain't it?"

CHAPTER
SEVEN

Bob Burns screwed up his nose. "You had a shower yet, lad?"

Andy Green smiled sheepishly. "I got one of the boys to nip out and get me a take-away Ruby Murray for my supper last night. I mean, I was really Hank Marvin. Never had nothin' to eat since the bully beef and pickled onions wi' the fried eggs and baked beans in the canteen at teatime, like."

Bob sat down at his desk and fumbled about in the bottom drawer. He produced an aerosol can and gave the room a generous spray. "What the blazes kind of curry was it?" he gagged. "Skunk Tikka Massalla or something?"

"Nah, too short o' readies for anything that fancy. Just had the mince Vindaloo wi' a half portion o' curried peas. Oh! and a pile o' garlic poppadums. Magic!"

"And you slept in here after scoffing *that* lot?" Bob fired off another few blasts from his spray can.

Frowning and blinking, Andy sniffed the air. "Heh, boss — that aerosol stuff. It smells like fly killer."

"It is! But it's a helluva lot more pleasant than the stink you're giving off!"

Detective Sergeant Jimmy Yule entered the room, his face drawn, his eyes bloodshot.

"Morning, Jimmy," said Bob. "Christ! you look *well* rough. Had a heavy night, did you?"

"Aye," Yule yawned, "I was sitting in intensive care in the infirmary all bleedin' night, just in case the old North Berwick GBH victim regained consciousness."

"And did he?"

"He did." Yule then nodded askance at Andy Green. "Just for long enough to mumble plenty that might interest you, son."

"Oh, aye? Such as?"

"Such as the cheque with your name and address on it."

"Oh, aye?"

"Aye. The old guy couldn't pay it into the bank on Monday, because it was a holiday, right?"

Andy Green swallowed hard, a creaking sound emanating from his chair as he shifted uneasily.

Jimmy Yule scowled at him, then investigated the soles of his shoes.

"No, you haven't stepped on something," Bob Burns assured him. "Green had a weapons-of-mass-destruction curry last night, that's all. Now, getting back to the point — you were saying that the old guy still had Green's cheque in the house when the break-a-leg brigade called . . ."

Yule shook his head. "That's the lucky bit for young Green here. The old man said he'd given it to his daughter on Monday night, long before the heavies turned up. His daughter works in the bank, so he'd asked her to pay it in for him in the morning, to save him the bother of going out specially."

Andy Green puffed out his cheeks and exhaled a raspberry of relief.

Taking no chances, Bob stood up, walked calmly over to the window and opened it wide. "So you're saying that the old chap got Green off the hook and, for his trouble, took a hammering for him as well, correct?"

"Not quite," Yule replied.

Andy Green held his breath again.

"No," Jimmy Yule continued. "Bear in mind the daughter had the cheque at her house when her old man was having the daylights knocked out of him at his own place just round the corner. *That's* why he didn't say a cheep. It had bugger all to do with saving Green's hide."

Bob nodded his head. "Scared to tell the heavies his daughter had the cheque, because of what they might do to *her*, eh?"

"That's it. In fact, as soon as they'd flashed their baseball bat, and before they even laid a finger on him, the old boy had spouted everything he could remember about Green."

"But the bastards gave him the full treatment anyway," Bob muttered through clenched teeth. "Nice people."

The blood drained from Andy's cheeks. "Aw, no," he groaned, "if the old boy grassed me up, it's me next for the universal knee joints!"

74

"Maybe not," Jimmy Yule said on his way back to the door. "The old guy's memory, you see. Not what it used to be."

Green's face was a picture of confusion. "But, eh, how does that like help me, Sarge?"

"Because he told the heavies your name's Black and you're in the fuckin' fire brigade, that's how."

It appeared to Andy that there may have been a hint of resentment in the way his superior had said that, but he was too relieved to be overly bothered. He slumped into his chair and fanned his face with both hands. "Aw, what a break," he sighed. "I'll send the old gadgie a bunch o' grapes."

"Save your pennies, son," said Yule as he opened the door. "The old fella whistled *The Last Post* half an hour ago." He half turned towards Bob. "Oh, and I almost forgot to tell you, boss — before he died, he whispered something about the rats who beat him up."

"Uh-huh?"

"Yeah, there were three of them — all with foreign accents."

"No descriptions?"

Detective Sergeant Yule shook his head. "No time."

"OK, Jimmy," Bob Burns said. "Write up your report, then get yourself some shuteye. I'll take it from here."

There was a distinct devil-may-care air about Andy Green now, which wasn't too surprising, given that a potential contract on him had been switched fortuitously to some other poor sucker. "Heh, why don't we get Interpol in on the act, skipper?" he cheerfully suggested. "I mean, two stiffs now, and all them Eyeties an' that . . ."

"Yeah, yeah, we've already contacted Interpol," Bob mumbled. He stroked his jaw with his thumb. "Hmm, but we haven't got much of a brief for them, have we? Three guys, *possibly* Italian, but no descriptions. And a fast dolly bird, *probably* Italian, who *maybe* wears *Femme* scent, who dumped a hundred K in a message bag in a small-town petrol station and drives a red Alfa Romeo Spider."

"Here, what *about* the Spider woman?" Andy Green gasped, panic returning to his eyes, his fingers massaging his knee caps. "Heh, ye've got to find her, skipper! I mean, she got a good look at ma mug, remember?"

Bob shook his head glumly. "We've got plenty bods working on it, but without a reg number for her car . . ."

Andy grabbed at the most obvious straw. "The Fiat Punto, then . . . the one that was torched at North Berwick?"

"Same story. All we know is that it was a left-hooker, and the engine and chassis numbers had been ground off."

"Ground off? How do ye mean, like?"

"I mean it's a doddle it was nicked." Bob kneaded his brow. "Yeah, but nicked from where? Let's face it, it's a big left-hand-drive world out there." He opened a file and pulled out a small cellophane envelope, then stared pensively at the contents. "Hmm, the Ardenstooshie and Muckle Floggit Ferry Company. I reckon it's all down to the number scribbled on this ticket stub now."

Andy Green was flummoxed, and he looked it.

Bob looked at his watch. "Nine o'clock. Start of the day's play in the financial sector." He reached for his phone. "OK, time to get some of our desk-bound gumshoes on the case!"

MID-AFTERNOON THAT SAME DAY — ON A BRITISH AIRWAYS FLIGHT FROM LONDON, ENGLAND, TO EDINBURGH, SCOTLAND . . .

"I don't like it," Franco Contadino griped. "I'm a blacksmith, not a sculptor. *Dio mio*, what do I know about statues?"

Laprima Frittella laid a scarlet-taloned hand on his and purred, "If Max Plantano says you're a sculptor, *piccino mio*, you're a sculptor. Likewise, if Max Plantano says you're dead meat . . ." She paused to draw her fingernails slowly over the back of Franco's hand, leaving four livid lines etched on his skin. ". . . then, you're dead meat. Capeesh?"

Franco forced a bravado-loaded laugh. "Ay-y-y, who are *you* trying to kid? Come on, this is my Uncle Massimo you're talking about." He faked another laugh, this one sounding even less convincing than the first. "He'd never hurt me. We're *casata* — family!"

"*Casata?*" Laprima gave a derisive little snort. "Huh, forget it, honey! Max would have you creamed as quick as that!" She snapped her fingers. "So, you better get used to it, *amico*. As from now, you are Dannato

77

Cornamusa, multi-millionaire sculptor of international repute . . . *and* owner of your very own sporran." She lowered her sunglasses and gave him a cautionary wink. "And when I say *owner* and *sporran*, I am talking —"

"I know, I know, you're talking 'capital A'." Franco held his head in despair. What a mess! How the hell, he asked himself, had he ever let Massimo hustle him into this? Money, of course. Money was the simple answer to that stupid question. Money — or, more accurately, the lack of it. Franco inhaled a great, shuddering sigh. There was no escape now. His Uncle Max had him firmly by the pubes. Franco knew it, Max knew it and the foxy Laprima Frittella knew it. But Franco still didn't like it. He hunched his shoulders almost to his ears. "But what happens when people ask me about sculpture and art and things?" he whined. "I mean, what the hell will I say?"

Laprima settled back into her seat, closed her eyes and muttered uninterestedly, "You're *Siciliano*, aren't you?"

"*Si, certamente!*"

"So, do what comes naturally. Bullshit your way out of it!"

MEANTIME, AT EDINBURGH POLICE HQ . . .

So far, the day hadn't been going too well for Bob Burns. First of all, the Italian Consulate in Melville Street had confirmed that the passport found in the car boot of the young murder victim at Tantallon Castle was false. There had been no such person as Gaetano

78

di Scordia; a depressing piece of information which, nevertheless, Bob had always suspected would prove to be the case. Why else would the killers have been so careless as to have left the passport behind? So, the only way forward now, it seemed, was the laborious one of circularising copies of the passport picture to police forces in Britain and Italy; although the fact that the guy could speak Italian — according to his North Berwick landlady, anyway — didn't necessarily mean that he came from that country. However, there was still a chance that Interpol would be able to come up with something on him, but only if the young guy's picture happened to match one of the many thousands of mug shots on their files. Not good odds. Bob was beginning to get a gut feeling that the more he dug into this one, the bigger the hole he'd be getting himself into.

Now the press were hassling him for further details on what the early edition of the Edinburgh *Evening News* had already dubbed, "The North Berwick Serial Killings". But, to date, the only real connections that could be made between the murders were two white Sierra cars and a hundred thousand pounds in used banknotes, and Bob wasn't about to make that information public — yet. Not that he wasn't already mulling over a plan to use that knowledge as bait to hook the Alfa Romeo Spider lady, but the timing had to be just right.

To add to his woes, a check with Lothian and Borders Fire Brigade had revealed that they had no less than four officers by the name of Black serving at their various fire stations throughout the region, and keeping those men covered in case of impromptu visits by the elusive hit squad was putting an extra and unwelcome strain on Bob's already hard-pressed manpower resources. The number written on the ferry ticket stub wasn't turning out to provide the easy lead that he had hoped for, either. The major Scottish and English banks had already ascertained that the number didn't relate to one of their accounts, so the telephone 'tecs were now busy checking out all the smaller institutions, both mainland based and offshore. Bob needed a break and he needed it quickly.

"Got it, skipper!" Andy Green shouted, barging into the office waving a piece of paper. "It's an account at the —"

Bob grabbed the paper and squinted at the scribbled words. "*The Waverley-King's Cross Commerce Bank.* Who the blazes are they?"

"It's one o' them highfalutin merchant bank outfits," DC Green keenly revealed. "Head office in George Street here in Edinburgh."

"Whose name's the account in?"

"Wouldn't say on the phone. Said they can't divulge any details without a warrant, either."

Bob lifted the phone. "One warrant coming right up. Yeah, so get one of the traffic boys to bring a car round, Green. You're on your way to George Street." He checked the time. "Oh, and don't bother coming back here when you're through. Get all the info you can, then see me at the Bailie pub along in Saint Stephen

Street. I've had enough of this bloody place for one day!"

THE BAILIE BAR, STOCKBRIDGE, EDINBURGH — 5.45p.m. . . .

Julie poked a finger into Bob's midriff. "You're starting to develop a beer belly, Kemosabe."

"Hallelujah! God knows I've been trying long enough." He took a luxuriantly long slug of his Belhaven Best. "Yeah, I was only fifteen when I bought my first pint of beer in the Castle Inn at Dirleton. Twenty-three years ago — fifty pence or something — earned it flogging plums I'd nicked out of the big house gardens at Archerfield Estate. Happy days . . ."

"Under-age drinking with the proceeds of stolen goods, huh? A truly apt kick-off for a future Detective Inspector, I must say!"

"Absolutely. After all, it takes one to know one, right?" Bob smiled nostalgically. "Yep, that's how I made my first bust as a rookie DC. Collared a pair of sixteen-year-old neds bevvying in the Captain's Cabin roadhouse out at Gracemount."

"That was a shade hypocritical, wasn't it?"

Bob pursed his lips. "Ah, but I never charged them, though."

"Conscience get the better of you, did it?"

"Nope. Their big brothers took me outside and beat the crap out of me in the car park." Bob nodded pensively. "Yeah, that's the Gracemount gadgies for you — a law unto themselves, and natural tutors of the

81

novice lawman. Mmm-hmm, what was it the man said? Something like, *God grant me the serenity to accept the things I cannot change, the courage to change the things I can, and the wisdom to distinguish the one from the other.*"

Julie cast him a puzzled frown. "But that's the prayer of Alcoholics Anonymous!"

"I rest my case." Bob raised his glass. "Cheers!"

It was then that a whey-faced Andy Green appeared in the doorway of the bar, which was already bustling with after-office-hours imbibers, all noisily talking everything but shop. He shoved his way through the melee to the corner table where Bob and Julie were sitting.

"I suppose a bar snack's out of the question, Chief?" he puffed. "I'm feelin' a wee bit peckish, like."

Bob made a help-your-bloody-self gesture towards the bar.

"No, Chief, it's, well — I mean, I don't suppose ye could see yer way to . . ." Andy patted his silent trouser pockets. "I'm totally Cap'n Flint, see. Ehm, so I thought maybe exies would be —"

"In order? To cover your half-mile trip in a police car up to George Street and back?" Bob shook his head in disbelief, but lobbed him two tenners, all the same. "You'll have to sign a receipt for that in the morning," he grunted. "Now, what's the news from the Waverley Whajimacallit Bank?"

DC Green slapped his notepad on the table. "All in there, boss," he grinned, then took off for the bar as if attached to the end of a contracting bungee line.

"Thank God he's printed it," Bob sighed when he'd found the appropriate page. "Green's attempts at joined-up writing still resemble the meanderings of a drunken bluebottle with a severe case of Montezuma's revenge." He scanned the page. "Let's see now . . . The account's in the name of Top Banana Enterprises, registered in the Cayman Islands. Joint signatories . . . what's this he's scrawled here? Dannato Cornamusa and . . .?"

Julie craned her neck to read the notes. "It looks like . . . Laprima Frittella!" She burst out laughing. "They can't be serious! I mean Dannato Cornamusa seems daft enough, but Laprima Frittella, in colloquial Italian, means something like —"

"Heh, boss, take a gander at this!" Andy Green called out. He was weaving his way back from the bar, one fist clutching a pint of beer, the other hand supporting a platter heaped with a random selection of Scotch eggs, sausage rolls, chips and multifarious other items of indiscriminate stodge. Tucked under his arm was a newspaper, which he dropped on the table in front of Bob. "It's the late edition of the *Evening News*, see. It was lying on the bar, and I noticed this on the front page." He deposited his pint and pointed to the headline:

MUCKLE FLOGGIT WELCOMES NEW OWNER.

"Muckle Thingmyjig," Andy affirmed. "That's that island you were on about, intit? The one the Doc here used to go to on her summer hols or somethin'?"

"So what?" Bob said.

Andy Green was pop-eyed with excitement. "The picture! Take sights at the photie!" He stabbed his finger at the caption. "There! Beside the helicopter — the new laird — the new owner o' the island. It's him in ma notes there! Dannato Corny-whatsisname!"

"Well, I'll be buggered!" Bob admitted quietly.

"Well! Nice-looking guy!" Julie commented keenly.

"Well spotted, Green," Bob added kindly.

Andy stuck out his chest. "Aye, well, the lassie at the bar dropped one o' ma pickled onions on it, like."

"Convey my compliments to your tapeworm, then," Bob said, deadpan. "The creature's got the making of a good detective."

"Aw, thanks, skipper." Andy Green was almost bursting with enthusiasm now. "But that's not all!"

Bob raised an inquisitive eyebrow. "Tell me more, lad."

"See the bird lookin' out o' the chopper window?"

Bob and Julie nodded in unison.

Andy's eyes were on sticks. "Well, it's her! The bint in the red Alfa Romeo Spider! The drop-dead stotter that dumped the hundred grand at the North Berwick pumps!"

Bob and Julie exchanged knowing glances, then duetted, "Laprima Frittella, *if* I'm not mistaken."

"Heh!" Green ejaculated, "that's the other name on ma notes there!"

Julie covered her lips with her hand and sniggered, "Somebody's *got* to be pulling our legs here."

"How come?" Bob frowned.

"Well, for starters, if my modest knowledge of Italian serves me correctly, Dannato Cornamusa means *Damned Bagpipes*, or such like. And, as I was about to tell you before, the name Laprima Frittella means . . ." She giggled aloud. "Laprima Frittella, loosely translated, is . . . *high-class crumpet!*"

"Loosely translated nothin'!" Green objected. "I could never have described her better maself, like! Aw, I'm tellin' ye," he drooled into a pork pie, "what a belter!"

Julie was in stitches now.

"What the hell's tickling *your* tootsies?" Bob enquired.

"It's that name — Laprima Frittella," Julie tittered. "You see, I've just thought that maybe an even more accurate translation would be . . . *grade-one grease-stain!*"

Perplexed, Andy Green pondered his pie.

Bob Burns' face was expressionless, save for a barely-discernible upturn at one corner of his mouth. He beat a steady tattoo on the tabletop with the fingers of his right hand. He was thinking fast. His evolving ploy for snaring the Spider woman had taken on a new and unexpected twist, and he liked it.

"Have you got a kilt, Green?" he asked, his finger-drumming slipping into a jaunty Highland rhythm.

"Aye, I've had one since I used to play in the Boys' Brigade band."

"You mean you're a bugler?" said Julie politely, her poise now fully recovered.

"Nah, a piper! Aye, and I've still got a set o' bagpipes an' all!"

Bob clapped his hands together. "Even better! OK, Green," he grinned, "I think you and I are Hebrides bound!"

Julie cleared her throat. "Uhm, excuse me, Kemosabe," she ventured, "but would you happen to need, per chance, a forensic scientist who knows Muckle Floggit like the inside of her test tube?"

Bob was already on his feet. "Just grab your chemistry set, Tonto. We're all taking the road to the isles!"

CHAPTER
EIGHT

LATER THAT SAME EVENING — DRAMGLASS VILLAGE HALL, ON THE HEBRIDEAN ISLAND OF MUCKLE FLOGGIT, OFF THE WEST COAST OF SCOTLAND . . .

Angus MacGubligan and three other senior members of the local Council — including the Reverend Dick, the parish minister — sat proudly on the platform with their new landlord. All five of them were going through the motions of listening appreciatively to the Reverend's wife contraltoing an unaccompanied rendition of the island's anthem, *Muckle Floggit, I Adore Thee* (in Gaelic, of course). On the floor of the hall stood a yawning scattering of islanders, their meagre numbers augmented by a few Isle of Skye "mainlanders", who had ventured early over the Sound of Stooshie on Angus's ferry for the coming weekend's annual agricultural show and associated festivities. The half-hearted patter of applause at the end of Mrs Dick's performance echoed off the little hall's corrugated iron roof like the sound of a couple of diarrhoeic dairy cows doing what comes naturally on the floor of an empty byre.

"*Tapadh leat*. Thank you, Mistress Dick," Angus boomed in a lilting island brogue, while hoisting his lean, craggy frame to its full height at the podium and trimming the lie of his chain of office over the wide lapels of his blue serge Sunday suit. "It is always a great *plessure* to express our gratitude at the end of one of your songs. Yes, yes, so it is, right enough."

"Aye, thank the holy Christ that's over with," came an anonymous grunt from the body of the hall. It was followed by ripples of laughter mingling with whispers of, "*Isht, isht!* The minister will hear! Are you wanting to get us all flung out at all?"

Angus coughed circumspectly and twirled a whirl of heathery eyebrow between forefinger and thumb. "It behoves me," he declared, "as Provost of Dramglass village and Chairperson of Muckle Floggit Island Council, to extend the warm hand of welcome to our new laird here, the world-famous sculptor . . ." He turned and bowed stiffly in Franco's direction and snatched a surreptitious gander at the relevant phonetically-transcribed detail of his notes as he did so. "Ehm, eh, the world-famous sculptor, Seenyour Tomato Cornmoose."

"Ah-*hum*! It's DANNato Corna*MUSA*," the Reverend Dick prompted in a stage whisper indiscreet enough to bestir the drowsiest of congregations from Sunday morning snoozes.

Fresh titterings rose from the floor.

"Aye, chust that, right enough," Angus conceded with official aplomb. "Yes, and it is a fine honour to be welcoming such a grand foreign chentleman as him here into the basoom of our simple wee community."

"Hear! hear!" the platform party muttered in awkward unison, to the accompaniment of another sparse splattering of applause from the audience.

"Tell him about our outside lavvies!" one cynic shouted from the back of the hall.

"Aye, and what about the sheep shite in our water supply?" goaded another.

"Enough of that!" Angus admonished at the top of his voice, his eyebrows twitching as if suddenly invaded by a clutch of grouse legging it through the heather on 12th of August. "Chust youse hold on a minute there! There is a time and a place for saying such things. This is maybe the place, but if it is, it is not the time. And when it is the time, it is me myself and the other Council members — speaking as your democratically-elected representatives — that will be after doing the saying!" His wee black eyes glinted like chips of jet set deep in a granite cliff. "So youse can all chust hold your wheesht for now!" He turned to Franco again and flashed him a provostly smile. "You will notice that we are having this wee public conflabbation in the English and not in the Gaelic, Seenyour Cornmoose. Yes, for we want to make you feel at home, so we do."

Unable to understand most of what had been said, Franco nodded his confused acknowledgement. Unseen, Laprima Frittella watched the bizarre proceedings from the curtained shadows at the side of the platform.

"Anyway," Angus went on, "I am sure to be speaking for every man, wumman and bairn on Muckle Floggit when I say to our new laird here that the news of his grand intenshuns to invest so *chenerously* in our little

89

wee community has came as a great relief — especially after all the driech years of damned stinginess we endured at the hand of yon jaggy-haired eejit of a rock-and-roller!" Angus was beginning to get carried away with himself, but a tempering cough from the Reverend Dick soon reined him in. He cleared his throat and re-adopted his avuncular Chairperson-of-the-Council manner. "But I say to you, Seenyour Cornmoose — or may I chust call you Tomato?" (The minister raised his eyes in silent prayer) "— that the chenerosity that you offer so, eh, *chenerously* will not be chust a one-way thing at all. Och, no, for there's nobody knows better than us folks of Dramglass here the mess yon Sid Sloth and his damned dope-fiend disciples were after turning the big house into up on the hill there." (A rhubarb of assent rippled round the hall). "Aye, it's chust a fair midden now," Angus continued, "what with all yon physiodelic paintings on the walls and all them funny West Indian weeds growing all over the place and even in the rodydendrums and everywhere. Damned heathen mary-joanna!"

Franco pricked up his ears at the mention of the mary-joanna word.

"Aye, aye, but never you fear, Mr Tomato," Angus smarmed, "you'll be finding us poor folk of Muckle Floggit are not the ones to take a good man's chenerosity for granted. Nah, nah, never such a thing! For, by the stars, we will rally round and we will give you all the assistance you will ever be needing to restore old Dramglass House to its former magnificence and glory, the likes of which it hasna seen since God knows when." Facing Franco, he spread his arms and declared munificently, "Man, all you have to do is chust ask!" He smiled warmly and added in hushed tones, "Yes, and you will find that my terms is *very* competitive indeed."

"Speak up, MacGubligan, ye conniving shite ye!" came a cry from the floor of the hall. "Man, mind thy bluidy self, right enough!"

The Jack Spratt-like Reverend Dick took this as his cue to rise and take his turn at the podium, his steady, slow march over the creaking boards of the platform giving the lie to the liberal quantity of communion wine that had passed his lips in the hallowed sanctuary of his vestry immediately before the event. He perched his pince-nez low on his nose, rheumy eyes surveying the gathered assembly one by one, a tight-lipped smile that was both benign and malignant creasing his cheeks and lending him the facial appearance of an anaemic lizard with constipation. Rolling his head back, he cast his eyes heavenward and clasped his hands tightly in front of the wrongly-buttoned waistcoat of his grey suit.

"My loyal friends and faithful parishioners," he monotoned, his vocal pitch dropping at the end of the phrase with the funereal intonation that is a hallmark his profession, "we are gathered here tonight to honour and receive with open hearts — and, ehm, hands — a man who is not only to be our new neighbour, but whom fate has decreed will also be the new head of our cherished community." He coughed discreetly into his dog's collar, then added the qualification, "Uhm, *secular* head, that is to say." The crucial word reverberated round the hall like the voice of Moses from the Mount. "I have little to add to Provost MacGubligan's eloquent, if not to say articulate, welcoming speech — except, perhaps, to mention to those present who may not share my love, my *scholarship* of the fine arts, that it is a rare privilege indeed to have our humble island home not only owned, but also graced by the resident presence of a maestro of the immense international stature of *Il Signor* Cornamusa."

Franco shrugged modestly and exposed the palms of his hands in response.

"Never heard of the bugger!" was the loud reaction of an unknown heckler.

"Tuts" of disapproval from the platform group, chuckles from the floor.

With a silent gesture of apology to Franco, the Reverend Dick continued, "And so, *Signor* Cornamusa, may I express my personal delight, and that of my more *enlightened* fellow islanders, that you have chosen as your home our beautiful, if — until now — sadly deprived little gem of God's wondrous works of creation. And may I just add, before inviting you to address the assembly here gathered in your honour, that the door of my church is always open to you. Indeed, it is my fervent wish that you will join the faithful in worship this very Sunday morning." He squeezed out a patronising chortle. "You see, *signor*, I am proud to say that the Dramglass Parish Kirk here on Muckle Floggit is a true haven of ecumenicism. Everyone, no matter what his colour, creed or caste, no matter what his faith or denomination, is ever welcome to join us and to contribute *wholeheartedly* to the, ehm, praise of our Lord."

"Aye, and to auld Holy Dick there's collection box!" quipped another faceless wag.

"Indeed, the parlous state of our church roof has for many years been a matter of the *gravest* concern," Holy Dick himself confided as an aside to Franco during the ensuing short interlude of congregational sniggering. Then, apparently deaf to all but his own voice, he resumed at full volume: "And now, ladies and gentlemen, good people of Muckle Floggit, I invite you to show your appreciation — albeit in advance — to our benevolent new laird in a hearty round of applause." With outstretched hand, he gestured theatrically towards the cringing Franco. "I give you . . . DANNATO CORNAMUSA-A-A!"

The ovation from the floor outstripped that from the platform this time, it being fairly obvious from the petrified look on the new laird's face that an opportunity to take a rise out of this bleach-haired foreign freak was about to be presented to the plebs at last.

As the keenly-clapping Reverend Dick continued to beckon him, Franco raised his hands in mute objection. But a chance glance into the wings, where Laprima was miming a slow disembowelment with a long, scarlet fingernail, quickly persuaded him that compliance was the name of the only game in town. He stood up and, amid wild whistling and cheering from the body of the hall, shuffled uncomfortably to the podium.

A gravid silence descended upon the place. Franco could hear his heart thumping, yet he managed to contrive a wooden smile. Bracing himself, he opened his mouth to speak, when, in the gloom at the far corner of the hall, someone (perhaps a schoolboy?) trumpeted a soft, purring, one-note fanfare into his trousers. A conflict of giggles and gasps of abhorrence sprang from the relevant camps.

Cristo! Welcome to Muckle Floggit, Franco thought. Still, faint heart never won forty thousand dollars. He was *Siciliano*, wasn't he? *Si, certamente!* So, go for it! Eyes staring straight ahead, he strained his rictus-like grin even wider. "What can I-a say?" he said for openers.

"How about *arrivederci?*" came the cutting riposte from the floor.

Inwardly flapping, but outwardly unflinching, Franco proceeded: "First, I must-a say *grazie*, thank you, for the beeg-a welcome from the mayor and-a the, uhm . . . priest."

Aghast, the Reverend Dick spluttered wordlessly, while his pasty cheeks turned a distinctly un-ecumenical purple.

Someone whistled, as if signalling a sheepdog on the hill. "Hey, Dannato!" he yelled. "How about rustling me up a quick fish supper — plenty salt and nippy sauce — aye, and a couple of ice creams for the bairns and all?"

Although neither fully understanding the question nor, consequently, the reason for the ensuing communal mirth, Franco — to his credit — laughed along with the rest. He raised a hand. "OK, my-a friend," he beamed directly at his heckler, "because the mayor he been-a so kind to, how you say? *conflab* in-a the English instead of your Garlic just-a for me, I gonna try reply in-a the Scotch just-a for you." Pressing a cogitative forefinger to his temple, he dredged up memories of those nights when the *Bella Siciliana* restaurant on Edgeware Road had been invaded by visiting Scottish football fans, then cockily proclaimed, "See-a you, Jeemy! Any more-a snash outa you, ya poultice, and Ah'm gonna stick-a the bloody heid right oan ye!"

The Reverend Dick, eyes downcast, muttered into his tightly-clenched hands a prayer for deliverance, while the entire assembly of plebs dissolved into paroxysms of raucous laughter.

A delighted, if slightly hysterical, Franco led the merriment, while milking his audience's acclamations, arms-outstretched, atop the podium. All at once, he felt like *Il Duce* of the Isles. This feeling of relief-engendered euphoria soon got the better of him, however. Inspired by the sudden recollection of the pizza-gobbling Jocks' predilection for the randomly-placed expletive, he allowed his natural Italian exuberance to carry his oration in Scots right over the top.

"Ay-y-y! I love-a youz all, my chinas!" he pronounced. Then, as those magic sporting phrases came drifting back, he punched the air and roared, "We *are*-a the people, OK! So, up-a the proud Edward army and up-a the Keeng Beely boys!" As a grand finale, he turned and made a flamboyant sweep of his hand towards the quailing Reverend Dick, then bellowed with unfortunate innocence, "AND-A TOO-RA-LOO-RAL, KICK-A THE FUCKIN' POPE, EH!"

9am THE FOLLOWING DAY — THE TERRACE OUTSIDE THE MORNING ROOM OF DRAMGLASS MANSION HOUSE ...

Franco eased one denim-clad cheek onto the stone balustrade and took a tentative sip from his steaming cup. *Dio!* how he needed this, and *mamma mia!* what he'd give for a real thick-as-tar espresso instead of this instant, wishy-washy excuse for coffee. Yet, to be fair, he had to admit that, coffee apart, these Muckle Floggit people didn't have much to learn about beverages — certainly not in so far as the alcoholic variety was concerned. Franco had learned that the hard way the previous night, when, immediately following the welcoming reception in the village hall, a group of his hecklers-turned-chums had spirited him off for an impromptu celebration in the public bar of the little Dramglass Hotel, down by the pier.

Strangely, the bar had reminded him of the run-down drinking pit which he used to frequent over the street from his blacksmith's workshop back in Sicily, this particular island establishment being just as spartan, every bit as aesthetically charmless, yet, in every *visible* way, totally different. Instead of cheap, white, lavatorial wall tiles, there was cheap, wood-effect hardboard wall cladding, and instead of dusty, bland terrazzo flooring, there was featureless, fag-end-pitted linoleum. But the hands-across-the-continent whiff of stale cigarette smoke, beery urine and commercial disinfectant formed the common denominator that made him feel almost at home. The clientele, too, was curiously similar; a men-only mix of, in the main, self-employed and unemployed local artisans and labourers, every one a dedicated social drinker with a bar-widow wife waiting sullenly at home. Franco recognised them all. Only their complexions and language were different from their Italian counterparts.

Though he had been unable to remember the given names of all the many faces introduced to him in the bar, Franco had noted that an inordinately large proportion of them shared the same surname. There was MacGubligan the woodman, MacGubligan the fisherman, MacGubligan the hen man, MacGubligan the coalman, MacGubligan the postman, MacGubligan the roadman, and the one MacGubligan whose first name he did remember, Hamish "Nip" MacGubligan, the on-the-sick distillery worker, who had led him on a guided, dram-at-a-time taste-tour of every one of a dozen or more single malts on the bar gantry. And that was before Franco's new coterie of *amicos* had introduced him to the island's unique liqueur, the mystical and head-poppingly potent *Saint Gubligan's Tears*. This was a sweetly-smouldering concoction which, he was told, local legend insisted was the true brew that enticed Bonnie Prince Charlie *Over The Sea To Skye* — en route, of course, to the source of this, his favourite tipple, on Muckle Floggit.

97

Franco had meant to enquire further into that alleged piece of history, but the commencement of a celebratory *ceilidh* (pronounced "kay-lay", according to Nip) and the progressive malfunctioning of a brain bemused by a surfeit of alien booze had put paid to that. All he could recall of the remainder of the night was a blur of ruddy faces, strange *he-darumming* and *ho-darumming* mouth music, and a piper (who sometimes self-multiplied before his swimming eyes into four perfect clones), skirling out selections of wild jigs and reels, before Franco himself succumbed to persuasion and contributed to the party-piece proceedings a communally-assisted version of *Dannato, Where's-a Yer Troosers?*.

Laprima had been waiting for him when he eventually staggered back up the rise to Dramglass House in the wee, small hours. If looks could have killed, Franco would have been dead meat as he ricocheted legless along the narrow hallway from the back door, through which he had been attempting a hush-hush entrance. Standing back-lit in the kitchen doorway, the nightgown-draped Laprima appeared to Franco like a seductive, out-of-focus dream. But his slavered and somewhat ambitious suggestion that they should spend the rest of the night making mad, endless *amore* was met with the derisory response that it deserved, followed by the unambiguous piece of advice that his Uncle Max didn't brook no lushes in the outfit.

"So dry out or get ready to be rubbed out, *piccino mio! Buona notte*, huh?"

For all that, Laprima had eventually paid a visit to Franco's room, but not until seven o'clock in the morning, and then only to haul him unceremoniously out of bed, with the hissed command to get his lazy ass into his pants and downstairs to the morning room, *pronto!* Awaiting him there, instead of the cool glass of freshly-squeezed orange juice and bubbling jug of Cona coffee that his hung-over system was screaming for, had been a tumbler of cold water, two Alka Seltzers and a half-hour refresher lecture from Laprima on who he really was, who he was supposed to be, and why.

But the *why* part of the equation still bothered Franco. Frankly, after being bombarded with all the "capital-A" double talk that he could take in, he really was no wiser about all this Muckle Floggit "sporran" business than he had been at the end of his Uncle Massimo's phone call back in Messina. Obviously, the island was somehow intended as a stash for some of Massimo's money — all ill-gotten loot at that, if Franco was any judge. But just why he had to masquerade as the owner *and* a rich sculptor, and what all the vague promises of benevolence to the islanders was about still puzzled Franco completely. Yet the only help Laprima would give was to repeat the theme of her original advice: "You're Sicilian, so bullshit your way through it!"

Here he was, then, the confused so-called lord of all he surveyed, perched on the terrace of his mansion, with hardly enough money in his pocket to buy a few slates for the roof.

The scenery was absolutely stunning, even to his drink-fuddled eyes. Beneath him, the wooded landscape fell gently northwards to the narrow strait that separated Muckle Floggit from its far-famed big sister, the magnificent Isle of Skye. There, the serrated ridges of the Cuillins reached heavenward, smudges of cloud drifting out from their summits like puffs of smoke into a clear blue sky. His eyes followed the slopes back down to the Sound, where the mountains were mirrored in the water on which Angus MacGubligan's toy-like ferry was already half way out on its first crossing of the day to the jetty at Ardenstooshie.

Franco had no idea when, if ever, he would see the menacingly-attractive Laprima Frittella again. All she had said to him, before leaving for the pier in the white limo that had been garaged in the stable block at the back of the house, was that he should use his brains, if he wanted to keep them intact, and await further instructions.

APPROXIMATELY ONE HOUR LATER — THE MAINLAND VILLAGE OF DORNIE, ON "THE ROAD TO THE ISLES", A SHORT WAY OVER THE SEA FROM SKYE . . .

Bob Burns and his two aides had just taken breakfast in the hotel dining room after a five-hour drive up from Edinburgh.

"Good idea o' yours to stop here, Doc," Andy Green said to Julie Bryson when she returned from freshening up. "Know what I mean, like — the view an' that?" He nodded out of the window. "Magic, eh?"

Julie sat down and poured herself another coffee. "Mmm, a step down memory lane for me. This is where we always stopped, my folks and I, for lunch or afternoon tea or whatever on our way to and from holidays on MF, as we called it." She followed Andy's gaze. "There may be other scenes as spectacular as that in the Highlands, but not too many, I fancy." She nudged Andy's arm and pointed. "See that old castle on the wee island out there in the sea loch? Well, that's Eilean Donan, one of the most photographed places in the world, I suppose. And little wonder. Just look at the overpowering majesty of those mountains rising up from the other side of the water there. You know, even great poets have been left speechless at the sight of all that."

"Aye, no bad, right enough," Andy agreed with typical understatement.

"Where's the boss?" Julie asked, still marvelling at the view.

Andy jerked his thumb towards the car park. "Out havin' a natter on the horn wi' DS Yule back at home base. Checkin' up on developments since last night, like."

After a minute or two, Bob re-entered the dining room, sat down at the table and checked his watch. "Yeah, time for one last coffee before we shove off again."

Julie duly obliged. "What's the latest word from Jimmy Yule?"

101

"Still nothing on the two cars, and still nothing on the Tantallon Castle murderee or his killers."

"And the Spider woman?" Andy Green enquired anxiously.

"Same story — nothing. They've got a blow-up of that press pic of her — *if* it's her — peeping out of the helicopter, and that's being shot off to all the UK constabularies and Interpol."

"And to the papers and the telly as well?" Andy Green urged.

Bob shook his head. "Nah, not yet. Don't want her to know we're on her tail, do we?"

Andy looked blank. "Aye, sure enough. Neither we do, eh?"

Bob stirred his coffee slowly. "DS Yule's already been up at George Street pumping the head guy at the Waverley Whatsit Bank this morning, though."

"And?" Julie prompted, catching the glint in Bob's eye.

"The Waverley bloke couldn't actually *tell* him anything else, but he did obligingly leave the office for a minute, having left a certain bank statement and associated memos conveniently placed on his desk. It goes without saying that Yule swiftly clocked the lot."

"And?"

"And the reported three million quid that Top Banana Enterprises used to buy Muckle Floggit appears to have been paid into the Waverley Bank in one lump. That was to open the account, just over two months ago — a transfer direct from the Cayman Islands, all paperwork AOK and legal."

"Well, well, well," said Julie, eyebrows raised.

"But there's more," Bob continued. "Two deposits, each of just over fifty thousand pounds in cash, were made in each of the two weeks immediately before the North Berwick filling station drop by —"

"The Spider Woman!" Andy Green spluttered, spraying coffee all over the white tablecloth.

"Nice piece of deduction," Bob said with more than a hint of cynicism.

"No!" Green's face was drained of colour, the whites of his eyes naked as he pointed frantically out of the window. "I mean, it's *her*! See, out there — that bint drivin' away in the big white Merc!"

"Hey, that's the flash babe I bumped into in the loo just a couple of minutes ago," Julie said. She thumped her fist on the table. "Dammit! I should've recognised the scent!"

"*Femme* by Rochas?" Bob suggested.

Julie stood up. "Correct! So come on — we'd better get after her!"

Bob calmly finished writing something on a paper napkin, then patted the seat of Julie's chair. "Sit down and finish your coffee. I've got her car number now, and there's only one long, winding road south from here. So don't worry, there'll be plenty of time to put out an APB on her once we're back on our way. I'll get the Fort William nick to set an unmarked car on her tail at Spean Bridge. Jimmy Yule can coordinate things by radio from then on." He looked over at Andy Green's ashen face. "Let's just hope she didn't recognise you sitting here when she came out of the karzi, kid."

Andy gulped.

Julie sat down and laid a reassuring hand on his. "I'm certain she didn't. In fact, I don't suppose she even looked near the dining room."

Bob couldn't resist a mischievous laugh. "All the same, if I were you, boy, I'd be wearing knee pads under that kilt of yours from now on." He signalled the waitress for the bill, then turned to Andy Green again, his expression serious now. "Before we go any further, though, are you sure you're up to this, Green?"

"Aye, no bother, Chief." Andy rolled his shoulders, attempting to look cool. "Nah, no sweat for me, like."

Bob wasn't that easily taken in, but he was stuck with the situation now. He looked Andy straight in the eye. "Just tell me one more time what the game plan is, then, OK?"

Andy inhaled slowly, fixed his stare at a corner of the ceiling and parroted, "I am Andrew Green. I have just inherited a multi-million-pound scrap business from my old man. I have got more money than sense. I am up here on holiday, and I am interested in starting a collection of sculpture — of which I know absolutely bugger all."

For the final leg of the journey, Bob deemed it prudent to have Andy Green take the wheel of Julie's BMW 328i drophead, the snazzy, bottle-green convertible having been requisitioned, as it were, to be passed off as the young scrap heir's personal pose-mobile. It was a necessary decision that Bob soon regretted, neverthe-less, as Green negotiated the ten miles of meandering

104

coast road from Dornie to the Skye Bridge at speeds and with a cavalier technique that would have been better suited to the Monte Carlo Rally. Bob's fevered back-seat demand to slow down, for Christ's sake, was met by Green's casual retort of:

"Listen, I'm supposed to be a thick-as-a-bottle-o'-shit scrappie, amn't I? OK, so I'm drivin' like one!"

Julie, perhaps because this was a driving style familiar to and, for that matter, favoured by herself in her not-so-distant wild and youthful past, was content to sit smiling in the passenger seat, the slipstream buffeting her dark tresses as she took in the breathtaking West Highland vistas opening out before them round every corner. These were sights that Bob could only snatch glimpses of through his blinkering fingers. And so it continued on the Isle of Skye, Andy Green determinedly overtaking everything that appeared before him — be it car, tractor, bus or sheep — from Kyleakin to Harrapool, from Broadford over the snaking ribbon of road round Loch Slapin, and on southward through Kilmarie to the coast at Ardenstooshie hamlet.

Angus MacGubligan was just completing the tricky task of guiding the laden brewery truck onto the cramped deck of his ferry (more of a motorised raft than a boat) when Andy screeched the BMW to a stop at the very end of the little wooden jetty.

"Chust you hold your horses there!" Angus thundered, then muttered under his breath, "Damned Sassenach eejit that you are!" He strode purposefully over the loading ramp, readying his shoulder-slung money-bag-cum-ticket-dispenser as he approached the car. "Man, man, it's surely in a terrible hurry that you're in," he frowned. "Chings me, the tide must turn terrible fast where you come from." He quickly scanned the car from front to back. "Anyway, that'll be the ten pounds single for your vee-hicle . . . *if* she's under the thirteen feet long, mind you. Yes, and the five pounds each for your passengers — driver free."

"How much if it *is* over thirteen feet?" Andy enquired, while prising an unusually fat wad of notes from his sporran.

"Och, the ten pounds chust the same. I'm not a greedy man at all."

Andy was patently puzzled. "So, what's the thirteen feet thing about?"

"Well now, if she was over the thirteen feet, you would chust need to wait until the next trip, you understand. Aye, for my vessel can only manage the one vee-hicle of thirteen feet or less when I have yon drinks lorry aboard, and that's a fact."

Andy hunched his shoulders. "I'll just have to drive on and see if it fits. I mean, I haven't a bloody clue how long the car is, like."

"Aye, aye, that'll be the thing to do, right enough then." Angus held out his hand. "And that'll be the ten pounds loading fee . . . ehm, deductible from the fare, of course, *if* your vee-hicle fits in."

"And if it doesn't?"

"Well, you would chust have to wait here for the next tide . . . or go away back home where you came from."

106

"And what would happen to the tenner loading fee if I did decide to shoot the crow?"

Angus opened his money bag. "Ach, I would likely spend it in the beer tent at the agricultural show tomorrow chust the same."

"Give him the money, for heaven's sake," Julie muttered. "The car's only twelve-foot-nine or something."

Angus arched his heathery brows, beady eyes glinting as they appraised Julie's appraisable parts. "By the stars! If it's not the wee lass of yon Bryson the boffin that used to be sometimes renting the wee house on my cousin's wee croft at the foot of Ben Doone over there. Well, well, *well*," he appraised afresh, "you've fairly grew into a fine, strong young wumman, so you have now. Mm-Hm-m-m . . ."

"You have a good memory, Angus," Julie smiled. She leaned over to shake his hand. "Nice to see you again after all those years."

Angus eyed Bob and Andy in turn. "And, eh, one of these chentlemen would be your husband, I suppose?"

"Actually, no. Mr Burns here is a professional colleague of —"

"And what profession would that likely be, then?"

"Uhm, science — like my father. Yes, Mr Burns and I are travelling together. Doing research, you know. Our car broke down back at Dornie, and Mr Green here kindly offered us a lift."

Angus shot a suspicious glance at Andy's kilt. "I never knew there was a Clan Green, Mr Green. Aye, and if I'm not mistaken, yon kilt of yours is the MacDonald tartan. Got Skye blood, have you?"

"MacDonald's ma mother's name," Andy lied. "Her granny came from Skye. Yeah, Lerwick it was."

Angus chose not to comment on the fact that Lerwick is the capital of the Shetland Islands, which are located some two hundred miles north-east of Skye as the seagull flies. "My, my, chust fancy that now," he crooned instead. His eyes then retreated back into their shadowy lair. "And what would *your* business be, Mr Green?"

"Scrap. Scrap metal."

"Chings me, the scrap metal, is it? Well now, you're after coming to the right place, and that's the truth of it. Aye, Muckle Floggit is fair littered with the stuff. Old cars that nobody would pay the ferry fare to get rid of when they was clapped out, you understand." He gave Andy a sly wink. "Maybe me and you could come to a nice wee arrangement, laddie . . . do you not think so?"

"Ye never know yer luck," Andy shrugged, "*if* ye can manage to squeeze this car onto yer tub, that is."

Angus tore three tickets off his role. "Ach, man," he chuckled, "something tells me that'll not be a problem at all." He held out his hand again. "So, that'll chust be the twenty pounds, please. Aye, I think we can dispense with the usual loading fee formality on this okayshun." He bagged the two tenners that Andy peeled from his wad. "*Ceud mile fàilte*, as we say in the mother tongue. A hundred thousand welcomes to youse all!"

CHAPTER
NINE

DRAMGLASS VILLAGE, THE ISLAND OF MUCKLE FLOGGIT — SATURDAY, AUGUST 10 — 9.30a.m. . . .

The day of the Muckle Floggit Agricultural Show and Highland Games was the highlight of the local year; the day when all of the island's eighty-five-strong population made their way from even the remotest crofts to Dramglass village for the grand occasion. It was also the one day of the year when Angus MacGubligan could be fairly sure of making an absolute mint on his ferry. If the weather was fine, as it certainly was today, hundreds of trippers from all over Skye would be guaranteed to descend upon the jetty on their side of the Sound of Stooshie to await transportation over the water to the festive proceedings, and Angus held the transportation monopoly. To maximise receipt potential, Angus always enforced a strict no-vehicles rule for this particular day.

From their seen-better-days rattan chairs in the "sun lounge" of the hotel, Bob and Julie had an unrestricted view of the Dramglass pier, onto which the morning's second batch of sardined passengers was already being urgently off-loaded by the little craft's delighted captain.

To the side of the hotel, a small, gently-undulating grass field — at various other times the home pitch of the Dramglass football and shinty teams, or a temporary holding paddock for ferry-bound livestock — inclined very gradually from the edge of the wooded grounds of Dramglass Mansion House to the shore. By some standards, a modest enough show venue, perhaps, but to the people of Muckle Floggit on this their annual day of days, this wee stretch of new-mown turf was Hampden Park, The Royal Highland Showground and the Esplanade of Edinburgh Castle all rolled into one.

Exhibitors, as varied in genre and substance as the West Highland distributors of Ford Tractors, the Forestry Commission, the Scottish National Party, the Bank of Scotland, and the Sponge-baking and Embroidery Circle of the Muckle Floggit Branch of the Scottish Women's Rural Institute, were already putting the finishing touches to their stands, titivating their tents, and generally setting out their stalls. Meanwhile, in the shade of the spreading trees on the perimeter of the big house woods, dandied-up stockmen were lovingly blow-drying shampooed Highland cows, pedicuring pampered pigs, or attempting — invariably without success — to transform wildly-indignant little Blackface ewes into serene and coiffured parade-ring ladies for the day.

The painful *skraitch* of bagpipes being tuned caught Bob's ear. "I hope to hell that isn't Green showing off," he grumped. "I told him just to get out there and mingle and sow the seeds of this sculpture-buying caper among the local chinwags."

110

Julie nodded towards a poster advertising the show, which was pinned to the wall behind Bob's head. "According to that, it's more likely to be the Portree Pipe Band warming up. They'd be the bunch of kilties that came off the ferry just now." She patted Bob's hand. "Just relax, Kemosabe. This is the Hebrides, the birthplace of *mañana,* so enjoy your cup of tea and take in the ambience. Andy'll get to your Signor Cornamusa bloke soon enough, never fear."

Bob still looked uneasy. "I wish I shared your optimism," he muttered. "Risking the outcome of a tricky case like this on Green's highly suspect sense of initiative somehow doesn't seem too clever an idea any more."

"You're only peeved because you can't now use him as live bait to hook the mysterious Laprima Frittella like you'd planned."

"Oh, yeah?"

"Yes, and while we're on that subject, it was a despicable thing to even contemplate. I mean, if she'd still been here and had recognised Andy, the poor young guy could well have been stiffed by now."

"I should be so lucky. But it looks like we're gonna have to cast our net a lot wider now in any case."

"How d'you mean?"

"I had a chat with Jimmy Yule on the blower before breakfast."

"And?"

"I didn't want to say anything in front of Green. Some things he's better not knowing. But the pay-off to the various tails we put on Signorina Frittella yesterday was that Jimmy Yule ended up posing as a traffic cop himself. He pulled her over just as she was approaching Edinburgh Airport. Spun her the usual line that she had a brake light on the blink or something."

"But for heaven's sake, why didn't he just come right out with it and arrest her on suspicion of aiding and abetting a murder — or two?"

Bob gave her a tolerant little smile. "If only it were that straightforward."

"Oh, I don't know!" Julie was in assertive mood. "Surely there's enough circumstantial stuff that could have been —"

"Think about it," Bob butted in. "We have absolutely no proof — only Green's word, for what it's worth — that she was the woman in the red Alfa Romeo at the North Berwick filling station, right? So, if DS Yule had suggested that she was, she'd only have denied it, *and* she would have rumbled that we were wise to her. No, I still say she's of more value to us on the loose."

"But in the meantime, we're no further ahead. That's the plain truth of the matter, isn't it?"

Bob raised a shoulder. "Who knows? Yule had a good butcher's at her driver's licence — American, in the name of Laprima Frittella. That's already been checked out, by the way, and it appears to be kosher."

"What about the car she was driving yesterday — the white Merc?"

"Nothing untoward there either. It's just as she told Yule. The Merc was included in the lock, stock and barrel purchase of this island. DVLC confirmed that the registration of ownership is already in the process of being transferred from Sid Snot — or whatever the name is of the rock pillock who used to own this place — to Top Banana Enterprises, of which Ms Frittella is a director. Her motor insurance is as watertight as a crab's bahookie as well."

"And you say she was bound for Edinburgh Airport?"

"Yep. Took off for Malaga on a normal holiday charter late yesterday afternoon."

"Malaga? Why Malaga?"

"Your guess is as good as mine. Jimmy Yule's got our Guardia Civil chums in the south of Spain keeping discreet tabs on her movements until we can dispatch a couple of our plain-clothes guys out there on the next available flight."

"Getting to be an expensive exercise this, isn't it?" Julie frowned.

"Tell me about it! Anyway, all we can do is hope Green's red Spider woman doesn't turn out to be only a red herring . . ."

Mrs MacGubligan — Flora MacGubligan, née MacGubligan, the wife of gardener-handyman-chauffeur Shooie MacGubligan — had been the housekeeper at Dramglass House for nigh on forty years, her career spanning the tenure of four successive absentee landlords, each one a bigger *scunner* (or pain in the backside) than the one before, in her informed opinion.

"Losh! I chust hope you're not going to be such a useless, lazy *sloonge* as yon Mr Sid, Mr Dannato," she said frankly to Franco as she placed a plate of bacon and eggs, black pudding and a crisply-fried slab of her home-made clootie dumpling before him on the otherwise deserted expanse of mahogany table in the dining hall. "Michty me, man, what time is this to be coming down for breakfast on the show day of all days? *Ochòin, ochòin*, and you the new laird as well. You should be down at the show field, engaging yourself in verbal intercourse with the masses by now, so you should."

Franco had already determined Mrs MacGubligan to be a kindly woman, but firm. Only last night, through his bedroom window, he had overheard her giving her husband a good Garlic roasting in their cottage beside the old stables. Franco hadn't understood one word of it, of course, but from the sound of old Shooie's slurred and feeble defence pitch, it was a cert that the root of the trouble was drink, a commodity of which the redoubtable Flora MacGubligan was clearly not in favour. Prudently, therefore, Franco decided not to admit to her that the reason for his late rising was that he was still recovering from his welcoming binge in the hotel bar the night before last.

Indeed, all he had managed to do yesterday was to take a gentle, paracetamol-aided stroll through the house grounds en route to the nearby church on a pilgrimage of apology to the Reverend Dick for that unintentional F-word faux-pas at the climax of his village hall speech the previous evening. To Franco's dismay and confusion, however, the curiously-coy Reverend Dick had appeared reluctant at first to listen to his open confession. Only the insertion of a crisp five-pound note into the slot of the Rev's conspicuously-placed collection box had finally kindled the fires of holy forgiveness in his heart and had stimulated total absolution — albeit of the unofficial, no-penance Presbyterian variety. Still, the experience had helped Franco feel much less conscience-stricken.

"I still-a be tired from my journey to your-a bee-ootiful island," he fibbed, flashing Mrs MacGubligan a seductive Sicilian smile. "Please-a to forgive, *signora*, eh . . .?"

Flora melted. The *signora* appellation had gone straight to her knees. Never before had she been addressed in such a — dare she even think the word? — sexy manner. She threw Franco a quick, flirtatious smirk in response, doggedly keeping a stiff upper lip, lest her loosely-fitting top set of dentures should let her down again. Here at last, she told herself, was a laird she could maybe, ehm, get *on* with, so to speak.

Captivated, she watched Franco wolfing into her clootie dumpling. *A dhuine, dhuine*, she sighed inwardly, he was chust a laddie, so he was. Aye, chust a laddie. A wee bit mothering was what he needed. With a strange longing, she gazed down at the top of his Adonis-like head. "Mm-hmm," she silently mused, "and his roots doing as well . . ."

The absence of a resident police presence on Muckle Floggit was a situation that the islanders valued greatly; a status quo, which, to a man, they were set on maintaining. After all, there was no record of crime amongst the locals, no one even *thought* of locking a house or car door, and if any sticky-fingered visitor dared to nick anything from Dramglass's only shop, Mohammed Patel-MacGubligan's General Store, Boat Chandlery and Petrol Pump down by the pier, the eagle-eyed proprietor would be sure to have ample time to nail him and recover his purloined stock long before the departure time (variable in summer, sporadic in winter) of the next ferry. So, why have some daft dumpling of a polisman, and an outsider at that, plodding about the place, telling them what time to shut the bar at night, and generally poking his nose into their wee bits of personal "business"?

Although unannounced visits were sprung on them periodically by old Constable MacClue from Broadford on Skye, Angus MacGubligan made sure that the good folk of Dramglass and beyond knew all about it in plenty time by sounding a prearranged tootle on his ferry whistle well in advance of casting off from Ardenstooshie with said lawman aboard.

Show day was the one day of the year, though, when it was a foregone conclusion that the bobby would be about, so all necessary arrangements would have been made by the islanders well in advance of his arrival. Aerials for unlicensed TVs would have been whipped in through upstairs windows, "privately" imported brands of spirits would have been removed from bar shelves (or more likely, on this bonanza day for booze sales, would have been decanted into bottles with legal labels), and cars wanting tax discs would have been secreted quietly away.

"Why pay road tax to yon grabbie London government," canny islanders reasoned, "when there's not even a road that deserves the name on Muckle Floggit, apart from Dramglass main street, and that's barely fifty yards long?"

All this "confidential" information was being imparted to Andy Green by the blissfully-unaware and cheery Hamish "Nip" MacGubligan in the refreshments tent, where he and a small band of fellow worthies were keenly cultivating the friendship — and potential bar beneficence — of this stinking-rich young visitor. For his part, Andy was trying to mentally note every detail of old Nip's incriminating revelations, lest any future career move might involve a compulsory transfer to the remoter regions of the Northern Constabulary.

"But mind you, man," chortled Nip as he draped a comradely arm round Andy's shoulder, "the polis is usually about as bent as they're daft — leastways the ones we're after getting over here, anyhow."

"Gerraway?" Andy replied, while trying to repress his lawman's sense of affront. "How do ye make that out, like?"

"Ach, I've never seen one yet that wasn't on for a wee backhander — a wee touch of the payola, you know — chust to keep his gub shut."

Andy cocked an ear.

"Oho, Andra," Nip laughingly observed, "that's fairly made you prick your lugs up, has it not now?" He adopted a sombre expression, then leaned in to whisper, "Man, you would be surprised chust how

117

much polis silence can be bought with a bottle of the *Saint Gubligan's Tears* ... ehm, and one of them speshull handshakes from auld Holy Dick the minister. Aye, one of them handshakes that means so much to the ministers of the kirk and the polismen, you know." He gave Andy a sly wink before posing the cryptic question, "How's yer granny's trooser leg?"

When a gormless, "Eh?" was the only response, Nip altered tack.

"Well, well, that's chust me," he sighed, placing his empty glass on the counter, "going and letting the drink get the better of my tongue again. Man, man, another dram and I'd likely have gave away the secret of the Saint Gubligan's Cave as well, so I would."

"Barman, another dram for Nip!" Andy demanded with some urgency. "Aye, and the same for his mates, like!" He dipped into his sporran and pealed off another note from the rapidly diminishing wad.

The Highland Dancing Competition was really starting to appeal to Franco, his dismay at being invited to present the prizes gradually turning to delight with each ascending age group that took to the platform. It wasn't so much the foot-tapping rhythm of the accompanying bagpipe music that attracted him, nor even the intricate steps and graceful, antler-like arm positions of the dancers. It was the kilts — specifically those kilts of the senior girls' category — that had him going. Those deep folds of tartan swirling and flying thigh-high with every leap and *birl*, revealing long, lissom, firmly-muscled legs in white knee-socks, and presenting tantalising glimpses of regulation navy blue knickers. After this, they could keep their grubby porn movies in the bar over the street from his Messina workshop. *Santo cielo*, this was the biggest turn-on he had ever seen!

"Ay-y-y! *I miei complimenti!*" he beamed at the judges' choice of winner in the Female Over-fifteens. He looked deep into her cowering eyes while he lingeringly smoothed the champion's medal ribbon over her still-heaving velvet bodice, then whispered into her ear as he bent to kiss her cheek, "Nice-a one, *bella*! You are-a very bee-oo-tiful. *Si*, and I love-a your keelt!" He kissed her other cheek and took her hand, the new phrase that Flora MacGubligan had contributed to his English vocabulary at breakfast springing conveniently, if rather confusedly, to mind. "I am-a Dannato Cornamusa. I am *Italiano* and I would like to, how you say? . . . *si*, engage-a myself in mass intercourse with you after the-a show, eh!"

Whether or not it was merely a surge of emotion at winning the first prize that overcame the girl then, only she would ever know, but the last Franco saw of her kilt was the back of it, as she rushed tearfully from the platform and away into the milling throng to seek her mother. On the other hand, maybe she just didn't like being called Bella.

It hadn't been entirely without misgivings that Franco had finally yielded to Mrs MacGubligan's insistence that he should dress in suitable lairdly fashion for the occasion, but now that he was getting used to the rigout and the attention it was clearly

119

attracting from the crowd, he was beginning to warm to the idea. There was a distinct swagger to his gait now. He wandered regally to the ever-present skirl of the pipes from pig pen to handicraft stall, from caber-tossing contest to Shetland pony potato race, and from sheep-shearing competition towards the refreshments tent.

The red tartan trews of Mrs MacGubligan's late soldier-father fitted surprisingly well, as did his dark green Highlander's tunic with the sergeant's stripes. The white spats over highly polished black brogues were definitely a stylish touch, too, Franco felt, and he was particularly pleased with the entire ensemble being crowned by a tooried Balmoral bonnet with blackcock plume. But the heat that all this heavy clobber generated under the noonday sun (combined with the choking smell of mothballs) was beginning to get to him. He needed a reviving drink, and he needed it *pronto*.

"Oi! Neep!" he shouted over the sea of noisily-bevvying heads in the booze marquee. "How's eet-a going, uh?"

"Och, fair to middling, Danny lad," his erstwhile whisky-tasting tutor at the welcoming ceilidh shouted back. "Aye, it's fair to middling that I am, right enough." Nip MacGubligan couldn't believe his luck. To be in the company of one young millionaire in the bar tent at Muckle Floggit Show was miracle enough ... but two! "Come away over here yourself now," he yelled at Franco above the din. "Yes, yes, man, come

120

you away in here now and meet my new chum chust arrived up from the Lowlands."

By now, Bob and Julie had entered the tent unseen by Andy, and had taken up a strategic position at the crowded bar. They were within earshot of the young DC's whisky-amplified conversation, but outside his line of vision.

"Chings me! What a grand pair of young Highland chentlemen we have here, sure enough, boys, have we not?" Nip was heard to remark to his cronies with a convincing air of sincerity. The cronies happily grunted their assent into their dram glasses. Nip then addressed the young gentlemen themselves. "Chust look at you here, Andra," he said to Andy Green, "with your kilt and all, and the set of bagpipes draped over your left arm there. Aye, aye, a grand sight for sore eyes is what you are, sure enough." He then turned his attentions to Franco. "And you, Danny lad, all dinked up fine-and-dandy in the good-old Inverness Light Infantry uniform like the true officer and chentlemen that you are."

"*Si!*" Franco grinned, then proudly indicated his sleeve stripes. "*Sergente*, eh!"

"Fancy a dram yersel' like, Danny?" Andy eagerly offered.

"No, no, *grazie*," Franco pleaded. He removed his Balmoral bonnet and fanned his face with its blackcock plume. "*Una birra, per favore.* I prefer a nice-a cold beer, please. *Si*, I am-a in heat!"

Andy delved into his sporran yet again.

121

"God almighty," Bob muttered to Julie, "if Green keeps doling out money like that, the hundred grand he found'll soon be used up in exies!"

"Stop complaining," Julie countered. "He's doing a fine job, so just shut up and listen."

Nip MacGubligan took the wheel of the conversation again. "Yes, and chust fancy two young chentlemen like yourselfs," he said, steering a business-bent course, "meeting up in a wee, back-of-beyond place like this, and the two of youse with such a lot in common with yourselfs and everything."

"*Si?*" Franco replied offhandedly, for the moment more interested in quaffing his beer than indulging in polite chitchat.

But Nip was having none of it. "Man, it's the bluidy sculpchoor thing I'm on about!" he declared, his patience exhausted.

Franco threw him a puzzled look.

"It's yourself being the famous sculpchoor artist," Nip eagerly prompted, "and young Andra here being interested in making a wee bit purchase or two for his new collection and things . . ."

Franco wiped his mouth with the back of his hand and thumped his empty glass onto the bar. "*Salute, amico!*" he beamed at Andy, seemingly oblivious to Nip's over-enthusiastic attempt at commercial match-making. He burped gloriously, then slapped Andy on the shoulder. "Fuckin' great-a swally, china!" he enthused, the Scottish sporting phrases overheard during his time at Edgeware Road's *Ristorante Bella*

122

Siciliana having drifted back afresh on the bubbles of the beer. "All-a the fuckin' best, pal!"

"Fancy another one, then?" Andy asked him, with scant need for a reply.

Nip and his cronies seized the moment to express *their* grateful acceptance of Andy's kind offer, irrespective of whether they had actually been included in it or not.

"So," Nip persisted, "you, ehm, you think, Danny lad, that maybe you might chust see your way to selling one or two of your statchoos to young Andra here?" He winked conspiratorially, before divulging out of the corner of his mouth, "I've been hearing it said here and there that he has fairly *adequate* resources, if you understand what I'm saying."

"I have-a no statues for sale!" Franco haughtily declared, dismissing Nip's entrepreneurial probing with a sideways flip of his Balmoral.

Andy's spirits fell. The Trojan horse that his Chief had created for getting him in with the Eyetie gadgie had nosedived at the first fence.

"You sculpt strictly by commission, I take it?" Julie interjected, having taken it upon herself to move in and stuff a dyke-plugging digit into the hole. She extended her hand to Franco and batted him one of her Italian-waiter-grabbing eyelash flutters. "I don't wish to obtrude, but I couldn't help overhearing. Oh, I'm Julie Bryson, by the way," she added with a coquettish smile. "I'm an in*sat*iable art fan, and it's an unbe*lieve*able pleasure to meet such a great celebrity as yourself, Signor Cornamusa . . . uhm, in the flesh."

Bob was dumbstruck.

Andy was gobsmacked.

Nip was niggled.

Franco was bewitched. He lowered his lips to Julie's proffered hand. "*Piacere, bellissima!*" he murmured. "Ees-a always for me the beeg pleasure to meeting such a lovely lydee." He raised a suggestive eyebrow. "*Specialmente*, as you say, een-a the flesh."

If Franco hadn't *actually* been in heat before, it was plain for all to see that he really was now.

Suddenly feeling cut out, Bob was about to cut in, when a bespectacled young man in a Hemingway-style suit of crumpled beige linen beat him to it.

"Pardon my intrusion," he said as he handed Franco a dog-eared business card. "Euan Stewart — *Isle of Skye Herald*. I was wondering if an interview might be —"

"No chance-a interview!" Franco was adamant.

But Euan was persistent. "Just a minute of your time, then. A few little quotes, perhaps, for the inhabitants of your new dominion, Mr Cornamusa?"

"Chust you fuck off away out of it with your damned nosey questions, Scoop Stewart!" Nip strongly advised. "For your informashun, me and the two chentlemen here was in the middle of having a wee business confabulation." He inclined his head towards Julie and added acidly, "Aye, and in private, and all!"

Scoop ignored him. Notepad at the ready, he proceeded assiduously. "Was the young lady correct, Mr Cornamusa? Do you only scuplt by commission?"

124

Franco wasn't at all sure what all this "sculpt by commission" stuff meant. But he *was* Sicilian. "Yes!" he bullshitted, while replacing his Balmoral at a jaunty angle on his loftily-held head.

Bob dug a knuckle into the small of Andy Green's back, then hissed in his ear, "Commission the bugger, for Christ's sake!"

Green was even more gobsmacked now.

"Tell me, Mr Cornamusa," Scoop Stewart went on, "where can one see examples of your past work? My research has thrown up no evidence of —"

"No chance-a interview!" Franco bellowed. He folded his arms and jutted his jaw *Il Duce*-style.

"I think you'll find, Mr Stewart," said Julie, cannily poking another finger into the dyke, "that much, if not all, of Dannato Cornamusa's work is to be found — like the work of several of his contemporaries — in the *private* collections of a rather esoteric circle of international patrons of the arts."

Franco latched on smartly to Julie's sophisticated line in bullshit. "That's-a right!" he confirmed. "Strict-a private! I scalp-a by the commissions only!"

"Bloody well commission him, Green!" Bob growled behind his hapless subordinate's back. "Commission the bugger right now, or you're heading back to the Haddington lollipop patrol on the next bloody ferry!"

The magic words had been spoken. "Heh, Danny, I'll commission ye!" Andy blurted out. "I'm needin' somethin' to start ma collection, see. Yeah, and the money's no problem. I've inherited a big scrap business, so I'm loaded, like. Oh aye, just name yer price, mate."

Bob slumped over the bar, his head in his hands. "What a complete bloody twonk!" he groaned.

Scoop Stewart, meantime, was quick to leap through the conversational door that Andy had conveniently opened. "The gentleman appears to have made you an offer you can hardly refuse, Mr Cornamusa. An open cheque for an open commission?"

Nip MacGubligan sensed the initiative drifting rapidly away from him. "Now chust youse all hold on a wee minute here," he said, stepping into the developing fray like a boxing referee. "Open cheques is one thing, and fine and dandy they may be to some, but it would be much better, I'm thinking, to see the value of this here commission specified in advance — and in cash!" He looked hopefully at Franco. "And when we're talking about commissions, we had better not be after forgetting about the percentage variety, either!"

Scoop slipped swiftly into journalistic probe mode. "I presume, then, you're acting as Mr Cornamusa's agent, MacGubligan, are you?"

"No, no, no, he's-a not!" Franco quickly corrected. He was at a loss as to how he was going to get himself out of this deepening quagmire, but the thought of this grabbing little Scotch *bandito* getting his mitts on any money that might be involved appealed to him not one whit. "I already got-a agent," he bluffed. "*Si*, in-a New York."

"Bugger it!" Nip grumped under his breath. "Pipped at the bluidy post!" Still and all, he reflected stoically,

126

there was always the Saint Gubligan's Cave thing from which to make a wee bit financial *pauchle* at the expense of the young scrap merchant laddie. Ach aye, he would chust have to hold his horses a wee while longer.

But if Nip's nose had just been put out of joint, Scoop Stewart's nostrils were now sniffing at the interesting end of a good story here. He tapped his ballpoint on the rim of his specs. "I think MacGubligan's got something, though," he said provocatively. "A fee for the new sculpture should surely be agreed in advance."

"End of-a interview!" Franco flatly announced. "Feez ees-a my private beezness!"

"Come, come, Signor Cornamusa," Julie honeyed, "surely it would be in your own best interests to show good will to the local newspaper, particularly after the bad media relationships generated by some of the previous owners of Muckle Floggit."

Franco was cornered, stuck for words.

Julie advanced astutely into the breach. "From my knowledge of such matters, I would suggest that an equitable amount to ask of Mr Green here for a specially-commissioned Cornamusa would be somewhere in the region of, say . . . a hundred thousand pounds?"

Scoop scribbled furiously.

Franco began to perspire profusely. "*Si!*" his mouth declared, without resorting to consultation with his brain. "A hundred thousand-a pound? You're-a on!" He grabbed Andy's hand and pumped it.

"And, uh, you'll do the work right here on the island?" Scoop checked.

"*Si*, right-a here and right away," said Franco's grinning mouth, still on autopilot.

Bob grabbed Julie by the elbow and hauled her over to the corner of the tent. "What the hell do you think you're doing?" he snarled. "This isn't just some posh schoolgirl's jolly-hockey sticks prank we're playing here, you know!"

Julie produced a suitably jolly-hockey sticks giggle. "Take it easy," she said, then tweaked Bob's cheek. "And smile. Like I told you, we're in the Hebrides."

"Never mind the Hebrides, we'll be in the shite, if I let that crazy offer stand. A hundred thousand quid?"

"Well, you wanted Andy Green to gain the guy's confidence, didn't you? That's the ploy, isn't it — get Andy in there to winkle out some info?"

A vein rose pumping fit to burst on Bob's temple. "But the hundred grand!" he groused, his face scarlet. "That money's locked up nice and secure in a safe at Police Headquarters in Edinburgh, and there it stays until it's time to reunite it with its rightful owner. For Pete's sake, woman, we can't just go promising it holis-bolis to Dannato bloody Cornamusa, no matter how many statues he scalps!"

Julie laughed out loud. "But that's the whole point, don't you see? We've got Cornamusa out in the open now, but he's never going to sculpt *anything*." She tickled Bob under the chin. "Cheer up, Kemosabe. Go on, let your hair down — go and cadge a dram on exies from millionaire Green there. Believe me, this Italian guy's as phoney as his name and about as convincing as his peroxide hair."

"Oi! Signorina Julie!" Franco called over, feeling suddenly flush. "Let-a me buy you a drink." He threw Bob a cursory glance. "*Si*, and-a one for your old man too, eh!"

Leaving Bob to fume silently, Julie sidled over to Franco, and with a come-hither smile cooed, "Oo-oo, how kind. I'd do *anything* for a spritzer — rosé, if poss."

"OK, if you gonna do anything," he ginned, wasting no time at coming hither, "how about dinner at-a my place tonight?"

Julie waved a slow, hypnotic finger before his eyes. "Uh-uh, no can do," she murmured, then puckered her lips into a pout of disappointment. "I already have a dinner date, I'm afraid — with my old man there."

Franco shrugged. "Bring-a him too," he said, as if referring to her pet poodle. "For me ees-a no *problema*!" Handing her a tumbler of Vimto laced with vodka, which was presumably the Muckle Floggit Agricultural Show version of a rosé spritzer, he moved in close, his knee brushing her thigh, his eyes burning hers from beneath his rakishly-cocked Balmoral. "Tell-a me, lovely lydee," he croaked in a voice hoarse with pent-up passion, "have-a you got a . . . keelt?"

CHAPTER
TEN

THE DINING ROOM OF THE DRAMGLASS HOTEL — MONDAY, AUGUST 12 — 8.30a.m. . . .

Andy Green hadn't surfaced at all the previous day. Neither had Franco "Dannato Cornamusa" Contadino been seen at large since the latter stages of the after-show dance in the village hall on Saturday night. At that booze-fuelled function, Andy had delighted himself, if not the customers, by sitting in on bagpipes with the local ceilidh band for what he'd thought, in his unfamiliar whisky-inspired state, to be a really slick, jazzed-up version of *Scotland The Brave*, but in reality had sounded like the mass strangulation of a pack of Highland wildcats. Franco, whose blood-alcohol level still hadn't completely returned to normal when he'd made the fatal mistake of entering the drinks tent at the show, had been sorely frustrated by Julie's teasing rebuffal of his advances.

So upset had he been, in fact, that the pain-numbing quantity of drams (prescribed, at Andy's expense, by Nip MacGubligan) which he'd then consumed had even rendered him incapable of taking up an oft-repeated invitation from Clinger Baptie, the visiting vamp of Ardenstooshie, for "a quick wee lift of the leg" behind the village hall. Poor Franco had cut a pathetic figure as midnight, the Sabbath and the compulsory end, therefore, of the dance and all things enjoyable approached, slouched as he was in a dim corner of the hall, wailing a dewy-eyed rendition of *O Sole Mio* to Nellie, old Donald the hallkeeper's mesmerised Border collie bitch.

Taking pity on his new pal, the only slightly less inebriated Andy Green had then invested the dregs of his sporran kitty in a bottle of *Saint Gubligan's Tears* from Nip MacGubligan's closet bar in the gents' toilet. The two young "millionaires" were last witnessed supporting each other on a wobbly course towards the shore and ultimate sweet oblivion among the sand dunes.

This morning, Bob and Julie were having breakfast.

"If that useless young bugger doesn't make it into the land of the living today," Bob warned, while deftly filleting the last morsels of a kipper onto his fork, "I'll personally —"

"See to it that he's on the next ferry to Lollipopland?" Julie correctly anticipated. She'd heard all that stuff before. "Listen, as I keep telling you, this is the Hebrides and Saturday was the annual show day. *All* the healthy young bucks get pissed as farts in the booze tent and fall about stotious at the dance afterwards. Then they sleep it off on the beach or behind a wall or wherever. It's *normal*, for heaven's sake!"

"Green had two hundred quid in expenses in that bloody sporran when we left Edinburgh on Friday morning," Bob spluttered. Flakes of kipper were flying everywhere. "That was supposed to last him for the duration of this caper, and *then* some! I'm telling you this for nothing, if he's blown the lot already, I'll — I'll —"

"Yeah, yeah, yeah," Julie chanted wearily as she flicked a kipper flake from the back of her hand, "I know, I know. But it was you who dreamed up the idea for him to act the rich young thicko, remember, and you can't deny he's played the part perfectly so far."

"Aye, but only because it comes bloody naturally to him," Bob mumbled.

"Maybe so, but he's well in with Cornamusa already, so I reckon the exercise has been cheap at the price, even if he has done in the whole float." She gave a little snort. "And I'll tell *you* something for nothing — it would have cost you a helluva lot more to get *me* to wheedle my way in with that guy. I mean, I know all about Italians, but that one's got more feelers on one hand than a regiment of soldier ants!"

Bob, who until now had scarcely spoken a word to Julie since her brief dalliance with Franco in the refreshments tent, looked up from his kipper skeleton and grumped, "So why the blazes did you go and fling yourself at him like that, then?"

"Ha! So that's what's been wrong with you," Julie laughed. "You're jealous, that's what — even though I was only doing my bit to help. Yeah, *and* you took the hump because he called you an old man!"

"*Your* old man. There is a big difference, you know."

Julie couldn't help sniggering. "Exactly. It could mean he thought you were my father."

132

"Come off it! I'd've had to have been even more sexually precocious than that randy rake to have sired you at ten years old. Nah, he thought I was your husband, and he moved right in on you all the same. Bloody typical!"

Julie held out the third finger of her left hand. "I don't see any rings there, do you? No, so you can either put up with me being propositioned now and again, or do something about it, right?"

Silence.

"Uh-huh," Julie nodded, "I thought as much. The old once-bitten-twice-shy syndrome still rules, huh?"

"All I'm saying is watch it," Bob huffed, patently aware that Julie had hit the nail on the head, but pointedly avoiding her question, nonetheless. "That young Cornamusa rabbit would poke the crack of dawn, if he was up early enough. I'm telling you, *Hornymusa* would be a better name for him!"

Julie shrieked with laughter. "And you're a fine one to talk, I must say! I mean, I don't know why you even bothered to book yourself into a separate room here. Let's face it, the only thing you've used in it so far is the wardrobe!"

Bob allowed himself a mischievous little smirk. "Well, discretion is the better part of undercover work . . . if you see what I mean." He finished his coffee and stood up. "Now, if you'll excuse me, I'll go and give Jimmy Yule a buzz at HQ."

Smiling to herself, Julie looked out of the window. She could see the ferry docking at the pier, old Angus having completed his first shuttle of the day over the

Sound of Stooshie. Monday morning, she reflected —
he'd be bringing the Sunday newspapers. She was fairly
sure that had once been the routine, anyway, but a
wander down to the end of the pier would make
certain. She folded her napkin and placed it neatly on
the table. Yes, she thought, while glancing over the
limpid waters of the Sound to the sun-bathed summits
of the Cuillins, it was a perfect morning for an
after-breakfast stroll.

A group of young children rushed past her after she
left the hotel, laughing and shouting excitedly as they
raced to see what strange new folk the ferry might
deliver today. The sound of their laughter reminded
her of the happy times she had enjoyed on this idyllic
island as a child herself. She took a deep breath of
the invigorating smack of seaweed wafting up from the
shore. *The tangle o' the isles* was what the old
song called it. Her spirits high, she began to whistle
the familiar melody as she stepped lightly down the
cobbled slope towards the quay.

"Losh me, if it's not the wee Julie Bryson lassie
herself!" came the pleasantly-surprised exclamation at
her shoulder. "And still wheepling away like a heather
lintie too!"

Julie turned her head to see the matronly face of
Flora, the housekeeper at Dramglass House. She
returned Flora's warm smile, but faintly familiar as
those cheerful features were, Julie couldn't quite place
them.

"Aye, Angus told me you was on the ferry the other
day, right enough," Flora panted, "and I was chust

thinking it was maybe you coming out of the hotel there chust now. Yes, and that's why I wheeched on like to catch you up." She smiled broadly as she watched Julie's confused expression. "It's *me*, lass! Can you not remember? Mistress MacGubligan from the big house yonder!" She pointed up the hill. "You were coming often enough with your mother in times past to buy berries and things out of the kitchen gardens. Aye, and maybe a few eggs as well, when I kept the hens. Remember me now?"

"Flora!" Julie yelled, then threw her arms round the housekeeper's ample frame. "How could I forget you? It's just that, well, it's been twenty years, and you looked a wee bit different when I was gazing up at you from knee level."

"Och, my, you've fairly knocked the wind out of me with your cuddles," Flora gasped. She took Julie by the shoulders and held her at arm's length. "Let me be having a right look at you now. Well, well, chust as I thought — you've turned into a right bonnie young wumman. Aye, and you still whistling *The Road To The Isles* like you used to do for your party piece at the ceilidhs when you was chust a wee bit mite of a bairn as well."

"Never!" Julie chuckled. "Did I?"

"Oh aye, you did at that, so you did," Flora confirmed, her eyes glinting, her cheeks dimpled with glee. She nudged Julie's elbow and winked. "But you can hold the chune a wee bit better now, if I may say so myself."

They joined each other in a hearty laugh.

"So, how's your husband?" Julie asked at length. "Still driving the laird's cars, is he?"

"Shooie? Oh aye, he is at that . . . when he's kind of half sober, which is none too often, mark you." Flora nodded sagely. "Hmm, it's chust as well for him that there's not a polisman with one of yon breathalysation contrapshuns on Muckle Floggit all that often at all." She chortled quietly. "Otherwise, there's whiles there would be no man on the island who hadna lost his driver's licence . . . although, mind you, there's precious few ever had one in the first place." She chuckled again, then, with a look of wary curiosity, she canted her head and said to Julie, "Now that I'm on about it, though, was I not hearing tell from somebody a while back that you had joined the polis yourself?"

"Oh, no, no, not me!" Julie swiftly assured her. "No, no, a scientist me — like my father."

"Oh, a *scientist*, is it?" Flora lilted, wide-eyed. "Losh, what a clever lass, right enough." She pondered that momentarily, then said, almost as if to herself, "Mm-hmm, so not in the polis after all, then . . ."

Julie decided it was time for a tactful change of subject. "Anyway, how are you getting on with your new laird?" she asked. "I met him at the show on Saturday. Quite a hunk!"

"Hunk? Drunk would be more like it, I'm thinking." Flora frowned and tutted ruefully. "And there was me being fair taken with him at first, too. Such a bonnie lad, and with a right chentlemanly turn of phrase and all. Called me *signora*, would you believe? Me, a *signora*! Aye, aye," she reflected dreamily, "they know

136

how to make a wumman feal like a wumman, yon Italian chappies, so they do. Mm-hmm, we had a few of them imprisoned here in the Wumman's Rural Meeting Rooms behind the post office during the last war, you know." Then, quickly snapping herself out of her reverie lest any sleeping dogs might be imprudently awakened, she said, "Anyway, lassie, I'll need to be getting myself away into Mohammed's store now. Mr Dannato has a party of guests due to be arriving today. Yes, it'll be for the shooting they'll be coming, I think."

"The shooting! Who's gonna to be shot?"

"Na, na, na," Flora laughed, "it's not who, but what. The grouse, like — it being the twelfth of August today, you see."

"Oh, right, the Glorious Twelfth. I'd forgotten all about that."

A sour look came over Flora's face. "Yes, and I only got the phone call last night to say these folks was coming. No time for a body to get a blessed thing ready at all. Always the same — never a minute to breathe. Ach, but never mind," she sighed. "It's not for the likes of me to be criticising the lairds ... the useless, inconsiderate, drink-befuddled sumphs that they are, the lot of them!"

Having first made Julie promise to pay her a wee visit right soon, Flora then ambled unhurriedly on her way.

Approaching the end of the pier, Julie noticed that there appeared to be only one car aboard the ferry this morning. There was nothing unusual about that, of course, but it was the size and colour of the car that caught her eye. It was white and very large. She walked closer, while Angus shooed half a dozen sheep into a waiting trailer on the jetty before striding back onto his vessel to conduct the tricky operation of marshalling the car over the ferry's narrow ramp, which was rising and falling with the gentle swell.

"Your right hand down, sir," he politely directed. "Aye, you're doing chust fine. Now left a wee bit. LEFT, I said, *LEFT*, ye deef eejit that ye are! By the stars," he bellowed, "the water's more as twenty foot deep here with the tide being in!"

Crouching low, Angus jinked about to check the alignment of the car's wheels, first at one edge of the ramp, then the other. That was when the three-pointed silver star atop the distinctive Mercedes radiator grille came clearly into Julie's view. Her first inclination was to dash back up to the hotel to warn Andy Green that his dreaded Spider woman was back on the scene. But no, it couldn't be her. She was in the south of Spain, for heaven's sake . . .

No sooner had the Merc's rear wheels cleared the ramp than the driver stepped on the gas. The big car surged forward, its tyres screeching for grip on the slippery paving as it hurtled along the pier. Julie flattened herself against a stack of lobster creels to avoid being knocked down by the refugee from *The Blues Brothers* behind the wheel. She just had time, as the car gathered speed, to catch a glimpse of its other occupants. A second Blues Brother, in black trilby and shades identical to the driver's, was in the front, while in the rear, a diminutive Dapper Dan wearing a beige fedora and camel-hair overcoat was ensconced beside a pretty blonde with big blue eyes and an innocent smile.

Julie already had the *Sunday Express* lying open at the appropriate page when Bob joined her in the hotel lounge.

"MUCKLE FLOGGIT'S NEW LAIRD NETS £100,000 ART DEAL," the headline ran.

Bob scanned the article. "That Stewart guy from the local bugle must have got off his mark bloody smartly to feed this out to the nationals as fast as this," he muttered.

Julie agreed. "But old Angus says the *Skye Herald* has all the latest communications kit over at Broadford. All set up fine and dandy for commuterising to cyberspace like the very clappers, as he puts it."Bob was engrossed in the article. "What does it say here?

A young Scots art collector, who chooses to remain anonymous, yesterday threw down a £100,000 gauntlet to the enigmatic Dannato Cornamusa to create a sculpture in full view of the islanders of Muckle Floggit. This is a feat the art world will surely monitor with great interest, given that my researches — including calls to leading dealers in Florence, the traditional home of the visual arts in Cornamusa's native Italy — have failed to locate anyone who is prepared to admit to having seen any of this multi-millionaire sculptor's work . . ."

Bob stroked his brow. "The shit's about to hit the fan now, all right."

"How so?"

"Because this sleepy wee backwater is gonna be crawling with press hacks and TV news crews from all over the shop in no time flat, that's how."

"What's the problem with that? Surely it's only going to help force our Cornamusa boy to expose himself as the fake he really is."

Bob looked less than totally convinced. "Whatever," he shrugged, "it's out of our hands now. Yeah, and we'll just have to pray that Green doesn't make a total arse of it. God almighty, the thought of him being grilled by some of those hard-nosed news hounds gives me the complete heebies!"

"Oh, ye of little faith," Julie chided. "Come on, give the guy a break. He'll come through with flying colours, you'll see."

Bob glanced at his watch. "I've already battered on his door three times this morning, and if he's not down here in ten minutes, it'll be skin and hair that's flying, never mind his bloody colours!"

"Yeah, yeah," Julie groaned, "we know all about that. But more to the point, what's the news from Jimmy Yule?"

"Two steps forward and three steps back, or three forward and two back. I haven't worked it out exactly yet."

"So, is it classified CID info, or can you confide in your humble forensic sidekick?"

"Not that much to tell, really," Bob replied cheerlessly. "They've had dozens of responses — from this country and Italy — to the photo we circularised of the young Italian murdered at North Berwick, but so far no two identifications have been the same. It'll take weeks to check them all out."

"But that phoney name on his passport — Gaetano di Scordia . . ."

"Uh-huh?"

"Well, Scordia's a place in Sicily. Didn't Jimmy Yule follow that up?"

"It may surprise you, *Doctor* Julie darlin', but us thick-heided polismen do occasionally manage to latch on to the bleedin' obvious. *Yes*, Yule made a point of targeting Sicily, because that was also where the fake passport claimed the guy was born, if you remember? But *no*, the authorities there have come up with absolutely zilch." He massaged his chin. "And that bothers me." After a few moments of pensive silence, he went on: "But I think we *may* have identified the Fiat Punto the killers used. Not that it's any help now, though."

"No? How come?"

"Just that a couple of French tourists reported their identical car missing when they got back to Edinburgh Airport from a trip to Shetland yesterday. Naturally, the silly buggers had left their parking ticket in the glove box."

"So, you're really no further forward."

Bob shook his head. "No, but it makes you wonder why the villains nicked a left-hand-drive car in this country."

"Maybe they just felt more comfortable with it, if they really were Italians. But what's the difference, anyway?"

"Maybe none, but that remains to be seen."

"Well, at least you've now got a possible link between the killers and the mysterious Laprima Frittella."

"You mean Edinburgh Airport?" Bob shook his head again. "Nah, a bit too tenuous that, I reckon." He thought about it briefly. "Still, it won't do any harm to get Jimmy Yule to put a stakeout on her white Merc in the airport car park."

Julie couldn't resist a vengeful little gibe. "It's a bit late even for something as bleedin' obvious as that, *Detective* Inspector Burns!"

Bob glowered at her. "What the blazes are you getting at?"

"It's only that said white Merc rolled off old Angus's ferry ten minutes ago, with what looked like four characters out of an old Al Capone movie inside. House guests of Signor Cornamusa, it seems. Over for the grouse shooting; according to his housekeeper."

Bob was intrigued. "Did she say who they were, by any chance?"

"She didn't, but Angus told me that the boss man, a little smout who looks like a mixture of Edward G Robinson, James Cagney and Danny de Vito all rolled into one camel-hair coat, introduced himself as Doctor Max Marsala — an American."

"Marsala . . . ," Bob mused, then said in unison with Julie:

"Sicily again!"

"Are you thinking what I'm thinking?" Julie asked.

"I was tempted to for a second, but I've forced myself not to." Bob shook his head. "The Mafia on Muckle Floggit? Nah, no way! That really would be taking the bleedin' obvious just a bit *too* far."

Julie gave a stranger-things-have-happened shrug, then asked, "What's the latest on Laprima Frittella, then? Her car's found its way back here, but what about the *femme fatale* herself?"

"Well, there's good news and bad news."

"And?"

"And the good news is that she's just saved Lothian and Borders Police the expense of sending two 'tecs out to tail her in Spain."

"And the bad news is?"

"That she's given the Guardia Civil the slip."

"You surprise me. I mean, it's not often our colleagues in the Spanish police let a good-looking bird out of their sight."

"They didn't. Quite the contrary, in fact."

Julie rolled her eyes in exasperation. "But why all the mystery? Just tell me what happened!"

"No mystery. The boys in green kept close tabs on her during the one day she was in her hotel in Marbella."

"And?" Julie urged again.

"And she didn't even leave the place for one minute, before getting into a cab and heading straight back to Malaga Airport."

"I didn't know they did one-day excursions from Edinburgh to Malaga."

"They don't. Miss Frittella was on the usual two-week package deal."

"So why the sudden taxi ride back to the airport?"

"To hop on an internal flight to Madrid, that's why. The Malaga Guardia Civil got their mates in the capital to put a tail on her the minute she got off the plane."

"Then?"

"Then she wandered about Madrid Airport for a while, before checking onto another internal flight . . . to Vigo."

"Vigo? But that's a big fishing port on the north-west coast of Spain. Hardly a typical holiday venue for a ritzy piece of crumpet like Andy Green's Alfa Romeo Spider lady, is it?"

"Not unless she fancied a fishing holiday."

"Oh, har-de-bloody-har-har!" Julie scoffed. "Very droll!"

"I'm not kidding. That's *exactly* what she did — buggered off on a big deep-sea fishing boat last night."

Julie frowned in disbelief, then, realising that Bob really wasn't kidding, she asked, "And bound for where, for heaven's sake?"

"Bound for the Grand Banks of Newfoundland off the east coast of Canada, according to the boat's agents in Vigo."

"Can we check that out?"

"Not unless our budget can stretch to hiring an RAF Nimrod surveillance jet, we can't. And before you suggest it," Bob swiftly added, "the Spanish coastguards are no help either. Their interest in the boat ended when it left their territorial waters."

Now it was Julie's turn to do a spot of meditative chin-stroking. "So, *cherchez la femme* comes to a sudden, watery end," she finally concluded.

"While you're toying with foreign languages," Bob suggested, "you may be interested to know the name of the boat she sailed off into the sunset in."

"Tell me do, Kemosabe."

"It's called — wait for it . . . *La Patella*."

"*La Patella*?" Julie piped in amazement. "Hey, now I *know* you're pulling my leg!"

"Nope. Never been more serious, in fact."

Julie's astonished expression morphed into one of sheer incredulity. "But this is bizarre," she frowned. "In Italian, *La Patella* means *The Limpet*, which is an understandable enough name for a boat."

"But?"

"But another meaning in Italian *and* in medical lingo is —"

"I know," Bob interrupted. "Jimmy Yule looked it up. Signorina Frittella has gone fishin' in a boat romantically called . . . *The Kneecap!*" Then, on seeing Andy Green enter the lounge, he put a finger to his lips. "Sh-h-h!" he hissed at Julie before she could say anything more. "Keep schtum about the fishing boat and you-know-who. He's better kept in the dark about all that for now."

"'Morning, Andy," Julie duly smiled. "'Fraid you've missed breakfast. Want me to see if the kitchen will whip you up some toast or a bowl of cornflakes or something?"

Andy clutched his stomach and groaned, "Aw, no thanks all the same, Doc. Naw, I still couldnae face any grub."

"That's a pleasant change," Bob commented, while surveying the bedraggled, kilted apparition standing before him. "God, you look even more horrible than usual, Green. I mean, just look at your eyes. They're like the rear view of two kittens drinking out of the same saucer of milk!"

"Aye, well, you should see how they look from the inside," Green grunted. "Tellin' ye, skipper, that's the last time I'll ever down a gutful o' whisky, then hit the *Saint Gubligan's Tears*. Tears?" he whimpered. "It certainly brings them to your eyes. Bloody rocket fuel!"

Bob's brows gathered into an inquisitive frown. "What's it all about anyway, this *Saint Gubligan's Tears* stuff?" he asked Julie. "Have you heard of it before?"

"Never. I didn't know it existed before I saw the locals nipping away at it in the booze tent at the show on Saturday. Come to that," she confessed, "I'd never even heard of Saint Gubligan before, either."

They both looked at Andy, who had slumped into an adjacent easy chair.

"Well, ye see," he confided through a pained grimace, "it's all very hush-hush. But Nip MacGubligan told me a wee bit about it, like. Says the hooch drips out o' some rock or other in a place they call Saint Gubligan's Cave, somewhere on the island here. Wants me to invest money so they can build up the business. Make the cave a tourist attraction. Flog more bottles o' the tears an' that. Supposed to be takin' me to see the place after dark tonight." He placed his hand very gently on his forehead. "Aw shite . . . I'm no gonny to drink any more o' that stuff, though!"

"Saint Gubligan's Cave?" Bob asked Julie.

She raised her shoulders. "Search me. I thought I knew this island like the back of my hand, but that's a new one on me." Through the open lounge door, she noticed old Angus the ferryman delivering a cardboard box to the reception desk. "There's the very man, however. Hey, Angus! Can you spare a minute?"

That was one thing about Angus — he was never short of a minute to spare, particularly if he thought there might be a wee bit *pauchle* (or "money on the side") in it.

"Och, I'll always be having enough time to have a wee bit blether with you, Julie lass," he said, looking directly at Andy and deliberately sitting down next to him. "And if it's not young Mr Green his-self again," he said with an optimistic smile. "Man, I've been keeping one eye open for you ever since Friday, so I have."

"Our friend Andy's been a bit indisposed, I'm afraid," Julie advised. "Too many rich venisonburgers at the show, maybe."

"Oh, the venisonburgers, was it?" Angus acknowledged dubiously, his wee black eyes glinting beneath bracken-like brows. "Mm-hmm, and I hear you play a braw set of the bagpipes as well, Mr Green. Aye . . . even if the chunes themselfs is not so bonnie."

Bob decided to cut through the small talk and get right down to brass tacks. "What we wanted to ask you about, Mr MacGubligan, is the Saint Gub —"

"Chust you call me Angus, Mr Burns," Angus butted in, his eyes still fixed on Andy. "Chings, if you're calling a man *Mr* MacGubligan on Muckle Floggit, Mr Burns, you'll likely get half the island answering you." With that piece of valuable information out of the way, he concentrated on the business in hand. "Now then, young Mr Green, about all yon scrap cars that's lying about all over the place here — is it not about time me and you got down to a wee bit commercial confabulation? Aye, for I'm thinking that maybe your money would be better spent dealing with a square-cut chentleman like myself here than throwing it away a hundred thousand pounds a go on a falderal, fantoosh statchoo that you've not even catched a blink of yet."

Andy blanched as the memory of the hundred-grand commission he'd given Dannato Cornamusa came staggering back into his befuddled brain. "Sorry, mate. Some other time, eh?" he mumbled. He raised a hand to cover his mouth as he struggled to his feet and stumbled towards the door. "Ah think . . . Ah think Ah'm gonna bark again . . ."

"Aye, it'll be the venisonburgers," Angus nodded knowingly at Julie. "Terrible rich for the Lowland digestchun, I suppose." He tutted in despair, then turned to Bob. "Now then, Mr Burns, you was chust about for to ask me about something, I think."

"Yes, well, it was about this Saint Gubligan thing that I —"

"A great and famous man, so he was," Angus declared with an emphasising jerk of the head. "Aye,

148

great and famous was what he was indeed. Mmm-hmm, chust that, chust that."

"I've never heard of him," Julie stated bluntly, "and I read Scottish History at university."

"Aye, well, of course," Angus chortled long-sufferingly, "that's the trouble with your universities and your history professors and your scientific boffins and your highfalutin chootors and the like."

"*What's* the trouble with them?" Julie came back, stone-faced.

"Och, man, they can only learn you what they know themselfs," Angus stated with a dismissive shaking of his head, "and that's not very much when it comes to the history of Muckle Floggit, by the sound of what you're chust after saying, lass. Chings me," he scoffed, "the Reverend Dick could lose the whole chingbang of them, and that's the truth of it!"

Nicely wound up now, Angus went on to reveal how the local minister had come across these old parchment scrolls a year or so back, when the dry rot men were ripping out the wainscoting in the kirk vestry. The amazing story of the hitherto forgotten Saint Gubligan had then been pieced together by the Reverend Dick, painstakingly translating the faded script from its queer mixture of Latin and ancient Erse, like the learned chentleman that he was. Saint Gubligan, Angus continued, had paddled all the way over the sea from Ireland in his wee coracle and had landed fortuitous-like on Muckle Floggit (known then only by its Gaelic name, *Reic e Mòr*), where he had sheltered in a cave and had wept for his departed homeland, before setting forth in his wee bit boatie again to spread the faith all over the Highlands and Islands of Scotland.

"Sounds uncannily like the legend of Saint Columba and the island of Iona to me," Julie sceptically remarked.

"Oh aye, there was plenty of yon other saint chappies as well," Angus readily conceded, "but when the Reverend's researches is finished, they'll all be playing second melodeon to Saint Gubligan of Muckle Floggit, chust you wait and see!"

Bob was trying to keep a straight face. "And *Saint Gubligan's Tears?*" he queried.

"Chust a miracle, Mr Burns. Chust a fair miracle, right enough." Angus's face couldn't have been straighter if it had been drawn with a ruler. It had only been a few days after the minister's startling discovery in the old scrolls, he explained, that he, the Reverend himself and Nip MacGubligan just happened to be fishing from a rowing boat, "round the island a wee bit", when a sudden squall had blown up, and they'd been forced to put ashore and take refuge from the rain in a certain cave — the same cave, it would be revealed, in which Saint Gubligan had rested his weary body those many centuries before.

Julie stifled a smile. "And this was where the miracle happened, I take it," she prompted, trying to sound as fascinated as possible. "Right there before your very eyes in the cave?"

"Chust that absolute very thing, lass," Angus affirmed, his voice lowered to a dramatic rumble. "There was me saying I hadna been in yon cave since I was a wee chiel in short breeks. Aye, and there was Nip saying chust the same. And then the minister says *Wheesht!* And, chings me, in the ensooing silence we hears this sound, this sobbing-like sound, chust sighing and wailing like the very wind itself outside, but coming from away back in the dark deepness of the cave, where none the three of us had ever set foot before at all."

Now sitting slack-jawed despite themselves, Bob and Julie motioned Angus to continue.

It was all the encouragement he needed. "Ah, but it was then," he droned, "that we seen it, the three of us all at once, like. Aye, it was catched fair full in the beam of Nip's big flashlight — a shuge big rock the size of a man, lying there fair recrumblent-like at the back of the cave, chust like the scrolls had said. *A dhuine, dhuine!* Me and Nip was feart for a terrible minute that the minister was going to be after crossing his-self!" Angus paused to chortle softly. "But, na, na, he's no as ecumenical as *all* that!" Clearing his throat, he resumed his theatrical air. "And then we seen the tears — drip, drap, dreepling down from yon saintly stone face, and gathering into a grand wee puddle right there on the floor of the cave in front of us." Angus's granite outcrop of a chin began to tremble with emotion as he solemnly lowered his head. "Man oh man, the three of us chust fell to our knees in spontaneous obesity."

Julie managed to convert a spontaneous snigger into a pseudo sneeze, just as Angus was raising his eyes to assess the effect his virtuoso performance had made on his audience.

"Bless you, my child," he monotoned clerically, though stopping short of making the sign of the benediction — but only just.

Bob reckoned it was about time to snatch proceedings back from the verge of pantomime. "And these drops, these *tears*," he said, "they turned out to be the highly alcoholic brew that almost sent young Mr Green here to join the saints himself on Saturday night, right?"

"The very exact same, sir," Angus sagely confirmed. "Aye, and they should be consumed with due circumcision, the *Saint Gubligan's Tears*, chust like the most powerful of holy waters that they are."

His curiosity well aroused now, Bob decided to play the old fellow along. "But how can you sell this strong liquor to the public without paying duty?"

"Och, laddie, laddie," Angus coyly crooned, "we're chust simple island folk. We have no knowledge of such sophisticated mainland things as yon." A divot of heathery eyebrow was hoisted to expose a beady eye of suspicion. "Ehm, you wouldna, by any manner of means, be connected with the Customs and Excise in your own chob, now would you?"

Julie hurled herself swiftly into the ensuing conversational hiatus. "One thing I don't get, Angus — what's the point in Nip trying to raise capital to cash in on this phenomenon, when the cave and, therefore, the source of all merchandisable goodies belongs to the laird of Muckle Floggit, whoever he may happen to be at any given time?"

152

"Ah, well now, lass, when I said we was chust simple island folk, I didna quite mean that we was *that* soft in the head!" Angus was a man affronted. "Oh, no, no, no! You see, the Reverend Dick, being the well-ejoocated chentleman that he is, got the previous laird, yon punk sloonge Sloth, during one of his physiodelic trips on yon acid stuff, to sell the cave to the folk of Muckle Floggit for the princely sum of one pound." Angus indulged himself in a smug grin. "And the administrashun of all things pertaining to the cave is to be administered by the minister of Dramglass Parish Kirk and — chust to make sure there is no chiggery-pokery — by the senior elder of the Kirk Session . . . who chust happens to be me myself."

Both Bob and Julie were temporarily at a loss for words.

Angus stood to take his leave. He smiled benignly as he shook Bob's hand. "And, eh, what was it you said you was researching here on Muckle Floggit, Mr Burns?"

"The flora and fauna," Julie chipped in rapidly. "Yes, the indigenous flora and fauna."

Angus gave her an avuncular pat on the shoulder. "Well, I wish you the best of luck, lassie, but I wouldna hold out too much hope, if I was you. Na, na, I've lived hereabouts all my days, and I've heard of such things as yon that you're on about, but I've never clapped eyes on one of them even the once."

"We can only live in hope," Bob said dryly.

"Chust that, Mr Burns. Oftwhiles it's the only thing for it, sure enough." Angus turned away, then hesitated.

"Oh, but mind you to tell young Mr Green to come down to the pier and see me when he's boaked up the last of his venisonburgers, for there's scrap metal and holy water business to be done. Aye, *slàn leat* — cheery-bye to youse both now."

CHAPTER
ELEVEN

LATER THAT SAME MORNING — THE GROUNDS OF DRAMGLASS MANSION HOUSE . . .

"Ya got holes in yer head or somethin'? Whaddaya mean ya accepted a friggin' commission to make a goddam statue?"

Franco didn't like it when his uncle was in this kind of mood. He liked it even less when the little guy whipped off his shades to reveal those steel-hard, ice-blue eyes. It made Franco feel like a rabbit being stared out by a homicidal snake. "But a hundred thousand pounds, Uncle Massimo," he pleaded, metaphorical ears clapped submissively down his back.

"SCREW a hundred thousand mother-humpin, Limey pounds! That's chicken shit, kid!"

"But Laprima, she said I was to act the part of a famous *scultore* . . ."

"Actin' is one thing, bein' is another, and you *bein'* a sculptor ain't never been in the script, capeesh?"

"*Si*, but what could I do?" Franco hunched his shoulders, exposed the palms of his hands. "I mean, this rich young *tipo* makes me the offer in front of witnesses and —"

"And you was too friggin' greedy to knock him back. Ya shoulda upped the ante to half a million, and

155

that woulda gotcha offa the hook, but fast!" Max replaced his shades, ambled forward and jabbed his finger into Franco's breast bone. "I'm tellin' ya, Frankie boy, I had ya figured as a smart kid, but this half-assed commission deal has got me wonderin' if yer friggin' elevator goes all the way up to the goddam penthouse!"

Franco inclined his head apologetically. "*Si*, I can see I made a big *errore*, and now we got big *problemas*."

"U'-uh! Correction, kiddo! *You* got problems, not we. In this outfit, my lootenants is paid to gimme solutions, not friggin' problems. Ya get where I'm comin' from? Yeah? OK, so *you* stuck your good-lookin' Eyetalian nose in the shit, and now *you* can lick it off." He reached up and clipped Franco's cheek with the flat of his hand. "Enjoy, Frankie boy, enjoy. Like, *buon appetito!*"

Franco was devastated. He had discredited his Sicilian heritage in public — or he soon would, if he couldn't manage to work out how to bullshit his way out of what he had so easily allowed himself to be bullshitted into. He'd have to think fast.

But before Franco's first thought had even reached the embryonic stage, Max said thoughtfully, "Hey, Frankie boy, I been thinkin'. A hundred thousand pounds, huh? Yeah-h-h, that figure seems kinda familiar." He made a facial shrug. "OK, so life is full a' coincidences, I gotta admit, but nine times outa ten the coincidences is only coincidental 'cos some smartass sonofabitch is coincidizin' the action . . . agreed?"

Franco agreed, although he wasn't quite sure with what.

Max's thin slit of a mouth contorted into a menacing sneer. "Yeah, kid," he croaked, "I think maybe I should meet wid this piece-a'-shit Scotch schmuck, but real soon."

"HALLO-O-O-OA there, yourselfs! Man, man, I've been looking for youse all over the place!" was the sunny greeting of old Shooie MacGubligan, Flora the housekeeper's handyman husband, today wearing his gamekeeper's hat. This was an additional item of estate headgear to which he had fallen heir since the rightful wearer resigned his position following an all-night rave-up by Sid Sloth and a group of his dopehead disciples, during which they broke into the gillie's hen run and Ozzy Osbourned a hundred of his hand-raised pheasant chicks.

"Come away with you now," Shooie shouted. "I've got the wee all-terrain vee-hicle all kindled up and ready to go." He held up a shotgun in each hand. "And look see, I'm after bringing youse a few old twelve-bores out the gun room. Aye, they've maybe seen better days, right enough, but they'll still knock the stoor out of a few grouses . . . if we get near enough the wee buggers, eh?"

Max brushed aside the offered shotgun. "Save it, Mac," he mumbled, then nodded at the shiny black case in his left hand. "I came carryin' already!"

IN THE GRAVEYARD OF DRAMGLASS PARISH KIRK, MEANTIME . . .

"We're supposed to be genuine rubbernecks," Bob muttered to Julie. "The Rev's probably watching our every move, so try to look interested, for God's sake!"

"I *am* interested!"

"Why the big, cheesy grin, then?"

"Who ever said that reading inscriptions on old gravestones had to be a funereal pastime? Lighten up, Kemosabe. I'm sure all the MacGubligans lying in here are happy enough. Look around — there's not one of them who didn't live to be well over eighty, no matter how far you go back."

"Yeah, so bang goes the theory of the benefits of hybrid vigour." Bob took her elbow. "Come on, this is giving me the creeps. Let's wander over to the church and see if we can flush any useful info out of this old Reverend Dick character. On an island like this, if there's anything worth knowing, the minister'll know it, if anybody does."

Inside, the tiny village kirk was a model of Hebridean Presbyterian austerity; the bare stone walls a grey as drab as winter mist, age-jaded pinewood pews straight-backed and cushionless, the frosted glazing of the narrow, lancet-arched windows unadorned by even one stained-glass pane. In fact, the only concession to colour in the whole church was a solitary vase of dejected lupins, placed dead centre on the little communion table that stood subserviently beside the dominating solemnity of the pulpit. All was silent, chilly, musty.

"Jeez, all this place needs is a stool of repentance down the front and a set of thumbscrews on the wall," Bob said. "Imagine cowering in here every Sunday morning, listening to some old Holy Wullie bellowing hellfire and damnation at you for drinking yourself rat-arsed and getting your leg over the neighbour's wife the night before."

"Language! And some respect!" Julie whispered, covering a smirk with her hand. "You're in the house of God, for heaven's sake!"

"Aye, and He's lucky He's got plenty more to choose from," Bob hissed back, "because I reckon He'd only take up residence in this one as a last resort."

Brandishing her fist in Bob's face, Julie linked arms with him and slow-marched him down the aisle, halting outside the closed vestry door. Bob's firm knock brought from within the sound of clinking bottles, the rattle of drawers and the clunk of a door being hurriedly closed.

"COME!" boomed the sombre invitation at last.

Bob creaked the door open and shepherded Julie through. "I hope we're not disturbing you, Reverend," he said as he extended his hand over the cluttered desk. "Robert Burns is the name, and this is my colleague, Julie Bryson. Ehm, *Doctor* Julie Bryson, that is. We're naturalists, visiting the island to do some research, and we've become fascinated by the folklore surrounding this charming little church of yours."

The Reverend Dick's stiff smile stretched the wine stain on his top lip into an upwardly-curving purple moustache. "Ah, yes indeed, Mr Burns," he intoned, while raising his hands to the four walls. "As your immortal namesake so eloquently put it, 'From scenes like these, old Scotia's grandeur springs.' Yes, from *The Cottar's Saturday Night*, I believe."

Bob cast his eyes quickly round the joyless interior of the fusty little room. "Absolutely, and another of Rabbie's lines also springs appropriately to mind."

"Indeed?"

"Yes, 'Churches built to please the priest', I think it goes. From *The Jolly Beggars*, I believe."

The Reverend Dick tilted his head with a look of puzzlement on his beaky face, which lent him the appearance of an anorexic blackbird patiently waiting for a worm to surface. "Indeed?" he queried again.

Julie coughed, then smiled demurely. "He means that the serenity, the inherent Highland fortitude of the building, is clearly reflected in your own demeanour," she flannelled.

"How kind," the Reverend responded in a hushed voice, eyes closed, his scrawny torso inclined forward from his seat in a bow of acknowledgement. "Yes," he added, "and how very true." His ego suitably inflated, he turned again to Bob. "You mentioned the folklore, Mr Burns. And, uhm, which *particular* aspect of it fascinates you, may I ask?"

"Saint Gubligan, or the legend of *Saint Gubligan's Tears*, to be precise."

Instead of the stunned look that Bob had fully expected his bluntness to provoke, the minister's pinched face opened into a smile of genuine delight. "Ah, you must be the friends of young Mr Green that Angus and Hamish have been telling me about," he gushed.

"Hamish?" Bob asked.

"Nip, they call him locally. A worker at the whisky distillery over in Skye, you see . . . er, *when* he's working, that is." The Reverend Dick laughed woodenly.

Bob forced out a polite, reciprocal laugh himself. "Now I get it," he said. "Whisky — Nip. Yes, *very* witty."

"But these scrolls that you found . . . ," Julie prompted.

"Yes, absolutely," the minister replied. "They were found right here in this very room." He leaned back in his chair and tapped the darkly varnished wainscoting. "In a lead casket, tucked into a niche in the stone right behind there, in fact."

"And may we see them?" Julie enquired

The Reverend Dick shook his head gravely. "I'm afraid not, Dr Bryson. Some day, perhaps, the public will be given the opportunity to view the scrolls, but in the meantime they are locked securely away where no harm can befall them." His tone then brightened. "There is, however, a videotape of the scrolls, complete with close-ups of all the writings and illuminations, which I made with a camcorder borrowed from the road manager of our previous landlord, the epithetical Mr Sloth."

"So, can we see *that*?" Bob asked.

An almost imperceptible smile passed over the minister's lips. "When the time is right, Mr Burns, the video will be offered into the public domain. But the time — and, uhm, the commercial considerations — *will* have to be right, hmm?"

Bob got his drift; build up the popular interest, then flog the TV rights of the video to the highest bidder. The wily old bugger . . .

Julie was right on his case, however. "But without *some* proof of the scrolls' existence, and checks on their authenticity — carbon dating and so on — it'll just be assumed that this entire Saint Gubligan thing is nothing but a hoax," she argued. "I mean, with due respect, Mr Dick, the public's hardly *that* gullible."

But the minister wasn't about to be so easily balked. "Come, come, Dr Bryson," he smiled, "lack of scientific authentification hardly seemed to do the Turin Shroud any harm in the public's eye, did it? Quite the contrary, in fact, and that went on for hundreds of years. Plus, *we* have the rock effigy of the Saint in the cave, with the tears flowing from his eyes, just as recorded in the scrolls. That will be there for all to see — er, once we have the necessary facilities in place."

"And this is why you want somebody like Andy Green to put up the venture capital," Bob speculated.

The minister dipped his head to indicate the affirmative.

162

"Forgive my prying, Mr Dick," said Julie, "but why don't you raise the money from conventional sources — Western Isles Council, Highlands and Islands Enterprise, the banks, the National Lottery, the laird? I mean, surely it would even be in the interests of the establishment of your own Hebridean Free Presbyterian Church to come up with the necessary out of *their* own resources?"

The minister respectfully declined to answer.

Because he's looking for a bloody patsy, Bob told himself — a pea-brained bloody soft touch who won't dig into the facts too far, and Green fits the bill perfectly. He scrutinised this grey-suited beanpole of an island parson in his wine-smudged dog's collar for a moment. Mmm, he mused, maybe he had the feckless appearance of a secretly-tippling cartoon crow, but under those tatty feathers there lurked a mind as crafty as a fox's. "These scrolls of yours," Bob said at length, "— they're probably similar in content to the ancient Book of Kells, which the monks on Iona wrote about Saint Columba, are they?"

"Probably," the minister replied, not being drawn, "although the monks who wrote our Dramglass scrolls seem to suggest that Saint Gubligan may have set foot on these shores some fifteen hundred years ago — perhaps half a century before Saint Columba's arrival on Iona. I still have some work to do on that, however." He peered academically at Julie over the wire rims of his spectacles. "The translations, you will appreciate, Dr Bryson, are most labyrinthine."

"Doesn't it follow, though," Bob proposed, "that if it was monks who wrote about Saint Gubligan, there would be some record in the Vatican of the man's existence?"

Narrowing his eyes, the Reverend Dick moved his lips into a practiced apology for a smile. "Well, if this wee kirk were one of the Vatican's own," he calmly responded, "I'm sure they'd find some kind of a record soon enough."

"Maybe so," Julie conceded, smiling inwardly at this piece of ecclesiastical cattiness, "but, as this wee kirk belongs to the Hebridean Free Presbyterian Church, it must follow, then, that the scrolls are their property and —"

"And I should have handed them over to the Kirk Synod in Portree," the Reverend Dick put in, "instead of keeping them to ourselves here on Muckle Floggit?" This time there was a trace of self-satisfaction in the minister's starchy smile. He clasped his hands, then sermonised, "You neglect to consider the feudal conditions which have pertained on islands such as this for centuries. Since the Reformation, you see — or shortly after," he stated smugly, "this building belonged, not to the Hebridean Free Presbyterian Church, who were merely its rent-free tenants, but, like every other building, like every stone, leaf or blade of grass on Muckle Floggit, to the laird."

"So, as the scrolls were found in this church, they now belong to Dannato Cornamusa," Bob deduced.

The minister gave him an admonishing look. "You clearly were not paying adequate heed to the tense I

164

employed in my explanation just now," he said in the manner of a Victorian schoolmaster reprimanding a pupil. "Had I been using the present form instead of the past, I would have said that Dramglass Parish Kirk *belongs* to the people of Muckle Floggit, and has done since one of the few charitable lairds the island has known bequeathed it to them at the turn of this century."

A tidy set-up for the Rev, Bob thought, recalling what old Angus had disclosed about the recent change of ownership of Saint Gubligan's Cave and the *admeenistration* of all things pertaining thereto by himself and the minister.

Julie decided to keep things polite, however. "It really is very good of you to answer all these questions of ours so fully, Mr Dick," she smiled. "I only hope you don't think us too forward."

The minister closed his eyes again. "Not at all, young lady. An enquiring mind, in my opinion, is a Godly one."

And a policeman's mind is a suspicious one, Bob reminded himself. "Quite a coup for Muckle Floggit, then," he ventured, "— it being the scene of the world's first Free Presbyterian miracle."

"Quite," the Reverend Dick concurred, with a suitably thankful lowering of his head.

"Yes, and involving the first alcoholic saint, at that," Bob pointed out. "I take it his tears go dry on Sundays — or at least turn to water?"

So jolted was the minister by Bob's unexpected barb that his pince-nez dislodged themselves from the end of his nose. In his lunge to prevent them falling to the floor, he sent a concealed wine glass flying, its contents splashing a flamboyant design over the featureless, yellowing wallpaper.

"Ah-uhm, a forthcoming communion," the Reverend flustered. "The wine must, of course, be scrupulously tested in advance."

"Oh, abso*lutely*," Bob agreed deadpan, then added under his breath, "You wouldn't want some old psalm-singing granny accusing you of slipping her a mickey."

"I do hope you'll forgive my colleague's glib remarks, Mr Dick," Julie implored, while giving Bob's ankle a surreptitious kick with the side of her foot. "It's just his quirky sense of humour, I'm afraid. No offence intended."

The Reverend carefully replaced his specs. "None taken, I assure you."

Bob put on a serious face. "So, how long have you been bottling up these tears?" he asked.

"Oh, not very long," the Reverend replied, still giving nothing away. "And in no significant quantity, I must stress. Only a few bottles for local consumption."

"What a splendid idea to develop the whole concept commercially, though," Julie provocatively enthused.

The minister smiled coyly, but said nothing.

"But doesn't the idea of profiting from the sale of alcoholic beverage clash with your ethics as a man of the cloth?" Bob probed.

"Oh, absolutely not, Mr Burns." The minister was resolute. "Why, the Benedictine monks and others of their ilk have been doing just that for aeons, after all."

166

"Ah, so the current trend towards ecumenicism doesn't just begin and end in the pulpit," Bob reasoned.

The Reverend Dick chose to let that observation pass without comment as well.

"Talking about Dannato Cornamusa," said Julie, deftly changing the subject, "do you know much about him or his work, Mr Dick?"

"Do *you*?" the Reverend craftily parried.

There was a moment of hush while Julie searched for a return shot in her mental armoury. "No," she finally rallied, stuck for anything more worthwhile to say, "not a thing."

"My position also," the Reverend owned up, "and I do pride myself in my considerable knowledge and appreciation of the arts." He paused to carefully weigh his choice of ensuing words. "But in my capacity as spiritual leader of this little community, it behoves me to cement the best, the potentially most *fruitful*, relationship with each new owner of the island as he happens along. And so, in the case of Signor Cornamusa — Bagpipe, a strange name for an Italian, don't you think? — I shall treat him as a famous sculptor until such time as it appears not judicious so to do."

"And in *what* hypothetical circumstance would you judge it not judicious so to do?" Bob prodded, a mite too sharply for the Reverend's liking.

The distant rattle of what sounded like a pneumatic drill caught the minister's attention and presented him with a timely escape from Bob's increasingly irksome questioning. "Strange," he said, cocking his ear towards the window. "That seems to be coming from up Ben Doone."

"Road works on the mountain?" Julie said, a puzzled look on her face.

"It can't be," the minister muttered, a look of bafflement on his. "There's been no road round Ben Doone since the landslide took it away during the bad winter of 'Sixty-two . . ."

BACK IN THE HOTEL — DR JULIE BRYSON'S BEDROOM . . .

"Did you get in touch with DS Yule like I told you to?" Bob asked Andy Green.

"Yeah, did it on the car blower like you said. More private, like. Bad signal here, though. Keeps fadin'."

"OK, but you managed to tell him to run a check on this Dr Marsala geezer, did you? That's all I'm bothered about right now."

"You bet, boss. All done. In fact, you just missed DS Yule. He was back on the blower just before you came back from the church. Got most of the info you wanted."

"Christ, that was quick! We've hardly been gone an hour!"

"Yeah, the miracle of modern communications and computerised records, Jimmy Yule says."

"Aye, well, I've had enough of bloody miracles for one day from old Dipso Dick the minister, thank you very much, so just tell me what Yule said, OK!"

168

"OK, he got a couple of WPCs to phone round the transatlantic airlines, right. Got them to check their recent passenger manifolds for a Dr Max Marsala, like."

"Manifests."

"Eh?"

"Manifests. It's passenger *manifests*."

"Yeah, whatever. Like I says, he kept fadin'. Anyway, WPC Geggie — that's the wee lassie in Detective Sergeant Yule's team wi' the ginormous honkers — know the bird I mean? Best pair o' thrup'nies in the whole —"

"JUST bloody well get on with it, Green! Even if such things are difficult for you to grasp, I can assure you that the size of WPC Geggie's knockers is hardly likely to prove crucial to this particular investigation!"

"Sorry, Chief. Right, as I was sayin', wee Janette Geggie hits the jackpot wi' her first call. British Airways flight, New York to London. Max Marsala, travellin' alone last Friday."

"And that's it?"

"No, DS Yule then gets on the blower to his contact in the NYPD for a character reference on Marsala, and the guy gets back to him within twenty minutes. Max Marsala, respectable New York businessman, no police record, clean as a whistle. The Doctor tag's a load o' shite, though. Just patter, likely, eh?"

Bob nibbled his top lip for a moment. "Hmm, clean as a whistle . . . Too clean, too slick . . . I don't like it. Anyway, what did Jimmy Yule say about Dannato

Cornamusa? Anything back from the Italian Passport Office yet?"

"Yeah, he faxed them that newspaper photo like you told him, and they've been back on to say it's all dead gen. Even got his profession down as a sculptor."

"Address?"

"Some luxury apartment in a fancy district of Rome. DS Yule's got the details. He got the Eyetie bogies to nip round and take a butcher's, like. All locked up, but nothin' suspicious. Belongs to somebody else, but the neighbours say a guy answerin' Dannato's description has been livin' there off and on until quite recently."

Bob nibbled his lip again — the bottom one this time. "Too neat . . . Too tidy . . . ," he muttered. "It stinks."

The far-off clatter of a pneumatic drill reverberated through the still air, causing Julie to look up from a map of the island that she had been pouring over at a table by the window. "You know," she said, "it was hearing that drill thing earlier that set me thinking." She beckoned Bob over. "When old Holy Dick mentioned the road round the mountain being swept away all that time ago, it reminded me of when I went hillwalking to that exact spot with Mum and Dad many years later. We were going to follow the road — just a rough cart track, really — all the way to a little fishing village at the other side of the island." She pointed to the spot on the map. "That's it there — Kildoone — no more than a scattering of wee cottages, actually. Deserted now. Totally cut off without the road. Not that I ever got there, mind you. I mean, we didn't even

170

know the road was out until we reached the landslide, and Dad decided to go no further. Too dangerous, he said. You got a fantastic view down the mountainside to Kildoone, though. Beautiful spot."

Bob looked at her, waiting for the rest of the story. "Is that it? Beautiful spot? Bloody hell! How've I managed to struggle through thirty-eight years of my life without being privy to that essential piece of information?"

"*Look* before you get sarky!" Julie snapped. She tapped the map with her index finger. "Can't you see what I'm pointing at?"

Bob screwed up his eyes.

"Oh, for heaven's sake!" she rasped. "Come on, you look, Andy. At least *you* haven't started to go blind yet."

"More's the wonder," Bob mumbled.

Andy took a swift gander at the map. "Aw, heh, do me a favour, Doc!" he protested. "The name's in Gaylick, intit!"

"Oh, I *do* beg your pardon," Julie chaffed. "I forgot that most of you east of Scotland folk are completely illiterate when it comes to your own country's native language!"

"Cut the bitchy Glasgow-versus-Edinburgh stuff and get on with it," Bob growled. "Go on, little Miss Polyglot — what the blazes does it say?"

"It says *Prince Charlie's Rest*, as it happens. It's a cave. I remember now. It's one of the things my folks were taking me to see that day."

"Cosmic!" Bob grunted.

"No, don't scoff!" Julie countered. "I've checked every square inch of this map, and there's no mention of another cave anywhere on the island." She indicated the point on the map again, then looked up at Bob. "Don't you see, this has got to be the alleged Saint Gubligan's Cave, right?"

"So what? Green here's gonna be taken to see it later in any case, so the *secret* location will be revealed then, wherever the hell it is. Who cares, anyway? It's plain enough to see now that none of this Saint Gubligan gobbledegook is gonna contribute one iota towards solving the two North Berwick murders, which, in case you'd forgotten, is why we came here in the first place!" Bob was clearly not a happy policeman. "Nah, I'm not gonna be sidetracked by any more Muckle Floggit so-called legends," he grumped, pacing the floor. "All this boulders-oozing-booze rubbish. It's nothing more than a corny, money-making scam, cobbled up by that old chancer Dick and his cronies. Once we're through here, I'm gonna report their illicit little caper to the Customs and Excise and that'll be an end of it. Six months in the slammer'll sort the buggers out!"

"You rotten spoilsport!" Julie scowled. "You wouldn't be so mean!"

Bob glared at her. "Do I need to remind you, Dr Bryson, that I am a law-enforcement officer, and selling bootleg bevvy is hardly regarded as a sport in the eyes of the judiciary!"

"But where's your sense of romance, your spirit of adventure?" Julie was horror-struck. "This is a Hebridean island, one of the last bastions of that innate

Scottish independence of character, of that untameable Scots freedom of spirit, that brave-hearted Celtic pride that won the day at Bannockburn, that rebellious ability — *need*, even — to raise the middle finger to stuffy old party-pooper law-enforcement officers and their like and tell them to spin on it! Report them to Customs and Excise? Hell, in my opinion, enterprising folk like the Reverend Dick, old Angus and Nip deserve medals for what they're trying to do to set their exploited wee island on its feet. *Medals*, not a stretch in the cooler!"

"Typical woman," Bob retorted. "Your spirit of romance has just gone bloody ballistic. Let me know when you come back down to earth, will you?"

"Uhm, excuse me, skipper," Andy Green interjected hesitantly. "Anything you want me to do on the, ehm, reason-why-we're-here front?"

"Yes!" Bob barked. "You can go down to the pier and have an investigative natter with the medal-winning Angus MacGubligan. Find out if the murdered Italian with the white Sierra was ever on his ferry. See what he's got to say about red Alfa Romeo Spiders. Anything! Talk about *anything* that might give us a lead in this damned case! But remember, you're a scrap metal dealer, *not* a cop, so play it cool, OK?"

Green nodded and was gone.

"Look, I'm sorry," Julie said in distinctly more placid tones as soon as the door had closed. "I know you're uptight about the total lack of progress you seem to be making on this one, but I just felt I had to speak up for the locals who're trying to help themselves to be less dependent on all these selfish arseholes of absentee landlords that they've had to suffer for so long, that's all."

Bob raised a conciliatory hand. "Yeah, I know. And, don't worry, I've got a sneaky admiration for the imagination and sheer cheek of those old guys too, believe me. But I can hardly go upholding their illegal booze business in front of young Green, can I?"

Julie adopted a remorseful look. "Right, I was well out of order there. Should've kept my big trap shut, huh?" She slapped her own wrist. "Silly me!"

Bob wandered over to the window and looked down at Julie's map again. "Kildoone . . . abandoned fishing village, you say . . ." The fingers of his right hand began to drum a slow, steady rhythm on the paper. "Kildoone," he said again. "A harbour there, is there?"

Julie shrugged. "I never got there, remember? And I don't suppose I paid much attention to what Dad said about it at the time. I was only seven or eight at the very . . ." She stopped, straining her ears to the noise of a pneumatic drill that had started up again in the distance.

Bob looked out towards the towering bulk of Ben Doone. "Road works where there's no road," he said quietly. "Bloody weird, that . . ."

"Mmm, it's got my curiosity fired up, too," Julie admitted.

They exchanged glances.

Julie canted her head inquisitively. "Shall we?"

"Aye, bugger it, why not? It's a fine day for a ramble in the heather, and there's nothing better to do around here at present, anyway." Bob started to fold up the

174

map. "Besides, I think having a wee peep at that beautiful spot of yours is beginning to appeal to me after all."

"Oh, meh!" Julie twittered in mock Miss Jean Brodie consternation. "Eh take it you're referring to the view over Kildoone, Mr Burns, and not to a spot on meh person?"

"Fetch the midgie repellent, Dr Livingstone," he said. "I'll grab the binoculars."

LATER THAT DAY — ON THE SLOPES OF BEN DOONE . . .

The air was soft with a gentle drizzle by the time Bob and Julie stopped for their first breather. They had picked their way along an ill-defined sheep track meandering upwards through the bracken, the line of the path often hidden completely under a blanket of green fronds.

"We should be wearing gas masks for climbing through this stuff," Bob puffed. He slumped his back against the crumbling stone wall of an abandoned shepherd's hut, the roofless interior of which had also been invaded by the ever-advancing army of ferns. "It's the spores under the leaves," he explained. "I read somewhere recently that they're supposed to be bad for you. Bloody lethal, in fact."

"Yes, that's what they're saying in scientific circles these days. But I shouldn't worry too much. If we're lucky enough to live as long as most of these bracken-leaping islanders in the graveyard down there, we'll be doing all right."

From where they now stood, the graveyard with the little church standing foursquare in the middle, the nearby hotel and the general store by the pier looked like matchbox miniatures in a toytown village. Over the sound, meanwhile, the Cuillin Hills of Skye had taken on a melancholy, brooding mood, their steep flanks bathed in pools of shadow, their jagged peaks caressed by fingers of mist.

"Too bad the weather's taken a turn for the worse," Bob remarked, pulling a can of beer from his rucksack and popping the ring-pull. "God, it's muggy!" He slapped the back of his neck. "And these damned midgies!"

"Ah, but that's the magic of it," sighed Julie, lavish as ever in her praise of the wild Hebridean beauty that surrounded them, despite the midges. "Just look at how unspoiled it all is. Mile after mile of sandy beaches down there, and not a soul in sight. Imagine, if it weren't for the unpredictable weather, you'd probably be looking down at a concrete jungle of Scottish Torremolinoses and Benidorms all the way along that spectacular coastline. Heavens," she shuddered, "what a nightmarish thought!"

Bob offered her his can. "Fancy a slug?"

"No thanks." She produced a plastic bottle from her kagoul. "I'll stick to water. Quenches your thirst better."

"To each his own," Bob shrugged. He stood resting for a while, pressing the cool can to his cheeks between

176

reviving gulps of beer, and joining Julie in her silent admiration of their surroundings. As she had suggested, it was impossible to resist marvelling at how the rather dismal weather somehow complimented, rather than detracted from, the tranquil majesty of the place. "Haven't heard the phantom road works for a while," he said at last.

"Well, maybe it's just another of the Reverend Dick's fake phenomena, dreamed up to kick start the Muckle Floggit tourist business."

Bob laughed. "Yeah, *The Ghost Roadman of Ben Doone* — a battery cassette player with a time switch and a powerful loudspeaker stashed away up here somewhere. Wouldn't put it past the old bugger."

Julie put her water bottle back in her anorak pocket, then looked at her watch. "Talking about roads, we'd better press on if you want to get to the rockfall and back before the light starts to fade. We don't want to be stranded up here after dark." She motioned towards the cloud-shrouded summit above them. "Particularly if the weather closes in, the way it often does in these parts."

Once they had cleared the uppermost limits of the bracken, they entered a landscape of heathery braes, strewn with boulders lying semi-concealed in the scrub like sleeping turtles. Every so often, the gradient would level out, the thick heather carpet giving way to rough grass and sedges. There, the peat underfoot squelched and sucked and dipped away into hollows, where water trickling from the enfolding crags gathered in boggy pools. As Bob and Julie trudged on, moorhens and ducks rose in alarm, voicing their startled protest to the humans who had dared enter their secluded domain.

"Jeez, I'm knackered," Bob wheezed. He swatted at a swarm of midgies that had taken a particular fancy to him. "I thought you said that splashing plenty of vinegar over my exposed parts before we set out would keep these little bastards at bay." He clawed at both of his bare and bitten forearms in turn. "Christ," he griped, "all it's done is make me smell like a fish supper, and I'm *still* being eaten alive!"

"You should've taken my tip and stuck to water back there at the shieling," said the midge-free Julie.

"Oh yeah? What difference would *that* have made?"

"It's the beer that's attracting them, you see. It'll be oozing out of your pours like nobody's business just now. Yes, and these wee beasties will never pass up the chance of a free bevvy." She giggled delightedly. "I mean to say, they *are* Muckle Floggit midgies, after all!"

Bob was still swatting frantically. "Thanks for the timely advice," he muttered. "I'll know better next time!"

It said much for Julie's sense of direction, and even more for her memory, that they found the location of the old landslide at all, for the narrow, un-metalled road which led to it had been all but obliterated by decades of neglect and the perennial ravages of the weather. The overcast skies had started to brighten, however, by the time Bob and Julie were clambering over the rocky scree that had reclaimed man's puny work for the mountain. The western sky was a random

178

wash of pale mauves and turquoises, speared by shafts of gold and red where the late afternoon sun was filtering through the lifting gloom.

Bob selected a flat slab of stone that had been protected from the drizzle by a low overhang, and gently lowered his aching body into a prone position on this improvised viewing platform. "I only hope this beautiful spot of yours turns out to be worth all the pain of yomping away up here," he grunted while attempting to make himself comfortable.

"Well, now's the time to judge for yourself," said an annoyingly unwearied Julie as she flopped nimbly down beside him and nodded her head towards the wide vista that had opened out before them. "For me, if I never saw anything more fantastic than that, I'd die a happy woman."

Her assessment required no endorsement from Bob. No Constable or Turner, and no wide-screen, three-dimensional film could ever have come close to reproducing the breathtaking panorama now regaling his eyes with such diversity of light, such subtlety of colour and such grandeur of scale. It was one of nature's inimitable masterpieces. The eternal, protecting arm of Skye's Sleat Peninsula reached away to the east, its rocky shores shimmering pink in the evening sunshine. The grand, sombre peaks of the Isle of Rum rose in the south, floating dark and mysterious on an alabaster sea, on which silver ripples danced and glittered on winding currents of grey. In contrast, far away on the western horizon, the silhouettes of the Outer Hebridean sisters of Uist and Barra and their scatter of satellite islands defined the hazy divide between ocean and sky.

"No bad, eh?" Julie suggested, then added, "as the eloquent Andy Green would say."

Bob savoured the views in silence for a few moments more, then quietly confirmed, "Aye, no bad, right enough." He allowed his gaze to descend to the cove that curved outwards far below; a tiny horseshoe of water, embraced by sheer cliffs and sheltered at its mouth by a small island.

Julie had followed his gaze. "That's the islet of Eilean Doone, another of the bolt holes where Bonnie Prince Charlie was tucked away by Flora Macdonald when he was on the run from the redcoats . . . *if* we believe local legend."

"Probably truer than a couple of the more recent ones we've been asked to swallow," Bob hazarded. He reached for his binoculars and focused them on a deep crescent of green bordering the bay immediately below.

"And that's the ghost village of Kildoone," Julie informed him. "Just a sprinkling of wee cottages, as I said."

"And no harbour," Bob noted, panning the glasses to his left, "— only a stone jetty and a slipway alongside. The water's likely to be fairly deep in that cove, though, judging by those cliffs."

"Mmm, no doubt," Julie replied indifferently.

Bob passed her the field glasses. "What do you make of those?" He pointed a finger. "See — those little box things dotted about on the grass beside that cottage near the pier. Yeah, the only cottage that looks as if it's still got a roof on."

Julie adjusted the focus. "They're . . . they're beehives."

"Aye, that's what I thought as well."

"And, wait a minute . . . YES!" Julie squealed. "There's somebody down there . . . just coming out of the cottage." She moved the binoculars slightly. "That's right! 'Cos there's his boat, tied up at the jetty steps. A rowing boat, with an outboard motor!"

"Give us a look," Bob demanded, grabbing the glasses and raising them to his eyes. "*Yeah*, and he's carrying something on his shoulder towards the water." He studied the figure for a few seconds, then gasped, "Nah, it can't be. Hell's bells, it is! He's humping a bloody great hind quarter of beef or something down to his boat!" Bob continued to watch until the haunch of meat had been duly deposited on board, then handed the binoculars back to Julie. "Here — he's coming back, and you're the one with the twenty-twenty eyesight. Any idea who he is?"

Julie fine-focused the right-hand eyepiece. "Let me see . . . Damn, he's turned his head away . . . Good, that's it. Now I can see you. Steady . . . Well, well, well . . . What do you know!"

"Come on, don't keep me in suspense! Who the hell is it?"

Julie lowered the binoculars and raised her eyebrows. "It's none other than Andy Green's local investment adviser himself, would you believe?"

"You mean . . . Nip MacGubligan?"

"The very man. Here, look for yourself."

Bob readjusted the focus. "God, you're right. It *is* Nip." He hesitated. "But — but I don't get it. I mean, he's supposed to be taking Green to see the cave with the hooch-weeping saint tonight. And the cave's right down there somewhere, according to your theory, while Green's still back in Dramglass."

"No probs. They won't be travelling overland like we've just done, remember. Nip can scoot back round the coast in his boat, pick up Andy and be back here in an hour — maybe less, when the sea's as calm as that."

"Is that a fact?" Bob said, a distracted note to his voice now. He trained the binoculars on the cottage. "He's gone inside again. Wait a minute . . . Hell, he's lugging out what looks like a whole slaughtered sheep this time! How much butcher meat is that old bugger gonna try to load onto that wee tub of his?"

"It's what he's going to do with it that intrigues me," Julie laughed.

"Well, it's nobody's business but his own," Bob said with surprisingly un-policemanlike lack of interest.

"Nobody's but Dannato Cornamusa's, maybe," Julie suggested.

"How's that?"

"Because, on Muckle Floggit, all the cattle and sheep are *technically* the property of the laird, if my memory of such things serves me correctly."

"A bit like the queen and all the swans in the country," Bob deduced.

182

"Something like that. Anyway, I'd wager my chemistry set that our peroxide-blonde sculptor, so-called, knows nothing about what Nip's up to."

Bob had a little chuckle to himself. "So, old Nip's a rustler as well as a bootlegger, eh?"

"*And* a beekeeper, by the looks of things."

"Yeah, that's a real strange one." Suspicion was writ large on Bob's face. "Why have his hives hidden away on the far side of the island here, when it'd be so much handier for him to look after them back home near Dramglass somewhere?"

"You've got me there, Kemosabe. Seems nuts to me, I must say."

Suddenly, Bob slapped Julie's elbow with the back of his hand. He lowered the binoculars. "What the blazes is *that*?" he gulped, pointing seaward. "Look — that huge hulk nosing out from behind the wee island there. God almighty," he exclaimed, "they really *have* raised the Titanic!"

"Wow, it's massive!" Julie gasped. "Titanic's right — and, hey, check the state of the corrosion on the hull. What a mess!"

They looked at each other, nodding their heads in unison as the penny dropped.

"Klondiker!" they chanted together.

"One of those Russian factory ships that lurk about these waters processing the fish catches from fleets of smaller boats," Bob said. He scratched his head. "But I wouldn't have thought they'd do much business at Kildoone . . . unless Nip's got his bees on a fishmeal diet, that is."

They looked on while Nip's meat-laden boat put-putted gunwale-deep out over the bay and on past Eilean Doone. A yawning hatch opened in the rust-scarred side of the huge factory ship as its diminutive visitor approached. It was impossible to see what then transpired in the dark cavern of the Klondiker's belly, but within minutes, Nip was bow-waving his way back to Kildoone. His little craft was still riding low in the water, but laden now with what appeared to be a cargo of cardboard boxes. Bob and Julie took turns at the binoculars, while the old fellow tied up at the pier, unloaded, then stalwartly carried two cartons at a time into the same cottage that he'd lugged the meat from.

"So, now we can add smuggler to the lengthening list of occupations on Nip's CV," Bob commented with a wry smile.

"Oh, be fair!" Julie objected. "It doesn't have to be hooky Sekonda watches or anything like that. It could just be jars of pickled herring or something. Hardly a hanging offence, surely!"

Bob held a finger to his lips, while inclining his head towards the mountain. "What's that — that *sound*?"

Julie cocked an ear. "That? Oh, that's only a whaup, a curlew. You get lots of them around here."

"I know what a bloody curlew sounds like," Bob retorted. "I do actually come from the sticks myself, remember?" He cupped a hand to his ear. "I'm talking about *that* sound! Can you hear it?"

Julie listened hard. "I can now," she whispered. "It's a sort of droning sound . . . like a motor of some kind

. . . coming round the mountain." Her voice was rising now, her eyes staring. "And it's coming this way . . . *fast!*"

A rapid burst of percussive banging echoed out from the same direction.

Bob jumped to his feet. "I'm gonna see what the hell's going on," he growled, before ducking smartly down again as a brace of low-flying grouse whirred at full speed over the rock canopy on a collision course with his head. "Holy shit," he muttered, "that was a close shave!"

Julie sniggered.

Bob made to stand up again, but this time he hadn't even straightened his legs when an object much more substantial and potentially head-damaging than the grouse launched itself ski-jump-style from the protruding rock shelf above. As if caught in slow motion, an Argocat rough-terrain buggy sailed out into the void, its engine screaming, its eight chunky wheels a blur of spinning rubber as it flew on to land with a bone-shaking thump on the face of the rockfall a good twenty metres below.

Julie had ample time to identify old Shooie MacGubligan, a maniacal grin on his face while he held grimly on to the Argocat's steering wheel with one hand and, even more determinedly, to a raised hip flask with the other. In the open rear of the little vehicle, two black-suited heavyweights in dark glasses and Frank Sinatra trilbies sat impassively rigid, supporting between them the sagging form of a patently travel-sick Dannato Cornamusa.

Yet it was Shooie's front seat passenger who really caught the eye — *and* ear. He was a short man, wearing shades, a camel-hair shooting jacket and beige velvet deerstalker. Bizarrely, he was standing Rommel-like at Shooie's side, firing from the hip at the fleeing grouse with a sub-machine-gun, while yelling sideways down towards Kildoone and the hastily-departing Nip:

"Hey-y-y, get offa the fuckin' island, ya goddam, trespassin' piece a' shit! Yeah-h-h, get the hell outa there, ya mother-humpin' asshole!"

As the Argocat lurched and bucked headlong in the other direction in pursuit of the long-gone grouse, Bob looked knowingly at Julie. "Dr Marsala, I presume?"

"And I do believe," she said with a discerning nod of her head, "that he's now worthy of the alias of *Ghost Roadman of Ben Doone* as well!"

Having journeyed this far (and all up hill), Bob quickly came to the conclusion that his curiosity, not to mention his complaining leg muscles, would be best served by scrambling over the rest of the scree and onwards down to Kildoone. The chance of starting and being engulfed by another landslide now seemed marginally less daunting than running the risk of contracting a terminal lung disease by retracing their steps back through the bracken, or, more realistically, of inadvertently stopping a stray salvo of bullets from Max Marsala's highly unorthodox grouse-shooting weapon en route. Bob's idea was to gain access, if possible, to the cottage where Nip had secreted his cargo, and to confirm his suspicion of what the boxes from the

Klondiker might contain. Returning to Dramglass after that would simply be a matter of waiting for Nip to arrive with Andy Green, and then cadging a lift back in Nip's boat.

"One problem," said Julie, while delicately negotiating her way between two precariously balanced boulders, "— what happens if I'm wrong, and Prince Charlie's Rest down there isn't the cave Nip's taking Andy to tonight after all?"

Bob took her hand and helped her jump a cluster of rocks made green and slippery by water from the burn whose tortuous course down the mountain they were attempting to follow. "Call it my blind faith in your map scouring capabilities," he replied, "or maybe it's just my policeman's intuition, but I'd put my pension on Prince Charlie's hideaway down there having a saintly squatter in it."

"And if it hasn't?"

"Then we spend a romantic night with the spooks in Kildoone."

Julie shuddered. "We'll be joining them before long if I've made a boo-boo about the cave." She looked up at the steep, crumbling terrain they'd already descended. "Without proper climbing gear, the chances of us making it back up there are slim, and the only other way out of here is by sea. We'd be marooned in Kildoone, and it could be weeks before we're found."

"Don't worry," Bob blithely assured her, "Nip'll be back to see to his bees in a day or two, whatever the case."

"Oh, a great comfort, I must say! And what, pray, do we live on in the meantime — seaweed?"

Bob gave her a hand down the last few feet of stony incline that ended at the back of a deep apron of green skirting the shore.

Now that they were actually there, the serene beauty of Kildoone that they'd looked down on from above was tinged with a certain melancholy. The plaintive cry of a lone gull circling slowly above the cove seemed to sound a lament for the people who had once inhabited this isolated little corner of the island. Forgotten people, whose women had scraped a meagre subsistence from the thin soil, while their menfolk sailed off in small boats to glean what they could from the capricious sea.

Without speaking, Bob and Julie wandered past one derelict cottage after another, their footsteps silent on the thick turf that now carpeted what had once been little fields yielding meagre crops of oats and potatoes, or, if the summer was kind, a kyle or two of hay to help sustain a shared milk cow during the long Hebridean winter. Down at the shore, a sickle of silver-white sand was lapped by waves sighing for those long-departed folk, whose souls still lingered among the sleeping ruins of Kildoone.

A short way beyond the pier, the sand surrendered to rocks, where, in a low cliff face just above high water mark, there appeared the mouth of a cave. The opening was crudely, though effectively, barricaded with two old harrow leaves that were chained and padlocked to iron rings set into the rock on either side.

188

"I think the no-messing blockade work says it all," Bob remarked as he peered into the dark interior of the cave through the trellised steel of the harrows. "Strikes me there's more in there than airy-fairy memories of Bonnie Prince Charlie." He chuckled quietly again. "Yep, it's odds on that Saint Gubligan is weepin' his rocky eyes out up the back there somewhere."

"Phew! I'm *well* relieved," Julie admitted. "But I'm telling you, I still won't be happy until I see Nip cruising in with our transportation out of here." A shiver ran through her body. "Yes, pretty as it is, there's something about this place that gives me the creeps!"

"The spirits of Kildoonians past, eh?" Bob let out a ghoulish chortle, then took a patently unamused Julie by the arm. "Come on, then. It's time we had a look at that mysterious wee cottage of Nip's just above the cave here."

For an islander whose fellow inhabitants still boasted that there was no need to lock up their houses at night, Nip MacGubligan appeared to have effected something of an over-kill in the case of this back-of-beyond shack. The door was double-bolted and padlocked, the two small windows boarded up with thick plywood criss-crossed with bits of old shuttering. Determined not to be foiled after allowing his curiosity to take them this far, Bob walked over to a nearby ruined cottage and rummaged about in the rubble, returning a few minutes later with a long, rusting poker and the hand grip of a broken oar. He handed the latter to Julie.

"Here, you hold this flat against the wall just under the window there. That's it. Now, if I can only get the tip of this poker in behind the shuttering here, I think I should be able to lever it off. It's only nailed on, see, not screwed."

"Breaking and entering, huh? Oo-ooh, tut, tut, tut!"

"I'm only an honest police officer going diligently about my duties, madam." Bob gave the handle of the poker a hefty thump with the butt of his hand. "There, that's got him! OK, hold the bit of oar nice and steady and I'll see if I can prize this corner of the board out first."

The stratagem worked. A couple of minutes, a few bruised knuckles for Bob and some choice oaths later, the square of plywood finally clattered to the ground.

"U'-oh!" said Julie when the window was revealed. "It's an old sash and case job, and it's fastened inside. You're still stymied, fingers!"

"Nah, there's always a way," Bob pooh-poohed. "Just a matter of taking a leaf out of the housebreaker's manual, that's all."

Julie stepped back, aghast. "Hey, come off it!" she bridled. "You can't seriously be thinking about flinging a brick through it or something." She held her hands up. "Count me out. I'm not aiding and abetting if there's going to be any vandalising of the man's —"

"Don't get your goody-goody, posh school knickers in a fankle," Bob butted in. He pulled a penknife from his pocket, then opened the blade and pushed it up between the two window frames, manipulating it back and forth against the catch, easing the stem round on its pivot until it eventually clicked fully sideways.

"Very impressive," Julie cynically admitted. "All the delicate skills of the seasoned cat burglar, I see!"

Bob gave her a sly wink. "As I've told you many times, it takes one to know one." He raised the lower half of the window fully and squeezed himself headfirst through the narrow opening, then beckoned Julie to follow. Sweeping the one-room interior of the cottage with his flashlight, he could see the cardboard boxes that Nip had brought from the factory ship stacked in one corner. Next to them was a corrugated iron enclosure, in which a cluster of steel hooks were suspended from the ceiling above two battered and lidless chest freezers, each connected to its own gas bottle.

Julie peered inside the enclosure and shook her head in disbelief. "One cold store, Kildoone-style," she said. "Ingenious, but hardly a masterpiece of energy efficiency."

"Enough to keep a few sides of hanging meat fresh for a day or two, though, and that'll be all our intrepid traders are bothered about." Bob moved over to the pile of cartons and lifted the top of one that had already been opened. "Just as I thought," he muttered, extracting a bottle of clear liquid and shining his torch on the label. He showed it to Julie. "Half the letters are arse-for-elbow, see, so I presume it's in Russian, right?"

"You guessed it. *Vodka*, it says. *The Old Babinski Effect — Full-Proof*, to be precise."

"Which means?"

"Well, in medical circles, the Babinski Effect is known as a pathological condition that results in the toes curling upwards. And I suspect that drinking this stuff will do just that to your tootsies — not to mention your teeth."

"And there must be twenty or more cases of the stuff in here — enough to fuel a NASA moonshot." Bob directed the torch beam to the opposite side of the room, where stood an old metal filing cabinet. Beside it was a long wooden trestle, on which was arranged a curious selection of bowls, basins, jugs and funnels. He turned to Julie. "You're the scientist, so what do you make of this lot?"

"The mind boggles, but I don't think it would be too wild a guess to say that it'll probably have something to do with bringing tears to a saint's eye, hmm?" She stepped over to the filing cabinet and tried the top drawer. "Wow, we're in luck! It isn't locked. Now then, what's all this?" She lifted out a glass jar and unscrewed the top, sniffed the contents, dipped the tip of her finger in and tasted. "Honey — heather honey, and first-class stuff at that. Look, there's loads of it in here." She opened the next drawer and folded back a wad of muslin. Under it was a small hessian sack, tied at the neck with string. Undoing the bow, she delved in and brought out a handful of tiny dried flowers. She took a sniff, then offered them up to Bob's nose. "Heather again, agreed?"

"Seems like it," said Bob, fascinated.

Julie pulled open the deep bottom drawer of the cabinet next and brought to light an old enamel bread bin, full to the lid with coarsely-milled grains. She bent down and took a pinch of the dusty particles between

192

finger and thumb, following the same sniff and taste routine as with the honey. "Oatmeal!" she declared without hesitation.

Bob nodded his head. "Vodka, oatmeal, heather flowers and honey," he contemplated aloud, then laughed to himself. "No offence, Dr Bryson, but I don't think I need to be a forensic scientist to suss what's going on here."

"And your conclusion?"

"Well, substitute vodka for whisky, and I'd say that Nip the distilleryman had assembled the basic ingredients for concocting some kind of Soviet *Drambuie* liqueur here, wouldn't you?"

Julie was already deep in thought, surveying the rough-and-ready apparatus laid out along the trestle. "I've heard about the occasional worthy in these parts who claimed to have cracked the secret *Drambuie* formula — or near as dammit." Pensively, she stroked the bridge of her nose, then murmured, "You'd need a heat source, though." She took the torch from Bob and shone it round the room. "And that's it! See, the open fire with the big black kettle hanging above, and the pile of peats at the side?" She was becoming quite excited now. "I mean, I'd need to run a few experiments to get the quantities right, but the procedure must be something like . . . soak the spirits in the meal for a while, squeeze the liquid out through the muslin, mix with honey and water over a gentle heat, at the same time drying the meal out over the peat fire — plenty of smoke — add the heather flowers to the dried meal, then soak the vodka-honey-water mixture in it again, filter well, and eureka — *Saint Gubligan's Tears!*"

Bob shook his head in amazement. "And the only outlay is a couple of quid for a tin of oatmeal . . .'"

"Yeah, and that's probably cattle feed," Julie laughed, "nicked, like the cattle it's intended for feeding, from the blissfully unwitting absentee landlord."

"Just a pity it's all totally illegal, Bob said," the smirk on his lips betraying a hint of secret admiration for the pawky audacity of it all. "And I suppose we can assume that the gas canisters in the chillroom there will have found their way here from the laird's kitchen?"

"I think that would be a reasonable deduction," Julie concurred. She glanced towards the open window and nudged Bob with her elbow. "Look outside — it's getting dark. Come on, we'd better get out of here before Nip arrives on the scene."

"I think you're beginning to forget just who's on which side of the law, aren't you?"

Julie didn't even attempt an answer to that one.

"But, yeah, you're right," Bob then conceded. "No point in letting Nip know we're on to their scam just yet. I've a hunch that letting this wee caper run for a while might be to our advantage at the end of the day."

"Really? What makes you think that?"

Bob winked. "Polisman's intuition again. But anyway, let's just have one last look at this place before we shoot the crow." He panned the torch beam slowly round the walls. "*That's* what I'm looking for!" he cried, then strode over to a recess in the far corner, where a small plastic barrel was wedged into the broken seat of an old wooden chair. Attached to a tap at the bottom of the barrel was a length of clear plastic pipe that curved downwards to disappear through a hole in the dirt floor. Bob dusted off his hands, a satisfied smile on his face. "OK," he said, "let's crawl back outside and bash that board back over the window while there's still some light left."

With no moon, and only a few stars occasionally visible through the thickening cloud, desolate Kildoone became cloaked in a ghostly mantle of shadows as darkness fell, only the hushed lapping of the waves and the distant, shrieking call of an owl hunting somewhere on the mountain above breaking the eerie silence that had settled on the cove. Although he would have been loath to admit it to her, Bob was probably every bit as relieved as Julie when at last the purr of an outboard motor was heard rounding the headland, heralding the arrival of the entrepreneurial Nip MacGubligan and his little syndicate's prospective financial backer.

Bob and Julie hid at one side of the pier, while Nip tied his little boat up by the steps at the other. A paraffin storm lantern was his only means of illuminating the way along the short stretch of beach and up over the rocks to the cave. No doubt it was a path that Nip himself could quite easily have negotiated blindfold, the lantern being mainly for Andy Green's benefit and, more crucially, to finally impart the most dramatic lighting effect on the awaiting stone "saint".

From where they stood, Bob and Julie could just make out Nip's muted conversation with Andy amid the clanking of chains and the scraping of metal on rock as the improvised portcullis was removed from the cave entrance.

He was chust fair vexed, Nip was saying, that it had been necessary to make the boat trip from Dramglass in the black dark, but it was right important, as Andra would likely understand, to keep the exact whereabouts of the Saint Gubligan's Cave a bit secret-like, until a proper wee business agreement had been agreed between theirselfs, as it were. "Aye," Nip concluded, "money on the table is a grand revealer of secrets, is it not?"

Andy's casual response was that it was no sweat, 'cos he hadn't a Scooby Doo which direction they had sailed in anyway, and he was just chuffed he never barked up his dinner on the boat. "Crap sailor, like."

Bob waited until the jabbering duo had entered the cave. Then, with Julie in tow and flashlight cautiously deployed, he stealthily followed Nip's footprints along the sand. Careful not to disturb one single tell-tale rock, they picked their way up to the mouth of the cave and stopped, one on either side of the opening, backs to the cliff, holding their breaths until they were certain that their presence was undetected. Only then did they venture inside, taking one furtive step after another along the narrow passageway, round a curve, up a slight gradient, then on towards a sharp bend, where the glow from Nip's lantern was glinting on the moist rock wall. Bob switched off his torch, and they tiptoed the final few yards in the lantern's reflected light.

They could hear the drone of Nip's voice now, his words becoming more discernible as they drew ever closer to the bend in the tunnel. He seemed to be describing the main physical features of the rock effigy of the sleeping saint. First Bob then Julie hazarded a peep round the corner, their cheeks pressed hard against the cold stone, little more than the tips of their noses protruding beyond the entrance to the vaulted cavern.

Nip and Andy were standing with their backs to them, their contrasting squat and gangly frames silhouetted against the flickering gleam of the lantern, which Nip had strategically placed on the floor between themselves and the weird rock formation that constituted the rear wall of the cave.

"So, you can see it all now, Andra lad," Nip was saying, "— the head yonder to the left, chust above yon wee ledge that would be the pillow, so to speak. Aye, and look you, there's his shoulder next, chust a wee bit higher up, because he's lying there on his one side and everything." He paused to check that Andy was suitably enthralled, then continued: "Uh-huh, then you come to his waist and the folds in his goonie — his monk's habit, you would maybe be calling it in the Lowlands — kind of flapping open a wee tait there, see, with the one leg bent and poking out and the knee chust pointing down. Mmm-hmm, and his arse is kind of up in the air there, if you see where I'm pointing at." Nip succumbed to a mischievous chortle. "Aye, his arse in the air . . . Man, man, I've never let dab to the minister, mind, but between me and yourself, I think yon saint

197

chappie there has likely been in the process of having a sleekit fart to his self when he was petrifized, like. Do you not think so at all yourself, Andra?"

Although he couldn't see Andy Green's face, Bob instinctively knew that it would be a study in total bamboozlement. For, although Nip's reading of the distorted rock formation could have been regarded, with a slight stretch of the imagination, as just about feasible, the so-called saintly shape he'd described could equally well have been interpreted — by a visiting Cajun, say — as a pair of hunchback alligators fornicating in a Louisiana swamp.

But Nip was uncompromising in his conviction, *and* in his convincing . . .

"Now then, Andra, all that chollity apart now — because we mustna forget that the pair of us is stood standing here in a holy shrine — are you not chust fair capsized sporran-up at the miraculous vishun of yon tears seeping fair steady-like from the eye of Saint Gubligan there?"

Andy was speechless.

Nip wasn't. "Aye," he went on, "and a wee bit half bottle of them teardrops is capable of felling any good Christian man, the likes as if he was stoned as bad as John the Baptist his self!"

Andy shuffled hesitantly forward to take a closer look at where the opaque liquid was oozing out of the rock and dribbling down to be collected, drop by viscous drop, in a galvanised bucket on the floor. He half turned back to Nip, providing Bob with an opportunity to confirm that his hapless sidekick's expression was, indeed, one of serious confusion. "But listen, Nip," he said, pointing a finger at the wall, "you just said the saint's head was over there."

"Aye, chust that, sure enough."

"But look! The tears are comin' out under that bit *there*, the bit you said was a flap in his goonie. And they're runnin' down his leg!" Perplexed, Andy frowned. "Heh, a funny place for a tear duct, eh?"

Nip stepped into the lantern light to conduct a closer inspection. He scratched the crown of his Harris Tweed bunnet. "Michty me, man, is that not chust a fair miracle itself!" he declared, the pitch of his voice modulating upwards. He cleared his throat and drew Andy away to his former, less critical, vantage point. "Ach, aye, but I've seen yon happen a couple of times before, now that I'm thinking about it," he bluffed. "But, na, na, never you worry, Andra, the tears will be back coming out of the saint's eye again tomorrow, chust as soon as — ." He pulled himself up, faking a cough.

Bob put his lips to Julie's ear. "Just as soon as Nip yanks a couple of feet of hosepipe back through the floor of his shack up there."

Nip finished his cough, then stated with a reassuring smile, "Chust as soon, as I was about to say, as it takes the saint's fancy, like. Aye, aye, Andra lad — chust like the good Lord His self, Saint Gubligan moves in strange ways."

Julie was struggling to contain a giggle. "His bladder certainly does," she whispered, her legs tightly crossed.

"Yeah," Bob whispered back, "and calling the miracle liquid *Saint Gubligan's Piss* would hardly have the same pilgrim appeal, would it?"

As Nip then launched himself wholeheartedly into a finance-raising sales pitch, Bob pointed back towards the cave entrance. "Let's go," he murmured to Julie. "You look as if you'll be emulating the strange ways of the saint there yourself if you're exposed to much more of Nip's duff patter. Yeah, and I don't suppose you thought to stuff a pair of dry knickers in your kagoul pocket, did you?"

Nip was still giving his capital-luring spiel big licks when his swinging lantern finally came into view along the beach. In the still night air, Bob and Julie could hear every word of his summing-up from where they were patiently waiting at the top of the slipway . . .

"And so then, that would be about the chist of it in a nutshell, Andra. We'd be needing a fine-like cabin cruiser to cart maybe twenty-five or thirty passengers a go round from Dramglass, a nice boardwalk kind of affair from the pier yonder to the cave back there, and a good, stout set of steps up to the entrance, where we would need to be constructing the souvenir shop, of course. *Buy Your Bottles Of The Saint Gubligan's Tears Here*, the sign would say. *Chenerous Discounts For Purchases By The Case*. Oh aye, and then, in addishun, we'd be needing a dinky wee diesel chenerator to run the fancy lighting effects inside the saint's chamber and everything. Oh! and for powering the piped music and all. Mmm-hmm, choosing the

200

chunes would be fairly crooshull as well, right enough."
Nip gave that a bit of consideration, then said, "Aye,
well, maybe something like a few CDs of yon dreich
Enya stuff would be the thing. Uh-huh, something a
wee tait churchie-like like that would be chust the very
dab to impress the pilgrims, would it not now?"

"Time to make our entrance," Bob told Julie. He
switched on his torch and led the way along the sand
towards the approaching lantern. "Hello there!" he
shouted. "We've just come down from the mountain.
Got a bit lost, I'm afraid. We saw your boat —
wondered if we could bum a lift back to Dramglass, if
you're heading that way."

"Chesus! What in the name of the holy Christ!" Nip
spluttered, raising his lantern to get a proper look at
who the hell this daft gumph was. "Up Ben Doone in
the dark?" he piped. "Man, you're not right in the
bluidy head!" He peered at the advancing couple, a grin
gradually spreading over face. "Well, well, well, Andra,"
he sing-songed, "would you ever believe it? It's yon pair
of Lowland chums of yourself themselfs, so it is!"

Bob sensed that if Nip had had both hands free, he
would have been rubbing them together. Undaunted,
Bob said brightly, "That's right, we met you at the
show on Saturday. Bob Burns — Julie Bryson."

"Aye, I mind fine enough," Nip replied, a calculating
edge to his tone. He favoured Julie with the lantern for
a second or two, then said, "Mm-hmm, the bonnie wee
lass who kind of scattered the tidy bit of statchoo
business I was busy brewing away at between Andra
here and young Danny-boy Cornmoose. My, my, now,

chust fancy that . . ." He cocked his head to one side. "So, it's a wee hurl back to Dramglass in my boatie there that you're after, Mr Burns, is it?"

"If you're heading that way," Bob confirmed as nonchalantly as he could.

Nip gave Bob's back a manly slap and pronounced that it would be a right pleasure, sure enough. Then, lantern held courteously low, he guided them along the little pier, stopping at the top of the steps that led down to his boat. He lifted the lantern to breast pocket height and looked Bob straight in the eye. "Aye, and the special night-time fare is the twenty pounds, sir."

Bob took a deep breath, exhaled slowly, dipped into his wallet and extracted notes of the required value.

"Ehm, that would the twenty pounds *each* that I was talking about!" Nip briskly advised.

Another two tenners were duly, though grudgingly, handed over.

"Eh, just lob him my fare when you're at it, Bob," Andy Green chirped, smartly exploiting the moment of immunity from punishable familiarity. "Yeah," he continued, "I just explained to Nip earlier that the old sporran got cleaned out on Saturday. Should've cashed a cheque at the hotel before I came out tonight, of course. Never mind, Bob mate," he smiled. "Square you up when we get back, eh?"

His eyes firing daggers at Green, Bob whipped a twenty-pound note from his wallet and stuffed it into Nip's hovering hand.

"Aye, well, that's paid for Andra getting here, thank you very much," Nip said, his hand still hovering, "but

202

he'll be needing the return ticket now as well, I'm thinking." He stopped Bob before his fingers had quite re-entered his wallet, cleared his throat and added, "And there will also be the fee for the excloosiff guided tour that young Andra has chust underwent hereabouts, of course." His voice oozed neighbourliness as he suggested to Andy: "We'll chust get your good friend here to pay for that now and all, and you'll likely settle up between yourselfs later on. Is that the way of it, Andra?" Nip answered his own question. "Aye, and why not indeed?" he smiled. "Man, what is friends for at all if they can't be helping a body out in a emerchency?" He turned back to Bob. "So that, sir, will be the round forty pounds more." Then, struck by a sudden afterthought, Nip raised his receiving hand into the "halt" position. "But here!" he exclaimed. "Wait a minute now — I'm taking all your change, so I am!" He handed back the crumpled notes already pocketed. "Now then, Mr Burns," he smarmed, eyeing Bob's open wallet, "I see you have a bonnie hundred-pound note tucked away nice and cosy in your wee leather spleuchan there. Aye, well, that will do me chust dandy," he chuckled, "and you can keep your wee notes for spending in the bar at the hotel when you get back." He gave Bob a crafty wink, moved in close and murmured in his ear, "Mind you at the same time, I'm thinking the drinks will all be on young Andra tonight. Man, man, what a grand business opporchoonity I've chust been after presenting him with!"

CHAPTER
TWELVE

THE SUN LOUNGE OF THE DRAMGLASS HOTEL — TUESDAY, AUGUST 13 — 10a.m. . . .

Having just been taken to the cleaners by the wily Nip MacGubligan and, worse still, having had an extra sixty quid of de facto expenses winkled out of him by a surprisingly quick-witted Andy Green, Bob had been in need of some quiet comfort on returning to the hotel the previous evening. But instead, he'd found the little establishment teeming with reporters and photographers from several national newspapers, all swapping dirty jokes and downing copious quantities of booze in their profession's accepted manner of getting their faculties sharpened up for the next day's assignment. On this occasion, their mission was to get the low-down on the island's new owner, the "famous sculptor", Dannato Cornamusa.

Bob had immediately hustled Andy Green straight upstairs to his room, with firm instructions to stay put with the door locked until further notice. He'd then seen to it that any of the press corps who wanted to interview the filthy-rich, scrap-dealing, young patron of the arts were to be informed by the hotel staff that he was indisposed, with strictly no visitors allowed.

To make matters more frustrating, it had transpired that Andy's casual chat with old Angus the ferryman in the afternoon had yielded absolutely no information of any use to the case, Angus's primary concern being how much he could screw out of Andy for transporting Muckle Floggit's burgeoning population of scrap cars off the island for him. Andy had had the feeling, moreover, that no potentially-valuable information of *any* kind would now be forthcoming from Angus until a tongue-loosening deal had been clinched. Money on the table, to quote his crony Nip, was a grand revealer of secrets, so it was.

Bob had already surreptitiously ascertained from the hotel register that no guests called Gaetano di Scordia or Laprima Frittella had stayed there this year, so how the ferry ticket stub had come to be in di Scordia's car at the time of his murder was still a mystery. Since any further indiscriminate quizzing of the local population on the subject would only generate suspicion and risk blowing his cover, Bob had come to the conclusion that the best way forward on that front would now be via Julie. She would have to pay a visit to her old friend Flora, the housekeeper at the big house, for a cup of tea and a chinwag — and the sooner the better!

There was, however, more on his mind that morning as he stomped into the sun lounge after making his customary call to HQ in Edinburgh.

Julie took one look at Bob's dark expression and commented, "I take it that the news from Detective Sergeant Yule has been less than encouraging."

"*Don't* mention those police handles in here, for Christ's sake!" Bob growled back through clenched teeth, then slumped angrily into a chair beside her.

"This place is crawling with damned newshounds, remember!"

"Oh, relax!" Julie said, giving the air a dismissive swat with her hand. "They've all gone out. I had a chat with a couple of them coming out of the bar. They thought they'd better tear themselves away from their Bloody Marys and go and hustle up some copy on Dannato Cornamusa's hundred-grand sculpture challenge before they missed their deadlines. Honestly," she laughed, "what a bunch of reprobates!"

"Yeah, well," Bob grumped, "that mob of pissheads are the least of my worries right now, as it happens."

"Really?"

"Yeah, I've just been told that Jimmy Yule, my right hand man on this case, has taken a couple of days' off. Compassionate leave, they informed me."

"Oh dear," Julie frowned. "What on earth's happened?"

"Apparently, his mother's dying, so he's shot off to Ayr or wherever she lives. I mean, would you *credit* it? Right in the middle of a bloody murder investigation!"

"Oh, *very* inconsiderate of the old lady," Julie sardonically replied. "She might at *least* have waited until you had a suspect or two locked up."

But Bob wasn't even listening. Drumming his fingers nervously on the arm of his chair, he announced, grim-faced, "My boss came on the blower himself. First time. Doing his nut. Wanted to know exactly what we're supposed to be achieving away up here. Wants some results, and bloody smartly at that. Yeah, two more days and we're outa here, he says."

Julie took a deep breath. "Well, I don't want to rub salt into the wound, but the man *has* got a point. I mean, apart from rumbling the little *Saint Gubligan's Tears* stunt, which really has nothing to do with us, what *have* we achieved by coming up here?"

Bob glowered at her briefly, then conceded, "Yeah, you're right. This is beginning to look like a total wild goose chase. Even the bait of the hundred-thousand-pounds petrol pump loot has failed to attract a single nibble. And that can only mean one of two things — either the villains know what we're up to anyway, or we've stumbled into something so big that the owners getting back a paltry amount like a hundred grand can be left in abeyance . . . until it suits *them*."

"Fair enough, but either way, *you're* still up shit creek without a paddle."

"Tell me about it! And don't think I've forgotten that the only reason I paddled up this particular creek was Andy Green's assertion that the bird who dumped the hundred grand at his feet and the mercurial Laprima Frittella are one and the same."

"You really think he could be mistaken?"

"Well, I always reckoned that the only way to find out for sure was to set it up for her to have a good look at Green, then see what transpired — which, to go back to where we came in, was the why we came up here in the first place."

"OK, so *that* nasty little ploy of yours didn't work, but as least Andy's still got his kneecaps intact!"

Bob allowed that remark to pass without response, but it had got him thinking, nonetheless. "Kneecap . . .

Yeah, and that's the name of the boat Signorina Frittella exited the Vigo stage in." He shook his head. "Too weird. Then there's her name and Cornamusa's — blatant, take-the-mickey pseudonyms. Yet the relevant authorities have said they're straight up. And now we've got this Max Marsala — a guy who arrives on a sleepy Hebridean island with two Neanderthal minders and goes shooting grouse with a machine gun, while the New York police vouch for him being one of their city's respectable businessmen." He looked up to meet Julie's sceptical stare. "You don't have to say it — it's all crap! *Somebody* has got a lot of official people in his, or her, pocket, and until we find out who that somebody is . . ."

A commotion down at the pier caught his eye.

Julie stood up to take a look. "I suppose that'll be your man Cornamusa's new speedboat arriving. Those newspaper guys were saying there was a buzz going round the bar about it last night. It's likely to be quite a beast, by all accounts."

"A *speed*boat!" Bob exclaimed. He got to his feet. "And here's me worrying about how I'm gonna justify blowing a hundred quid in expenses for no apparent reason last night. It's an ill-divided bloody world, right enough." Sighing, he held out his hand. "Anyhow, any chance of borrowing your car for a few hours? I want to catch the next ferry and drive up to Broadford over on Skye."

Julie produced the keys from her purse. "Be my guest. But, if I may be so bold, what in heaven's name are you going to do there?"

208

Bob tapped the side of his nose. "Let's just say I'm going to visit young Scoop Stewart at the *Isle of Skye Herald* office and see if he'll let me — to borrow the words of Angus MacGubligan — do a bit of 'commuterising to Cyberspace'."

The melee at the pier comprised a fairly equal mix of locals and press people, all jostling to get a better view of the sleek, white craft berthed below. The proud new owner and his bizarre little entourage had already descended the metal ladder on the wall to join the delivery captain aboard. After taking a sneaky look at the newspaper squad from the door of the hotel bar the previous evening, Bob had decided that, as he didn't recognise any of them, it followed that it was a pretty safe bet that none of them would know him. They were most likely a Glasgow bunch, he'd reckoned. It made geographical sense, as there was no way any penny-pinching editors would send journos from their Edinburgh offices away over here on the opposite side of the country. Still, he would keep a low profile all the same; just drift about inconspicuously on the periphery of the scrum to see if he could pick up any useful info.

"That's a *Sunseeker Manhattan* or *Renegade* or somethin'," one adjacent hack said to his photographer. "Twenty-two, twenty-three metres long — somethin' like that. Worth a bloody fortune. It'll go like shit aff a shovel an' all, like. Aye, no for wee boys playin' wi', that wan!" He gave his mate a wink, then shouted, "Heh, Dannato pal, what are ye gonny use yer new boat for — beltin' up tae Ullapool for a taste o' the high life on

Saturday nights, or a wee dash doon tae the fleshpots o' Tobermory, maybe?"

General laughter from the assembled throng.

"For-a feesh!" Franco shouted back good-naturedly. "*Si*, I gonna use for-a catch the feeshes!"

"Aye, fair enough, ye'd need a racin' boat like that, son. Fast wee buggers, them Scottish herrin', when they've twigged ye're efter them!"

More raucous merriment on the jetty.

Bob moved a bit closer to the edge. Wow! Julie's information had been right. It *was* quite a beast, this — elongated prow thrusting phallically forward, sheer power oozing from every inch of its sleek hull. On board, Franco and his Uncle Massimo were sporting identical navy blue yachting caps with a gold anchor emblem on the front and a surfeit of scrambled egg round the peak. They were being given a lesson on the controls by the delivery captain, while, at the stern, Max's two dark-suited bodyguards were sitting stiff and expressionless on a deeply-upholstered couch. Between them was perched a curvy little blonde in a mink jacket draped over a *Good Mornin' America* T-shirt. No matter how sartorially diverse the Cornamusa crew, however, it was obvious that sun glasses were mandatory for all.

A ringer for a bunch of stereotypes out of some ancient gangster movie, Bob thought. Bloody hilarious . . . if it hadn't been for the genuine air of malice that the poison-dwarf-like Max Marsala exuded, even with his head lowered to shield as much of his face as possible from prying zoom lenses above.

"Excuse me, Dr Marsala," one smirking reporter called down to him, "but can you tell us, please, what exactly you're a doctor of, sir?"

Without looking up, Max rasped, "Doctor of Philosophy. My philosophy bein', kiddo, that if ya don' stick yer goddam nose into other people's friggin' business, ya ain't liable to get it busted! Capeesh?"

An exaggerated, "Oo-oo-ooh!" rose from the totally unfazed press corps.

"And which particular American university did you graduate from, sir?" the smirker pressed. "The Al Capone Memorial College of Grace and Charm, was it?"

"Don' push yer friggin' luck, ya piece-a'-shit Limey schmuck!" Max snarled back amid concerted press sniggering.

"Kevin Keevins, *Daily Express*, here, Mr Cornamusa," one keen-looking youth then called out. "Can you tell me more about this hundred-thousand-pounds sculpture commission that you've accepted? What, for example, is to be the subject of the work?"

"Ees-a top secret," Franco bluffed.

"Like all your previous work?" another reporter goaded.

"Yeah," shouted someone else, "how come nobody's seen any of your creations, Mr Cornamusa?"

The questions now started to rain down thick and fast from all angles . . .

"Aye, and where's yer studio in Italy?"

"That's right! Nobody over there seems to know anything about you!"

"Another thing — is this Dannato Cornamusa moniker your real name, or have you just taken it on for a dare?"

Franco held up a hand to stem the deluge of questions. He was thinking hard to recall the exact bacon-saving words that Julie had used when he was facing a similar grilling from Scoop Stewart in the refreshments tent at the show on Saturday . . .

"Like I say-a to Scoop," he finally replied, "my *clientela* is-a all very rich, but is-a all very liking to hide away the stuff too. *Si*, so they stash-a my statues in their — uhm, how-a you say? — erotic places."

"Surely you mean esoteric?" an upmarket scribbler from the *Sunday Times* cynically enquired.

"That-a too," Franco grinned. "*Si*, I respeck-a their privates."

"Eh, Ah'm Alex McClarty, *Daily Record*, by the way," one bleary-eyed hack then called out. "So when ye gonny start sculptin', big man?"

That did it. "No chance-a more interview!" Franco immediately announced. "I am *artista!*" he haughtily declared. "I can only start-a scalp when I got-a the inspirings!"

"Yeah," Max grunted, "and the sonofabitch hundred big ones in yer mitt!"

This presented keen Kevin Keevins an opportunity to journalistically pounce on behalf of the *Daily Express*. "Aha! So it's money up front, is it?" he smirked. "You don't trust the financial integrity of our Scottish art collectors, eh?"

Franco waved his hands to subdue the rumble of hostile mutterings on the pier. "No, no, I trust, I trust — please-a believe!"

"OK, so when ye gonny start sculptin', then?" Alex McClarty persisted.

Stuck for words, Franco gazed up at the battery of expectant faces staring directly at him. He then looked appealingly to Max for backup, because it was he, after all, who had lumbered him with this crazy sculptor tag in the first place. All he got back, though, was a don'-gimme-no-friggin'-problems shrug. Franco's forlorn gaze returned to the army of eyes peering down from the pier.

Alex McClarty was first in with the verbal boot. "Can we quote ye as sayin' ye'll start sculptin' ramorra, which is Glaswegian for *mañana* in Italian, by the way, or is the *Record's* headline gonny be . . . EYETIE CHANCER BOTTLES IT?"

Although Franco didn't fully understand the headline, he didn't much fancy the sound of it either.

"Tell the goddam sonofabitch he should go hump a sheep," Max advised out of the corner of his mouth.

But Franco suspected that his Sicilian sense of honour was being called into question by this scruffy scandal ferret in the stained Humphrey Bogart mac. His head held high, his hackles rising and obviously so, Franco rummaged rapidly through his memory banks for the cogent English phrase his Uncle Massimo had drummed into him during that fateful transatlantic phone call to his workshop in Messina . . .

"Ay-y-y!" he shouted, preparing to quote. "When Dannato Cornamusa say he gonna friggin' do something, he friggin' gonna do it! *Si*, and don' you forgetting it!" He stuck his chest out and bellowed at McClarty, "OK, *amico*, so now I tell-a you thees — no way I gonna bottle, *capisci*?" While Max groaned in despair, Franco doffed his yachting cap, clasped it to his heart and boomed heavenward, "I, Dannato Cornamusa, will start-a to scalp . . . *RAMORRA!*"

Flash bulbs popped and pencils scribbled.

But keen Kevin Keevins persisted. "And so I repeat my question, Mr Cornamusa — what is to be the subject of this new sculpture?"

His tongue adrenaline-driven now, Franco's voice performed a brain bypass and loftily pronounced, "To the glory of-a the peoples of-a thees bee-oo-tiful island, I gonna make for subjeck . . . *THE EAGLE-BIRD WITH-A THE SALMON-FEESH!*" Then, his subconscious prudently injecting a squirt of caution into this adrenaline free-flow, he attached the rider: "In-a the abstrack, *naturalmente!*"

"Jesus H Christ!" Max grunted at him. "Button yer goddam lip before ya swallow yer own friggin' asshole!"

But Franco's trip down the path of self-undoing had now reached the point of no return. His mind may well have been searching for reverse gear, but his mouth was firmly locked in overdrive.

"Medium?" Kevin Keevins enquired, pencil poised.

"No chance-a medium!" Franco shouted, before spreading his arms into something ominously reminiscent of the crucifixion position. "FUCKING-A VAST!"

"Perhaps I didn't quite make myself clear," Keevins patronisingly continued after the ensuing uproar of hilarity had abated. "What I actually meant was, what material will you be working in — marble, sandstone, granite?"

"Or maybe pizza dough?" McClarty taunted.

Franco elevated an admonishing forefinger and waved it from side to side. "No chance I gonna use *any* them materials. No, no, Dannato Cornamusa scalp only with-a the *cliente* in mind." A smug smile traversed his face. "For, like-a you Scotchmen saying, he who name-a the tune, pay-a the bagpipe, eh!" Then, ignoring the grimacing Max, he added flamboyantly, "So ramorra, for-a my *patrono* Meester Andy Green, I gonna scalp in . . . SCRAP!"

Bob had slipped away from the baying pack of newshounds in response to old Angus's call of "ALL ABOARD FOR ARDENSTOOSHIE!" from the other side of the pier. To suit the tide, Angus was using the slipway to load his ferry this morning. To ensure his place on board, Bob had taken the precaution of parking Julie's BMW in good time right at the water's edge, but he needn't have bothered. When he got to the top of the slipway, he could see that the BMW was still the only car in the queue, the only other passengers being a handful of pedestrians and four scrawny Rhode Island Red hens in a wire cage. The hens, Angus informed Bob, after he'd gone through the usual over-the-top performance of guiding him over the ramp, were ancient, off-the-lay boilers of his wife's that she knew he wouldn't risk his jaw muscles on, and were bound, therefore, for the Indian take-away in Ardenstooshie — "at chust the right price to suit both parties".

Leaning on the rail of the little ferry as it chugged over the channel between Muckle Floggit and Skye, Bob was stirred to reflect on how an island and the sea had also featured in another murder case, the successful conclusion of which had ultimately led to his being elevated to his present rank after languishing for years as a Detective Sergeant. He didn't hesitate to admit to himself that he'd been a bloody good Detective Sergeant, mind you, but one whose dour determination to do things his own way and never to kowtow to any superior officer had seen him sidelined in the promotion game for far too long. Although it was probably too much to hope that lightning might strike in a similar situation twice, it was, nevertheless, interesting to recall that Julie Bryson and Andy Green had figured prominently in helping him bring that particular investigation to a satisfactory conclusion as well. The three of them had been thrown together on a Mediterranean island under fairly unlikely circumstances, and Julie's rather privileged background had provided some invaluable skills, which, although more indicative at times of a hooligan upbringing, had been instrumental in setting up the circumstances that had led to the culprit's ultimate demise.

Yet it had been young Andy Green's fearless actions, his selfless bravery in the face of grave personal danger, that had finally been responsible for the capture of the murderer and for saving the life of his second intended victim. Bob chuckled inwardly. OK, so that had been the press and TV version of events, but the real truth of the matter had been that Green's swashbuckling exhibition of heroics had been a total flook, a freakish happening over which he'd had no control, and which, in all probability, had left the seat of his underpants resembling the surface of the pit lane at Silverstone on Grand Prix day. For all that, it had resulted in Bob moving up the ranks at last, and it had also been responsible for Andy Green — until then a bottom-of-the-heap beat bobby — being given his chance to prove his worth in the CID. And what had Julie got out of it all? Well, she had got him, Bob modestly supposed; or as much of him as he was prepared to surrender, for the present at least. For him, as Julie had reluctantly grown to accept, it was still "once bitten in the nuptials, twice shy".

But anyway, here the three of them were again, though with a double murder to crack this time. And they had damned little to build on, except a paper carrier bag and an old ferry ticket, which both smelled vaguely of *Femme* perfume. There was still the intuitive sleuthing prowess of Bob's nose, however, and those talented nostrils were beginning to smell a rat.

Unfortunately, he would now be obliged to risk taking Scoop Stewart into his confidence with regard to who he was and why he wanted access to *The Skye Herald*'s communications equipment. The deal would be Scoop's silence in return for something like a twelve-hour exclusive on the outcome of the case; that, plus the threat of a stretch in the slammer for non-cooperation with the police if he didn't play ball. An unconventional, if not downright reckless, way of going about things, perhaps, but desperate situations call for like measures.

Bob felt a tap on his shoulder.

"Bob Burns? Well, well, imagine bumping into you here!"

Bob turned his head, and his heart sank as he found himself looking into a vaguely-familiar face — one that he couldn't quite put a name to, but the face of a bloody newspaperman, of that he was certain. Dammit!

"Come on, Bob," the face smiled, "I haven't changed that much, have I? It's me — Mike Gibson of *The Scotsman*, remember?" He gripped Bob's hand and gave it a hearty shake.

"Yeah, yeah, of course I remember you, Mike," Bob said, trying not to appear put out. "It was just that, you know, I haven't seen you at any of the Edinburgh police press conferences for yonks."

"Ah, well, that's because the paper transferred me through to their Glasgow office a few years ago. Not as grand as the old George 1V Bridge HQ, of course, but it has its compensations. I mean, I'm more or less my own boss now. More or less *The Scotsman's* roving reporter in the west, you might say." He grinned and gave Bob's shoulder a slap. "And belated congratulations, chum! Yeah, I read all about your exploits in the Med a while back. Some story! And some happy ending for you, eh? Imagine, a year or so ago it was still the same old Bob Burns, the perennial

Detective Sergeant, and now they say you're in line to be a bloody Detective Chief Inspector, for Christ's sake!"

Bob signalled him to keep it down. He doubted that any of the other passengers or old Angus in his wheelhouse were within earshot, but he wasn't about to take any chances. "Look, Mike," he murmured, while glancing furtively right then left, "it's vital that you keep shtum about who I am, right? See, nobody around here knows what my job is, OK?"

Mike gave him a knowing wink. "Undercover in the Hebrides, eh? On the trail of an international sheep-shaggin' ring, are you?"

Bob faked a coy little smirk, then nudged the reporter with his elbow. "Come on, Mike," he winked, "you're a man of the world, mate . . ."

"Ah, now I get it," Mike whispered with a sly smile. "A dirty day or two in the isles with one of your sexy wee WPCs, right? Yeah-h-h," he growled, returning Bob's nudge, "all black stockings and handcuffs, eh? Oo-ooh, nice work if you can get it!"

Bob altered his coy smirk to one of smugness. "Well, you know how it is, Mike. But listen, just do me a favour and keep it dark that you saw me here, all right?"

Mike let out a bawdy guffaw. "Frightened the wife finds out, eh!" Then, noticing Bob lowering his eyes, he cleared his throat and said awkwardly, "Aw look, I'm sorry, Bob. Honest, I heard about your wife dumping . . . I mean, that is, about you and your wife breaking up and the divorce and all that. I, uh, I just forgot there, that's all."

Bob faked a nonchalant look. "Forget it, mate. All water under the bridge now. Anyway, enough about me. How about your reasons for being away up here? No, don't tell me — you've been covering the story about this sculpture thing involving Muckle Floggit's new laird, right?"

"Nah, the Sundays had the best of what there's likely to be on that for a while." Mike pointed back to the press contingent still swarming round the speedboat at Dramglass pier. "Look at that bunch of stupid buggers. They're still trying to pump something worthwhile out of the guy. Bet you somebody's asking him right now about the millions he's supposed to have said he'll spend on improving conditions for the islanders and providing jobs and so on. A waste of bloody time. Whatever answers they get, it'll all turn out to be bullshit."

"What makes you so sure?"

"Because it's the same old story every time some mysterious multi-millionaire buys one of these islands. Yeah, it's all sweet words and extravagant promises at first, then fuck all! The place is just a big playground for them until they get fed up with it — usually after a couple of crap summers in a row. Then they flog it to some other selfish ponce, and the locals can go and raffle themselves. Take it from me, mate, most of these absentee landlord guys don't give a monkey's about the human element. All they're interested in is having fun with their new toy for a while, then buggering off,

220

probably with a tidy profit, to somewhere else that takes their fancy. Nah, there's nothing Dannato Cornamusa's got to say that would interest me. I've heard it all before too many times."

"OK, so if it wasn't to interview the new laird, what did bring you up here?"

"The island's in the news because of him — I'm not denying that. But listen, I've spent enough time snooping about backwater, west-coast places like this to know that, if there's anything *really* worth knowing that doesn't hit everybody in the face, there's only one person who's guaranteed to know it."

"Uh-huh?"

"Yeah, and that person is the local minister."

Bob laughed.

"Laugh if you want," Mike said, "but I'm telling you, they're better than having a stringer in every village, these nosey old Holy Wullie guys."

"Is that a fact?" Bob replied, feigning astonishment.

Mike took the bait. "You bet," he enthused, clearly bursting to admit how astute he was compared to his peers back there on the pier, "and that's why, when the other scribes and snappers were guzzling their liquid breakfasts in the bar this morning, I was off to see the Reverend Dick at the kirk."

Humouring him, Bob arched his eyebrows. "Really?" he said. Then, not wishing to show *too* much interest, he leaned his elbows on the rail, gazed out over the sound and chuckled, "Well, if nothing else, it'll maybe have done your soul some good."

"More than that, mate!" Mike retorted, obviously desperate now to tell something of his skill at winkling out an inside story. He leaned back against the rail and inclined his head towards Bob. "Listen," he said out of the corner of his mouth, "I'll keep shtum about your wee, ehm, *flirtation* with the WPC, if you'll promise to keep this under your hat until it comes out in tomorrow's *Scotsman*, OK?"

"Fair enough," Bob shrugged, still trying to keep any outward sign of curiosity in check.

Mike moved his head closer. "The Reverend Dick, would you believe, has discovered scrolls — two of them — that may contain proof that Saint Columba *wasn't* the first Christian missionary to arrive in Scotland from Ireland fifteen hundred years ago!"

"Gerraway!" Bob scoffed. "You're bloody at it!"

"No way!" Mike was adamant. "Honest — I'm telling you, I've seen stills from a video the old bugger's got." He patted his breast pocket and winked. "Got the neg of one of them right here."

Bob shook his head and gave a mocking laugh. "Yeah, yeah, very good, mate. Very droll." He punched Mike playfully on the shoulder. "Come on, you'll be telling me next that somebody's witnessed a miracle on the island. The Bleeding Madonna of Muckle Floggit, or some such crap!"

Mike folded his arms. "Take the piss if you want," he shrugged, patently miffed, "but that's exactly what *has* happened."

"A bleeding Madonna?" Bob pooh-poohed. "Yeah, pull the other one. It plays *Ave Maria*!"

222

Mike rolled his shoulders uneasily. "Yeah, well, not *exactly* a bleeding Madonna, maybe, but, uhm-ah — ." He was fumbling for words. "Ehm, I mean, old Dick the minister wouldn't divulge the *precise* details — not at this stage, anyhow."

"Why not?"

"Well, just 'cos he knows it'll turn the island into a Mecca for Jesus-freak sightseers once the full details come out."

"So?"

"So, he's keeping them dark until he's got all the necessary commercial facilities in place. Says he's negotiating with a financier right now, in fact."

Bob trumped up a look of utter disbelief. "And you swallowed all this tripe?"

"OK, it all sounds a wee bit far-fetched, I know," Mike replied defensively, "but —"

"But you won't allow a load of far-fetched tripe to stand in the way of a good story, right?" Bob laughed. "I didn't think upright publications like *The Scotsman* went in for that sort of thing."

Mike cast him a you-can't-be-serious glance. "Investigative journalism, it's known as. A bit like your game. You get half a clue that you might be on to something, and if your nose tells you to go with it, you do. Simple as that." He was getting on his high horse now. "Don't kid yourself, mate, I'll get a helluva lot of mileage out of this scrolls thing. Yeah, and what's more, I'll be cultivating old Holy Dick back there as if he was a bed of prize roses." He nodded his head emphatically. "Have no fear — whatever else breaks in this story, I'll be the one he tells about it first!"

Bob was tempted to comment, "Unless one of the tabloids starts dangling silly money in front of him for an exclusive," but he didn't. The last thing he wanted right now was to antagonise this guy with a snide quip. Mike Gibson's discretion was too important to him. "And if the whole thing turns out to be a hoax?" he said, hoping to keep the subject going without being too contentious.

"Then I'll be the one to expose it, wont I?" Mike smirked. "Yeah, this scrolls-and-miracle thing is going to give me a mile of column inches, whatever happens. On top of that, the Reverend Dick and his faithful flock of Muckle Floggites will be on to a tourist bonanza like they never dreamed of, hoax or no hoax, 'cos that's how bloody gullible certain sections of the pilgrim brigade are. So," Mike smugly concluded, "we all come out winners, no matter what, right?"

Bob was obliged to nod his agreement, because Mike's prognosis was more or less the way he had read the situation right from the start himself. He couldn't help admiring, though, the canny way that the foxy old minister had jumped at the opportunity of feeding these appetising titbits of information to a reporter from what was generally regarded as the high-principled bastion of the Scottish press. The Reverend would be well satisfied now that the widespread media interest generated by the release of this choice morsel of publicity would surely jolt his potential financial backer into a flurry of cheque signing. Little did the

224

poor old sod know, however, that his ostensible scrap-dealing benefactor was meanwhile locked in his room at the Dramglasss Hotel, not only as skint as one of the mice that doubtless lived behind the wainscoting in the Rev's own vestry, but also substantially in hock to the bank for the purchase of a second-hand white Ford Sierra that he was now too scared even to be seen near.

Oops-a-daisy, Bob thought, this was all going to end in tears for someone, and he just hoped like hell that it wasn't going to be for him.

"ARDENSTOOSHIE PIER!" Angus bellowed through the open window of his wheelhouse as he clunked the little ferry's engine into reverse for the final approach to the jetty. "ALL DRIVERS OF MOTOR VEE-HICLES PLEASE PROCEED IMMEDIATELY TO THE VEE-HICLE DECK TO PREPARE FOR DISEMBARKASHUN!"

As there *was* only one deck with one car on it, Bob wondered at the relevance of this announcement. But that was only until he looked up to behold the imperious jut of Angus's jaw while he delicately edged his tiny vessel, inch by inch, towards the slipway, all the while muttering inaudible commands to the non-existent team of subordinate officers on his bridge. For, although this appeared to the casual onlooker as merely the do-it-with-his-eyes-shut routine of an old ferryman steering his comical little raft shorewards, in Angus's own mind, he was the master of one of those grand Caledonian MacBrayne inter-island steamers, easing his mighty vessel alongside

225

the crowded wharf at some great, bustling seaport, like Ullapool, or maybe even Oban.

THIRTY MINUTES LATER — THE MORNING ROOM OF DRAMGLASS MANSION HOUSE . . .

"One sure-fire way to get yer ass in a sling, Frankie boy, is to put yer own friggin' neck in a noose, which is precisely and exactly what ya just done by allowin' them noospaper bums to railroad ya into doin' this sculpture crap. Ya shoulda priced yerself outa it, like I friggin' told ya, for cryin' out!" Max wasn't messing. He stubbed out a cigar and snapped his fingers to attract the attention of the curvy little blonde who was sitting legs-crossed, painting her fingernails on a high stool by the French windows. "Hey, Lulu-May, doll face, get yer sweet, little, lily-white butt outa here and go fix some coffee, huh? I wanna talk some business wid the kid here — in private already."

"Sho' thing, Maxie honey. Anything you say, big boy." Lulu-May let out a silly giggle and wiggled off. She paused at the door and half turned, hand on hip, chin resting on a raised shoulder. "But tell me, Maxie baby, why'd ya call Danny boy Frankie boy just then, hmm?"

"Because," Max exploded, "his goddam middle name's friggin' Frankenstein! Why the hell else do ya think I would call him Frankie, ya dumb broad? Now, get the hell outa here like I told ya!" He lit a fresh cigar and blew the smoke into Franco's face.

226

Julie heard the resultant coughing and spluttering from where she was sitting by the big open fireplace in the kitchen downstairs.

"There's something a wee bit funny-like about yon chimney," Flora the housekeeper confided in a hushed voice, while pouring Julie a cuppa from a big, brown, enamel teapot. "You'll maybe have heard of a dumb waiter?" she enquired. "Well then, yon chimney there is more of a talking one. Mm-hmm, it can be fair amazing the things a body can accidentally hear chust sitting here quiet-like." She poured herself a cuppa as well, then settled down in her easy chair at the other side of the hearth to "accidentally" eavesdrop with her guest.

"I guess I'm gonna have to spell it out to ya in woyds a' one friggin' syllabub," Max could be heard saying upstairs. "The reason I fixed it for ya to be known to them Scotch Limeys as a famous friggin' sculptor, Frankie boy, was *not* so you could come over here and make a goddam asshole a' yerself in public by doin' sculptin', OK? *That* much I had allowed myself to assume ya was intelligent enough to savvy widout bein' told. But I was friggin' wrong, right! Yeah, so permit me to elucidise . . ."

Max proceeded to explain that, when he had told Franco that he had bought a sporran, he had actually meant — in "capital A" lingo — that he had acquired, not a sonofabitch Scotch faggot's handbag, but a receptacle, figuratively speakin', into which sums of mazooma from his various *business* interests could be legitimately stashed bank-account-wise. And in order to keep the identity of said *business* interests off the figuratively-speakin' record (that bein' a golden rule of the organisation), the kosher source of any said sums of mazooma would be declared, if any snoopin' piece-a'-shit fed or revenoo people should stick their noses in, as having resulted from the overseas sale of a Dannato Cornamusa original. "An original," Max stressed, "which don't exist, capeesh?"

But why, the mystified Franco wanted to know, had he not been told all of this at the start?

"Because, Frankie baby, another golden rule a' the organisation is that none a' my lootenants gets to know Jack Shit he don' need to know. Yeah, and only one goddam person in the outfit knows everything, and that one goddam person is ol' Max here. That way none a' my lootenants can spill no embarrassin' amounts a' beans if they get shoved around by, figuratively speakin', the other side — whomsoever they may happen to be. Ya get where I'm comin' from?"

Flora MacGubligan passed Julie a buttered scone.

And so, Max's voice continued, all Frankie boy had needed to do was to do some play-actin' to the shit-for-brains local peasants for a few days every month or so, then, between times, he could disappear to enjoy his forty grand hand-out back in the old country or wherever. And the more mazooma that went into Max's sporran, the more — like he'd said before — would go into Frankie boy's. "Simple, huh? Yeah, friggin' simple, until *you* went and goofed it all up, ya dumb schnook!"

Franco was then heard to weakly protest that he hadn't been paid the forty thousand dollars yet. In fact, all he'd had to date was the travelling money he received from Luigi back at the travel bureau in Messina, and all but the last dregs of that had been spent at the show on Saturday.

"Now just listen up, kiddo, and listen up but good!" Max's grating staccato rattled down the chimney like the lead weight on the end of a sweep's brush. "My name *ain*'t friggin' Kriss Kringle, dig? Yeah, and nobody gets forty big ones outa me by actin' like some kinda jive-ass jerk! So, ya better haul yer good-lookin' Eyetalian hide outa this public sculptin' crap smellin' like roses, or ya gonna be back doin' what prematurely stiffed yer old man, but wid yer legs in plaster also!"

A muted whimper.

"Now," Max barked, "I want ya should get that piece-a'-shit Limey that offered ya the hundred grand round here pronto. Somethin' about that guy smells bad. Yeah, and I ain't even met the sonofabitch yet!"

"Well hiya, Mrs Mac honey," Lulu-May drawled from the kitchen door. "Ya think Ah could trouble ya for three cups a' coffee?"

CHAPTER
THIRTEEN

THE DINING ROOM OF THE DRAMGLASS HOTEL — 8.30p.m., THE SAME EVENING . . .

With the last of the press contingent long since departed for Ardenstooshie and the long journey homeward to Glasgow, tranquillity had once again descended upon Dramglass village, though it was a tranquillity now spiked with a strange kind of expectancy. Tomorrow would bring the commencement of Dannato Cornamusa's work on his new sculpture, and there wasn't a soul on Muckle Floggit who hadn't been gripped by a rather morbid curiosity as to how this enigmatic new laird of theirs was going to tackle what seemed a distinctly weird artistic project. There was, however, more than the prospective creative credibility of the young Italian to occupy the minds of the last two diners in the hotel tonight . . .

Bob had been in a brown study all through the meal, *his* mind clearly still back among the high-tech communications gear of Scoop Stewart's newspaper office over in Broadford. Although dying to hear what, if anything, of value his mission had yielded, Julie had left him to chew over his thoughts, along with his fillet of Ben Doone venison, while she concentrated her attentions on extracting the flesh from the bodily nooks and crannies of a freshly-caught Sound of Stooshie lobster.

Politely declining the waitress's sweets-trolley offer of a slice of Muckle Floggit Vodka Cake (another of Nip MacGubligan's "trading" offshoots, Bob suspected), he finally said to Julie, "So, you really don't know if Max's floosie, Lulu-May or whatever she's called, sussed that you'd been listening in to his upstairs conversation down the flue in the kitchen?"

"Well, I could hardly ask her, could I? But, even if she did, I doubt that it would matter that much. I mean, she's one of those real southern-belle bimbos, a bit like Elly May Clampett in the Beverley Hillbillies. You know, all boobs, bum, blonde curls and a brain-donor certificate stuck to what little forehead she has."

"She obviously made a favourable impression on you," Bob observed dryly. He smiled a lopsided smile. "Yeah, I got a glimpse of her down at the pier. Quite a spectacular piece of stuff!"

"Certainly is," Julie granted, "*if* you like them thick and tarty!"

Bob reached over the table and patted her cheek. "No, I prefer them clever and catty . . . I think. Anyway, what about Flora MacGubligan? If I know country women, she's liable to have told every gossip on the island what Max said by now."

"She'll have been sorely tempted, I'll give you that. But, no, I've a feeling I managed to seal her lips. After Lulu-May shimmied off with the coffees, I took Flora to the opposite side of the kitchen from the fireplace and lied that I had inside information on Dr Max Marsala. I said he was suspected of being a homicidal maniac with a penchant for rubbing out people who rub him up the wrong way."

Bob struck up one of his meditative finger tattoos on the table. "Who knows, you may not be too far wrong at that," he provocatively hinted.

Julie narrowed her eyes. "You mean, if Lulu-May *did* cotton on to what we were listening to, Erased is likely to be my middle name. Is *that* what you're saying?"

"Nah, you'll be all right," Bob said. "Just don't get yourself into any potential murderee situations immediately before ferry departure times. That's the only way off the island for Max's Merc, remember."

"Forget the Merc!" Julie retorted, shocked by Bob's apparent lack of concern for her welfare. "He's got a bloody great speedboat at his disposal now, so I reckon I need some heavy-duty police protection here!"

"You've got young Green and me," Bob muttered offhandedly. "What more protection could you want?"

"Do me a favour! A pair of unarmed Jock rozzers versus a homicidal Yank midget with a machine gun and two cavemen in bullet-proof suits?" Julie's voice had ascended to a twitter of disbelief. "You have *got* to be joking! I'm telling you straight, if you've come up with something that puts that little creep into the dangerous-to-humans category, I'm outa here until the cavalry arrives. Don't forget, Kemosabe, I'm only with this wagon train to act as a scout!"

Bob let out a laugh that had the waitress peeping through the little window in the kitchen door to see what she was missing. "There you go again," he told Julie, "getting your posh school knickers in a fankle. Just relax." He gave the back of her hand a comforting pat. "Don't worry, I'd be sending for reinforcements soon enough if I thought Max and his minders were a threat to *anybody*. But the info I've picked up suggests the opposite."

While the still-sceptical Julie nibbled nervously on an After-Eight, Bob attempted to reassure her further . . .

Bypassing the New York Police Department contact that DS Yule had been using, he had gone straight to the head honcho at the relevant office in the FBI. Although the fed concerned had appeared unwilling, or unable, to give away too much at this stage, he *had* divulged that Dr Max Marsala sounded typical of the many aliases used by one Massimo "Messina Max" Plantano. This top-drawer New York lowlife had long been known to have had his fingers immersed in every kind of racket, from the old faithfuls like prostitution, gambling and extortion to "owning" union leaders, judges and high-ranking politicians, and possibly, more recently, of masterminding an international crime network of awesome proportions. The "Doctor" title was one that this Plantano character had been known to use in the past, for no other apparent reason than to feed his own ego and as an attempt to legitimise his image in certain circles. Also, the Marsala surname did square with his Sicilian extraction — as did, of course, his "Messina Max" underworld nickname.

"And you're telling me not to get my knickers in a twist about the possibility of this evil little slug being tipped off by his moll that I've rumbled him!" Julie was twisting her After-Eight wrapper into a knot. "My God, if what the FBI guy says is right, this pygmy psychopath wouldn't think twice about bumping Flora and me off!"

Bob had to concede that there was probably little doubt about that. The only consolation was the fact that, in over forty years of concentrated hoodlum activities, Max Plantano had never once been collared by the law for anything more serious than dropping a cigar butt in the street. Beatings, slashing and murders galore had been credited to his bidding often enough, but Max had always been cute enough to ensure that he was never directly implicated. For him, taking the rap was an option not even worthy of consideration. On that basis alone, he was hardly likely, in Bob's considered opinion, to risk all by having a couple of women wasted in what was, for him, an exposed location like this. He flashed Julie a mischievous smile, then added, "Unless, of course, the two ladies concerned were daft enough to sing to the cops."

"Thanks, *Detective* Inspector Burns," Julie muttered. She compressed the knotted After-Eight paper into a tiny ball and chucked it at him. "That makes me feel a *whole* lot better, I must say!"

Supplanting the good news with the bad (or vice versa, depending on your point of view), Bob then advised Julie that the FBI had mentioned, interestingly enough, that the trademark of a Max Plantano-ordered "hit" was the tactic — if an element of initial persuasion were called for — of re-designing the victim's lower legs with a baseball bat.

"Which could link his mob with the North Berwick murders?" Julie gulped, at a loss as how to distinguish the bad news from the even worse.

Bob stroked his chin. "Could be, except that neither the Italian police nor Interpol have yet been able to offer anything on the real identity of Gaetano di Scordia, the first North Berwick victim. I checked that out personally, and it tallies exactly with what Jimmy Yule came up with . . . nothing!"

"Some of Max's *employees* in those august investigative bodies raking over the traces for him, maybe?"

"Only time will tell." A cunning little smile played at the corners of Bob's lips. "Unless, that is, Andy Green comes up with something on that score tonight."

Julie frowned. "I don't get you."

"I went to his room when I got back from Broadford tonight — just to see how he'd survived his day in solitary — and he told me he'd had a message from Dannato Cornamusa, inviting him up to the big house for a bite to eat tonight. So, since all the newshawks had bolted the course, I told him to go right ahead — enjoy himself."

"I don't know what you're up to," Julie scowled, "but I already don't like it."

Bob shrugged that off. "Anyhow," he said, "what did old Flora have to say about Laprima Frittella?"

"Like what?"

"Like, for instance, had she ever clapped eyes on her before the day young Cornamusa arrived on the island in the helicopter?"

"Once before, as it happens. She remembers it distinctly. Just a few weeks back — turned up with some bloke from the estate agents. And before you ask, Laprima Frittella *was* the name she used."

Intrigued, Bob pouted pensively.

"Flora didn't take to her, though," Julie went on. "Too hoity-toity for her liking. Too *nippit*-like, she said. Fancied her barra, as we say in Glasgow."

"It accounts for our *Femme*-scented ferry ticket, though," Bob pointed out. "Did Flora say anything about a red Alfa Romeo Spider, by any chance?"

"Nope. Came in the estate agent's Range Rover."

"Hmm, still the mystery woman, then . . ."

"Couldn't your FBI guy come up with anything on her?"

"Well, he didn't, although I had a sneaky feeling that maybe he *could* have. Same applied to Dannato Cornamusa." Bob thought for a moment, then said, "But maybe I'm being unfair to the bloke. If he *does* know anything about them, it could be that he has good reason for being a bit tight-lipped . . . under the circumstances."

Julie's eyes narrowed again. "Under what circumstances?"

Bob took a deep breath, leaned forward and folded his arms on the table. "OK, it's only fair to tell you, I suppose. You see, the FBI guy eventually admitted that they knew Massimo Plantano had flown into London last week. However, they purposely didn't tip off Scotland Yard that they were monitoring his movements."

"But why not, for heaven's sake?"

"The old usual. They didn't want to risk Plantano twigging that he was being watched."

"So, who *is* watching him?"

"All my man at the FBI would say is that they have an agent working undercover in this country. So, their agent will now be informed of our activities, and if *our* Dr Max Marsala does turn out to be *their* Massimo 'Messina Max' Plantano, we'll be contacted when their agent decides the time's right to break cover."

Oddly, for one who only a few moments earlier had been teetering on the verge of panic, Julie was now managing an impish little smile. "Massimo Plantano," she mused. "Massimo Plantano . . ." Her smile broadened and she began to laugh.

"A joke we can share?" Bob enquired.

"I was just thinking about that name. It's like another of those leg-pull handles that keep cropping up. You know, Dannato Cornamusa meaning Damned Bagpipe, or Laprima Frittella for High-class Crumpet or whatever."

"And?"

"And Massimo Plantano, loosely translated from the Italian, could mean — wait for it — Top Banana!"

Bob nodded his head slowly, his eyes glinting no less brightly than those of Archimedes must have done when thoughts of a screw suddenly came to him in the bath. "And Top Banana Enterprises, if I remember correctly," Bob proffered, "just happens to be the Cayman Islands company — supposedly headed by

Dannato Cornamusa — which now owns Muckle Floggit." He slapped Julie a high five.

"Eureka!" they yelled in concert.

"A breakthrough?" smiled Julie.

"Two brandies!" Bob beamed, gesturing with raised fingers to the flummoxed face still peering through the window in the kitchen door. "We're celebrating!"

MEANTIME, IN THE DRAWING ROOM OF DRAMGLASS MANSION HOUSE . . .

Max was sitting in a high-backed leather armchair by the huge fireplace, one hand gently swirling a generous measure of malt whisky round the inside of a crystal glass. His other hand was holding a large, unlit cigar, while resting on the exposed thigh of Lulu-May. She was tucked up on the overstuffed arm of his chair, her knees on his lap, one arm draped round his shoulders.

The recently-finished meal had been a strange experience for young Andy Green; a nervy hour or so spent sitting in the formal dining room, which still bore the evidence of the previous owner's taste for aerosol "art" on its oak-panelled walls. Max and Lulu-May had been seated at opposite ends of the vast mahogany table, with Andy and Dannato facing Max's pair of dark-suited minders on either side of it. The two Blues Brothers lookalikes' only gesture to etiquette had been the removal of their black porkpie hats, which they'd placed within comfortable reach immediately to the right of their place settings.

238

Despite the tense atmosphere generated by Max's very presence, Dannato, while making no attempt to stimulate conversation, had appeared relaxed throughout. Andy had thought, in fact, that he'd appeared relaxed almost to the point of being amused — though in a queer, detached sort of way.

Although nothing could be seen of Max's eyes behind the impenetrable mirror lenses of his shades, Andy had instinctively known that he was being watched incessantly; every nervous twitch of his face, every furtive glance of his eyes being studied and analysed by the intimidating figure at the head of the table.

As if sensing that a measure of levity was called for, Lulu-May had tried periodically to break the ice with some giggling triviality or other, only to be gruffly told by Max to, "shut yer hole, except for insertin' the friggin' meatballs!" Naturally enough, meatballs and spaghetti, being Max's favourite chow, had been the sole items on the evening's bill of fare. Although the recipe had previously been alien to her, Flora MacGubligan had striven diligently to prepare it according to Max's earlier instructions. She was soon to learn, however, that the path to successful spaghetti-making can be a rocky one, particularly with Dr Max waiting at the end . . .

"What the hell kinda garbage ya call this?" he'd snapped at her, his fork twirling the long, steaming pasta strings from the first plate served up to him. "Don'cha know the spaghettis is supposed to be cooked *al dente*, for cryin' out! Chrisakes, I told ya often

239

enough already — *al dente*, to the goddam tooth, like so there's some bite left in the stuff! I mean, I don' want ya should go takin' this personal or nothin', but if I had a dog threw up a mess like this, I'd be treatin' him for goddam worms!" He thrust the plate back at her. "Here! Go stuff this up yer haggis or somethin', and fix me the spaghettis the way I friggin' told ya!"

Struggling to hold back the tears, Flora, chin a-quiver, had then looked to her precious Dannato for support, or at least for an encouraging word of sympathy. All she got, though, was a glazed smile and a wave of a limp hand. So, with an indignant toss of her head, she had swept out of the room like a galleon in full sail, returning, to her credit, only twenty minutes later with a heaped platter of perfectly *al dente* spaghetti and individual bowls of meat balls. Everything was just the way, she hoped, that Max had demanded.

"Hey-y-y," he'd grinned at the end of the meal, "even if yer pasta-cookin' technique was strictly Grade Zee 'til I learned ya better, I gotta hand it to ya, Mrs Mac, yer meatballs is the plumpest I ever seen." He'd then pinched her well-upholstered bottom and added the distinction, "Just like yer Highland fanny!"

Flora's blush of embarrassment, tinged with a stinging sense of insult, did not go unnoticed by Max.

"BOYS!" he yelled at his two silent stooges. "How about that? The old Scotch broad here gotta natural bent for fixin' Eyetalian balls, huh?"

A deathly hush prevailed until a guttural chortle from Max cut through it like the croaking of a bullfrog with laryngitis. Only when the chortle had graduated

240

into a full-blown guffaw did the two heavies deem it prudent to join in.

"The old Scotch broad gotta natural bent for fixin' Eyetalian balls, get it?" Max wheezily reiterated mid-guffaw. "Now, tell me, boys, ain't that a goddam kick in the plums?"

Flora summoned up commendable reserves of dignity as she eased past Max to clear away his dishes. "Fine that," she smiled. "Chust as long as you enchoyed the meatball sauce as well, Dr Marsala."

"Yeah, you betcha," Max belched, shooing her away with his hand. "I'm tellin' ya, my balls ain't never been better sauced by nobody!"

Her voice masked by the ensuing raucous laughter from Max and his two otherwise-mute disciples, Flora whispered in Andy's ear while gathering his dishes, "Och well, at least he's liked *his* portion of the sauce a wee bit better than my Shooie's old Labrador bitch did. Aye, for she spewed it up on the kitchen floor while I was making the second batch of spaghetti." She gave Andy an impish wink. "Still, it's not lost what a chentleman gets, isn't it not?"

That canny dining room cameo of Flora's had temporarily eased Andy's overwhelming feeling of apprehension, but now that she had gone home for the night and he was alone with this collection of oddballs, his nerves were jangling again.

"So, kiddo," Max finally rasped, "ya wanna pay Danny boy here a hundred thou' for a piece a' original sculpture, right?"

Andy felt like a cornered rabbit. He opened his mouth to speak, but nothing came out.

Max signalled Lulu-May to give him a light for his cigar. "Ya deaf or somethin', Clyde?" he grunted at Andy between puffs. "I asked ya a friggin' question!"

"Aye, well, ehm, that was the price suggested," Andy warbled, glancing sidelong at Franco for moral support.

But, taking his cue from Max lighting up, Franco was now busy fishing what looked like a hand-made Roman candle from his shirt pocket. He stuck it between his lips and held a match to its twisted touch paper. Only a *minor* show of pyrotechnics happened, however. It was followed by a smell which reminded Andy of burnt lawn clippings. Franco contained a cough between pursed lips as the inhaled reek hit his lungs. He held his breath for several seconds, then leaned towards Andy and disclosed, tight-voiced, "The — how you say? — mary-joanna of Signor Sloth. *Si*, I been finding the leaves hanging for-a dry in the *attico*." He offered Andy a drag of his giant joint. "You like-a the wacky baccy, *amico*?"

Wrinkling his nose, Andy shook his head. "Naw, I'm no intae the Bob Hope, like."

"So, where does a hick kid the likes a' you get that kinda dough to throw about like it's piece-a'-shit toilet paper already?" Max demanded of Andy, paying no apparent heed to Franco's overt reefer routine, but disapprovingly eyeing Andy's less than suave-looking get-up of rumpled kilt and baggy Aran sweater.

"Scrap," Andy replied, oozing lack of confidence. "Aye, scrap metal, like."

242

Max elbowed Lulu-May off the arm of his chair and leaned menacingly forward, stubby hands clasping mohair-trousered knees. "Oh, yeah? And what's the price a' recycled steel on the Tokyo market today, huh?"

Andy was in a flap, and Max knew it.

"Come on, Clyde, gimme a friggin' answer, will ya? Ya want I should go senile waitin' or somethin'?"

"Ehm, well, ye see, there's not any internet facilities in the hotel here," Andy spluttered, somewhat surprised by the quality of his own ad-lib. "Not even Teletext or nothin'. Yeah, ye get out o' touch when ye come on yer hols to wee, back-o'-beyond places like this. Still, even multi-millionaires need a wee break, eh?"

Max stared at him in taut silence for seconds that seemed like eternity, then probed, "Where ya from, kid?"

"Eh, Scotland," Andy replied through an innocent smile.

"DON'T gimme no smart-ass answers!" Max bellowed, a gold tooth flashing between thin, snarling lips. With studied calm, he settled back in his armchair and drew deeply on his cigar, his eyes scrutinising Andy's face from behind those ever-present shades. "Now, lemme guess," he eventually grunted. "Yeah-h-h, now I got it. Ya come from a boondocks place they call North Ber-wick, don'cha, Clyde?"

The butterflies which had been fluttering in Andy's stomach mutated instantly into fruit bats, a whole flock of them knitting string vests with his gutful of Flora's *al dente* spaghetti. "Naw, n-never been there," he

243

stuttered. "West coast gadgie me. Place they call Aberdeen."

Either Max's knowledge of Scottish geography was as flawed as Andy's, or he simply felt that the rabbit-paralysing effect of his foxy question had been satisfactorily achieved. Whatever the case, he fed Andy more line to twitch on by rising slowly from his seat and ambling casually out of the room. He was followed obediently by Lulu-May and the shuffling Neanderthal twins in dark suits.

"Bloody hell, Dannato!" Andy gasped as soon as the door clicked shut. "That wee bugger can fairly put the shites up ye! And, heh, who the hell does he think he is anyway, carryin' on as if he owned the place?"

By now, Franco was in orbit round planet Zomboid, his zeppelin-size spliff having been reduced to finger-singeing proportions by some concentrated inhalation exercises. He started up a slurred, chuckle-punctuated vocal rendition of his favourite, *O Sole Mio*, while Andy rummaged in his sporran for a folded sheet of paper that Bob had given him back at the hotel. It was one of the small posters showing the passport picture of Gaetano di Scordia, which had been circularised to police stations in the UK and Italy after his murder at North Berwick. Andy opened it up and held it in front of Franco's rolling eyes.

"See this?" Andy said for openers. "Well, somebody gave me it. Said the guy looks a wee bit like me, maybe. Aye, and he does an' all. Kind o' eerie, eh?" He kept glancing towards the door, while desperately trying to get the semi-zonked Franco to concentrate. "See," he

244

urged, "it says here he's Italian. I just thought ye might know him, like." He pointed to the picture, took a double take at Franco, then gasped, "Heh! Now that I have a proper gander at him, the gadgie looks a wee bit like you as well!"

Franco, not without some effort, managed to focus one eye on the poster for a second or two, before dissolving into hysterical laughter. "*Si*," he wept delightedly, "the dead guy with-a yellow hair . . . he look-a just like me!"

Hearing footsteps approaching the door, Andy swiftly re-folded the poster and shoved it into Franco's shirt pocket. Max strutted back in, his pair of permanent shadows in line astern. The little procession had a businesslike look about it. *Dirty* businesslike. Some of Andy's gastro fruit bats dropped a stitch or two.

"OK, Clyde," Max said, quickly adopting a posture of authority in his high-backed chair, with his heavies standing arms-folded on either side, "I been checkin' the friggin' map a' Scotland, and you been jivin' my goddam shorts off wid yer Aberdeen-on-the-west-coast chicken shit!"

"Aye, well," Andy gulped, "what I was *really* meanin' was —"

"SHUT yer bugle, boy! Ya lied once al-friggin'-ready, and now I don' wanna hear nothin' outa ya except the whole truth and nothin' but, capeesh?"

Andy could only nod, as a rush of panicking bats tried to escape up his windpipe.

"OK," Max continued, "first I wanna know why ya offered Danny boy here a hundred grand. A hundred — not eighty or ninety, but a hundred!" He raised his cigar and jabbed it threateningly towards Andy. "One, nothin', nothin', nothin', nothin', nothin' just happens to be my very unfavourite combination a' numbers right now, so how come ya just happened to pull that one outa the goddam hat?"

Andy still couldn't untangle the flapping bat wings from his vocal cords.

Max smiled a snake-like smile. "Yeah," he snarled, "ya ain't got no friggin' answer to that, have ya? Well, surprise, sur-friggin'-prise!" He leaned forward again and held out an upturned hand. "I'm tellin' ya, Clyde baby, as Danny boy's manager, I wanna see them hundred big ones slapped right here in my dainty mitt before *any* goddam sculptin' is even talked about again!"

"B-but the newspaper gadgies," Andy managed to yodel, "they'll be comin' back expectin' Dannato to —"

"SCREW the sonofabitch noozpapers! Who the hell gives doodly squat about them shit-sniffin' pigs anyway!" Then, as though a hidden switch had been thrown, Max instantly assumed a relaxed manner. He settled back into his chair and lowered his voice to a pseudo-genial murmur. "Ya *do* have the dough, don'cha, Clyde?" he smiled.

Andy coughed, cleared his throat, then coughed again. "Oh aye, nae bother," he said, his voice breaking like an adolescent schoolboy's. "Yeah, a hundred grand's nothin' for the likes o' me, like."

246

Max savoured the sight of his fidgeting victim massaging his Adam's apple for a while, then, with an almost convincing warmth to his voice, said, "Hey-y-y, Mr Green, ya look a tad peakish there — a tad *green* about the gills, if ya pardon the pun." He leaned further back into his chair, opened his arms and drawled affably, "Come on, come on, come on, unlax, kid. We're both businessmen, huh?"

Andy nodded in green-gilled silence.

"Hey, I got it," Max beamed, as if suddenly struck by an idea bursting with conviviality. "Maybe we need some music to get the right atmosphere goin' here." He reached up and snapped his fingers in the face of the minder on his left. "Go put a record on, bub. And, hey, make sure ya pick somethin' ya think our guest here would appreciate already. Yeah, somethin' to *pump* up his spirits . . . if ya get where I'm comin' from." Max sucked contentedly on his cigar and smiled malignantly at Andy, while the minder lumbered over to a hi-fi cabinet by the door. There was the plastic rattle of a cassette being selected, then being clumsily inserted into the player.

Andy waited, his heart pounding, as the minder pressed the play button and ambled back to his sentry post by his boss's side. A gun shot rang out, causing Andy to jump in his seat, and jolting Franco into a re-entry trajectory from his armchair orbit. A second shot rang out . . . and three more! Then the introductory bars of *You Always Hurt The One You Love* exploded into the room. The harmonic havoc of Spike Jones and His City Slickers reverberated round the garishly painted walls as if to remind the previous punk-rock owner of the house that his generation hadn't been the first to go musically ape. Not by a long chalk.

Andy felt physically sick.

It showed, and Max noticed it. He grabbed the remote control from his stooge and hit the volume-down button, stood up, then swaggered across to Andy and looked down at him crouched in his chair, his face a picture of misery.

"I see ya share my taste in music, Clyde," Max croaked. "A Spike Jones fan, huh? Friggin' unusual for a kid a' your age, ain't it?" He prodded a finger into Andy's stooped shoulders and barked, "Stand up, ya sonofabitch! I wanna see yer eyes!"

Andy did as he was told, but even in his droopy state, he still towered above his vertically-challenged adversary.

Max, of course, had a pathological aversion to this sort of genetic privilege. "What height are ya, boy?" he snapped.

Andy was holding a hand to his mouth, trying not to throw up. "Six-two or three or somethin'," he mumbled through his fingers.

"Which means yer legs is about a foot too long for the good a' yer health." Max jerked his head in the direction of his two thugs. "But maybe the boys there can do somethin' to remedy that ailment for ya!"

Feeling in sudden need of a booster burn to put the brakes on his impending feelgood splashdown, Franco was meanwhile fumbling in his shirt pocket for another reefer. "Wot's-a thees?" he muttered, pulling out the police poster and unfolding it, "*Gesù Cristo!*" he exclaimed as the dope-induced mist cleared from his eyes. "He's-a dead! All murdered and-a dead!" He clapped a hand over his heart and wailed, "Franco Contadino, my little cousin from-a the States, all murdered and-a dead. *Dio mio*," he sobbed, "my Mamma she got-a his picture from the christening on the mantelpiece, 'cos they name-a him after me." He started to beat his chest in anguish. "And now he's-a dead . . . all murdered and-a dead!"

Max pounced forward and snatched the poster from his hand. "Where the hell d'ya get this, for Chrisakes?"

Franco was too busy working up a deluge of grief-stricken tears to answer.

Max glared at the poster, then at Andy.

Andy started for the door, gagging. "'Scuse me," he mumbled between retches, "but I've really got a honk comin' on . . ."

It took but a snap of Max's fingers to set his minders on Andy. Each grabbed one of his arms and wrenched it up his back while frogmarching him back to their boss.

"Honest," Andy pleaded, ashen-faced, "I really am gonna puke. No kiddin'!"

"That bein' the case," Max snarled, "I reckon the boys here better take ya for a breath a' sea air." He snapped his fingers again. "Ya know what to do, boys, and if the sonofabitch don' feel like singin' the full lyrics a' the hundred-grand song for ya on the way, beat out the rhythm on his goddam knees before he goes for

249

his swim. Yeah," he growled, "that oughta loosen up his friggin' voice!"

The Blues Brothers lookalikes didn't have to be told twice. They exchanged sadistic smirks. This was a little chore they were going to relish. Twisting his arms upwards until his shoulder joints were on the verge of popping, they bundled Andy out of the room and down the hallway. Even as they reached the back door, the grating sound of Max's violent tongue-lashing could still be heard raging above Franco's pathetic whimpers — whimpers which erupted into a howl of agony following the dull thwack of fist against face.

But Andy was too preoccupied with the welfare of his own bones just at the moment to be bothered too much about Franco's problems. In a flurry of grunts and shoves, he was hustled out into the moonless night, round the side of the house and into the pitch darkness of the old stables. One of the heavies pulled a small flashlight from his pocket and shone it at the rear of the big white Mercedes, which was parked just inside the door. He opened the boot and peered inside, a look of bovine puzzlement extending over his face, his mouth gawping goldfish-style before he finally mumbled, "Hey, man, where's the fuckin' ba —"

WALLOP!

The torch fell from his hand and clattered onto the cobbled floor, its beam quickly smothered by the collapsing body of its owner.

WALLOP!

Andy felt the iron grip on his other wrist slacken then slip away, as the second heavy groaned and slumped unconscious on top of his partner. Instinctively, Andy turned quickly, raising his arms to protect his head. But there was no-one there, only the muffled sound of footsteps hurrying over the gravel into the night. Then he noticed it. Propped against the door jamb, its shape just visible in the reflected glow of the car's boot light, was a bloodstained baseball bat . . .

CHAPTER
FOURTEEN

10a.m., WEDNESDAY 14 AUGUST — IN FRONT OF THE BLACKSMITH'S WORKSHOP, BY DRAMGLASS PIER . . .

Donal the blacksmith was a man after Franco's own heart. He was a small, sturdy man of perhaps twice Franco's age, but a man who recognised the young Italian's knowledge of his demanding trade and shared his distaste for it. They had met hazily in the hotel bar on the night of Franco's welcoming ceilidh, and although Donal had found it difficult to fathom how an arty-farty sculptor could know so much about the mysteries and aggravations of the blacksmith's craft, he had allowed a liberal intake of drams to put the conundrum out of his mind on the night. The subject hadn't revisited his thoughts until an hour or so ago, when Franco had turned up to ask if he might hire — on deferred payment — Donal's oxyacetylene cutter and welder, together with multifarious other metalworking tools, for the purpose of creating his new work of art. Heavy lifting gear had also been on Franco's shopping list, so Donal had sent him along the road to Dramglass Home Farm, where his brother, Dougal the cattleman, might have "chust the very exact item" he needed.

Donal was now standing discussing this whole turn of events with old Angus the ferryman, when Franco came back into view, athletically driving a clapped-out Ford tractor along the main street of the village. The ancient machine, although diesel powered, looked and smelled — according to the plume of black smoke belching from its funnel — as if it were burning a mixture of coal and old tyres. The steering, meanwhile — if Franco's flailing arm movements were anything to go by — appeared to be on the suicidal side of dodgy. But thrusting upward from the front of the old Ford was the accessory so essential for Franco's needs — a hydraulic loader, complete with dung fork, which, for Dougal, took the backache out of the once-dreaded task of mucking out the cattle sheds every spring.

"Man, man, Seenyour Cornmoose, yon's a terrible sore-looking keeker you have on your face there this morning," Angus observed as Franco reined in the clattering old steed, his black eye contrasting vividly with the shock of bleached hair dangling above it. "When you was at the farm along there," Angus continued, "you should chust have got Dougal to carve a nice slice off of the arse end of a bullock for it, so you should have now. Chings me, the new laird would never have missed a wee bit rump steak from one of his beasts!"

Franco joined in the good-natured laughter that followed Angus's shaft of Celtic wit, though, as usual, not really understanding much of what had been said. "Ah, *buon giorno*, Meester Mayor," he grinned, raising a hand to the clear, blue sky. "*Fantastico* day for-a the size of the town, *si*?"

Angus's whin-bush eyebrows converged into a scowl of curiosity. "And Donal here tells me, Tomato — if I may be so familiar at all — that you are about to be embarking yourself into an act of creative concepshun with a welding rod."

"No, no, *signor*," Franco replied, clueless as to what Angus had said, but ready with his answer, anyway, "I only gonna start-a scalp my new statue, the Eagle-Bird With-a Salmon-Feesh." He pointed to a wedge of grass between the blacksmith's shop and the foreshore. "And weeth your permission, Meester Mayor, I gonna scalp him right there!"

Donal was quick to voice his opinion. "Man, Angus, it would be grand for all to behold the statchoo there as they sail away over here from Ardenstooshie on your wee ferry, would it not at that?"

"Aye, well, that's as may be, Donal," Angus cautiously granted, "but, in my offishul capacity as Provost of Dramglass and Chairperson of Muckle Floggit Island Council, it behoves me to keep the head when making civic deesishuns unilateral-like." Angus squared his shoulders and gripped the lapel of his sea captain's jacket with his left hand. "I mean to say, there could be matters pertinashus to the Town and Country Planning Act involved here."

Franco was impressed. He didn't know what a Town and Country Planning Act was, but it sounded important and *very* dignified. In fact, it was just the sort of quality endorsement he desperately needed to add some credence to his first attempt at doing anything more artistic than fashioning a piece of steel reinforcing rod into a number for someone's gate. He laid a hand on Angus's shoulder. "I gonna tell you thees, Meester Mayor — you feex thees Town-a Country beez-i-ness, and I gonna give ten *per cento* of-a my fee to your charity *favorito*." He slapped Angus's shoulder. "How you like-a that?"

Angus liked that fine. Ten per cent of a hundred thousand quid meant ten thousand for him, on the tried and tested basis of charity beginning at home. His home. "Well now, Tomato," he lilted unctuously, his twin black beads of eyes glinting beneath their canopy of shaggy brows, "I'm chust after thinking that I might chust be able to carry a wee machority of the council planning committee with me, sure enough." He turned to Donal and told him in the Gaelic that, if he kept his bloody trap shut about this to the other greedy buggers on the council, there would be ten per cent of his ten per cent in it for him.

Donal sealed the covenant with a calculating wee smirk.

Angus gave Franco a toady smile. "Aye, Tomato," he smarmed, "I was chust saying there to my good friend Donal here — and I hope you will pardon me slipping inadvertent-like into the mother tongue for a wee minute and all — that, being the modest chentleman that you are, you will likely not be wanting any publicity for the chenerous donation so chenerously promised to my, ehm, favourite charity. Will that be right now?"

"And the Town-a Country beez-i-ness ees-a all feex up?"

Angus gave an affirmative dip of his head.

Franco slapped his back and shook his hand. "Nice-a one, Angoose," he grinned, then climbed back aboard the tractor. "Now I gonna go pick up some-a scrap cars!"

Angus was horrified. "Scrap CARS?"

"Si! For scalp-a the scalpture." Franco made a sweep of his hand landwards. "Look, the whole place ees-a crawl with them." He laughed aloud as the significance hit him. "Hey-y-y! Dannato Cornamusa, your-a new landlord, he no just gonna scalp, he gonna clean the place up as well, eh!"

In an instant, Angus saw the deal that he had been so assiduously cooking with Andy Green sliding swiftly down the pipes. But what was a man to do? You couldn't have the nine thousand nett in the paw from Cornmoose for nothing *and* have the profits for shipping the scrap cars off the island too. "Ach, well," he told himself philosophically, his mind clicking into senior-elder-of-the-church mode, "the Lord giveth and the Lord taketh away, right enough. Aye, and an absolute pure bugger it is and all!"

While all this was happening at the smiddy, Bob and Andy were still in the hotel sun lounge, going over and over the traumatic events at Dramglass House the previous evening. Julie, meanwhile, had been dispatched on the first ferry of the morning in her BMW to Broadford air strip with a carefully-packaged baseball bat to be sent on the daily flight to Glasgow, and thence via police courier to her forensic colleagues in Edinburgh. But, even in the absence of the baseball bat, Andy was still anxious for the immediate and long-term integrity of his limbs and, perhaps, his more vital bodily parts as well . . .

"Honest, skipper, that Dr Max gadgie's got ma number. Tellin' ye, it was uncanny! He could see right through me like he had x-ray eyes. Talk about yer Clark Kents!"

"Yeah, and it's not as if there's anything transparent about you, Green, is it?"

Andy failed to perceive the irony. "That's right, boss. Bloody uncanny, intit! Anyway, now that ma cover's knackered, maybe I should just disappear until this is all over, eh? I was thinkin' somewhere like New Zealand would be no too bad. I mean, I've got an auntie there and everything. Yeah, Auntie Senga, ma mother's sister, like. Lives in a wee place called Glen Aft —"

"Forget it, Green! We've got a job to do, and you're staying put right here until the death — figuratively speaking or otherwise. Now, think hard. What was the name that Dannato Cornamusa came out with for the guy who was stiffed at North Berwick?"

"I cannae remember."

"*Try* to remember, for Christ's sake! It could be the key to everything."

"Yeah, but that Max bampot and his two gorillas up at the big house — they're gonna be comin' after me any minute now, and then what am I —"

"For*get* Max and his gorillas! How many times have I got to tell you — the housekeeper told Dr Julie on the phone this morning that the two bozos are basket cases, all safely tucked up in bed with concussion, OK?"

"OK, but why don't ye just go up there and arrest their boss? Nick him for threatenin' a police officer or somethin'?"

Bob took a deep breath and counted to ten. "Because, Green, it's only your word against his that you *were* threatened. And also, he still doesn't know you're a copper, does he? Think about it. It's more likely that he might just decide to charge *you* with GBH against *his* two minders!"

"But I keep tellin' ye, Chief, I never touched them."

"I know, I know, Captain Midnight materialised out of nowhere, felled them, then did a runner. Tell that to a jury, especially with your dabs on the felling weapon."

Andy's face fell. "But I thought I was doin' the right thing," he said disconsolately, "like bringin' the bat back for evidence an' that."

"Yeah, yeah, you did well, Green. It's just a pity you hadn't wrapped a hankie round the bat handle, that's all." He put on a solemn face. "And you better say your prayers that neither of those two heavies kicks the bucket."

Bob knew only too well, however, that the main threat to Andy Green would be Max's keenness, in the light of the bungled attempt to extort information from him about the missing money from the North Berwick filling station episode, to have the "exercise of persuasion" revived at the earliest opportunity. From Bob's point of view, though, he either had to gamble

258

that Green would be in no danger for as long as Max's two hit men were incapacitated, or he had to play safe and send him back to the relative security of Police HQ in Edinburgh, thus risking the loss of the one good lead that they'd had to date. All things considered, there really was only one option open to him, the trick being to keep young Green from losing his nerve while still using him as a human carrot. Confuse and control — that had to be the maxim.

Andy Green was already confused, though perhaps not quite enough, in Bob's opinion. So, no time like the present to put that right . . .

"You can bet your kilt, Green," he said flatly, "that Max or his moll will be watching the pier from an upstairs window in the big house all day now."

"Christ! Expectin' backup heavies, are they?"

"No — in case you shoot the crow on the ferry. Then it would just be a question of how far back down the road from the isles you'd get before you were wasted by one of Max's mainland mob." Shaking his head gravely, Bob pursed his bottom lip. "Yeah, I reckon you wouldn't get any further than Glen Shiel, twenty minutes maximum from the Skye Bridge. You'd be away in the lonely moors between the mountains — a perfect place for a sniper to pick you off. Could be weeks before your body was found in the wrecked BMW at the bottom of one of those deep gulleys there."

Green swallowed hard, as if trying to down a golf ball. "So, I'll just need to lock maself in ma room here again, right?"

"*Au contraire*, lad," Bob blithely countered. "High profile — that's the name of your game now. Yes, see and be seen, mix among the locals, tell them you've decided to hang about here indefinitely, keep dishing out the millionaire scrap-dealer patter, give them a tune on your bagpipes occasionally. Believe, me, that's the way to bamboozle hoods like Max — let 'em know they don't scare you."

"But he *does* scare me! Honest, skipper, if I had anything left in ma guts after chuckin' up outside the big house stables last night, I'd be shittin' bricks right now."

Bob conjured up a calming laugh. "Nah, you've got *no* worries, son. Guys like Max Marsala never dirty their own hands with the victim's blood, and there's no way that floozie of his could kill a man." He gave Andy a playful punch on the shoulder and added suggestively, "Except over a long period of time, maybe, and then only in the nicest possible way, eh?"

The wisecrack was lost on Andy. "Whatever you say, Chief," he mumbled dolefully. "Just tell me what you want me to do . . ."

Bob looked out of the window towards the smiddy, where the tractor-mounted Franco was about to deposit the first chunk of rusting motor car onto the grass. "Well, for starters," he said, intrigued, "you could get yourself down there and see what your chum Cornamusa's up to. Oh, and one other thing — for God's sake try to wheedle the real name of that North Berwick murder victim out of him again." He grabbed Andy's arm as he stood up to leave. "But bloody well remember it this time, OK — even if you've got to carve it on the palm of your hand with the business end of your sgian-dhu!"

TWO HOURS LATER — THE BAR OF THE DRAMGLASS HOTEL . . .

Julie had made her return journey on the ferry that brought the daily newspapers over from Skye. Angus had shipped a bigger consignment than usual today, due to the local interest generated by the articles centred on the new laird.

"£100K JUNK JUNKET" one headline ran, "WEL(D) DONE, CORNAMUSA" another, "SCRAP ART OR 'S CRAP ART?" asked *The Daily Record*, while the stately *Scotsman* contrarily announced, "PRE-COLUMBAN CHRISTIAN ARTEFACTS FOUND IN HEBRIDES".

Julie read one of the typical tabloid pieces to Bob:

"The sexy Italian sculptor, Dannato Cornamusa, interviewed exclusively aboard his luxury motor yacht while cruising round his Hebridean hideaway island of Muckle Floggit yesterday, pushed a lock of golden hair back from his tanned forehead and said:

'Sure, you can compare me to Michelangelo, only I'm much younger, a lot better looking, and I can pull the birds easier!'

When asked his opinion on the work of Britain's Henry Moore, he replied:

'Great! Magic! I loved everything the guy did, but for me, Sean Connery will always be the 007!'

Even allowing for language difficulties, it has to be said that Dannato Cornamusa — apparently unknown in his native land, despite his claimed international reputation — failed to give satisfactory answers to any of the more important social questions which I then put to him. Questions like:

How much do you really intend to spend on improving living conditions for the locals on Muckle Floggit?

Is it a fact that you sprinkle powdered rhino horn on your spaghetti Bolognese instead of parmesan cheese?

Is the whisper that you regularly have sex up to fifty times a week with as many partners really true?

Did you truly once enter an All-Italy Mr Penis Contest and come first, second and third?

These and many more probing questions were fielded and skilfully kicked into touch by Cornamusa's no-nonsense manager, the dynamic New York entrepreneur, Dr Max Marsala, among whose many past celebrity clients, I can exclusively reveal, have been Champion The Wonder Horse and Lassie — neither of them noted for their great sculpting talents either.

And it was on this artistic note that my interview ended. Dashing Dannato, a bronzed, muscular arm encircling the scantily-clad, curvaceous body of his latest live-in sex kitten, Hollywood

262

starlet Lulu-May (38-22-36), then announced in his macho Italian accent that he would earn the £100K fee offered by a mystery millionaire scrap metal dealer by starting work on his new sculpture today, in public and . . . IN SCRAP METAL!

Watch this column, folks, to find out if Dishy Dannato comes good by sculpting a steel masterpiece, or bombs by dropping a king-size clanger."

"Scintillating stuff, Bob yawned. He opened *The Scotsman* and scanned Mike Gibson's piece on the supposed Saint Gubligan's Scrolls.

Julie tapped her tabloid with a finger. "When the guy here says, 'watch this column', how can he cover the continuing sculpture saga when he's not even here?"

"Same as his mates on the other rags. They use Scoop Stewart as a stringer." Bob tapped *The Scotsman* with his finger. "Mike Gibson here told me about it."

"You mean Scoop scoots down here from Broadford to check on progress occasionally, then beams the griff to the various papers in Glasgow or wherever?"

"That's it — the old usual. They get a snippet or two from the stringer and make the rest up. Scarcely need to leave the pub. Nah, you won't see any of that bunch up here again, unless something big breaks." Bob read his paper for a minute, then whistled through his teeth. "Yeah, and this article of Mike's could well be what triggers it off!"

"How come?"

Bob pulled pensively at his top lip. "I'm not sure yet, but if my hunch is right, mad Max up at the big house isn't going to be a happy camper when he reads this."

At that, Andy Green slouched in through the door from the street. He headed straight for the table by the lobby door where Bob and Julie were seated.

"Aw, heh, glad I found ye in here," he puffed. "I'm Christmas crackered — totally shagged. Been helpin' Dannato, see." With a heart-rending look, he appealed to Bob, "Any chance o' a sub for a pie and a pint? All that liftin' and humpin's got me well Hank Marvin again, like."

Bob got to his feet quickly. "No, no, I insist," he said aloud, in an effort to negate any of Andy's indiscreet request for an advance that may have been overheard by ever-alert local ears at the bar. "My round, definitely! You've already been *much* too generous since we met on this trip. Pint, was it . . . and a pie?"

"OK, if ye really insist," Andy replied at a similar volume as he flopped onto a chair. "But, ehm, on second thoughts, make that *two* pies and a packet o' cheese and onion crisps as well as the pint for me, Bob. There's a good lad."

Ignoring Julie's smirks, Bob bent down and muttered in Andy's ear, "You better have some useful info for me, boy, or two bloody pies and a packet o' cheese and onion crisps'll be taking the short route to your large intestine!"

On Bob's return from the bar, Andy took the wise precaution of rapidly ingesting the snack conventionally

264

before declaring, "I *tried* to pump him about the name o' the croaked North Berwick Eyetie. Honest! I mean, that's why I've been so long helpin' him an' that. But he just clammed up. Wouldn't even tell me how he got a black eye. What a brammer, by the way! Aye, he just kept smilin' and sayin' he couldn't remember anything about last night. Says he was too stoned." Andy shook his head. "He's tellin' porkies, though. Oh aye, I could see that easy enough, like."

While Bob silently fumed, Andy Green went on to recount at great length how Dannato had only been interested in getting his assurance that the one hundred thousand pound fee was going to be forthcoming as soon as the sculpture was complete, no matter what. In reply to Andy's query as to why he had decided to proceed with the work against his manager's instructions, Dannato had explained that he was Sicilian and, therefore, a man of his word. He had then confided that, despite the outward trappings of wealth, he would be "right in-a the shit" without that fee.

"Which means he could be nothing more than a front man," Bob quietly reasoned, "and a front man with financial problems at that."

"That would square with what I overheard when I was having the cuppa with Flora," Julie said.

"Search me," Andy shrugged. "All I know is that I felt a right turd, standin' there promisin' I was sound for a hundred grand." He looked appealingly at Bob. "I mean, what in the name o' the wee man am I gonna do when he finishes his statue?"

"How long did he say it would take?" Bob asked.

"Coupla days, top whack."

"Which gives him one day more to do his work than we've got to do ours. So, I wouldn't worry too much about welching on the deal, Green, because if we haven't cracked those North Berwick murders by tomorrow night, we'll be on the first ferry out of here the following morning — with you hidden in the BMW boot, *if* that'll make you feel any less of a turd."

Julie, who had been sitting thinking during all of this, suddenly thumped the table with her fist and called out, "FRANKIE BOY!"

Bob and Andy, along with the gathered ensemble over at the bar, turned their heads to see who had just come in.

"No, no," Julie said in more discreet tones to her two companions, while simultaneously flashing a contrite smile to the curious coterie across the room, "I wasn't saying hello to somebody, I just remembered a snatch of the verbals I picked up down the kitchen chimney when I was having that cuppa with old Flora. Frankie boy — that's what Max kept calling Dannato Cornamusa." She turned to Andy. "Does that jog your memory any?"

Andy's eyes widened. "FRANCO!" he yelled, causing the bar brigade to look to the door once again.

"Keep it down, Green, for God's sake," Bob muttered behind his hand.

Andy lowered his voice to almost a whisper. "Yeah, but that's what Dannato said his stiffed cousin was called, see. Franco somethin'!"

266

"OK, we're halfway there," Julie said. "Just keep saying Franco to yourself, Andy. Let your mind go blank and the surname will soon come to you."

"His mind's permanently bloody blank," Bob curtly reminded her. "Come on, Green. *Think!* What was that damned surname?"

Andy Green closed his eyes tightly and rolled his head back into the thinking position. "Franco . . . Franco . . . Franco," he droned hypnotically. "Franco . . . Co . . . Ca . . . Cu . . . I'm goin' through the alphabet here." A smile of impending success slowly spread over his boyish features. "Yeah, Franco Cu . . . Cun . . . Cunt-somethin'," he grinned. "That could maybe be it!" He re-opened one eye and glanced hesitantly at Bob for a reaction.

"Franco Cunt-something," Bob repeated in a stunned monotone, his expression one of explosive incredulity.

"I *don't* think so, Andy," Julie interjected, a note of humane deliverance in her voice. "I mean, without a dictionary, I can't be absolutely certain, but I'm *fairly* sure that C — U — N — T isn't a progression of letters to be found in the Italian language, except in some colloquial context that I'm maybe not familiar with, of course."

Glowering at Green, Bob Burns stifled the temptation to use that very progression of letters in a context that *he* was certainly familiar with — in English. "Get a grip," Green, he growled, the rein on his patience now strained to breaking point. "Try to dredge the guy's surname out of that cesspit of a mind of yours!"

Julie decided to give the scholarly approach a go. "Let's go back and try the other vowels instead of U, Andy" she suggested. "I and E are out, because in Italian that would make the C sound like C-H, as in *cheese* and *checkers* respectively. So, that leaves us with A and O." She gave young Green a primary schoolteacher's smile of gentle encouragement. "Now, does that help you a bit?"

Andy Green gave a slack-jawed shake of the head in return. "Eh, just hang on a minute, Doc. I'm still tryin' to work out the cheese and checkers stuff, like."

The hotel receptionist popped her head round the door. "Phone for you, Mr Burns. Euan Stewart from the *Isle of Skye Herald*."

Julie gamely persevered, albeit fruitlessly, with her alphabet work on Andy while Bob took the call at reception.

"Franco *Contadino*," he said brusquely on his return, sitting back down at the table and giving Green a how-does-that-grab-you? look.

Green was amazed. "Heh, bull's-eye, boss! But — but how did ye manage to —?"

"Scoop Stewart just told me on the phone there," Bob said matter-of-factly.

Julie was astounded. "Wow! I mean, I've heard of extrasensory perception, but this is ridiculous!"

"Nah, just a happen," Bob said, a well-pleased smile on his face. "And he wasn't telling me it as Cornamusa's cousin's name. He knows nothing about that angle. No, he was telling me it as Cornamusa's *own* name. Seems Scoop's had the London office of the *Wel(d) Done, Cornamusa* tabloid on the blower. They ran the piece, complete with mug shot, in their English editions this morning, and they've had several people — a bank manager, a bookie, the owner of an Italian restaurant in Edgeware Road, and some Irish bird — on the phone to say they recognise him from the photo. They all said they might've been fooled by the dyed blonde hair, but the dark-coloured yachtie's cap blew the disguise."

"So, who or what is Franco Contadino, alias Dannato Cornamusa?" Julie asked.

"An ex-waiter in London is all we know so far."

Julie didn't seem particularly surprised. "What now, then?"

"Scoop Stewart and his Fleet Street mates are going to sit on the Cornamusa-unmasked story until they've raked up all the muck they can on the guy in London and Italy. It'll make for a more sensational exposé that way, they reckon — more journalistically attractive to the discerning tabloid reader." Bob hunched his shoulders. "Not that it matters to me one way or the other. It's the *dead* Franco Contadino I'm interested in." He looked at his watch. "Mmm, still only half-seven in the morning New York time. Better give it another couple of hours, then I'll get my man in the FBI on the case." Rubbing his hands together, he grinned, "OK, so even if one swallow doesn't make a summer, it's a damned sight better than none in the bush. Let's have another drink!"

Julie's attention was drawn to someone peeping round the street door. It was old Flora MacGubligan, gesturing urgently to her. Catching on fast that Flora didn't want to run the gauntlet of the worthies at the bar, Julie signalled her to join them by coming round by the main hotel entrance. This Flora duly did, though the final two steps from the lobby to their table were taken with obvious reluctance.

"Losh me," she panted, all of a fluster as she sat down with her back to the pointing, muttering huddle at the bar, "I've never once set foot in one of these here places in my whole life, so I've not!" She fanned her burning cheeks with a beer mat.

Bob offered her his hand. "I was just about to order," he said. "Burns is the name — Bob Burns."

"MacGubligan," Flora replied. "Mrs."

"And, uh, I think you've already met our friend Mr Green here," Bob continued. "So, ehm, can I tempt you with a drink? Nice cooling gin and tonic, maybe — plenty ice and lemon?"

"Certainly *not*, Mr Burns!" Flora was fair black-affronted, and she said so. My goodness to heavens, she had never allowed strong drink to pass her lips in her whole life, so she hadn't, and she was *not* about to start now at her age. So, she would have nothing at all, thank you very much — not even a glass of water — for it was bad enough to be seen in one of them here places without being seen drinking in it as well! She cast Julie an apologetic glance, then added, "Mind you, it's different for your cheneration, lass — more free and easy altogether, what with yon pill thingamychig and all them other modern personal appliances and everything like that." Flora was obviously ill at ease.

Julie laid a reassuring hand on hers. "What's happened, Flora? I've never seen you so hot and bothered."

"Och, it's yon Dr Max," Flora panted. "He's got me fair up to high doh with all his sweary words and his bad manners *and* his buttocks-nipping chinks behind your back when you're not even looking." Flora dabbed a tear from her eye. "If it wasna for our wee tied cottage and my Shooie's chob, I would be tendering the resignation of my services right away without further notice." With her forearms, she nudged her cardigan-clad bosoms into a more comfy lie and divulged, "Mind you, though, it's not me myself that I'm bothered about, for losh knows the heathen things I've witnessed and tholed without a word of complaint when Mr Sid was the laird. No, no, it's chust the ill-kinded kind of way Dr Max treats poor Mr Dannato that fashes me something terrible." Flora looked at Andy. "You likely thought I was away home chust after I cleared away the dishes last night, Mr Green, did you not now?" Andy nodded his affirmation, and she went on, "Well, I was *not* away home at all, for I was still in the big house, in a place where I could fine hear what was going on in the parlour, as I like to call it. Aye, aye, and I can tell youse all this fair and square-like that it was Dr Max his-self that was after skelping Mr Dannato on the keeker after you was bundled out of the house by yon two muckle sumphs, Mr Green. *Ochone*," Flora lamented, "the scandal of it all!" She took a moment to compose herself, then warbled, "Michtie me, good, God-fearing folk shouldna have to enchoor such terrible ongoings as that." Flora was getting well wound up now, her upwardly-nudging forearms rhythmically engaged as she prepared for delivery of the climax of her address. "I'm telling you this, Miss Julie lass — even although you gave me the wink not to get yon Dr Max's birse up for fear of my very life, I'm right sore tempted all the same to get on the telephone to Constable MacClue at Broadford and report the man for his malishus, heathen-like ways."

Sensing that Bob was about to blurt out something that, as a supposed naturalist, he really shouldn't, Julie quickly put in, "Uhm, no, contacting PC MacClue wouldn't be the thing to do, Flora. Not just yet, at any rate." She then nipped the old woman's attempted objection in the bud by adding, "You've got to trust me on this one, Flora. Forces even greater than PC MacClue are at work on the shady dealings that are attributed to Dr Max Marsala." She gave Flora a stern look and said in a matching voice, "Your continued confidentiality is *essential*, OK?"

Flora shot Julie a quizzical look and *replied* in a matching voice, "Are you *sure* you're not in the polis, like somebody was maybe saying to me a while back?"

Julie merely put a finger to her lips and repeated, "Confidentiality *essential*. Trust me."

Flora took a tense sideways glance at the bar, then whispered to Julie, "Remember you said I was to tell you if ever I was hearing anything suspeeshus-like coming down the chimney in the kitchen?"

272

"Uh-huh."

"Well, it's chust that . . ." Stopping short, she looked nervously at Bob and Andy, then murmured to Julie, "Ehm, your friends here, and what you were saying there about the confidentiality being essential and all . . .?"

Julie assured the old woman that anything she had to say could safely be said in front of her two male companions.

Her confidence bolstered, Flora poked a work-worn finger and thumb into her cardigan pocket and pulled out a little piece of paper. Handing it to Julie, she confided, "I heard Dr Marsala saying that a wee while ago. Talking on the phone at the time, he was."

Julie ran her eyes over the message, then passed the note to Bob.

Fascinated, he read it out: "Eight — fifteen — one — twenty — thirty — fifty-seven — seven — six — nine . . ."

"Pickin' his lottery numbers for next Saturday, was he?" Andy Green quipped.

"No, no, Mr Green," Flora corrected in all seriousness, "somebody was reading the numbers to *him*!"

"And you're sure this is all correct?" Bob checked without taking his eyes off the paper. "You got it all down verbatim, did you, Mrs MacGubligan?"

"Oh aye, absolutely all correct, Mr Burns. Yes, there's no doubt about that at all. You see, he was saying the numbers terrible slow-like, as if he was maybe writing them down, and him maybe not too good at it, kind of ways." Flora was resolute. "Oh yes, yes indeed, the numbers is all chust as they came down the lum, and no doubt about it!"

Bob kneaded his forehead as he scanned the numbers again. "Weird. I just don't get this." He looked over the table at Flora's flushed, apprehensive face and said, "And that was it — end of telephone message?"

"Well, no, there *was* one other daft wee thing he said after the numbers was finished — kind of slow-like again, as if he was maybe writing it down as well, you know."

"And that was?"

"And that was . . ." Flora let out an unexpectedly girlish giggle. "And that was, 'The Sporran Connection'!"

THE MORNING ROOM OF DRAMGLASS MANSION HOUSE, MEANWHILE . . .

Max was already in a sour mood, and Mike Gibson's article in *The Scotsman* did nothing to sweeten it.

"What the fuck's all this chicken-shit baloney about anyway?" he barked, then hurled the newspaper over the coffee table at his two groggy minders, both nursing bandaged heads on the couch opposite.

As reading, even in a non-concussed state, would probably have been a problem for them in any case, it was no real surprise that they merely looked at the crumpled paper, but said nothing.

"A load a' friggin' good you schlubs is turnin' out to be! First ya let a goddam beanpole Limey kid mug ya wid yer own friggin' baseball bat — which, in addition also, has been snitched by said beanpole — then ya crawl outa yer stinkin' bunks at noon and sit there lookin' at me like ya just pissed yer pants or somethin'!" Max then turned his attention to Lulu-May, who was filing her fingernails while perched on her favourite high stool over by the French windows. "Hey, sweet lips, haul yer cute little ass over here pronto and read me that friggin' noozpaper story one more time, will ya?"

After an unhurried inspection of her nails, Lulu-May obliged.

"Yeah, yeah, yeah," Max butted in before she'd even completed the first sentence, "ya can skip all that holy-scrolls crap and get to the bit about the piece a' this island them dumb natives is supposed to own!"

Lulu-May obediently skipped to the relevant paragraph . . .

"The Reverend Richard Dick, while refusing to be drawn on the exact location, then revealed to me that a small area of the island, which had been sold to the islanders for a nominal sum by the previous laird, has since been discovered to be the site of what the Reverend Dick would only describe as a unique and recurring spiritual phenomenon. It is the Reverend's avowed intention to raise sufficient capital, not merely to open the site to the public, but to create facilities at the spot commensurate with the enormous numbers of visitors that he anticipates will be drawn there from all over the world, once the full story of the Miracle of Muckle Floggit has been told. It would appear that —"

"OK, button it! I heard enough already!" Max stomped over to the phone, while at the same time shouting over his shoulder to Lulu-May, "In that drawer there — yeah, in that sideboard by the window — dig out the sale schedule on this place and shout me the real estate agent's number, will ya?" Max ponderously punched in the digits as Lulu-May read them out. "Hello! Smythe, Hoare and Shaftesbury? . . . Yeah, I wanna speak wid the guy who clinched the sale a' Muckle Floggit wid Laprima Frittella. Nigel somethin', his handle is . . . "DON'T gimme none a' that in-conference baloney! Just tell him it's Max, Miss Frittella's broker, capeesh?" . . . "Yeah, that's it — Max, *Doctor* Max Marsala."

While the "hold" Musak tinkled in his ear, Max snapped his fingers at Lulu-May and growled, "Bring them sale particulars here, baby, and find the map a' the island. It's at the back a' the folder there somewhere."

"Hello! Hello, is this Nigel I'm speakin' wid?" . . . "OK, now listen, kid!" . . . "Ya trust *what*?" . . . "No, everything ain't hunky-friggin'-dory! What's wid all this crap I been readin' in the papers here — all this bullshit about them Scotch Limeys here ownin' a hunk a' this island or somethin'?" . . . "It's on the title deeds? Ya mean Laprima was wise to this?" . . . "Ya *thought* she was? Well, ya know what thought did, don'cha? Yeah, he shit his pants and thought he'd only whistled *Dixie* through his ass! Yeah, so don' gimme no *thought* crap!" . . . "Only a *tiny* cave, ya say?" . . . "And the patch a' land and one small cottage immediately above it?" . . . "And un-*what?*" Max looked as if he was about to self-combust. "Unfettered and unlimited access thereto from the pier, ya say? WHAT goddam pier?"

Max signalled Lulu-May to fetch him a blood pressure pill . . . two!

"Yeah, yeah, hold yer friggin' horses, bud!" he bellowed down the phone. "Lemme find it on the map here, for Chrisakes! South coast, ya say?" . . . "Prince Charlie's Rest, near the village of?" . . . "Uhm, yeah-h-h, now I see it. Kildoone." Max's face turned crimson, the veins at his temples throbbing and pulsing like a tangle of earthworms doing the conga. "KILDOONE?" he shrieked, horror-struck. He slammed the phone down and roared at his two stooges, "Youse guys get down to that church and bring this dickhead padre up here on the double! Yeah, and find me that Green kid wid the hundred grand. That mazooma's mine and I want it BACK — along wid the sonofabitch baseball bat!"

The heavies stumbled to their feet and headed for the door.

"And hey, get this but good!" Max snarled after them. "Screw up this time, and I gonna dress ya up as grouses, let ya loose on the mountain there, and use ya for friggin' target practice!"

A LITTLE LATER — BACK IN THE HOTEL BAR . . .

Andy Green having been sent forth once more to mingle with the local populace and generally keep a high, ostensibly-fearless profile, and old Flora having proceeded on her unenthusiastic way to Mohammed's Stores for more spaghetti-and-meatballs ingredients, Bob and Julie were left to ponder the cryptic possibilities of the numbers that the elderly housekeeper had overheard Max reciting on the telephone.

"Eight — fifteen — one — twenty — thirty — fifty-seven — seven — six — nine," Bob repeated for the umpteenth time. "I mean, if we assume that they're not phone or bank account numbers or anything as obvious as that, what are we left with? Lottery numbers, as Green suggested? Not British ones, anyway — the fifty-seven rules that out. Could be American or Irish ones, though — not that I'd know, of course. Then again, if Max really is this Plantano hood, maybe it's all something to do with some kind of New York numbers racket."

Julie, who was busy tapping away at a pocket calculator, looked up and frowned in disbelief. "You're joking, of course! Surely all that numbers-racket stuff went out with Elliot Ness and *The Untouchables* on black-and-white telly!" She returned to her computations. "No, Kemosabe, if there's anything illegal about these numbers, it'll be something a lot more subtle than that, I fancy. Hmm, there doesn't seem to be any obvious sequence involved, though. OK, let's have a look at some permutations, then . . ."

"Nah, forget all that advanced maths stuff. You're only flying round in ever-decreasing circles like the legendary ooya bird, and you know where that ended up." Bob's nose told him that a guy like Max didn't think like some boffin code-maker/breaker, so whatever these numbers meant, it was a cert that deciphering them would hardly require degree-level calculus. "Let's couple them up in pairs," he suggested. "Yeah, let's see what that throws up."

"That's exactly what I'm doing," Julie snapped, "but there are so many combinations."

"No, no, never mind your permutations and combinations." Bob grabbed the calculator and switched it off. "We aren't dealing with bloody Einstein here, you know!" He pointed to Flora's piece of paper. "Forget about adding, subtracting, multiplying and dividing. Let's just *look* at the numbers, two at a time at first."

"Whatever you say, Kemosabe," Julie shrugged. "You're the gumshoe."

"OK, eight and fifteen — what does that say to you?"

"Naff all!" Julie muttered, patently huffed. Stuffing the calculator back into her handbag, she added tartly, "I'm only a humble scientist, after all — totally unversed in the intellectual sophistications of high sleuthery!"

"That's right, so you are," Bob said, poker-faced. "But never mind, just pay attention and you might learn something. Right then, let's tag the next number on. That gives us eight — fifteen — one."

Julie scratched her head.

"No, *don't* think about it," Bob said. "Just tell me the first thing that comes into your mind. Eight — fifteen — one, OK?"

"Could be tomorrow's date — August 15th, 2001."

"There you are then. The first rule of sleuthery — don't think too much. Right, let's take a gander at the next two. Twenty — thirty. Anything spring immediately to mind?"

"Half past eight, twenty-four hour clock-wise?"

"Clever girl! See how brilliant you can be when you don't use your brains?" Bob pulled a wry smile. "Maybe you could teach the trick to Green. He should be a natural."

Julie had taken a liking to this numbers game. "Come on," she urged, "hit me with the next two. Go on, I'm not thinking, so just shout them out!"

"OK, fifty-seven and seven."

"Uhm.. nothing!" Julie shook her head in frustration. "No good, I'm starting to think about them. Quick, give me the next pair."

"Six and nine."

Julie shook her head again. "Nope, still zilch. Maybe your no-think theory's a bummer after all, huh?"

"I don't think so . . . if that's not a contradiction in terms."

"You mean you've sussed what the last four numbers mean?"

"You tell me. You're supposed to be the map-reading expert."

Julie nodded her head slowly. "Aha, *now* I get your drift. We've got a date and a time. Now we need a place, and you think these numbers are a map reference, right?"

"I'm trying not to think, but I *think* they could be . . . if you see what I mean. Are you still carting that map of the island around with you, by any chance?"

Julie rummaged in the side pocket of her handbag. "Here we are — one OS map of Muckle Floggit." She unfolded it on the table, then, glancing at Flora's piece of paper, murmured, "Fifty-seven degrees, seven minutes . . . that'll be north. OK, got it. Now, six degrees, nine minutes west." She ran her finger over the map. "That's it. Right, let's see where that leads us." Using a square beer mat as an improvised ruler, she plotted the two references until they met. She then marked the spot with a cross and pushed the map over to Bob, a glint of intrigue-tinged surprise in her eyes.

"Well, well, well," Bob smiled, "it seems Kildoone isn't such a forgotten village after all, eh? Mmm, I reckon we'd better make some discreet arrangements to get ourselves around there before half past eight tomorrow night."

The street door clattered open, and there stood Max's minders, silhouetted against the distant Cuillin Hills like a couple of baddies in a spaghetti western. They lingered there for a few moments, unmoving, but presumably surveying the spartan interior of the bar from behind their dark glasses. Total silence and several pairs of suspicious local eyes followed them as they swaggered over to the bar.

"Scotch! Two shots!"

The barman indicated the admirable range of whiskies on the gantry behind him. "Would there be any particular brand you fancy, chentlemen? We have everything here from the best Islay single Hebridean malt to yon blended stuff from places on the mainland like Perth and —"

With no more than a sideways flick of a hand, the spokesminder directed him in no uncertain manner to cut the spiel and pour the drinks. "The padre," he grunted. "We been lookin' for him at the church. Ain't there."

"Ah, well now, if it's a wee bit spiritual uplift you're looking for," the barman said with a congenial smile, "it's likely you'll need to be waiting a wee while yet. Aye, for the Reverend went over to Skye on church business this morning. Dropped in here for his usual wee stomach-settler before the sea voyage, so he did. Mmm-hmm, said he wouldna likely be back until the evening. Ach, but never mind, lads," the barman beamed, "you can replenish your spirits chust fine here in the meantime." He inclined his head gantrywards and winked. "It's a wider selection of the uplifters we have here than you'll be blessed with at old Holy Dick's in any case. Do you not think so?"

"Green," the more verbose of the two heavies rasped. "The scrap guy. He in?"

"Och, man, but you've chust missed him," the barman said, then gestured towards the table where

Bob and Julie were seated. "But look you over yonder. Aye, maybe his two chums there can tell you where he's went."

Julie had to fight hard to restrain herself from whistling the theme from *The Good, The Bad and The Ugly* as the thugs ambled towards them and stopped in front of Bob.

"Green," the head heavy reiterated. "Where'd he go?"

"Mr Green?" Bob replied offhandedly. "Haven't a clue, mate."

The two pairs of dark glasses were then re-directed down at Julie.

"Me neither, boys," she shrugged. "Who wants to know, anyway?"

"Me!"

"And who, pray, are you," Julie enquired with an exaggeratedly lofty air, "apart from being poor imitations of *The Blues Brothers*, that is?"

Bob could visualise the four eyes narrowing into squints of befuddled rage behind those dark glasses. Farcical figures as they appeared, it would have been a rash person indeed who ignored the mindless violence a couple of goons like this could be capable of.

"You want Mr Green, do you?" he chipped in, judiciously adopting a more interested attitude this time. "I'd try down at the blacksmith's, if I were you. He's probably checking on how his hundred-thousand-pound commission's coming along." Then, unable to resist a provocative jibe, he said, "Yes, you'd scarcely credit it, but he can hardly wait to see it finished, because the money's burning a hole in his sporran."

As Julie gave Bob's ankle a kick under the table, the drone and skirl of bagpipes striking up oscillated in through the open door. All heads turned towards the source of the clamour — the patch of grass down by the pier, where the metallic foundation of that selfsame hundred-thousand-pound commission had earlier been laid. Andy Green, it appeared, had decided to take out the insurance of adopting the highest of profiles by leading a lunch-break procession, headed by Franco and followed by half-a-dozen delighted children, up through the village.

The two thugs thumped their empty glasses on the table and made a beeline for the door.

Julie prepared to follow them.

Bob grabbed her wrist. "*Hold* it! The two gorillas aren't gonna risk touching Green with the whole of Dramglass looking out of their windows." He nodded at her handbag. "Got any paper hankies in there?"

"Yes. Why?"

Bob stood up, shielding the table from possible prying eyes at the bar. "Pick up these two whisky glasses nice and carefully," he whispered, "then wrap them in some tissues and stash them in your handbag, swift as you like. We'll get these down south to our fingerprint mates on tomorrow's mail plane from Skye."

It was then that the distressed squawk and yowl of bagpipes being unwillingly deflated gave the lie to Bob's belief in Andy Green's temporary immunity from danger. The two heavies had apparently deemed it less hazardous to pounce on their victim in full view of the villagers than risk their boss's wrath by returning empty-handed. Followed by a clutch of worthies from the bar, Bob and Julie ran into the street in time to witness the start of a good-going free-for-all. The two thugs were already struggling to unravel Andy's flailing arms from a tangle of bagpipe drones, while a few of the more daredevil children punched, kicked and pulled at the assailants' legs. Franco, meanwhile, shouted words of encouragement to the *bambino* battlers — in Italian and from a shrewd distance.

"Stand back!" Bob shouted at Julie, who had already started to sprint towards the fracas. "Leave this to me! I'm trained for it." With that, he prised two battling wee boys off the spokesminder's legs, then attempted to put a half-Nelson on him. However, a viciously-delivered elbow to the solar plexus immediately had Bob lying flat on his back at Julie's feet, struggling for breath, his mouth opening and closing like a newly-netted haddock's.

"Stay there!" Julie yelled down at him. "You'll only get yourself hurt!"

Although barely up to the thug's shoulders on her tiptoes, Julie pluckily sunk a stiletto heel into his instep, choked off his resultant howl of agony with a karate chop to the throat, kneed him in the groin, and, as he buckled over in agony, finally sent him to sleep with a rabbit punch.

"It pays to be able to look after yourself if you're wee," she informed the prostrate and purple-faced Bob

Burns, while dusting off her hands and preparing to have a go at the second heavy. It was only then she saw that Flora MacGubligan, on her return journey from Mohammed's Stores, had already launched an attack on him herself.

"Try that sauce for your meatballs!" Flora yelled as she swung a string shopping bag loaded with two large tins of plum tomatoes, a netful of onions and two pounds of mince through a hundred and eighty degrees. The missile clunked with a nauseating squelch into the second heavy's wedding tackle, setting him up perfectly for Julie to deliver her second rabbit punch of the day. No further action was necessary.

"There's chust far, far too much violence about nowadays," Flora sighed while checking her tomato tins for damage. "I mean to say, a body isn't even safe walking the street here in the broad daylight now." She glanced disdainfully down at the decked duo, then commented, "Aye, what with wild animals like this pair on the rampage and all."

"Ay-y-y, nice-a one, *Signora* Flora!" Franco gushed as he stepped boldly forward to give her a congratulatory kiss on both cheeks. "You now being the lady world-a champion!" He threw his arms around her. "*Si, campionessa mondiale*, eh!"

"Och, Mr Dannato," Flora fluttered, cheeks ablaze, "you've went and got me all flichtered-like again with all yon romantic foreign words of yours and everything." Reluctantly freeing herself from Franco's hug, she pulled herself together enough to say to Andy, "And now you can chust get your bagpipes sorted out for a nice wee skirl again, Mr Green." Then, as an afterthought, she added, "Yes, and there's been no harm done at all, for I noticed your big drone was out of chune anyhow!"

CHAPTER
FIFTEEN

It was an assertive crowd of islanders who met the Reverend Dick off the evening ferry. Word of the shameful incident in the village that afternoon had reached even the remotest crofts, and it seemed that at least one representative from every family on the island had gathered on the pier to demand action from the two leaders of their little community, the minister and the Provost-cum-ferrymaster himself. Naturally, the deferential Angus had already briefed Mr Dick on the dreadful affair during the short crossing over the Sound of Stooshie. Although the Reverend had been tippling away discreetly at the whisky-laced tea in his Thermos flask during the tedious bus journey back from Portree, where he had been summoned by senior members of the Kirk Synod to explain his Saint Gubligan's Scrolls revelations in *The Scotsman*, he was, as ever, still very much in possession of his faculties. Taking up his pulpit stance at the open window of Angus's wheelhouse, he addressed the disaffected congregation below . . .

"Dearest friends and fellow citizens of this God-given island —"

"Aye, but God gave it to the bluidy laird," a voice interrupted from within the gathered assembly, "and not to us citizens!"

That released a deluge of mutterings of support . . .

"Right enough, and it's high time something was done about it!"

"Down with these damned lairds and their scunners of hangers-on and everything!"

"That's it! Muckle Floggit for the people!"

"Chust see today's papers! Not a word about improving *our* lot!"

"Aye, too true! They had plenty to say about bluidy hundred-thousand-pound scrap statchoos and yon Yankee lassie with the page three mess-yoorments, but never a cheep about getting shot of our outside lavvies and the sheep shite in the water supply!"

"Damned lairds! Chust lies and broken promises from the lot of them all the time, so it is!"

The Reverend Dick raised his hands to quell the mounting pandemonium. "Be at peace, my friends," he intoned. "I beseech you to be of calm hearts, for I am with you, and your sorrows and sufferings also are mine."

"Aye, but you can count *your* sorrows in comfort," came an anonymous call from down on the pier, "for you have the electric heating in the manse, and most of *us* haven't even got the electricity at all!"

"Correct!" shouted someone else. "And while the most of us ones is on the dole, you have a damned good minister's wage for to be doing your suffering on!"

The minister lowered head and shook it gravely. "Ah, but I fear not for much longer, my good man. You see, I was warned by my superiors today that, following the revelations published in the *Scotsman* newspaper, my post as pastor of this fine parish could be in jeopardy, if I do not agree to apportion a considerable percentage of any potential revenues from our Saint Gubligan's miracle to, uhm — for want of a better name — head office."

An astounded hush fell upon the gathered islanders.

Clasping his hands below his scraggy chin, the Reverend Dick closed his eyes and said in lugubrious tones, "My future, kind folk, is in your honest hands alone."

Nip MacGubligan's voice was the first to rise above the ensuing mumblings. "Any miracle money that will be coming in is ours, and we want the Reverend Dick to stay on and manage the business for us!" he proclaimed, ever mindful of the likely amelioration of his own financial fortunes as the "creator" of *Saint Gubligan's Tears*. After all, the miracle, without the complicity of the churchman whose finding of the scrolls sparked its discovery, would be no miracle at all.

"Hear! Hear!" Angus shouted from the doorway of his wheelhouse, his own motives for standing by the Reverend even more mercenary than Nip's. As head elder of the Dramglass Kirk Session, he would be jointly responsible with the minister for the administration of any future miracle moneys, after all, so he promptly declared, "By long-standing endowment from a chenerous laird of yesteryear, the Dramglass Parish

290

Kirk belongs to the people of Muckle Floggit, and if we say the Reverend Dick stays as our minister, then, by the stars, the Reverend Dick stays as our minister, no matter what the Cheneral Assembly of the Kirk Ecksecutive away over in Portree says!"

"And who is it that's going to be paying his wages, though?" someone hollered.

"Saint Gubligan, ye daft eejit that you are!" Angus boomed. "Who in God's name else would you expeck to be paying his bluidy wages?"

Muted mutterings of, "Better the devil you know when it comes to ministers," and similar irreverent sentiments rippled through the crowd. Therefore, when Angus called for a show of hands to approve this unilateral declaration of independence from the Kirk Synod, a clear majority were raised, albeit somewhat grudgingly.

The Reverend Dick then cast his eyes heavenward and sermonised, "Praise be, for this is the most moving, the most humbling, the most blessed moment of my life, dear friends. For lo! the flock has come to the rescue of the shepherd in his hour of peril." He buttressed his fingers and droned, "Ah yes, we have here a parable fit to have been told by the Saviour Himself."

"Aye, well, now that you're to be working for us," a cynical voice piped up, "how about getting yourself up to the big house with the Provost there, and tell that young laird and his bunch of hard cases chust what we think of them!"

Another upsurge of vocal support rose up from the pier . . .

"Damned right! We've had enough of yon machine guns scaring the daylights out of our wee birdies up on Ben Doone."

"Aye, and we've had enough of gangster-like chappies chumping on tourists on the street — especially ones playing the pipes!"

"You've said it! And don't you be forgetting to get stuck into the laird about all yon idle promises. We want money spent on our amenities right *now*, or he can go to hell, so he can!"

"Well said! If he thinks he can bugger us about like the rest of his ilk before him, we'll run him off the island — him and his thug pals and the whole chingbang of it!"

The roar of assent that erupted from the crowd had Angus's eyebrows flapping up and down like bunting in a gale. All this sudden laird-expelling talk did not augur well for his chances of ever picking up the ten percent of said laird's hundred-thousand-quid sculpture fee for "arranging" official permission for it to be erected on the wee green just up from the pier.

"Control yourselfs, for Christ's sake!" he thundered, then threw a belated nod of apology in the minister's direction. "There will never be any civil disobedience in Dramglass for as long as *I* am the Provost!"

"Is that a fact now?" yelled a resolute citizen. "Well, you better chust get what we want from the laird, Mr Provost, or we'll vote you out chust as fast as we've chust been after voting old Holy Dick there back in!"

FIFTEEN MINUTES LATER — THE DRAWING ROOM OF DRAMGLASS MANSION HOUSE . . .

"The preacher! Hey, the very guy I was wantin' to talk wid," Max said from his high-backed armchair as Lulu-May ushered in the minister, closely attended by old Angus. "Grab a pew, padre, if ye'll pardon the expression."

The Reverend Dick smiled coldly and asked to see Mr Cornamusa.

"The lord of the manor has retired early to his bedchamber," Max enunciated in mock butlerspeak, before reverting to his nasal Bowery twang to add, "but there ain't nothin' ya can say to him widout first sayin' it to me, so shoot!"

The Reverend shrugged then proceeded to impart the views of the islanders, as instructed.

"Hold on a goddam minute there, padre, if ye'll excuse the language," Max butted in before the minister had gone much beyond his preamble. "Mr Cornamusa ain't responsible for what no noozpaper bums say about what he is or ain't gonna spend on his investment here. Capeesh?"

"Yes, but irrespective of that," the minister protested, "he does still have an obligation to improve the living conditions of his —"

"Obligation nothin'! The people here been livin' wid them conditions long before my client hit the scene. Correct or otherwise? Yeah, correct! So, even if he don't do nothin', they ain't gonna be no worse off than they was before. Correct? You betcha, correct again!"

"Perhaps, but —"

"Perhaps, but zilch!"

Angus cleared his throat and started to chip in his pennyworth. "As Chairperson of Muckle Floggit Island Council, it behoves me to inform you that a dim view is taken of the use of machine guns for the grouse shooting, and I have to advise you that —"

"Blanks! I was firin' blanks! Any law against that?"

Angus had to think about that one.

"Correctóla, Mac! I'm innocent, as friggin' usual!" Max then crouched forward into the attack posture. "Now get this straight. I ain't here to knock off yer goddam grouses, for which I don' give Jack Shit anyway, and in addition also, I ain't here to act as no Santy Claus for no goddam natives. All I'm here for is to see that my client's investment is up and runnin' smooth, then I'm outa this sonofabitch place faster than you guys can hump a haggis." He held up a cigar-toting hand to silence the minister's attempted interruption. "But on the subject of improvin' livin' conditions for the natives here — which, I repeat, my client ain't under no obligation to do — there could be a deal lined up for ya to help them help themselves, if ya get where I'm comin' from."

Both the Reverend and Angus indicated that they neither got where he was coming from nor, indeed, where he was going to.

"OK, allow me to elucidize." Max settled back in his chair and explained through billows of cigar smoke how it had only just come to his attention that a certain insignificant dot on the map, a certain piece-a'-shit cave

294

called Prince Charlie's Rest, had been excluded from the subjects of sale when his client's company bought the island, and while this cave was worth diddly squat to anybody, his client would be willing to make a generous offer for it. "Just so as to keep the subjects of his investment *virgo intacta*, to use the Eyetalian legal term," Max said in conclusion.

The minister swapped a sly glance with Angus, then enquired, "And, ah, just how *generous* an offer did your client have in mind, Doctor ehm . . .?"

Max hunched his shoulders and grunted speculatively, "We was thinkin' maybe somethin' like a hundred grand."

"American dollars?" Angus and the minister chorused.

"Limey pounds. See, I got a bad debt outstandin' for that precise sum, which I intend to personally collect, but real soon."

"A hundred thousand pounds," the minister repeated pensively. "What a coincidence!" he said through a smile that was as naïve-looking as he could muster. "Why, isn't that the same amount that Mr Cornamusa is reported to be due to receive from young Mr Green on completion of the new sculpture on the foreshore?"

"You got it, padre." Max let out a pernicious little chortle. "Now ain't that just a kick in the pecans?" He clapped his hands together. "So whaddaya say? Ya gonna go along wid the deal for the cave?"

The Reverend Dick and Angus maintained a canny silence.

"Come on," Max urged, "just think a' the indoor johns ya could stick in all them peasant shacks here for that kinda bread. Chrisakes, them natives would be crappin' in comfort like they only ever seen in the friggin' movies!"

While Angus glowered in outraged silence, the Reverend Dick smiled stiffly again and said that, while the offer was indeed a generous one, he felt he could safely say on behalf of the, uhm, *natives*, that they would not be selling their cave for a hundred thousand pounds, or even ten times that amount. Prince Charlie's Rest, quite simply, was not for sale.

Max choked on his cigar smoke. "Nobody, but nobody, refuses an offer like that from me! I'm tellin' ya, preacher man," he wheezed, "that flock a' yours is gonna have frost-bitten assholes from here to friggin' maternity if ya don' clinch this deal wid me. Think about it — a hundred grand for a goddam hole in the ground!"

The minister stood up and extended a courteous hand. "I think we both know where we stand now, sir. It is somewhat unfortunate, but I'm sure my ever-stalwart parishioners will endure a touch of winter chill around their, uhm, *hurdies* yet a while. Indeed, as you yourself so eloquently put it, Doctor Marsala, they been livin' wid them conditions long before yer client ever hit the scene. Capeesh?"

CHAPTER
SIXTEEN

There was more than a hint of resentment in the mood of the dozen or so villagers who had gathered on the grassy verge to look on in confused wonder while Franco (in Dannato Cornamusa guise) cut, hammered and joined lumps of old car parts into shapes which, to them, looked more grotesque than artistic. Yet their state of mind sprang, not from any basic dislike of the young Italian, for they had found him to be an amiable sort of chap, if a bit flamboyant and overtly-randy by their standards, and he *had* lent his vocal support (if nothing else) to old Flora and the Julie lassie when they were duffing up the two thugs who had attacked Andy Green. No, any animosity they felt towards Franco emanated from the fact that it seemed he could earn enough money cobbling up this type of unintelligible metal hotch-potch to actually own *their* island and them with it, while being unwilling, according to his manager's reaction to the requests of their civic representatives last night, to spend a penny on a few basic human comforts for them and their families. They'd experienced this type of treatment at the hands of successive lairds for as long as any of them could remember, of course, but until now had never actually seen first-hand how their feudal superiors had managed to become so obscenely rich. Under the circumstances, therefore, they could hardly help feeling that young Mr Cornamusa, whether intentionally or not, was now rubbing their noses in the how-the-other-half-lives dirt.

They, like their fellow islanders who had assembled with them on the pier the previous evening, were also feeling distinctly crestfallen that this Dr Marsala character had successfully called their bluff of threatening to run the new laird off the island. For, in the final analysis, what good would it actually do them to get rid of this one, even if they realistically could? Another laird, just as selfish and probably not even as likeable, would only take his place. All they could do was bide their time, as the minister had recommended, and hope that his assertion that all would be well might yet turn out to be more than just another blast of hot Holy Dick air.

Scoop Stewart had just come off the ferry and was circling Franco's slowly-growing conglomeration of scrap, taking pictures from every conceivable perspective. He knew he'd earn a few quid from these shots, no matter how the so-called sculpture turned out, and maybe even a *right* few quid, if some sort of smut-and-scandal angle could be trumped up for the tabloids. Scoop had phoned Bob Burns from his office in Broadford earlier to tell him that some faxes and emails had arrived for him. Rather than take the unnecessary chance of reading them over the phone, which was one of the reasons Bob had asked to use his more secure communications facilities in the first place,

Scoop had said that he would bring them with him on this routine stringing trip.

Franco, meantime, was finding that he was beginning to get a real kick out of this free-form sculpting thing, and not just due to the very real consideration that busying himself with this work was keeping him out of the way of Max at the mansion house. There, following the two minders' repeated failure to nobble Andy Green and the highly unsatisfactory outcome of Max's meeting with the minister and Angus MacGubligan, the atmosphere was positively volcanic. In contrast, Franco could now visualise, almost miraculously, how this developing metallic shape was going to represent, in *his* mind's eye at least, his declared Eagle-Bird With-a Salmon-Feesh concept. He was really enjoying himself. And so was Donal the blacksmith, whose allotted task now was to buzz around the countryside on the ancient Ford tractor, fetching bumpers, bonnets and any other likely bits of abandoned old cars for the young genius on the welding torch.

But they weren't all agreeable thoughts that were filling Franco's mind this morning. He still worried about how long the bank in Messina would continue to allow his blissfully-unaware old mother to go on overdrawing their account without his depositing the forty thousand dollars promised by his Uncle Massimo. He also worried about his own wellbeing, following the vicious thump on the eye and accompanying threats from that selfsame uncle. More than anything, though, he was haunted by the news of his namesake cousin's horrible murder.

Grazie a Dio, he reflected, thank God for Andy Green's hundred-thousand-pounds commission. *Cristo!* as soon as he got his hands on that cash, he'd be off this crazy island (as much as he'd grown to love it) and back *rapidamente* to the comparative simplicity and safety of Sicily. *Si*, and Uncle Massimo could take his measly forty thousand dollars and stick them up his *culo!*

Bob Burns had thought it best to send Andy Green to accompany Julie over to Broadford airstrip with the two finger-printed whisky glasses, solely to keep his inept sidekick out of the way of further potential strife for a few hours. Bob had subsequently watched Scoop Stewart's arrival from the hotel window and had now made his way down to the smiddy green to meet him. Scoop was busy clicking off a final few shots with his camera.

"An expert on modern art, are you?" Bob asked the young newsman. "Looks like the result of a major motorway pile-up to me!"

"But not bad for an ex-waiter, eh?" Scoop replied with a conspiratorial wink.

Glancing furtively around, Bob hissed, "I hope the hell you've kept that under your bloody hat!"

"Aye, aye, relax. Like I told you, the London boys are sitting on it too . . . for the present, anyway."

Bob exhaled a breath of relief, then had a long look at Franco in action. "Must admit the guy can handle a welding torch, though — waiter or no waiter."

"Yeah, but maybe not so surprising at that." Scoop flashed Bob a taunting little smirk.

Bob was in no mood for games, however. "Come on, don't bugger about! If you've got anything new on him, I want to know smartish. I'm trying to solve a double bloody murder, so skip the Cluedo stuff, all right!"

"OK, OK, keep your kilt on!" Scoop handed him an envelope. "It's all in there. First fax of the three. Info dug up by a Fleet Street mate's contact in one of the Italian papers."

Bob silently read the message as Scoop rambled on . . .

"Once we had Cornamusa's real name and the Sicilian connection, it was a piece of cake. Which is why I still can't understand why you didn't just get your own CID blokes in Edinburgh to sniff this out for you."

"I have my reasons," Bob muttered, then started to read the fax aloud: "Blah, blah, blah . . . Franco Contadino . . . blacksmith's workshop in Via Antonio Scaletta in Messina, Sicily . . . blah, blah . . . modest financial means, but no local criminal record . . . Messina neighbours confirm identity from recent press photographs taken in Scotland." Bob gave himself a few seconds for it all to sink in, then asked Scoop for a frank answer: "How long are these Italian newshawks going to be able to keep the cork on this?"

"That *is* a problem," Scoop admitted. "I mean, they've promised my mate in London that shtum's the word until he gives them the all-clear, but having said that, the whole caboodle could be headlining on the news stands in the streets of Rome tomorrow morning." He shrugged his shoulders. "Sorry about that, but be fair, this sort of stuff's bread and butter to us struggling hacks, no matter what country we're in."

"Yeah, well, don't let it bother you," Bob sighed. "If this North Berwick murder thing hasn't been resolved right here on Muckle Floggit by the morning, the Dannato Cornamusa — alias Franco Contadino — story breaking in the Italian papers is going to be the least of my problems, believe me."

Scoop looked over Bob's shoulder as he ran his eyes over the second fax message. "Couldn't make head or tail of this one, though," Scoop said. "It's to you, from the FBI in Washington DC. Says the late Franco Contadino confirmed as Plantano's nephew." Scoop then gestured towards Franco, who was now happily semi-submerged in a cascade of sparks spurting from the screaming disc of an angle grinder. "He doesn't look very *late* to me." Scoop pointed to the fax. "And who's this Plantano guy? Yeah, and what about this bit . . . *local agent now confirms your Max is ours?*" Scoop grimaced. "All a bit cryptic, isn't it?"

Bob tapped the side of his nose. "That's the FBI for you. But never fear, you'll get your exclusive on it all soon enough."

So, that was that, Bob pondered, still staring at the fax. *Doctor* Max Marsala was this never-convicted New York hoodlum after all. And the young Italian murdered at North Berwick was his nephew, killed, as far as could be ascertained, because he was late for Laprima Frittella's hundred-grand money drop. Or, more likely, he'd been snuffed because she'd thought at first that, due to his resemblance to Andy Green, he really *had* made the pickup and had intended making off with the loot. Laprima Frittella, then, *was* the vital missing link, but she was apparently steaming across the Atlantic towards Canada on a Spanish fishing boat right now. Hell's teeth, Bob told himself, the sooner the FBI's alleged undercover agent on the case came out of the closet the better!

"And the third one's from your own HQ," Scoop said as Bob turned the page. "It's from your personnel department, and another real puzzler. What does it say again? Yeah, there it is . . . *The subject of your query was born Giacamo Giulianetti, arrived in UK with parents from Sicily, 1965, and changed name by deed poll at age eighteen.*" He gave Bob a dig with his elbow. "OK, give us a break, eh! What the hell's that all about?"

Bob shook his head. "No way, boy! At this moment, that's classified information, and between you and me, I hope it has to stay that way. Forget you ever saw that fax. Get it?"

Scoop sensed he'd be wasting his time to press Bob further. He slung his camera bag over his shoulder. "Well," he shrugged, "if there's nothing else happening here, I think I'll nip up to the church and see if the minister can be persuaded to leak any more dope on the Saint Gubligan's Scrolls crap that he fed Mike Gibson of *The Scotsman*."

Bob then paraphrased Scoop's recent taunting little remark: "Aha, but maybe not so much crap as *all* that . . ."

Scoop was suitably intrigued. "You mean you think you know more about this than Mike wrote in his piece?"

"Maybe I even know more than I think I know. That remains to be seen. But if you come away empty-handed from old Holy Dick — which I reckon you will, according to Mike Gibson — you can always try hanging about here on Muckle Floggit tonight." Bob tapped the side of his nose again. "The old sleuthometer here tells me that something tasty might be cooking."

HALF AN HOUR LATER — THE BAR OF THE DRAMGLASS HOTEL . . .

Bob was enjoying a pint of his favourite Belhaven Best and a casual chat at the bar with four young backpackers while he waited for Julie and Andy to return from Skye. By the sound of their accents, two of the lads were Australians, while the other pair were dyed-in-the-Clyde Glaswegians — all stretched vowels and "wee man" this and "big man" that.

"So, you say you all met up by accident in Fort William," Bob said. "A favourite haunt for hikers, is it?"

"Yer hillwalkers and mountaineers on the whole," said the first Glaswegian. "Ben Nevis, see. Highest mountain in Britain. Draws them like flies roond shite."

"And what are you guys," Bob asked, "hillwalkers or mountaineers?"

"Bit a' both," said the second Glasgow lad. "Ye've got tae be tae get tae where our sport takes aff, like."

"Skiers, then, are you?"

"Yeah, ya could say that, mate," said the first Aussie. "Euphamistically speakin', if ya know what Oy mean."

"Gotta be real careful what we say in our game," said his cobber. "They'd dob ya in to the coppers as soon as spit in yer eye, some a' the mongrels we bump into."

"Fancy that," Bob remarked, deadpan. "I didn't think there were many illegal things four guys could get up to up a mountain . . . even one called Ben Doone."

"Haw, don't get the wrong idea, pal," the first Glasgow lad smiled, adopting a slightly over-butch posture. "We're no a bunch a' shirt-lifters, like."

"Too right," the second Aussie confirmed. He grinned as he gave Bob's shoulder a manly slap. "Well, at least nobody can call *me* a mattress-muncher. Not with them three, anyway. Yeah, none a' them's good enough kissers for moy likin'!"

The bawdy laughter fairly bounced off the bar's bare walls.

"I'm no expert on mountains, of course," Bob said once all the guffawing had subsided, "but Ben Doone here shouldn't disappoint you, if spectacular views are anything to go by. I climbed up there the other day, but only as far as where a landslide took out the old road a while back, mind you."

"Aye, Ah know that bit, pal," the first Glaswegian said. "Been up there a coupla times masel', by the way. Matter a' fact, Ah'm thinkin' a' takin' the lads here up there in a wee while, like." He crooked his thumb towards their bulging backpacks lying inside the bar door. "Nice spot for oor game. Nice, big, slopin' ledge hangin' oot over the glen an' that."

Bob was none the wiser about what their particular game might be, but the possibility of their heading for that exact area of the mountain gave him an idea. "Have you got a place for an extra man on this expedition, lads?" he enquired, thinking fast.

Four pairs of sceptical eyes looked him up and down.

"Ya sure ye're up to it, mate?" the first Aussie checked. "Mean to say, no offence, but us guys'll be getting' up to some pretty strenuous stuff up there, ya know."

Masking his wounded machismo behind a forced laugh, Bob began to explain that it wasn't actually himself he was talking about. But before he could go any further, the four pairs of eyes were drawn to the doorway leading from the hotel lobby.

"Strewth! Take a screw at the foxy sheila, mates!" the second Aussie gasped, while joining his chums in ogling Julie as she pranced high-heeled into the bar. And she certainly was looking every bit the foxy sheila in her mini-kilt and flouncy white blouse.

"Stone the lizards!" the first Aussie remarked, pop eyed. "Fair dinkum!"

"Aye," one of his Glasgow companions agreed, "what a stockin'-filler tae find hangin' on yer bed end on Christmas mornin'!"

"Ah-*hum*!" Bob coughed. "This, gentlemen, is my colleague, Doctor Julie Bryson." He pretended not to hear one Glaswegian's muttered aside that she could feel his pulse any time. Then, to Julie's obvious

disappointment, Bob whisked her away to the residents'
lounge, having told the four hunks that they had some
urgent private business to discuss.

"Why the instant purdah treatment?" Julie objected.
"That looked as if it might've developed into a cosy,
wee swaree in there!"

Bob gave her a despairing look that probably wasn't
as feigned as it seemed, then went on to divulge the
faxed information about the true identity of Max
Marsala and his relationship to the young Italian they
had found murdered in his car at Tantallon Castle.

"His *uncle?*" Julie was astounded. "And you honestly
think he was implicated in the killing of his own
nephew?"

"That depends a lot on what this Sporran
Connection business that old Flora mentioned turns
out to be tonight. But if it happens to tie in with the
setting-up of the international crime ring the FBI were
on about, then anything could be possible."

Julie nodded her head. "Which makes what old Flora
told me outside just now even more significant."

"Oh, yeah? So, what was that?"

"Just that she was eavesdropping down the chimney
on a powwow old Holy Dick and Angus had with Max
last night. Seems Max offered them a hundred
thousand smackers to sell the cave and cottage at
Kildoone. Oh, and incidentally, she thinks the hundred
thou he offered is Andy's money, which Max now
intends to snaffle when the statue's been paid for.
Anyhow, the Rev refused the offer point-blank, and

Flora says Max has been going nuclear ever since. Really ripping his buttons, she said."

Bob stroked his chin. "So, whatever Max's own plans are for Kildoone, we can take it that he wouldn't fancy boatloads of tourists pouring into the cove every day of the year to gawp at an alleged miracle."

"Well, at least he won't have that problem tonight."

"He won't have a tourist problem, certainly, but I intend to poop his party all the same."

Julie gave him one of her seriously-incredulous looks. "And how, pray, do you plan to do that? Don't forget, there's only three of us on this team, and if it comes to physical hostilities, I have to tell you that I, as a professional forensic scientist, amateur scout and part-time interpreter, am only going along as a *strict* noncombatant."

"Max's two emasculated minders'll be relieved to hear that, I'm sure! Anyway, don't you concern yourself with how I'm going to put a spoke in Max's wheel. To be honest, I'm not that sure myself yet, but I'll think of something." Just then, Bob noticed his young Detective Constable passing the lounge door en route to the dining room. "Hey, Green," he said in a stage whisper, "come here! I've got a special assignment for you."

Andy was clearly less than enthralled by the prospect. "Aw, no," he moaned, "not another high-profile, mix-wi'-the-punters job. Honest, skipper, ma nerves would never stand it. And anyway, ma bagpipes are Donald Ducked!"

"Just sit down and calm down," Bob said placidly. "The job I've got in mind for you is going to keep you well out of the way of Max's hit men for the rest of the day, and it's going to threaten you with nothing more dangerous that a couple of midgie bites. Now then, there are four young backpackers through in the bar there, and you're going on a nice gentle hike half way up Ben Doone with them, OK?"

Andy Green said nothing, but his expression showed that he was still far from comfortable.

"That map of the island you have in your handbag," Bob said to Julie, "— spread it out in front of Green here, will you, please?" Bob waited until Julie had done as requested, then indicated a place on the map to Andy. "Right, lad, there's where you're going — that point on the old mountain road where it disappears under the landslide. Now, I'm going to give you a pair of binoculars, and make sure you have your mobile phone with you. All I want you to do is sit looking down into the bay of Kildoone there, where something — I don't know what yet — is gonna start happening about half past eight tonight. All being well, Doctor Bryson and I will be down there on the coast somewhere. You should be able to pick us out OK with the binos, and if you see us getting into any bother, I want you to phone this number." He handed Andy a piece of paper. "Got all that?"

Andy looked anxiously at his watch and clasped his stomach. "Yeah, but —"

"I know, I know," Bob cut in, "you'll miss your midday feed. But don't panic. Just go and get the cook to fix you up with a packed lunch, and I'll organise everything with the four lads in the bar."

Andy was about to protest again, but the steely look in Bob's eyes made him think the better of it.

"On you go," Bob told him. "See you through there in ten minutes."

"So," Julie said stern-faced as soon as Green had slouched off to the kitchens, "now it'll only be *two* of us versus the world. Honestly, I'm beginning to like the look of this less and less. I mean, let's face it, they never said anything about putting my life on the line for the furtherance of police work when I joined the forensic mob!"

"Fair enough," Bob nonchalantly replied, "just sit in here watching whatever depressing soap is on the telly tonight when all the fun and games are happening over at Kildoone . . . *if* you've lost your bottle." He stood up. "I'm off to give the coastguards a quick call. Catch you later."

Julie got to her feet then as well. "OK, OK, OK, you've talked me into it," she said with a resigned shrug. "No matter what happens at Kildoone, it couldn't be a fate worse than sitting in here watching *EastEnders*. Make your phone call. I'll be in the bar giving the four lads the pleasure of my company." She fluttered her eyelashes. "Wouldn't want to send them up the mountain disappointed, would we?"

A COUPLE OF HOURS LATER — ON THE SLIPWAY AT DRAMGLASS PIER . . .

Bob's initial approach to Nip MacGubligan for the self drive hire of his boat for the evening had been met with a frosty refusal. It wasn't that Nip didn't want the hire fee, because everyone knew that Nip would rent out his own kids for shark-fishing bait if the money was right, but rather because Bob had rashly let it slip that the purpose of the hire was to make a return visit to Kildoone. Nip certainly didn't want a stranger snooping about unescorted there, particularly a stranger like Bob, whose friend Andy Green was already privy to the whereabouts of the miracle.

So, as time rolled on and the hour of Max's mysterious Sporran Connection grew ever nearer, Bob decided that a fresh approach to the entire matter was urgently required. Secrecy was all very well, but diving headlong into an unknown situation at such a remote place, with only Julie for backup and a rookie DC perched high above armed only with a mobile phone, really was stretching stealth a bit too far. Also, the plan that was beginning to take shape in his mind called for the involvement of Angus the ferryman as well, so the time had come to brave all and bare, if not all, at least enough to persuade these two key locals to help him out. He slipped Nip a swift look at his Lothian and Borders Police ID card.

Nip blanched and was obliged to steady himself against the wall of the pier. "Cheesus Christ Almighty, the bluidy polis!" he wailed, as horrified as he would have been had someone just added a splash of water to his dram of single malt.

Bob clamped a hand over Nip's mouth. "Sh-h-h-h! Don't broadcast it to the whole bloody island!" he hissed. "This is life and death stuff!"

Nip shied away. "You'll not be attached to the Customs and Excise as well at all, are you? For even if you are, you canna pin nothing on me. Aye, and even if you do, I'll name names and bring them down with me and all!"

A great ally this windy bugger was going to be in an emergency, Bob told himself. But needs must. "Look, Nip," he said calmly, "I'm not interested in whatever you're on about. Murder's my game and —"

"MURDER?"

Bob covered Nip's mouth again and glanced nervously around. "Look," he growled, "there are people coming off the ferry up there, so just belt up, or I'll have you run in for obstructing a policeman in the course of his duties. Now, did you read in the papers recently about the two men who were clubbed to death at North Berwick, over on the east coast?"

Nip shook his head. He only ever looked at the racing pages, he revealed, and they made depressing enough reading at times without bothering about anything else.

Taking a deep breath, Bob proceeded to relate a suitably abridged account of the story so far, culminating in a purposely overemotional appeal to Nip's feelings of patriotism for Muckle Floggit in the light of the unsavoury future it *might* now be facing. For good measure, he also threw in a thinly veiled suggestion that rich rewards could be forthcoming to those who assisted in bringing this sordid and complex case to a satisfactory conclusion.

That ticked the right box for Nip. "Ah, well now, you can count on me, sir. There can be no place for folk like yon Max and his wicked-like chickery-pokeries on my wee island home!"

"Fine sentiments, Nip. You're a credit to Muckle Floggit."

Nip leaned in close, an inquisitive eyebrow lifted. "Aye, fine that. And, ehm, was that me hearing you mentioning something about a wee reward there chust now as well . . .?"

Angus's voice booming down from above spared Bob the embarrassment of having to own up that any reward was likely to be more spiritual than material.

"Oho, it's yourself, Mr Burns, is it?" hailed the ferrymaster. "Aye, so it is, right enough. Well now, is young Mr Green anywhere abouts, do you know?"

"No, he's away on a climb up the mountain with some other young blokes. Why?"

"Well, it's chust that he was after asking me the other day if I ever did spy the likes of a red Spidermobile in these here parts."

"Are you sure you don't mean a red Alfa Romeo Spider?"

"Aye, that'll be it," Angus laughed, clapping his hands together. "That's the very exact name of it you've came up with there, true enough now."

Bob was all ears. "What about it, then?"

"Och well, it's chust that one of them cars, with a wumman at the wheel, slinked terrible sleekit-like into the wee car park behind the inn over there at

313

Ardenstooshie when we was loading up a wee while back. Aye, and fair tucked away out of sight now, it is."

"And you're sure it was an Alfa Romeo Spider?"

"Chings, man, I wouldna know the difference between the make of yon machine and a double-decker bus, for cars is of no interest to a seafaring man like me. No, no, it was a bunch of young laddies was shouting and pointing at it fair excited-like, as if they had chust seen a wumman's bare arse on the picture house screen in Portree."

"And what about the woman who was driving the Alfa?"

Angus pushed his captain's cap back, thought a bit, then said, "No, she never had a bare arse!"

Bob had to keep his cool in silence while Angus and Nip indulged themselves in convulsions of wheezy laughter.

"Ach, that was only me having one of my wee bits of fun with you there, Mr Burns," Angus eventually said. "Aye, for the truth of it is that there was no wumman in the car at all. No, chust a man all by his-self, and he chumped into one of yon wee ski boats tied up at the Ardenstooshie pier yonder and steamed away chust as fast as you like, bearing east by south-east, near enough."

"And where would that course take him?"

"Straight head-first into the rocks south of Achnacloich or thereabouts, if he was daft enough not to steer to his starboard a wee bit sooner, like."

"But if he did turn to the right and right again, he would end up round the other side of Muckle Floggit, right?"

314

"Aye," Angus chuckled, "or Canada, if he's got enough fuel aboard. Man, that's the thing about the sea, you see — the world's your oxter, if you have yourself a good boat and the means to keep her moving."

Bob snapped his fingers. "And you've just reminded me of a wee favour I wanted to ask you, Angus. Half a tick, I'll be right with you." He started up the stone steps, turning to tell Nip, "Back here just after seven tonight, right? And remember, keep all this to yourself."

"Aye, aye, so I will at that," Nip muttered under his breath. "Chust like the rich rewards . . . if us island folk ever gets to clap eyes on them."

CHAPTER
SEVENTEEN

DRAMGLASS — 7.10p.m., THAT SAME DAY . . .

Bob's calculated risk that Nip and Angus's pledges of silence would not be worth the breath they'd been uttered with appeared to have paid off, for there was a larger than usual number of villagers wandering about quasi-casually in the vicinity of the pier when he and Julie made their way down from the hotel. Murmured asides and furtive nods of the head in their direction emanated from each little group as they passed.

Fortunately, though, it was evident that none of the gossip had filtered through to Max and his motley gang, who were already ensconced aboard the big Sunseeker berthed at the other side of the pier from Nip's little outboard-powered rowing boat. Max himself was too preoccupied with trying to remind a flustered Franco what the delivery captain had spelled out about how to operate this beast of a speedboat to be aware of anything else going on around him . . .

"Chrisakes! How come I get surrounded wid nothin' but shit-for-brains shmoes them days?" He gave Franco a shove. "GET yer goddam mitts offa the controls and lemme at 'em!"

"But, *Zio* Max —"

"SHUT yer ventilator shaft, kid! I shoulda knew better than trust an important mission like this to a

316

bunch a' half-assed schleppers like youse guys. Now get outa the friggin' way!"

"Interesting," Julie remarked quietly to Bob as they approached the steps on their side of the pier. "Dannato just called Max *zio*, and that's Italian for uncle."

"It follows," Bob reminded her, "seeing as how his Franco Contadino alias is the same as his late cousin's. Keep it in the family is obviously Max's motto."

"But, Max," Franco piped up again, this time prudently omitting the "uncle" tag, "if this is a feeshing trip, how come we got no feeshing stuff on-a the boat?"

Max didn't answer that one. He was furiously flicking switches and pressing buttons instead, though to no avail.

Comfortably seated between the two motionless minders at the back of the boat and seemingly oblivious to the pantomime being enacted only a few paces forward, the mink-draped Lulu-May was concentrating on the more crucial task of applying her lipstick. She paused momentarily to look up at Bob and Julie, waved her mirror and smiled vacantly, "Hi, y'all! Have a nice evenin' now."

"Likewise," Bob called back, while giving her a surreptitious wink on Julie's blind side.

Bob had invited Scoop Stewart along on the trip, more as an independent recorder of what might happen at Kildoone than as some extra muscle, should any be required. As he led Julie down the stone steps, he was pleased to see that the keen-as-mustard cub reporter was already sitting in Nip's boat with his camera bag snugly in his lap.

"Ahoy there, the both of youse!" Nip shouted. "Well, well, it's a grand evening for a wee sail, is it not now? Chust look at that water out there — flat as a witch's pap and smooth as the skin on a nun's bahookie, so it is."

"Charmed, I'm sure," Julie muttered under her breath, before detecting a not-unexpected whiff of whisky on *Nip*'s breath as he helped her aboard.

"Yeah, shouldn't take us long to get round to Kildoone in this weather," Bob said, "but the quicker we get going the better, Nip, just in case Max manages to fire up that speedboat's motors before we get a good head start on him. Oh, and if we can slip away from here without him noticing, that'll be even better, OK?"

"All yon things you menshun is absolutely possible, Mr Burns," said Nip with a reassuring smile as he cast off and pushed the little boat away from the pier. "Aye, absolutely no problem at all for me whatsemever." He made ready to pull the starter cord on the outboard, but hesitated. "Och, man, man," he said with a slow shake of his head, "there was me chust about forgetting, and here's us bobbing about and drifting further away from the shore and everything . . ."

"Don't tell me you've forgotten to fill her up with bloody juice," Bob groaned.

"Oh, no, no, no, never that, Mr Burns." Nip lifted a petrol can from under his seat and grinned. "There's likely enough two-stroke in here for to take us to

Mallaig and back, if we was of a mind. Aye, or one way to Tobermory, maybe."

"OK, what's the problem, then?" Bob snapped. "Let's get going!" He glanced at his watch. "Come on, it's twenty past bloody seven, so get a jildy on and pull that damned string!"

The little boat drifted still further from the pier, while the infuriatingly laid-back Nip casually produced a half bottle of whisky from the breast pocket of his jacket. "Anybody fancy a wee sensashun before we set sail — a wee splice of the mainbraces, sort of thing? You know, speed your churney, as they say . . ."

"Has Max Marsala lobbed you a bung to keep us bouncing about here like a cork in a lavvie pan while he makes the bloody sporran connection?" Bob barked, cut off as he was from Nip at the opposite end of the boat, but wishing he was close enough to grab him by the throat. "I thought you said you were on the side of the good guys!"

Nip took a leisurely slug from his bottle, then said to Julie, who was sitting immediately in front of him, "I hope you'll excuse me, lassie, if I take a wee drop of the nerve-settling solution. I'm chust not accustomed at all to all this high-speed excitement, you understand."

Bob's bellows of frustration were drowned out by the throaty roar of the big Sunseeker's engines erupting into life at the other side of the pier. However, their rumble was only to cough and stutter to silence again as Bob yelled out the last few words of his tongue-lashing to Nip: ". . . or I'll tie the starting string round your bloody neck!"

But Nip was still the epitome of all-the-time-in-the-world relaxation. "Well now, I never chust exactly catched what you was saying there, Mr Burns," he smiled, "but if it was you minding me that I was after forgetting to collect the fares, I think I would be much obliged to you — ehm, under the circumstances."

"How much, MacGubligan?" Bob bawled, brandishing his wallet. "Go on, sock it to me!"

"Och, only the usual twenty pound a head daylight return will be fine."

"Daylight bloody robbery, more like!" Red-faced, Bob peeled off three twenties and thrust them at Scoop to pass down the boat.

"Oh, and ehm, plus the ten pound a head night-time supplement, of course," Nip demurely advised. "Refundable in the event of return to home port before sunset, like. Eh, oh aye, and there would be the fifty pounds damage deposit, in case my wee west coast boatie here gets herself skaithed in the course of partaking involuntary-like in east coast polis business, so to speak."

By the time they had cleared the south-eastern cape of Muckle Floggit, Bob's temper had subsided, if not quite to a level of calmness to match the sea, then certainly to a degree of control which put Nip's neck out of danger — at least for the moment. In fact, Bob couldn't resist having a quiet chuckle to himself about the whole episode. In Nip's position, he'd probably have done the same thing himself, *if* he'd had the gall. But this had been the second time in the space of a few days that he'd allowed himself to be ripped off as easily as you like by this old pirate, and when you came right down to it, he'd only had himself to blame. Yes, he was learning the hard way that, no matter how frugal their living conditions and how of-necessity simple their way of life, opportunism was one item in which the good folk of Muckle Floggit most definitely were not wanting.

"Still no sign of the Sunseeker behind us before we rounded that last point," Julie said, "and it's nearly half an hour since we left Dramglass."

"Yeah, they're obviously not up to starting the brute," Bob replied.

"Aye," Nip agreed, "the contaminashun in the fuel will usually make things a wee bit tricky-like for the starting up, right enough."

"Contamination?" Bob queried.

"Oh, aye, a terrible thing! You see, yon Max chappie gave me four tenners to myself to slip away along to Mohammed's pumps for to fill up two five-gallon drums of diesel for him while I was standing about on the pier waiting for youse ones. Ach, and what with me being fair in a flichter about this here boat trip and all, I must have went and squirted a wee drop water in among the diesel by mistake. Michty me, man," Nip chortled, "what a right creel of herrings it has turned out to be!"

"And this crafty old bugger wound me up something hellish back at the pier there with all that time-wasting carry-on," Bob said inwardly, unable to suppress an admiring smile, "and it was all just to up the ante, because he already knew he'd put the mockers on the speedboat, anyway!"

Scoop Stewart took the news more seriously, though. "What the hell were you thinking about, MacGubligan? I mean, how can this Max guy make a connection with whoever he's supposed to at Kildoone if he's landlubbed at Dramglass pier?" He threw his hands in the air. "That's it — the whole damned story's down the pipes!"

"Na, na, never you worry, laddie," said Nip "They'll likely have their big boat kindled up by now, all right. No, it's chust that her top speed will maybe not be much better than this wee boat of mine until all yon water gets flushed out of her chubes and inchectors and such." Nip angled his head round Scoop to catch Bob's eye with a sly wink. "Maybe not so handy, though, Mr Burns, if Doctor Max is hoping to be making a quick getaway a wee bit later on, is that not right?"

Bob responded by returning Nip's wink and giving him an approving little nod of the head. The wily old weasel had already more than justified his grossly-inflated boat-hire bill, no matter how self-interested his true motives might yet turn out to be.

The sun was suspended low over the far mountains of South Uist, while spreading a burning blanket of red on the waters surrounding the islet of Eilean Doone, as Nip's little boat chugged round the headland and entered the silent Bay of Kildoone. It was in shadow now, save for the rugged eastern cliffs, which were still basking in the warm glow of evening and were reflecting a soft, almost spectral light on the ruins of the deserted village. Bob had asked Nip to slow his motor to a mere tick-over on entering the cove, and to put ashore well away from and, if at all possible, out of sight of the pier.

"There's a wee kind of inlet affair over at the foot of yon crags," Nip said, pointing away to his right. "We'll be able to hide the boat fine in there, and then chust make our way back over the rocks to the beach. Aye, you won't be finding it much of a bother at all."

Bob had had a gut feeling that the water ski boat in which Angus the ferryman had seen the driver of the Alfa Romeo Spider making off from Ardenstooshie earlier in the afternoon would have been moored somewhere hereabouts, but now that he had a clear view of the entire bay, he was obliged to concede that his hunch appeared to have been wrong. Odd that, he thought, though a considerable relief, nonetheless.

Persuading Nip to allow them to use the cave as a lookout post had taken Bob most of the journey round the coast from Dramglass, and Nip's permission had only been granted once a general undertaking had been made not to venture any further inside the cave than was absolutely necessary to keep out of sight. What's more, on no account was that Scoop chiel to be taking any flash pictures in there with yon fantoosh camera of his!

It had turned eight o'clock by the time they'd made their way back along the little curve of the bay and up to the mouth of the cave. Bob's anxiety was growing with every seemingly endless minute that Nip took to undo the tangle of padlocked chains that held the harrow-leaf "gates" over the entrance.

"Come on, Nip, for God's sake get a move on! If that bloody Sunseeker comes roaring round the headland now, we'll be caught standing here like a bunch of tailor's dummies in a shop window."

But Nip was as unflustered as Bob was exasperated. "Ach, man, don't you fash yourself, Mr Burns. Yon muckle boat will never be here for a good ten minutes yet. Aye, you chust mark my words."

Behind their backs, meanwhile, a small ski boat emerged furtively from the cover of Eilean Doone islet and slipped silently into the cove, hugging the shadows beneath the cliffs and finally anchoring in the shallows of a little creek, well out of sight of the cave. From the mountain high above, Andy Green watched the boat's sole occupant wade ashore, a wooden box under his arm, a revolver in his hand.

"OK, Nip," Bob urged once they were all inside the cave at last, "let's pull those harrows back over the opening, so at least it'll still look blocked up from a distance. Then it's just a matter of waiting patiently until the action starts."

They didn't have long to wait . . .

"Well, well, Sergeant Burns," said the man who suddenly appeared outside the cave, his outline silhouetted against the rosy evening light, "it's been a long time."

Bob peered through the metal grid, straining his eyes to make out the shadowy features behind the voice. "Yeah, but not long enough," he eventually said. "Don't tell me some soft-headed bloody parole board decided to give a rat like you remission. The beak gave you life, and that was only ten years ago."

"Where I've been, ten years *is* a lifetime, Burns, and I've wasted those years in a stinking shit hole of a cell in Saughton because of you, you bastard!"

"And never mind the old night watchman who spent the last years of *his* life in a wheelchair because you shot him in the back," Bob snarled. "If it was down to me, Joe, scum like you would be behind bars until you rotted — and even that's too good for you!"

The man threw his head back and laughed. "Except it's *you* who's gonna be rotting behind bars!" He raised his revolver and tapped it against the harrows. "The great, smart-arsed Detective Sergeant Burns, eh? Aye, but you're way out of your league now, pal, and I'm gonna make you pay for every day of the ten years of my life you owe me!"

If Bob was in any way fazed by that threat, he didn't show it. "You know, it's funny," he said casually, "but I was half expecting it to be your brother who turned up here tonight."

"Yeah, well, life's full of surprises, Burns, and you've got a few more coming, believe me!"

Bob turned to his three companions. "Please excuse my bad manners. I haven't introduced you. This *gentleman* is Giuseppe, better known as Joe, Giulianetti. One-time ace safe-blower and all-time prize slug."

Scoop Stewart wasn't slow to latch on to this. "Giulianetti. Isn't that the name on the fax that came in from your HQ?" he said to Bob. "The guy that came over from Sicily with his folks in 'sixty-five or something?"

"That's right — Giacamo Giulianetti, alias Jimmy Yule, my trusted right-hand man. Well, I *thought* I could trust him, until a few days ago. That was when he told me on the phone that he'd just been given certain information — duff, as it turns out — on Max so-called Marsala from his contact in the New York Police Department. Trouble is, it was only shortly after ten in the morning here, making it just gone six in New York. So, instead of being on the phone to Jimmy, his alleged contact would still have been tucked up in his scratcher."

"Wow, you're really brilliant, Burns!" Joe scoffed. "Fact is, though, you're so fuckin' dumb that you took all the bait Jimmy dangled in front of you to get you up to this island. After that, it was just a matter of letting your snooping copper's nose lead your head into our noose."

"I see jail's mellowed you a lot," Bob muttered.

Joe beckoned Nip to come forward. He then thrust his hand through the harrows and grabbed him by the lapels, ramming the muzzle of his gun into his belly. "Gimme the keys to these padlocks NOW," he barked, "or I'll drop you right here!"

"He means it," Bob said. "Better do as he says."

After Nip had done as instructed, Joe quickly padlocked the chains, tugged at the harrow leaves to make sure they were secure, then motioned Julie to step forward into the light. "Yeah-h-h," he drooled as he ran the back of his hand over her cheek, "the nights I've gone crazy thinking about a piece of stuff like you these past ten years." Julie shied away. "Don't worry, I'll be back for you, darlin'," he laughed. "Yeah, no point in getting rid of you with these three gits — not until we've had ourselves some fun at any rate, eh?"

Julie spat in his face. "Go play with yourself, lowlife! That'll be all you're good for after ten years in the slammer, anyway."

Joe wiped his face, his hand shaking. "You'll find out *all* about what I'm good for later on, your ladyship," he growled. "*And* you're gonna wish you paid me a little bit more fuckin' respect. That's a promise, right!"

The sound of a backfiring motor entering the bay caused Joe to turn his head. "That'll be Max now," he mumbled. "Thought the little bastard would never get here." He reached up to a ledge above the cave opening and lifted down a wooden box. He tapped its lid. "Know what's in here, Burns?" he smirked. "No? Well, you should, 'cos it's exactly the same gear I was about to use when that moron of a night watchman butted his face in. That's right — gelly — enough to reduce this cosy, wee grotto here to nothing but a mess of boulders and dust . . . with you lot, or what's left of you, underneath. What a beauty, eh? Perfect! It'd just be written off as a cave-in, and nobody would give a shit." He gestured towards Nip. "To finish the job, I haul the old guy's tub into the open sea and capsize it, and you berks are posted missing, presumed drowned."

"Nothing's changed," Bob muttered. "You're still one of nature's gentlemen."

327

Joe laughed again. "It's really sweet, isn't it? Max wanted me to destroy the cave so's the local peasants wouldn't get in the way of his future operations here, and getting rid of you, Burns, was gonna mean extra work. But not any more, eh?"

"Bullshit!" Bob countered. "Max doesn't even know who the hell I am, so why would he have put out a contract on me?"

"OK," Joe shrugged, "so he doesn't know who you are *yet*, but he will in a few minutes. Yeah, and just think how good it'll look for brother Jimmy and me when I present him with the arseholes who stumbled into his action at North Berwick and swiped his hundred grand."

It was Bob's turn to laugh now. "Hard luck, Joe, but the arsehole who really stumbled into his action isn't even here."

"You mean this pea-brained Andy Green twonk?" Joe scoffed. "Nah, no sweat. We'll deal with him in due course, in the same way Jimmy and I originally planned for you — over the side of a boat with a few concrete blocks chained round his fuckin' neck."

"That's still not gonna get Max his hundred thousand out of the police safe."

Chuckling to himself, Joe then clambered down the rocks and sprinted along the sand towards the pier, where the big Sunseeker was already spluttering to a halt in a haze of white exhaust smoke.

"Anybody fancy a nip?" said Nip, producing his half bottle again.

"Could be the answer," Bob replied, but declined the offer all the same. "I just hope Green's twigged we're in soapy here."

"What *was* that number you told him to phone, anyway?" Julie asked, a trace of apprehension in her voice.

"Broadford Police Station on Skye," Bob replied, a hint of unease in his.

Scoop Stewart was thunder-struck. "Broadford *Police* Station?" he echoed. "What the hell good is it gonna do phoning there? By the time old Constable MacClueless — *if* he's even on duty — gets himself the fifteen miles down to Ardenstooshie, tries to find somebody with a boat and then chugs all the way round here, we'll all be buried under thousands of tons of rock!"

"Yeah, well, I was merely intending Green to contact that number as a trigger for the appropriate emergency services," Bob bluffed, feigning a suitably confident detective-inspectorly air. "Normal police practice under such circumstances."

"*Emergency services?*" Scoop squeaked. "On *Skye?* What do you expect to trigger — the Cuillin Hills Mountain Rescue Team and Portree Fire Brigade, all steaming in to our salvation aboard old Angus's wee ferry? You have *got* to be joking!"

Still maintaining an unconcerned front, Bob replied, "Many a true word spoken in jest, lad."

"Yeah," Scoop retorted, "except I wasn't jesting!" He stomped over to the cave mouth and shook the harrow leaves. "Admit it, we're about to be yesterday's bleedin' newspapers!"

High above them on Ben Doone, Andy Green was also in a total tizzy. If the mobile phone signal down at Dramglass had been poor, up here on the other side of the mountain it was virtually non-existent. He punched in the numbers from Bob's note for the umpteenth time. Still nothing. "Shite," he said to himself, "what the hell am I gonna do now?"

Down at the jetty, meanwhile, Max was still barracking Franco for his inability to drive the Sunseeker properly, when Joe Giulianetti jumped on board and blurted out how he had skilfully trapped an undercover cop and how he planned to put him out of the way for keeps by killing several birds with one heap of stones. Max liked the sound of that. This was the kinda creative thinkin' he looked for in his lootenants, but seldom friggin' got.

"So," he told Joe, "you should get on wid doin' the deed, like pronto!"

Eager to get to work, Joe picked up a coil of rope from the deck of the Sunseeker and prepared to clamber back onto the pier.

At that, Lulu-May prised herself out from between the two minders at the back of the boat and wiggled up to Max. "Hey, sugar babe," she drawled, "can Ah tag along with Joey boy? Ah jus' *love* explosions . . ."

"Sure, doll face," Max replied. He then patted her butt as she attempted, without success, to maintain a modicum of modesty while climbing out of the

Sunseeker in her skin-tight micro-mini. "Ya'd only get in the friggin' way here, anyhow."

Joe Yule ogled her as she struggled, all knees, thighs and lace gusset, up the metal ladder. He clamped a hand to her backside, ostensibly giving her a boost up the steps.

"Oo-oo-ah!" Lulu-May squealed in undisguised delight. She paused seductively with one leg raised to look back down at Joe. "My, what strong fingers ya got, gran'maw! Wow, Ah jus' *love* strong fingers . . ."

From his lonely eyrie, Andy Green looked helplessly through his binoculars at Lulu-May and the stranger making their way back towards the cave. He hadn't a clue what was going on down there, but judging by the revolver and rope the guy was now toting, it certainly didn't look good for his boss and the Doc. He'd have to do something, and do it fast. But what, for heaven's sake?

With the mobile phone useless, he was totally cut off, a good hour and a half away from Dramglass back the way he'd come, with the only other option being a risky climb down that rocky mountainside to Kildoone. Chances were he'd never make it in time. And what if he slipped? He'd be no good to anybody lying in a mangled heap at the foot of the mountain. Hell, if only the two Glaswegian gadgies and their Aussie mates had still been around, maybe they'd have thought of something. But no, they'd gone higher up the mountain in search of even bigger thrills a while back, leaving Andy to mind their spare back pack for them.

Heh, maybe that was it, Andy suddenly thought. He'd watched how the blokes got into their gear and how they worked it. It didn't look *that* difficult. Stark, raving crazy, but easy enough. Not that different from the go he'd had at it on his hols at Benidorm that time, the only difference being that there'd be no speed boat pulling him here. He walked over and picked up the back pack. Aye, bugger it, he'd give it a bash!

As Joe and Lulu-May neared the cave, they were stopped in their tracks by a holler from Max, who was pointing excitedly to the entrance of the bay, where a big, ocean-going fishing boat had just appeared round the western flank of Eilean Doone and was heading straight for the pier. "Hey, Joe!" he yelled. "Get that blowin'-up business done fast, then get yer ass back here and give the boys a hand wid the merchandise!"

Bob and Julie were already peering through the harrow leaves.

"Can you make out the name on the bow yet?" he asked.

Julie nodded her head. "It's a long way from the Grand Banks of Newfoundland where Jimmy Yule said she was bound, but what you're looking at there is none other than the good ship *Patella* — or *Kneecap*."

Bob wasn't particularly surprised. "Yeah, well, when I phoned the coastguard earlier, they said she'd been logged lying at anchor off the Ayrshire coast last night — less than two hundred miles south of here. The coastguards thought nothing of it, of course. The waters off the west coast of Scotland are always swimming with Spanish fishing boats these days." He checked his

332

watch. "I just hope the customs boys at Oban were tipped off in time, though."

"Customs?" Nip gasped, panic rising through the soles of his boots.

"Relax," Bob told him. "I think they'll have bigger fish to fry here than any you've been catching." He gestured towards the approaching Joe Giulianetti. "And I reckon we've got more vital matters to be bothered with ourselves right now as well."

"Get back from the mouth of the cave, Burns!" Joe shouted. "Go on, and take the bird with you!"

Grasping at straws she may have been, but Julie decided she'd have nothing to lose by having a go. "But I thought you were going to take me with you, Joe," she purred.

She was wasting her time. "Go to hell, slag!" he snarled. "I was looking forward to teaching you some manners, but it's too late for that now. Go on — get back there with the rest of them!"

"That's right," Lulu-May pouted, while stroking Joe's biceps. "Joey boy's gonna be all mine, ain't ya, honey?"

Joe quickly undid the chains and heaved one harrow leaf aside. He handed the coil of rope to Lulu-May. "OK, darlin', tie the four of them up — hands and feet, then back-to-back in pairs. Tight as you like. We don't want them meddling with this gelly," he laughed. "They might get hurt, eh?"

"You're off your bloody rocker, Giulianetti, that's your trouble," Bob growled as Lulu-May fumbled at his ankles with the rope. "You're as crazy as that little runt

Max down there. I'm telling you, your only chance of getting out of this is by making a run for it now, before the —"

A sickening blow from the butt of Joe's revolver sunk Bob to his knees, blood oozing from a gash on his temple.

"OK, just one word from any of the rest of you, and I'll shoot you in the fuckin' head!" Joe barked. He motioned Lulu-May to get a move on.

"Ah can't, honey," she complained. "It's this rope stuff, see. Plastic or nylon or somethin'. Ah can't tie a knot in it. Aw gee, Joe," she wailed, "Ah think it's breakin' ma fingernails . . ."

Joe grabbed her arm and hauled her to her feet. "Let me at it, for Christ's sake, you useless slapper! Here, take the gun, and if anybody so much as moves a muscle, blow their fuckin' brains out!"

"Anything you say, big boy," Lulu-May cooed, then waited until Joe had crouched down to tie the rope, before pistol-whipping him on the back of the head — once, twice, then thrice for good measure. "A little present from a useless slapper," she added in a cultured Boston accent. She kicked him over sideways as he slumped to the floor, then dropped to her knees and started to undo the tangle of rope at Bob's ankles. "Agent Cindy Rudelski, FBI," she said. "Sorry I left it so late, but timing's everything in this job."

"Tell me about it," Bob groaned, then gingerly fingered the rapidly-swelling welt on the side of his head. "Why the blazes didn't you introduce yourself a bit earlier?"

"Too risky. That Max guy's as sharp as a razor."

Julie knelt down to help her truss up Joe Giulianetti with the rope. "My God," she said, "you deserve a medal for letting a stunted little creep like that crawl all over you. Talk about beneath and beyond the call of duty!"

"Max? No problem," Cindy laughed. "He's a watcher, not a doer. All porno videos and no action. Yeah, the occasional paw was the only thing he tried, and I could handle that. Take it from me, you get worse in the New York subway every rush hour." She nudged Joe's limp body with her knee. "I guess I'd've had a lot more to worry about in that department from this heap of garbage, though — if he hadn't fallen for the old rope-a-dope trick, huh?"

"So," Bob said through the twitter of cerebral birdsong, "it was *you* who felled Max's two bozos when they were about to take Andy Green for a midnight swim the other night."

Agent Rudelski gave him a blank look.

Bob shook his head and smiled a self-chastening smile. "Yeah, and there was me thinking it must've been old Flora the housekeeper who domed them with the baseball bat."

"Think what you like," Cindy Rudelski replied with a shrug. "I'm taking the Fifth Amendment in any case. Let's face it, those bozos could still file charges for assault and battery."

Bob was now leaning groggily by the cave entrance and looking out to where the big fishing boat was drawing alongside the Sunseeker at the jetty. "Anyway, do you FBI people know what Max is up to here?" he asked.

"Not too hard to guess," Agent Rudelski replied. "It's catching Max in the act that's the trick. Better feds than me have tried over the years, and no dice." She raised her head. "What's he doing now?"

"Standing on the pier with Dannato — I mean Franco. They're having some sort of argument, by the looks of things. A lot of arm-waving going on. A couple of guys have appeared on the deck of the fishing boat now. They've got packages, parcels, about the size of shoe boxes. They're throwing them down to the two stooges in the speedboat. Hell, there's dozens of packets now, being flung up from the hold of the trawler!"

As soon as they'd finished tying up Joe Giulianetti, Agent Rudelski and Julie joined Bob, standing with their backs to the wall just inside the cave entrance. Scoop and Nip had been told to keep well back out of sight. Meanwhile, the pile of packages continued to accumulate on the deck of *La Patella*.

"How the hell are they gonna manage to stow all that stuff in the speedboat?" Bob muttered.

"No problem is the answer to that," Cindy Rudelski said. "Everything that could be has been stripped out below decks — sleeping bunks, galley, shower, the works. Yeah, that Sunseeker's nothing but a high-speed floating removal truck now." She shrugged her shoulders. "Well, maybe not so high-speed at that. Motors need tuning, I guess."

336

"Aye, well, remind me to tell you about that sometime," Bob smirked, with an over-the-shoulder wink to Nip.

Scoop Stewart took out his notebook and prepared to write. "Not wishing to appear flippant, Agent Rudelski," he said, "but have you made arrangements for the US Cavalry to appear over the horizon any minute now — maybe in the shape of a Polaris sub lurking somewhere outside the bay there?"

Agent Rudelski shook her head. "U'-uh! No, I'm very much on a tightrope on this assignment, I'm afraid. Solo performance, no safety net. The last instruction I got from Washington via our man on Muckle Floggit was just to rely on and cooperate with the decisions and actions of Detective Burns here. We're both fighting the same enemy, maybe for different reasons, but our goal's the same."

Bob was frowning. "You said your man on Muckle Floggit . . . You mean there's *another* FBI undercover agent on the ground here?"

Cindy Rudelski smiled. "Not an *agent* exactly — more a contact man, a trusted go-between, you know. He spent some years as padre — chaplain, I guess you'd call it — to our guys at the US Navy Base at your Holy Loch right here in Scotland a while back. Yeah, it pays us to keep in touch with people like that. Never know when you're gonna need them, right?"

"Well, I'll be buggered," Bob muttered, "old Holy Dick's a G-man!" He gave that a moment's thought. "You — you mean he's known who Andy Green, Doctor Bryson and I were all along?"

Agent Rudelski shrugged, but said nothing.

"So," Bob smiled, "*that*'s why the crafty old git divulged all that Saint Gubligan stuff to us. Yeah, and *he* must've been behind Andy Green being brought round to this cave that night as well. All part of setting up a trap for Max." He looked round at Nip for tell-tale signs of collusion on his face. But there were none; only a look of genuine bamboozlement.

"Don't try to look too deeply into it," Agent Rudelski advised Bob. "All that matters is that you come out of this on the winning side."

"All that matters," Julie dryly opined, "is that we come out of this *alive!*"

Ignoring that remark, Agent Rudelski looked Bob in the eye. "OK, so what's the plan of action, sir?"

Bob tried not to look too caught-unawares. He checked his watch again. "Ehm, as you said, Agent Rudelski, timing's everything in this job. So, for the moment, we, uhm — we stay put and do nothing."

Down on the pier, Max and Franco had now been joined by a woman and a man from the trawler, the four of them appearing to be caught up in animated exchanges of words. Max was pointing askance at the cave. Suddenly, he turned and shouted, his voice just audible above the rumble of the fishing boat's idling diesels. "Hey, Giulianetti! Get that friggin' demolition business done and get yer asses back down here! The goddam merchandise is pilin' up here already!"

Telephoto lens to the fore, Scoop Stewart had now crept nearer the mouth of the cave and was busily snapping away at proceedings on the pier.

"Hey, can I borrow that for a moment?" Cindy Rudelski asked. "I wanna have a closer look at that woman's face down there."

"Be my guest," said Scoop.

She raised the camera and adjusted the focus slightly. "Hmm, at last . . . the elusive Laprima Frittella, or whoever she really is." She panned the camera round a bit. "Can't recognise the guy, though."

"Aye, but I've a feeling I'll know him," Bob said, his expression grim. "Can I have a look?"

"Be my guest."

Although he had been expecting it, the sharp image of the face framed in the viewfinder still sent a shiver down his spine. "I've always known his brother was a bad bastard," he muttered, "but in my book, this makes *him* even worse." He handed the camera back to Scoop, a look of disgust on his face as he said to Agent Rudelski: "The man's my own Detective Sergeant Jimmy Yule, brother of your erstwhile companion on the floor here. He must have got aboard the boat when it was off Ayr last night." Bob shook his head. "And he had the neck to tell the office he was visiting his dying mother."

"There you go," Agent Rudelski shrugged. "They're all *casata*, all family, all part of the old Sicilian Contadino clan, of which Max likes to think of himself as the godfather. Their kind of blood is thicker than *anything*, particularly when it's coagulated with the kind of haemoglobin Max promises to inject into their —"

"Sporrans?" Bob suggested.

"You got it."

The boom of a single shell shot echoed round the bay, prompting the reflex reaction in Andy Green of ducking his head, then cocking his ears for the first few bars of Spike Jones' *You Always Hurt The One You Love*. Those didn't materialise, so he got on with his preparations.

Far below, those assembled on the pier and at the cave mouth could see a puff of white smoke rising from the source of the bang — the entrance to the bay to the west of Eilean Doone islet. A second shot thundered out, and through its smoke appeared the sleek, grey hull of a fast-moving motor launch, its prow thrusting high out of the water as it sped into the cove.

"Right on cue," Bob smiled. His widening grin illustrated the extent of his relief. "That's *The Lynx* — latest anti-smuggling boat the Customs guys are operating out of Oban. Max's arse is *right* in a sling now!"

"What the friggin' hell!" Max croaked when he saw the cutter scything over the water towards him. "What the fuck's this — the goddam Scotch navy on a haggis-shootin' exercise or somethin'?"

"HER MAJESTY'S CUSTOMS AND EXCISE," came the answer over *The Lynx's* loud-hailer. "NO-ONE MOVE ABOARD *LA PATELLA* AND THE ADJACENT POWER BOAT. YOU ARE ABOUT TO BE BOARDED!"

Max seized Jimmy Yule by the shirt front and stabbed a finger in the direction of the approaching Customs launch. "How come?" he yelled. "You been double-crossin' me or somethin', ya cock-suckin' sonofabitch?"

"What's the difference now?" Laprima Frittella said. She grabbed Max's sleeve. "Let's get the hell outa here!" She then shoved Franco across the pier towards the Sunseeker. "Get down there and start up the motor — quick!"

Franco raised his hands and backed away. "Ay-y-y, no way I gonna start no *motore*! I already just been tell you — no way I gonna have nothing to doing with this kinda feeshing trips!"

Wobbling precariously on the edge of the slab of overhanging rock high above, Andy Green, his windblown kilt gripped between trembling knees, had closed his eyes tightly and was doing his utmost to generate a final upsurge of adrenaline.

Bob was taking the opportunity, while confusion reigned on the pier, to slip smartly out of the cave, closely followed by Scoop and the two girls. Nip elected to take the less impetuous option by ambling back along the shore towards the inlet where his boat was tied up, while the others made a mad dash for the hub of the action. The Customs men were already well on top of the job when they arrived on the scene. Franco (despite his persistent protests of innocence), Max's two minders and the crew of the fishing boat had been cuffed together and were standing in a forlorn line on the pier next to *The Lynx*. A Customs officer had knelt down in front of them to open one of the suspect packages.

Bob introduced himself.

"Ah, yes, thanks for the tip-off," said the officer. He dipped a finger into some powder that had spilled from the packet and dabbed it onto the end of his tongue. "Heroin — and there could be about a hundred kilos of the stuff here. On the street, twenty-five or thirty million pounds worth, give or take." He looked up and flashed Bob a smug smile. "Looks like we've stumbled on one of the biggest drug busts ever in this country."

"*Stumbled* on?" Cindy Rudelski gasped, looking distinctly un-federal-agent-like in her Lulu-May tart's garb. "Allow me to inform you, sir, that I've every reason to believe that this haul is part of a consignment my fellow agents have been tracking all the way from South America to Europe, via the Caribbean and North Africa, for the past two months!"

The officer did a double take at her, then looked enquiringly to Bob.

"Let me introduce Agent Cindy Rudelski of the FBI," Bob said. "She's been working undercover here — on the inside with the man suspected of masterminding this operation, and who may also be behind a double murder I'm investigating."

The Customs man took another incredulous glance at Agent Rudelski.

"Hey, don't let the outfit fool you," she said to forestall any likely comment. "Not my usual style, I promise you." She caressed her jacket lovingly. "But the up-side is I get to keep the mink."

"I take it you've already got the three ringleaders aboard your launch?" Bob asked the officer. "I don't blame you for not taking any chances, but I'll have to insist on interviewing them before you leave here."

The officer's face was a blank. "What three ringleaders?"

It was Franco who answered. "Look, there they-a go, Meester Burns!" he shouted, unable to indicate with his manacled hands, but nodding his head frantically to where Joe Giulianetti's little water ski boat, with Laprima at the wheel, was emerging from the creek just round the curve of the bay.

Bob muttered a curse.

Wasting not a second, the Customs man barked a command to the helmsman on *The Lynx*: "Get under way fast and head them off before they get out of the bay! Looks like they're making for the narrow passage to the left of that small island there!"

"Yeah, and fire a shot over their bows!" Agent Rudelski shouted. "And if they pay no heed, just blast them outa the water!"

"Sorry to disappoint, ma'am," the Customs officer said meekly, "but unless given specific orders from upstairs, we use the deck gun as a warning device only. No live ammo on this trip — only blanks, you know."

"I do *not* believe this," Agent Rudelski groaned. "Honestly, I figure you Brits woulda tried converting Al Capone from his criminal ways with readings from Enid Blyton's *Famous Five* stories over cups of tea and cookies after church on Sundays!"

As soon as they'd reached the open water of the bay, Laprima opened the ski boat's throttle wide in a desperate bid to outpace the Customs launch, which

Max could be seen pointing feverishly towards as it surged away from the pier. It soon became clear that Laprima was no stranger to piloting a speed boat, however. She hurled it first to the right then to the left in a wild zigzag course that had the more powerful but less-manoeuvrable *Lynx* struggling to keep up.

"They're going to get away," Julie said, her voice tense. "And the big Customs boat maybe won't make it through that narrow gap, anyway. Damn, it'll have to go the long way round Eilean Doone."

But suddenly, the ski boat was thrown into a U-turn, bucking and splashing back into its own wake as Laprima inexplicably changed course in a frantic attempt to make *her* way to the wider opening at the other flank of the islet.

Julie shook her head. "That doesn't make sense," she muttered. "She'd almost got away there . . ."

Bob let out a whoop and sprinted up to the end of the pier to get a better view. "*There*'s why she did a one-eighty!" he called back. He was grinning like a kid whose Christmases had all come at once. "Just look! And I was beginning to think the old bugger had bottled it!"

The unlikely object of his delight was now becoming apparent for all to see. The little Ardenstooshie-to-Muckle Floggit ferry was being positioned in the narrower of the two channels so precisely by Angus that only a bulimic mermaid would have had a chance of squeezing past. And there, appearing from behind the *opposite* end of islet, was a rope-linked convoy of small boats of every description but opulent. These

344

constituted the result, Bob confidently presumed, of the secret of this evening's covert operation being so badly kept by Angus and Nip among their Dramglass neighbours that afternoon.

"Look at that," he said, "they're actually going to try and form a human barricade across the other channel."

"Yeah, but they'll never make it," Agent Rudelski replied. "That ski boat's going too darned fast. And anyway, they should leave it to the Customs guys. They're the pros, and that launch of theirs'll eventually catch Max and his moll once they're outa the confines of this little cove here."

Maybe so, Bob thought, although he reckoned that the last thing the people of Muckle Floggit wanted was to owe the Customs and Excise any favours. That aside, he had to admit that it did look more likely by the second that Laprima and Max were going to reach the gateway to the open sea before the islanders had completed their blockade. What's more, with daylight fading fast, there was no guarantee that the Customs launch would overtake the smaller craft in these rock-ridden waters before nightfall helped the fleeing duo make good their escape. Like it or not, it was beginning to look as if the elusive Max Plantano was about to give justice the slip yet again. Bob's spirits were suddenly flagging as fast as they'd risen.

Then, from the sky behind him, there came a wild, Tarzan-like cry. All eyes were drawn upwards to where a kilted paraglider had just launched himself off the side of the mountain. The flight degenerated immediately into a series of uncontrolled plunges and stalls, of eccentric yaws and pitches, the canopy of the 'chute flapping and billowing alternately while the pilot fought an apparently-losing battle against the relentless force of gravity.

Bob looked up at the lanky, naked legs flailing about beneath the swirling folds of kilt tartan. "It can only be Green," he muttered despairingly. "The complete bloody bampot!"

"ANDY!" Julie screamed, her mothering instinct going into instant overdrive as she dashed back along the pier towards the estimated point of crashdown. "THE SHROUDS!" she yelled. "CONTROL YOUR DESCENT WITH THE SHROUDS!"

"WHAT'S A FUCKIN' SHROUD?" came the frantic plea from above.

"THE PARACHUTE STRINGS! THE CORDS! BUT STEADY — BOTH HANDS TOGETHER! FEEL IT! BE PART OF THE WHOLE!"

Under less fraught circumstances, Andy might well have attempted to fashion a crude quip out of that last piece of advice, but this was no time for whimsy. The green, green grass of Kildoone was approaching fast, and the nearer it got, the clearer it became to Andy that this daredevil stunt of his had been totally uncalled-for after all, since the Doc and the Chief now appeared to be in no danger whatsoever. And that was more than he could say for himself. He was dropping like a stone. He closed his eyes.

The Doc was still shouting instructions, her voice growing ominously louder. Which meant nearer! She was yelling at him to push the shrouds forwards. Or was it to pull them backwards? His panic-frozen brain wasn't even listening to his ears. Yet, somehow, his hands did manage to do something of their own volition, and he felt a scrotum-crunching jolt on the harness as the 'chute re-opened, halting his downward momentum and hurling him suddenly forwards.

Through one half-opened eye he could see that he was only five or six feet from the ground, hurtling pell-mell over the turf between ruined cottages towards the shore. There, the Doc was standing directly in his flight path, arms outstretched to stop him, and shouting at him not to worry. *Not to worry?* Christ! If he hadn't been wearing a kilt, Andy freely admitted, he'd have filled his pants several times already!

He closed his eyes again. His brain was now sending desperate SOS messages to his mouth, but all that emerged was another wobbly yodel that ended abruptly in a gulp of agony when Julie's head rammed into his sporran area and her arms twined themselves tightly round his knees.

Bob and the others on the pier looked on awestruck as a sudden up-draught caught the canopy of the 'chute and sent Andy and his would-be saviour soaring out over the bay. Bob's natural inclination was to laugh, except he knew this wasn't as funny as it looked. Their present trajectory was going to see Green and Julie end this flight splattered like a pair of windscreen bugs against the face of the cliffs on the west side of the cove.

"For heaven's sake, Andy, pull the left-hand shrouds!" Julie yelled up from under his kilt.

This Andy did, and the canopy banked to the left, swinging the suspended couple sideways in a crazy chairoplane ride. Julie tucked her knees up at the last moment to save her feet from smashing into a blur of rock.

"Now the right hand one!" she hollered, all the while jerking her head about to keep the flapping kilt tartan out of her eyes. "Now brace yourself! We're going down!"

Andy couldn't bear to look. On the pier, Bob couldn't bear to blink.

Unknown to Laprima, who had enough on her plate trying to outsmart the chasing Customs launch to even think about looking upwards, Julie's feet were now only a couple of yards above and behind the stern of the ski boat, and closing fast.

Andy felt the weight on his harness lighten suddenly as Julie released her hold on his legs, yet he was still hurtling forwards at the same velocity. He was suspended directly over the ski boat now, but unable to see down into it because of the billowing cloth of his kilt. Panic gripped his vocal cords once more, and another broken-voiced bellow escaped his mouth. Now Laprima *did* look up, her first worm's eyeview of a true Scotsman's dangly bits causing her to lose concentration just long enough for Julie to make her move.

She lunged forward from where she had landed at the back of the boat and forced her way between Max and Laprima, snatching the wheel from Laprima's grasp with one hand, while reaching forward in hope of closing the throttle with the other.

But Max was too quick for her. Cursing, he knocked her hand away from the throttle lever, then grabbed her by the throat and pressed his thumbs into her windpipe. The restricted space in the little boat left Julie scant opportunity to fight back. Max was hauling her over his lap by the neck, his knees digging into her as he strained to manhandle her over the side.

Her lungs bursting, Julie let go of the wheel. This sudden loss of resistance resulted in Laprima jerking the wheel the other way. The boat tilted over to one side and raised Max's head to a level approximately equal to that of Andy Green's flailing hiking boots. When the inevitable impact finally came, it propelled Max overboard, dragging the half-strangled Julie with him.

"For Chrisakes help me, ya dumb broad!" he gurgled at her as soon as they'd surfaced. "Can'cha see I can't friggin' swim already?"

While Max was floundering, Andy was heading for a fortuitous crash landing on Eilean Doone. The survivalist Laprima Frittella, meantime, had evidently decided to abandon her boss to whatever fate had in store for him. She charged the ski boat through what remained of the channel to the open sea mere seconds before the lead boat of the islanders' floating barricade could block it off completely. In so doing, however, they inadvertently made good Laprima's escape from the now penned-in Customs launch.

"The best-laid schemes, to paraphrase my great namesake," Bob Burns muttered ruefully, "gang aft right down the bloody pipes!" It then came to his mind that, amid all this furious activity, Jimmy Yule was nowhere to be seen.

The manacled Franco, once again, made the crucial indication: "Meester Burns!" he shouted. "There go the brother of-a the Joe guy!"

Bob wheeled round to follow Franco's wide-eyed stare towards the cave, into which Jimmy Yule was disappearing in an obvious bid to free his brother while everyone else's attention was drawn to the distractions unfolding out in the bay. Then, just as Bob was about to ask the Customs officers for some help in apprehending the two brothers, an almighty explosion burst from the mouth of the cave, throwing a cloud of dust, smoke and lumps of rock high into the air.

Nip MacGubligan, back in his wee boat, emerged from the inlet round the corner just in time to witness his versatile cottage collapse and tumble into a gaping pit that, until a moment ago, had been Saint Gubligan's Cave. It had also been his and his fellow islanders' only real asset, and potentially an *extremely* lucrative one, at that.

"Joe Giulianetti's gelignite," Bob muttered. "The bastard must've had it linked up to a timing device inside the box."

"Yeah," agreed Agent Rudelski, "and but for my little rope-a-dope trick, right now you and your good buddies would now be . . ." Her voice trailed away.

"It's OK, I know what you were going to say," quavered Scoop Stewart, ". . . we'd now be resting in pieces!"

CHAPTER
EIGHTEEN

At first light the following morning, the red Alfa Romeo Spider was found abandoned at Broadford airstrip on Skye, its engine still running, its headlights still on, and an empty *Femme* perfume bottle lying on the driver's seat. A nearby crofter told Constable MacClue that he had heard the sound of a light aircraft landing and taking off again at about 1a.m. It ultimately transpired, however, that the control tower, which was un-manned during the night, had had no such impending arrival notified nor any out-going flight plan logged for that time. Laprima Frittella, it seemed, had literally disappeared into thin air.

By mid-morning, Dramglass village was buzzing with activity, Scoop Stewart having blitzed as many news media night desks as he could with his sensational exclusive immediately upon returning to his office the previous evening. There were now reporters arriving on every ferry, with three TV helicopters already parked on the football pitch, their camera crews jostling for position with their pencil-wielding counterparts in the village hall, where a press conference had been hurriedly arranged. Not surprisingly, Andy Green, as the death-defying instigator of the capture of such an apparently-major international drugs baron, was the centre of attention, and Bob was pleased to let it be so.

Agent Rudelski had already left the island aboard *The Lynx* to escort Max and his minders to a high-security mainland jail, where they would await trial for drug running and suspected involvement in the two North Berwick murders. It seemed that Messina Max Plantano's legendary luck had finally run out.

Thanks to Bob's assertion that he had been no more than a pawn in his uncle's game, an innocent dupe, who, when the chips were finally down, had made no bones about whose side he was really on, Franco had been released by the Customs and Excise after a sworn undertaking had been made that he would stand as a witness for the prosecution when Max and his henchmen eventually appeared in court. The stark realisation, though, that he had been used in such a humiliating way had left Franco feeling foolish and hurt, feelings exacerbated by the revelation that Andy Green, whom he had looked upon as a friend as well as his hundred-thousand-pounds benefactor, was really a penniless policeman who had also been manipulating him for ulterior purposes. Andy's apology that he had only been doing his job and had actually understood very little of the machinations involved was cold comfort indeed for Franco.

However, as Andy himself would have said, "It's an ill wind, eh?". For Franco still had his pride and, despite the painful fact that his true identity and humble trade were about to be exposed to the world, he had decided that he would try to preserve at least a shred of his dignity by keeping his promise to the people of Muckle Floggit. He would complete his first and, in all probability, his last sculpture — in their honour, and for free!

So, while the media circus was otherwise engaged in the village hall, it was on the deserted green in front of Donal the blacksmith's shop that Franco was to be found, welding the finishing touches to *Eagle-Bird With Salmon-Fish*. He then sprayed the completed work with grey, navy-surplus paint that had been procured by Donal from Mohammed MacGubligan's Boat Chandlery in lieu of payment of some long-overdue bill or other.

"Man, but it's a spectacular thing now that it's all finished, right enough," Donal declared, standing well back with Franco to take an appraising look at the twelve foot-high abstract. "Aye, very individual-like it is — not chust your run-of-the-mill, poofy, wee Greek god with his naked bits and pieces all exposed-like and leaving nothing to the imaginashun at all." Donald nodded authoritatively. "No, no, lad," he affirmed, "you need plenty of the imaginashun to appreciate the modern art . . . now that I see it close up and everything."

Despite his blue mood, Franco couldn't help but feel extremely chuffed with what he had fashioned out of a load of old rubbish. *Si*, he told himself, this thing had style, it had . . . class! Unfortunately, it had also used up several oxyacetylene gas bottles and a few boxes of arc welding rods, not to speak of the diesel burned up by the old Ford tractor. Franco had *un problema*.

He turned to Donal. "Uhm, about the deferred-a payment, *amico* . . . ," he said in unconcealed embarrassment.

"Ach, never you bother yourself about that," Donal grinned. "Man, I've fair enchoyed myself, for it was a rare wee change from straightening out bent plough bits and welding patches onto old exhaust pipes and the likes."

It was then that the proverbial ill wind blew in, bringing with it Nip MacGubligan and two chiffon-neckerchiefed chrysanthemums, who had just come off the ferry and had stopped the passing Nip to seek the benefit of his local knowledge. As coincidence would have it, these were the same two arty-farty types that Bob had encountered in Edinburgh's Deacon Brodie Tavern at the outset of the case.

Nip was obviously in good fettle as he led the pair towards the village. "Oho, so it's there you are yourself, Danny lad!" he gushed on catching sight of Franco by the smiddy door. "Now then, I would like you for to meet my two colleagues chust up from London and Edinburgh and everywhere. Aye, for they were after seeing a picture that yon Scoop Stewart took of your half-done statchoo in the paper, and chust asked me at the pier there if I could maybe negotiate a wee bit on their behalfs for to —"

Nip was brusquely brushed aside by one of his two "colleagues", who then extended a limp right hand to Franco, his left one holding a gold-tipped Black Sobranie cocktail cigarette at shoulder height.

"Claude d'Arcy, *signor*," he sibilated. "And this is my partner Marcel." He proffered a pink business card. "Our firm — d'Arcy and Prévert, international art dealers, specialising in the avant-garde, the bizarre, the, uh . . . different. Quite, and we are particularly *intéressé* at the moment with ultra-modern metallic sculpture — with subtle Middle Eastern undertones, whenever possible." Claude d'Arcy then dropped any pretence of butchness that he may have been attempting, however unsuccessfully. "No *really*, luvvie," he said in an Old Compton Street accent that was as camp as a field full of boy scout tents, "if an artist's work even *whispers* The Desert Song to us, we're his, totally and utterly head-over-heels, bum-for-bollocks his . . . uhm, for a twenty-five points commish, of course."

Nip winced.

Claude minced. "Now, let's have a butchers . . ."

He and Marcel gasped in concert and clasped delicate hands to their colour-coordinated Hawaiian silk shirts as the full impact of Franco's scrap-metal effigy struck them. They chasséd daintily this way and that, crouching, leaning back, tilting heads, folding one arm with forefinger raised to lips, critically surveying, quietly conferring.

"Mm-m-m, bona!" Claude said aloud after a while. "Oo-ooh, yes, it's telling me Laurence of Arabia, Peter O'Toole, Omar Sharif."

"Peregrine falcons," Marcel enthused. "Arab stallions, flared nostrils, rippling leg muscles, *gorgeous* tight niagaras!"

Franco butted in with a polite cough. "Ehm, ees called Eagle-Bird With-a Salmon-Feesh, gentlemens . . ."

"You call it what you like, ducky," Claude twittered. "To me it's pure Rudolph Valentino, and that's as good as a da Vinci to our mate Ali."

The two art dealers took an arm of Franco's each and walked him out of Nip and Donal's earshot.

Claude didn't beat about the bush. "Same genre, different themes, darling," he said to Franco. "Four sculptures for our mate Ali — big ones. The hawk, the horse, the camel, the oil well. Forty grand apiece. Well then, how does that tickle your parts, sunshine?"

Franco did a quick bit of mental arithmetic . . . Eh, less twenty-five *per cento* commish, and the ten thousand pounds to Angoose for the Town-a Country Planning business, and not forgetting the equipment hire payments to Donal and Dougal . . . Hey, this was even better than the original hundred-thousand deal Andy had reneged on!

And so it was a distinctly up-beat Franco who was able to turn the tables on the press corps when they eventually descended upon him with a view to sinking the collective boot in. Not only would these genuine commissions establish the name of Franco Contadino as a *scultore* of international repute, but they would also enable him to pay off his debt to his former boss at the *Ristorante Bella Siciliana* in London's Edgeware Road, to get the London bookie off his case, to clear his overdrafts at the banks in London and Sicily, to rid Muckle Floggit of the rest of its unsightly rash of abandoned cars, *and*, when this was all over, to start converting the old farmhouse on the hillside overlooking Messina into the swankest country restaurant in Sicily.

"Ay-y-y!" he beamed, slapping a bemused Andy Green's back after he'd joined the inquisitive throng gathering on the little patch of grass. "As you have-a sometime say, *amico*, it is a ill-a wind, eh!"

"Oh yes, it is an' all, to be sure," a husky Irish voice whispered in the young Italian's ear. "Have ye missed me, Franco me darlin'?"

Franco knew that voice. He spun round, his heart turning somersaults, his eyes devouring every mouth-watering cubic centimetre of the flame-haired, emerald-eyed, Celtic goddess who stood before him. Kate O'Flaherty! *Santo cielo*, she was even more tantalising than he remembered from the time of his financially disastrous fling with her in the old *Ristorante Bella Siciliana* days! Had he *missed* her? *Gesù Cristo*! Did a starving man miss beluga caviar?

"*Cara mia*," Franco purred, "come back, *bella* . . . all is-a forgive!"

He threw his arms around her, crushing those exotic Hibernian contours against his thumping Latin breast.

"*Si*, and-a tell me," he finally panted through a volcano of pent-up passion, while struggling for breath after a two-minute tonsil snog, "have-a you got a keelt?"

Kate parted her smudged, crimson lips in a playful smile. "No, sure but *he* has, darlin'," she said in her silky Irish brogue. Disentangling herself from Franco's tentacle-like hug, she stood aside to reveal a little baby buggy that had been parked discreetly behind her back. She bent down and picked up the ginger-headed toddler who was sitting holding an Italian flag in his fist.

"Come away wit' ye now, Frankie, the little-wee lamb that ye are," Kate crooned, before handing her slavering bundle to a mesmerised Franco. "Yes, come away wit' ye now and say a nice, big hello to yer owld daddy . . ."

EPILOGUE

Angus's little ferry puffed and wheezed its way over the sound on the last crossing of the evening. The unsteady clank and thump of its ancient engine was sounding just a little more sprightly of piston, a little less arthritic of crankshaft in the wake of all the media attention that had been showered on the tiny craft following its epic voyage to blockade the eastern approach to the Bay of Kildoone the previous night. And the ship's master himself, Bob noted from the rail of the car deck, had an even more pronounced than usual air of self-importance about him.

Angus was standing, square-shouldered and granite-jawed, in his wheelhouse, staring Columbus-style out over the two-hundred-yard expanse of sea to Ardenstooshie. Clearly, he was now a living legend among seafarers, the MacGubligan name to rank in future with the likes of Drake, Cook and yon other explorer chiel who went on to make pushbikes and whose name Angus couldna quite remember.

"I still can*not* get over Detective Sergeant Yule," Andy Green frowned, patently perturbed. "Talk about goin' out wi' a bang!"

There seemed no appropriate answer to that, so Bob didn't attempt one.

Andy thought for a moment. "I mean, I still cannae understand why he never grassed to the heavies about me right at the off."

"Because he didn't know you'd copped for the hundred thou until after the old guy you bought the car off was beaten up. It was a Monday holiday, remember, and Yule had the day off."

"But how about all the info he passed on from HQ to us during this caper up here? OK, it turns out a lot of it was dodgy, but a lot of it was sound."

"It's called hedging your bets, lad — playing both sides against the middle. A dangerous game, because you can end up getting squelched, just like Yule did." Bob gave Andy a schoolmasterly nod. "Let it be a lesson to you."

"Yeah, but why did he let us mooch about up here on Muckle Floggit without tippin' off the Max gadgie who we were? Seems daft to me, that."

"Ah, but don't forget we'd never have stumbled upon this Muckle Floggit venture of Max's if Laprima Frittella hadn't dumped the hundred thousand at your feet by mistake. But once we were on the case, Yule either had to blow the gaff to Max — risking him shelving the whole project and meaning Yule and his brother would be in for a financial cut of nothing — or play us along, hoping he could snuff us out *in situ* and thereby gain a load more brownie points for himself from Max." Bob shrugged his shoulders. "That's more or less what his brother implied back at the cave, anyway."

Andy Green was getting the picture at last. "And that Agent Rudelski bird reckons Muckle Floggit was earmarked for bein' a major drugs distribution base, eh?"

"Well, makes sense, doesn't it? Remote place like Kildoone. The Spanish fishing boat slipping in there and unloading the stuff, unseen from the open sea. Then Max's people using their big power boat to rendezvous with other fishing boats, divvying up the dope for distribution." Bob shrugged again. "That's the FBI theory, and who am I to argue?"

"And ye say the stuff came in from Africa, up through Spain to that fishin' place — the same route Laprima Frittella took, like?"

Bob shook his head. "Maybe, but that trip of hers was more than likely only a red herring. No, the *Patella* boat probably picked up the consignment in North Africa, did a bit of bona fide fishing, unloaded the catch at Vigo to make everything look gen, then sailed off to Newfoundland . . . making a slight detour via Muckle Floggit, of course."

Pensively, Andy poked his ear. "Phwee! Pretty complicated way o' goin' about things, if ye ask me!"

"With upwards of twenty-five million quid involved in one delivery, you can afford to be complicated. In fact, you can't afford *not* to be."

"And what about the money Laprima Frittella dropped off at the North Berwick filling station, then? I mean, where did that come from? And then there was the other loot that was stashed into the Waverley thingmy bank a few other times . . ."

"Probably the rake-offs from smaller fishing boats at the bottom of the distribution ladder. That's how Laprima came to be at a place like North Berwick, we think. Small fishing ports like that all over the country would be part of the collection network that Max was setting up, with flunkies like the young guy who was murdered all part of a cell system."

"Cell system?"

"Yeah, it's an old ploy. Terrorist outfits, for instance, have used it for yonks. Never let the right man know what the left man's doing. That way, if one person in the operation is nicked, there's only so many beans he can spill."

Andy was impressed. "Amazin', eh! And ye reckon Max's two minders and DS Yule's brother were the ones that done in that young Eyetie and the old gadgie that flogged me the car, do ye?"

"Time, forensic evidence and a jury will tell, lad. But I wouldn't be surprised." Bob pondered the point for a second or two, then added, "Not that it'll make a lot of difference to Jimmy Yule or his brother any more."

Seemingly oblivious to this conversation, Julie was gazing forlornly back towards Muckle Floggit. The little village of Dramglass, with its stone pier, the daytime hub of village life, overlooked now by Franco's weird creation. The run-down mansion house on the hillside, with old Flora sipping tea alone now in front of a silent kitchen chimney. The tiny church, where the enigmatic Reverend Dick would probably still be testing the

362

quality of communion wine behind his closed vestry door. And above it all, the towering bulk of Ben Doone, its serene but brooding presence a permanent reminder of their lowly lot to the eighty-five islanders who lived in its shadow.

"It's such a shame," Julie sighed, her eyes misting over.

"What is?" Bob asked.

"The people of Muckle Floggit. They've seen their home almost raped, if you like, to satisfy the financial lust of that greedy little sleaze Plantano, they've seen their lovely, peaceful island invaded by press sensation-seekers, they've had themselves used as a means towards an end by here-today-gone-tomorrow police people from far-away places, and what have they got out of it all? Nothing." Julie then laughed a sad little laugh. "Even that beautiful *Saint Gubligan's Tears* scam of theirs has been destroyed before it even got going properly. Yes, it's such a shame," she sighed again. "They're back where they started, except more exploited than ever."

Bob put an arm round her shoulder and gave it a comforting squeeze. "Nah, I don't think you need worry yourself too much on that score." He nodded towards old Angus on his bridge. "I mean, does that look like a disconsolate man to you? No way!"

But Julie wasn't convinced. "I wish I shared your optimism for them," she murmured, her eyes downcast.

"Well, you *should* share my optimism," Bob said, a twinkle in his eye. "You see, I had a word with old Holy Dick before we left. He'd had a phone call from Agent

363

Rudelski this afternoon. Seems there's been a big reward on Max Plantano's head for quite some time in the States."

Julie gave him a quizzical look.

"Come on," Bob said, "you know the sort of thing the law gets up to over there — finger this bum for something that's gonna stick, and we'll see you all right, bud. And let's face it, it *was* the naval blockade set up by old Angus and the islanders that really did the business last night, right?"

Julie made no attempt to hide her opposition to the sweeping nature of that statement. "*If* we forget about near death by throttling and drowning experienced by one public-spirited forensic scientist," she ventured, "*and* the unbelievable birdman exploits of one intrepid Detective Constable, that is!"

"Yeah, well, I'll see you're both mentioned in dispatches," Bob said with exaggerated indifference.

It appeared that Andy Green had been listening intently to all of this, but, in truth, his brain had pressed its own pause button a few sentences back. "Ehm, ye said something about a big reward, boss?"

"That's what I was told."

"So, eh, how *big* a reward would that actually be, like?"

"The Rev didn't say, but I can tell you he was smiling a lot when he mentioned it. Of course, on top of that, there's the question of who owns the island now."

Julie inclined her head inquisitively. "How d'you mean?"

364

"Well, if you recall, it was bought by Top Banana Enterprises, an off-shore company headed by one Dannato Cornamusa, a person who doesn't exist. And, with only one other named director, Laprima Frittella, who, being absolutely realistic, is hardly in a position to press any claim, even if she had one . . ."

A slowly-spreading smile began to return Julie's hitherto glum expression to its normally-sunny state. "You mean the islanders them*selves* could become the owners of Muckle Floggit?" An instinctive frown of suspicion wrinkled her brow. "Hey, you wouldn't be pulling my leg, would you, Kemosabe?"

"No siree!" Bob was smiling now himself. "Think about it. The previous owner's happy — he's been paid for the property — and the company that paid him has, to all intents and purposes, done a self-destruct act." He gestured towards old Angus again. "That's why the Provost there's looking so sure of himself. I mentioned all this to him before we left Dramglass."

But there was still a look of concern in Julie's eyes. "Yes, but how would the islanders be any better off at the end of the day. You know what I mean — how could *they* possibly raise the money to do all the things that desperately need to be done on the island?"

"Listen," Bob said, opening the BMW door for her as the ferry neared Ardenstooshie pier, "as long as there's Klondikers on the sea and honey bees on the heather, Angus, Nip and old Holy Dick will find a way. Just keep watching Mike Gibson's column in *The Scotsman*. Yeah, I reckon it won't be long before a back-up Miracle of Muckle Floggit is revealed, alcoholic tears and all. Oh, but with the historic writings in Saint Gubligan's Scrolls having been suitably re-translated, of course."

Andy Green, who had been lost in thought since the subject of a reward was last mentioned, suddenly piped up: "Heh, Chief, that loot I picked up in the filling station at North Berwick . . ."

"Yeah?"

"Ye've still got that finders-keepers law to look into for me, eh?"

"Ah, that's right, boy, so I have. Which, ehm, reminds me . . ." Bob dipped into his jacket pocket. "This note was found by PC MacClue under the empty *Femme* bottle in the red Alfa Romeo Spider this morning."

Andy Green took the piece of paper and blanched as he read it aloud:

"A HUNDRED BIG ONES, *PICCINO MIO!* YOU OWE ME — CAPEESH?"

THE END

Also available in ISIS Large Print:

Tremor of Demons

Frederic Lindsay

Racked by fears for his daughter and her young son, at odds with his detective sergeant, and haunted by the worry that he is losing his grip, DI Jim Meldrum has to draw on all his resources of integrity and courage as he seeks to find the connection between the death of a one-time pentecostal minister and a call-girl. A darkly compelling psychological murder mystery, layered through with conspiracies and a sinister religious undertone.

ISBN 978-0-7531-7910-9 (hb)
ISBN 978-0-7531-7911-6 (pb)

Little Face

Sophie Hannah

Fascinating and original . . . beautifully written . . . oustandingly chilling   **Spectator**

Alice's baby is two weeks old when she leaves the house without her for the first time. On her eager return, she finds the front door open, her husband asleep on their bed upstairs. She rushes into their baby's room and screams. "This isn't our baby! Where's our baby?" David, her increasingly hostile husband swears she must either be mad or lying, and the DNA test is going to take a week.

One week later, before the test has been taken, Alice and the baby have disappeared. Run away, abducted, murdered? The police who dismissed her baby swap story must find out and, as they do, they find dark incidents in David's past — like the murder of his ex-wife . . .

ISBN 978-0-7531-7822-5 (hb)
ISBN 978-0-7531-7823-2 (pb)

The Mallorca Connection

Peter Kerr

A rare combination of suspense and humour, with a real twist in the tale

Peter Kerr writes with a combination of nice observation and gentle humour **Sunday Times**

Bob Burns is an old-fashioned kind of Scottish sleuth, more interested in catching villains than creeping to get promotion. So, when his enquiries into a brutal and bizarre murder are blocked by his bosses, should he risk losing his career by carrying on his investigations?

Encouraged by an attractive, though maverick, forensic scientist and assisted by a keener-than-bright young constable, Bob does it his way. The trail leads the trio from Scotland to Mallorca, where intrigue and mayhem mingle with the crowds at a fishermen's fiesta.

ISBN 978-0-7531-7844-7 (hb)
ISBN 978-0-7531-7845-4 (pb)

Cold Pursuit

Judith Cutler

When a colleague becomes seriously ill, Chief Superintendent Frances Harman delays her retirement to oversee an investigation into a recent spate of "happy slappings". Initially, she takes a back seat, but it is not long before she is close to the action again.

The wave of assaults has ignited a media furore and Fran is concerned that an atmosphere of mass hysteria is being generated. She soon finds herself having to spend as much time trying to control the media as trying to catch the criminals. However, the local reporter who initially broke the story, Dilly Pound, may have personal reasons for taking such an avid interest in the case.

As the crimes gradually escalate and the line between "happy slapping" and serious sexual assault becomes blurred, all mention of retirement is postponed until Fran can resolve the nightmare that has enveloped her.

ISBN 978-0-7531-7820-1 (hb)
ISBN 978-0-7531-7821-8 (pb)